BEYOND VALOR

❖ S. M. SAVOY ❖

بساله

Published by
Ace Lyon Books
June
2019

Books in This Series:
Valor
A Warrior's Fury
A Sun Priest's Magic
Beyond Valor
Upcoming Book: *A Rogue's Passion*

Books in Related Series:
Return of the Fae
Upcoming Book: *Enter the Frey*

Ace Lyon

Published by
Ace Lyon Books
Acelyonbooks.com
First Edition
Cover Design by S. M. Savoy
S. M. Savoy *Beyond Valor*
ISBN 978-1-947122-20-8
eBook 978-1-947122-22-2
Hardcover 978-1-947122-28-4

This is a work of fiction. Names, characters, businesses, places and incidents or events either are products of the Author's imagination or are used fictitiously. Any resemblance to actual events or locales or persons, living or dead, is entirely coincidental.

Dedication

To the men and women who dedicate their lives to make us all safe.

This book is a work of fiction. The places portrayed in it have no basis in fact. The officers taught at Annapolis were an inspiration for this story, their bravery, dedication and the sacrifices they make to serve their country, but the story itself is a complete fabrication, both the people and the place.

S. M. Savoy

Table of Contents

BEYOND VALOR

THE BEST LAID PLANS

Charlie glanced over as Hawk laid his bow on the counter beside his rifle.

"Guthrie is coming," Hawk said.

Charlie nodded acknowledgment and hit the target dummy one last time, rocking the leather-clad metal frame, before returning to the table where Sara and Oz sat surrounded by a mound of books. Both had laptops open before them and were typing so fast the soft clicks sounded like a continuous hum.

Stasia leapt past Charlie and ruffled Oz's hair before settling into the seat beside him.

Oz absently batted her hand away, and Charlie winked at Stasia who snorted with laughter. Both Sara and Oz had their own target dummies but rarely used them, staying instead at the table in the corner of the windowless room. A week ago the shelves behind the table had been empty but already they were crammed with books. Oz had hooked up a printer and two computer terminals on the counter that had held an assortment of weapons, putting the weapons into the boxes the books had come in and leaving the boxes stacked beneath the counter.

Charlie frowned thoughtfully as he sat. Oz and Sara needed more room and a nicer spot to study in than this windowless gym. If Guthrie denied their request to change schools, he'd make sure Oz and Sara got a room with storage space for their mountain of books and windows so she could sit in the sunshine while she read. His frown deepened. She likely wouldn't sit in a sunny window if he wasn't in the room. He'd have to find somewhere she felt safe when he wasn't with her.

Sara darted a quick glance at him, and he smiled and waved a dismissive hand. His spike of anger had alarmed her, but she smiled and closed her laptop before placing it into the bag at her feet. She began straightening the books, stacking them in small piles in the center of the round table.

Charlie stood as Staff Sergeant Guthrie entered.

Team Valor had been back in Pendleton for a little over a week and Charlie was nervous Guthrie wouldn't take their news well. A lot of effort had gone into moving Team Valor and their families across the country, telling Guthrie they wanted to move again, regardless of reason, might be too much to ask.

"This looks serious." Staff Sergeant Guthrie smiled in greeting.

Sara half turned away from Charlie to hide her guilty wince. It was a useless gesture when her guilt magnified his own. He said nothing. They'd spoken and agreed mentioning feelings they couldn't help when they knew the cause was pointless. He'd already told her he was worried about this move and why. He'd also told her a million times that she had nothing to feel guilty about.

Her cheeks flushed when she felt his exasperation, and he knew she was worried about upsetting him now.

Charlie stifled a groan and pointed to the empty chair at the table.

"Please, take a seat." He slid a stack of files forward and sat back down. "Thanks for meeting us. I know we aren't scheduled to meet again for another week when our classes start."

"So, what's this about, guys?" Guthrie sat in the indicated metal chair and folded his hands on the table.

"After talking things over, we've made plans of our own for the future." Charlie took Sara's hand and ran his thumb over her clenched fingers. "We want more input on what we're doing."

He bit back a snicker over her spike of lust from the small gesture. She was amused now, likely over his answering spike of lust, although her expression remained serious. He tried to keep his face straight and released Sara's hand.

"I see." Guthrie leaned back in the chair, rolling the pen on the table before him.

"We want to choose what we study and not all of us want a military career. We've talked about this a lot lately and have a plan I think will make everyone happy." Charlie pushed a folder across the table to the sergeant. "Stasia and I want to attend the naval academy in Annapolis this fall while Sara, Oz and Hawk attend Johns Hopkins. We've received our GEDs already. We've taken SATs last year and passed them. I'm sure we'll pass with even higher marks this year."

Guthrie's brow rose. "So, Stasia and you would like military careers, then?"

"Yes, Hawk too, but he plans to enlist later. He doesn't want to go through the academy without us and won't qualify for the age brackets. Stasia won't technically qualify either, but she'd only need slight rule bending."

"You know you can't be married and attend, right?"

"Yeah, but Sara and I aren't legally married, so it shouldn't be a problem." A small grimace crossed Charlie's face at the thought of being separated from her. She laid a hand on his arm, but it was her rising anxiety that made him glance at her. She gave him a reassuring smile and lightened her grip.

They'd agreed to accept nonverbal cues instead of asking for explanations over every emotional change, so he turned back to the sergeant. He'd ask her again later if she was sure about this plan, now they needed to present a united front.

"And Oz and Sara, what are your plans?" Guthrie turned to Oz who leaned back in his chair on two legs with his booted feet on the table and his laptop on his lap.

"I'll study mechanical and electrical engineering as well as math and computer science. Sara wants to study medicine and history and anything else she thinks will help her understand the magic. I plan on working on some computer programs I have ideas for and then studying the magic too."

"And Team Valor?"

Charlie cracked his knuckles and stretched. "We'll stay together, keep up on our training and do missions as needed, but only as a team, never separate."

"But you're okay with being separated like this though?"

"No, but it'll be temporary. Our schools will be close together, and we'll see each other as often as possible." Charlie handed Guthrie a map. "Security for Oz and Sara is a concern. They plan to find a house or apartment to share in this area here."

He took the map from the sergeant, spread it out on the table, and used his finger to outline the area they were interested in. "Stasia and I should be secure enough on campus, but they'll be traveling on and off their campus."

"When Captain Sanders spoke with my mom, he mentioned the possibility of using the GI Fund, and we were hoping we could get some scholarship money," Stasia added with a glance at her brother. "Johns Hopkins isn't a cheap school."

Guthrie turned to Sara. "Sara, you don't want a military career? You want to be a civilian doctor? The military has doctors too."

Sara's blue eyes squinted as she ran a hand through her long blonde hair and then nervously began to braid it. "I don't want to practice medicine. To study my magic, I'll need to learn everything I can about the human body. There's so much I don't know and not just about medicine. I'll be taking lots of different courses. Besides, if I joined, I'd have to go where I'm sent, and I can't do that because of Charlie. I need his magic. When he graduates, we'll legally marry, and I'll go wherever he's stationed."

"The minute I graduate." Charlie smiled and ran a hand over her bright hair, freeing the fingers that plaited the ends and holding her hands. Nervous and a bit afraid, her gaze locked on the sergeant.

"No matter what, we won't be separated," he added emphatically.

The fear he sensed from her eased as she turned to him. Since her abduction she was both fearful of being alone and worried her clinginess would annoy him. He did his best to reassure her and her magic who he was sure was magnifying her fear. Her magic craved him and sought him frequently. Crowds put her on edge and only exchanging magic with her soothed her. He hoped the magic would revert to its prior quiet existence soon and stop pressuring her.

"No, we'll marry the first Christmas after you graduate. That's our anniversary." Sara leaned over and kissed him.

Guthrie cleared his throat.

Charlie flushed as he broke from the kiss. Her emotions enthralled him. The simplest of touches captured his attention, his feelings merging with hers until they echoed so strongly between them he thought they might become visible to even those without magic.

"And you, Oz? You don't want a military career either?" Guthrie asked.

Oz smiled at Sara as he dropped his booted feet to the floor and leaned forward. "No, I never did. That was Charlie's plan, but I always thought I'd get into computer programming, video games maybe, something like that. Now I want what Sara wants, to study the magic, but I also want to work on my own ideas. I'll most likely go wherever they go. Sara and I will work together. None of us want to attend your school this winter. Instead we'll study for our tests to get into these colleges and work on our projects."

Oz tapped the folder before Guthrie, then rose his hands to scrape his blond hair off his cheeks. He fished an elastic from his jeans pocket and pulled his shoulder-length hair into a quick ponytail.

Sara licked her lips and slid another folder to the sergeant. "We'll need good recommendations. If we can't get scholarships, I can afford to send everyone."

"And if everyone doesn't get accepted?" Guthrie turned to her, his eyebrow raised.

Her nervous gesture made Charlie frown, he'd felt no spike in her emotions to account for it, but her rising assurance as she removed a stack of folders from her bag made him smile. She always felt better, more secure, surrounded by books and papers. They captured her attention, the more complex the subject, the more she relaxed as she puzzled it out. He made a mental note to buy her some new books before he left, and she glanced over, sensing his excitement. There was something else he wanted to buy her too. He winked, and she gave him a quick grin as she riffled through her stack of folders saying, "We have a backup plan, or I should say plans. It depends on who doesn't get in and why—"

Charlie interrupted, "All our plans require we stick together. We're willing to be separated only if we can remain close together. In no plan is Sara in a different zone then I am. None of my team can be in a different zone."

"What if you're ordered somewhere far away, to different service posts?"

Hawk straightened in his seat, his brown

eyes serious. "We've talked about being assigned to different posts far from each other. In the service, you go where you're told, and we'll do that once we join, but we'll never use Team Valor abilities when not in a team. If they want us to use them, they send us all. If they want regular soldier skills that's a different story."

Guthrie leafed through the file. The first pages were highlighted course lists they wished to take followed by a list of requirements to get into the schools of their choice. Another list of accomplished requirements lay beside it.

He flipped the file closed and stood. "Okay, I see you're serious about this. I'll pass it up the line and let you know as soon as I can."

General Campbell placed the file on his desk. "Well, we knew this was coming someday. Honestly, this is better for us than I imagined."

"Shall I tell them we approve?" Guthrie asked.

General Campbell rose, paced to his window and gazed out over the dusty Iraq landscape. Harsh sunlight had shriveled the transplanted greenery and no effort had been made to replace it. The desert climate was too harsh for nonnative species without constant care. Care that his ten thousand troops had no time for.

"We need more details worked out, but in general, yes. What's your opinion of Sebastian as a student? Do you think he's ready for the academy?"

"Is he smart enough? Definitely. Is he committed enough? I don't know. He hasn't shown the drive to be an officer like the other two. He's more introverted than his sister and has been content to let Chief lead."

The general returned to his seat and folded his hands on the desk before him. "Is he capable of command?"

"Yes, he commands the Scouts with a superb grasp of strategy, especially as it pertains to his and Team Valor's abilities," Guthrie asserted.

"Their fitness reports show aptitude in that area. You're sure Oliver and Sara have no interest in a military career?"

"They claim not to. Both want to be in charge of where they're sent and what they do, but they made it clear they're willing to work with us. Sara could be talked into attending the academy for Charlie's sake, but

I don't think we could sway Oz. But I worry about our rep with her if she attends and is unhappy. Our rep with her is already low and if we push it...."

The general nodded and tapped the folder in front of him. "Give them approval to proceed with their plan. Help them attend what classes they'll need or arrange tutors. Let them pick their own curriculum." He paused a moment, then continued, "Keep up with their fitness program and training. Don't let them get rusty, but we can cut the hours back and provide more time to study. I'll be looking into getting them into the academy this fall." The general leaned back and rubbed his chin with two fingers. "Security will be an issue. I'll see what can be done, and we'll work something out for any missions that might arise."

"And the scholarships they wanted?"

"Shouldn't be a problem. We did promise them access to education. You see about getting them ready to pass the entrance exams." He laughed when Guthrie snorted. "I realize Sara and Oz are overqualified but the other three might need tutoring. If they qualify, they can be presidential appointees. I'm sure we can get Sara and Oz into Johns Hopkins. I'm considering recommending they be allowed to attend the academy as civilians, or at least some classes there. I don't know though, there's a lot to work out. Tell them to carry on with their plans until I put something together."

"Yes, sir." Guthrie stood.

"Dismissed," General Campbell said.

Staff Sergeant Guthrie saluted and left.

A month later General Campbell attended a meeting in the Oval Office with the president. "We've gotten their test scores back. I think we'll need to send in fake ones." He handed the folder to the president.

"Really? I was sure they'd do well." President Carmichael opened the folder and leafed through the pages, a smile lighting his face as he read.

"They did— too well. No one does that good," the general said.

"No, use these, well, at least for the naval academy. I need to deliberate about this for the other college."

The president stood and gestured the general to a seat. "Please, sit. I assume you had a chance to read Major Harris' latest report?"

"I did."

"General Flores really lowered our reputation with the entire team but especially with Sara. Every effort is to be made to keep them happy and working with us. The superintendent has received his orders" –the president slapped his open palm on the files before him and continued— "our three will attend plebe summer and be admitted as midshipmen this fall. Their records will be sealed. Details are still being worked out, mostly security related. Oliver and Sara will be given access to classes that interest them. I want them to make friends, forge bonds, feel like part of the school. While on campus they'll be expected to follow the same rules as the midshipmen. New panic buttons, made to resemble wristwatches with beepers built in, will be issued and we expect them to wear them at all times. Keep the callouts to absolute emergencies to give them as normal an experience there as possible."

"And if Charlie's magic needs contact with Sara? Or she needs him?"

The president grinned ruefully. "We're going to play that by ear. It'd be best if they can wait until he has a legitimate leave, but it's imperative we keep all five happy. They'll be allowed access to a cell phone if they report to the infirmary during plebe summer. If he needs Sara, or anything else, they can call Staff Sergeant Guthrie or Majors Nelson or Harris, and they'll ensure they get what they need."

"I'm assuming the sports ban is still in effect?" the general asked.

The president grimaced. "Yes, it feels too much like cheating to me to let them compete. Nonparticipation will be a problem for them. I'm recommending they be given extra class work to justify their eschewal. Noncompetitive and intermural sports will be allowed. And, of course, they'll participate in the mandatory PE."

General Campbell's eyebrows rose. "I hope we're still having them keep their physical abilities in a normal range."

"Actually, I don't mind if they excel as long as it's not by so much that no one can keep up. Record breaking is fine if it's by a tiny amount, the same with their hand-to-hand training. It's fine if they always win if they don't do it too flamboyantly. We won't hold them back at all in academics. Give them whatever they can handle."

"And Sara and Oliver?"

"John Hopkins has agreed to enroll them. We, ah, falsified their transcripts. We had to do something to account for their genius. Both will take placement tests this summer to determine where they need to start. Security for them is still being considered. The naval academy will host them until we can be assured of their safety. A discreetly armored car will drive them to and from the campus. Agents will oversee them on campus too. All precautions must be taken to ensure their safety. We can't afford to lose them, they're too important. Pierce Taylor had a hell of job covering up this last abduction, and I despise needing to lie to my cabinet. If and when this becomes known to the public, I'm going to be vilified. So many lies and cover ups…"

The president stood and paced with his hands behind his back. After a few moments he resumed his seat.

General Campbell cleared his throat and continued, "Physical fitness training for Sara and Oz is also necessary. Can we get them access to the gym and track at the academy? We don't want them running on the streets."

The president rubbed his cheeks and then straightened in his seat. "Yes, I'll see to it. Tell them to wear what the others do so they blend in as much as possible. Acceptance letters should arrive within the month. I'll be speaking to them about what we expect from them as far as fitting in goes, but if you would as well that might be best. So far, they've been remarkably compliant with our requests. I don't foresee this being a problem, but if there are any, bring it to my immediate attention."

"They've been so compliant I almost believe they'd cooperate in Project Erasure if they thought the magic was harmful to the United States."

"I think so too, but we couldn't risk asking them. If it ever reached that point it would be much too dangerous," the president said.

"Well, we're nowhere near that, thank God." General Campbell stood to leave.

The president nodded his agreement, saying, "I'm still not convinced of the feasibly of that plan. There's no guarantee that killing the host will destroy the magic. In fact, I'm more and more convinced it wouldn't now that we've seen the magic trade hosts. Do your best to ensure they remain cooperative. Nightmares wake me when I think what could happen if we lose rep with them."

General Campbell placed a hand on his shoulder and squeezed before saluting and returning to his duty.

2

SAFETY CONCERNS

Three weeks later Team Valor held a private meeting. They'd gathered in Charlie's and Sara's apartment, sitting at a rickety cardboard table. None of the others had bothered buying any furniture. A cheap folding table and chairs in the center of the room and a giant cat tree with a small white kitten in front of the picture window were the only furnishings.

Most of the time they hung out at Charlie's parent's house or with Mrs. Morales.

Hawk's dog, Tank, dozed at their feet. With a regular diet and exercise Tank had already gained thirty pounds and his shaved coat was glossy black. The kitten eyed his tail in fascination. Lucky would pounce in moments.

"Tank won't hurt Lucky, right?" Sara

asked, correctly divining her kitten's intentions as it hunkered down, wiggling its hind end, preparing to pounce on the dog.

"Nope, she's perfectly safe. Let her play with him. He won't notice her." Hawk ruffled Tank's ears.

Everyone laughed as the kitten jumped and grabbed the dog's tail, trying to disembowel it, tiny legs kicking ineffectually. The dog didn't even pick up his head.

Charlie cleared his throat to get their attention. "Now that we've received our acceptance letters, is everybody still happy about this?"

"Except for Tank." Hawk rubbed his dog's stomach. Tank let out a happy groan and rolled onto his back, waving his paws in the air.

"Don't worry, Hawk." Sara smiled at Tank and patted his belly too. "We'll bring him with us all the time as part of our security. Oz and I'll take very good care of him."

Hawk nodded, but still appeared unhappy.

"It isn't too late to change your mind either," Oz said.

"I want to go, but I'll miss the big guy."

Sara heaved a deep sigh. "Not as much as

I'll miss Charlie."

"I'll miss you too. I'm counting on Oz to sneak us around." Charlie put an arm around Sara and gave Oz a hopeful glance.

"Of course I will. But if you're caught, they'll kick you out," Oz said.

"I know, and I'll try to hold out; I just don't know if I can. When Sara wants me, it's impossible to resist."

"Eww, too much detail." Stasia closed her eyes and waved her hands in front of her face while laughing.

"Not that kind of wants me, you dweeb, although I'd be an idiot to resist that. I meant her magic." Charlie threw an empty folder at Stasia. Her hand darted out with inhuman speed and plucked the folder from the air.

"They know that, and I'm sure there's a plan in place," Oz said. "And if there isn't, I'll help you guys."

"We'll all help you." Stasia punched Charlie's shoulder and slapped the empty folder down before him.

Sara grinned at Stasia before turning to Oz. "Oz, you and I will need to find a place. Somewhere pet friendly with a sunny outdoor space for Tank and I to share."

"Yeah, we should look for three bedrooms too so Stasia can have a room when she wants one. Hawk can share mine."

"And we'll need one more car. I can use Charlie's, but I'm sure our class schedules will be different, so we'll need another."

Stasia handed Hawk and Charlie a folder. "These will be our instructors. There's a list of their specialties in there just like a boss strategy. I recommend reading their published works to get a feel for them."

"Oh, that's a great idea, Stasia." Sara picked up Charlie's list and scanned it. "I'm going to do that too."

"Well, I'm not." Hawk didn't glance at the list, he continued to rub Tank's belly. "I'm just going to ask what you think."

Stasia rolled her eyes and grinned as she mussed his hair.

"Okay, each research three and then compare notes," Charlie said.

"Fine, three it is." Hawk sighed and flipped the folder open.

"Poor Stasia will need to cut her hair again," Oz said in real sympathy.

"Meh, I'm used to short hair now, it's all good. If I can survive bald, I can survive a trim." Stasia ran her fingers through her shoulder-length brown hair and examined the ends.

Sara leaned back in her chair, gazing contemplatively at Stasia. "Let's go there and see how the girls are wearing their hair. If we go early enough we can check things out, get moved in, and make it feel like home. You guys report June twenty-seventh, so let's go in May and take the entire month off to get settled in."

After the general met with them, they changed some of their plans.

"You want us to use academy grounds when we run?" Oz asked in surprise.

"Yes, you'll have permission to enter the grounds whenever you wish. While on campus you'll be expected to behave in the same manner as the midshipmen and dress appropriately. The gymnasium, weight rooms, tracks and exercise machines will be available to you. Don't use the equipment at Johns Hopkins."

"I guess that's okay, but it'll be weird for us." Sara bit her lip and looked doubtful. Charlie gave her an encouraging smile, and she winced and glanced away. He let his smile fade; she could feel his guilt all too clearly.

"Also, we want you to take Tank everywhere you go. Get him a working dog vest. Hawk assures me Tank's a well-trained guard dog. We want him to train another that will stay at your home." The general slid a folder to her. "We've rented you a top floor in this building."

Sara took the folder, leafed through it and frowned. She handed it to Oz who glanced through it and passed it to Stasia.

"We can't live there, thank you though." Sara reached for her laptop bag.

"The penthouse is perfectly secure with around-the-clock security guards," the general explained.

"It also has no room for Stasia and nowhere for Tank and I outside. This will be our home for a few years. Here, we can go outside and sit by the pool whenever we want. There, I'd need to leave my house to sit in the sun. No, I'm sorry, but we can't live there." Sara pulled out her laptop and opened a folder to show the general the houses they were considering. "We were thinking this one, but now that you say we'll be doing our exercising at the academy, this one would be better." Sara brought up the listing.

"Sara, that house is over a million dollars," General Campbell said.

"I can afford it, and it has everything we want. It's a bit bigger than we need, with one extra bedroom, but Oz can use that as his office. The yard is sunny and private, and it's already completely fenced. It's practically on academy grounds. We can walk there or just hop our fence. None of the houses next door can see into the backyard and it has off street parking for two cars. The driveway needs a gate and alarms for the walls, but that won't be hard to do. And John's Hopkins is only a thirty-minute drive, most of which is highway. We won't need drivers or anything."

Charlie's guilt eased as she spoke, and he let himself feel excitement over attending the academy. She'd be mere yards away from him. It wasn't as good as being in the same house, but she'd be close enough he could get to her within minutes if she needed him. She smiled at him, but she was concentrating now, and he couldn't tell if the smile were real or forced.

"I'll have my security team check it, and if they agree, we'll purchase it," General Campbell said.

"No, I will. I want it to be my home." She glanced at Hawk and corrected herself. "This will be our home. I have more than enough money to buy it, and it's a good investment,"

"Fine, easier for me," General Campbell agreed, "But, it has to pass our security inspection."

"We still want to go in May to settle in," Charlie said.

"That shouldn't be a problem. I'll get back to you on the house a soon as I can. If that one doesn't work out, I'll look for another one with an outdoor space for you and easy access to the academy grounds."

"With at least three bedrooms. Stasia needs her own room," Sara reminded him.

General Campbell made a note of the address. "I'll see to it. Be very careful who you allow in your home. This isolates you, probably more than you'd like, but it *is* necessary."

"Don't worry. We'll be careful," Oz agreed.

"Keep the panic buttons on. The superintendent and the commandant are aware of security issues regarding you, but they aren't in the loop. They've only been told you're academically gifted and attempts have been made to subvert you. Sara can bring Tank onto the grounds as long he remains well behaved. Arrangements have been made for Tank to attend classes with her as well."

"Is that okay with you, Hawk?" Sara rubbed Tank's head, which rested in her lap.

"Sure, he'll like hanging out with you." Hawk rubbed his dog's ears too. "I'll find you a good guard dog for our house. We could use two more panic buttons for them. I can train the dogs to use them if Sara or Oz can't."

"I'll see to it," the general agreed. "A panic button will be in every room of your home and both vehicles. Speaking of which, they'll both need to be armored with bulletproof glass. Agent Lewis will supply the cars and oversee the agents assigned to guard you. Both of you should vary your routes to classrooms randomly as well. Sara, keep your shield up when you're outside or sitting in windows. No one should notice it unless they come in direct contact."

The general turned to Oz. "Mostly, we're concerned about you. Attend as many classes as you can at the academy, those grounds should be relatively safe. When you're anywhere other than a secure location, keep in mind the possibility of snipers. One headshot and it's all over unless one of the others could rez you. Don't sit outside on steps or the grass for long periods of time at predictable intervals. Take seats away from windows and doors."

"Oz should keep a bandage on him," Stasia turned worried brown eyes on Oz and grabbed his hand. "If he's shot and has one on already, it would help."

"Fine, I'll put one on somewhere." Oz patted her hand and then put an arm around her. "Don't worry about me, I'll be careful."

"You all be careful." The general gave them each a hard stare. "If any of you think something is off, report it immediately. You're assets we can't afford to lose."

Sara cleared her throat and stared at her hands clenched in her lap. "If they'd kept me, nothing would've made me help them. I would've died first."

Charlie grabbed her hands and squeezed. "Never give up, Sara. We'll come for you. You fight, you hear me!"

"I will," she promised, not looking up.

Her distress made his magic flare from him. With a grimace, he forced the magic back and pulled her into an embrace, resting one hand on the pulse in her neck to reassure the magic. Usually, he could control it better, but her fear was too raw. The magic wanted assurance he was with her, he wanted to comfort her, to ease her fear.

"We know you'd never willingly assist terrorists, Sara, but having any of you to experiment on would assist them. Our scientists are learning a lot, theirs would too," General Campbell said.

"We'll be careful." Sara gave Charlie a

quick kiss on the cheek. She pulled away but kept his hand. He tightened his grip on her and didn't try to hide his anger from her. The talk about Oz's vulnerability had gotten him very angry. But his anger reassured the magic and he could beat the target dummies to release it.

"I'm glad you're all doing so well and look forward to seeing you soon," the general said as he stood.

Charlie escorted him to the door.

As soon as the general left, he leapt to his target dummy, landing beside it from across the room, and hit it, bending the thick metal frame slightly. He circled it as he attacked, knowing if he continued to hit it from one spot the reinforced metal would bend. His dummies lasted much longer if he hit them evenly from all over.

The others spoke for a moment, the low murmur of their voices somehow soothing but the fireball that flew past his ear and exploded against the dummy beside his made him grin.

Sara began to cast, the bright orange of her smites and darker spheres of her fear spell rolling through the air and lighting all the dummies as they impacted.

Team Valor attacked their dummies, the room echoing from the force of their magic, and smoke billowed in thick clouds from the fire spells.

Hawk air-bubbled them and they continued to cast until Charlie's rage was spent.

He felt much more relaxed when they exited the room, and he slung an arm around Sara's shoulder.

She grinned up at him and his smile widened. She felt nothing except lust now and an eagerness he shared.

He knew they'd have issues. She had needs normal girls didn't, and he didn't respond like a normal man. *But she wanted him to go to school*, he told the soft voice of his conscious, and going would keep her safer in the long run.

Somewhere out there a man had been willing to pay millions for her, and he knew ISIS would try again.

But I'll be better trained and have more troops to command, he told himself firmly to still the bubbling guilt. He leaned down to kiss his wife, letting her lust subsume his worry before it could make him angry again.

One step at a time, he reminded himself.

"We're getting better at controlling it," he murmured, holding up their clasped hands. Not a spec of magic had escaped them.

3

HOME-SWEET-HOME

The general contacted them a week later and gave approval to buy the house. A week after that Sara owned it sight unseen.

"Major Nelson is overseeing the instillation of the new security system, adding the gated driveway and alarming everything." Sara opened her laptop on the folding table and handed Stasia a stack of printouts and paint chips on a metal ring. "The major sent me pictures and video so we can decide who gets which room. He said we'll want to get it painted after they're done, so we need to choose the colors and stuff. No repairmen, or painters, or anyone like that can come inside the house unless he approves them first."

Stasia flipped through the color swatches and chose a light pink. "My room color. Which room is mine?"

With little discussion they picked out bedrooms and colors for them. "Are you guys sure it's okay that we get the biggest room?" Sara asked as she looked over the floor plan.

"Makes sense, there'll be two of you in it," Oz said. "Four if you count Lucky and Tank. Besides, it's your house."

"No, it's our house. All our names are on the deed." Sara didn't glance up from the plans before her.

Hawk scowled. "You don't need to do that."

"Too late, it's already done." Sara grinned at him. "If something happens to me, you won't lose your home."

"Nothing is going to happen to you." Charlie frowned at her, not liking her fatalistic attitude at all.

"I'll be careful, but you never know what can happen— we're living proof of that. No matter what, the people I love will keep their home."

"I appreciate it." Stasia slid a color chip to Sara. "How about this yellow for the kitchen?"

Charlie let it go and stood. She wasn't upset and harping about it would only anger him, which *would* upset her. "I'm going for a run. Anyone else want to come? You two, pick whatever you want."

Both girls laughed when Oz and Hawk jumped up and joined him. The boys ran to a local restaurant and ordered a pizza.

Hawk lounged in the corner of the booth. "That was close, I thought they'd keep us there for hours picking colors."

Charlie laughed and leaned back to let the waitress place the pizza on the table. "Let them enjoy it. They'll have fun deciding, and it's more likely to take days."

Oz handed the hot pepper flakes to Hawk before he asked and took a slice of pizza. "What will you do with your car?"

Charlie shrugged. "Leave it at my parent's house, I guess."

Hawk handed the parmigiana to Oz, speaking with his mouth full. "Our mother was thinking of moving to Annapolis, but we talked her into staying here. She's thrilled we're going to a good college, but she'll miss us."

"Yeah, my parents too." Charlie took a slice of the meatball pizza. Hot cheese dripped to the plate, and he waved his hand and blew on it before speaking. "It's safer for them here, and besides, they wouldn't ever see us anyway, even if they were living with you guys." Charlie indicated Oz with his head, his hands full of pizza.

"Yeah, this will be tough on all of us. We're so used to talking every day," Oz agreed.

"We'll be busy, that should help," Charlie said, trying to convince himself.

"I'm not worried." Hawk sprinkled more pepper flakes on his slice. "If I hate it, I'll quit."

"True, if we absolutely hate it, we can quit. It's not like we'll be forced to attend," Charlie said in a happier tone.

Oz laughed and glanced from one to the other. "Well, give it some time; the first few weeks are bound to suck."

Charlie groaned. "I miss her when I just think about it. I keep telling myself other people do it all the time, and she won't be far away. She's stressing about it too, and it's hard to separate her anxiety from mine."

"I'll be with her; she won't be alone," Oz said.

"Sometimes she has nightmares." Charlie glanced away unable to meet Oz's eyes, setting the pizza down, guilt making his stomach roil. "If you wouldn't mind, I was hoping if you heard her at night, you'd wake her and stay with her until she falls asleep again?"

A guilty flush heated his cheeks. The best way to stop her nightmares was his presence.

His breath on her neck or his body against her while he surrounded her in his magic could change a bad dream into a good one. Woken from a bad dream, she'd be fearful and embarrassed. The longer the dream progressed, the more afraid she'd be and the longer it would haunt her once awake. Comforted in her sleep, she wouldn't remember she'd even had a nightmare.

"Sure, and I'll get her a baby monitor she can sleep with for the first few nights at least. Make sure you work out a plan of some kind with Major Nelson in case she summons you in her sleep though," Oz said.

Charlie grimaced. He knew it was a risk. Being summoned could expose their secret. *But the risk is slight that his roommates would notice in the middle of the night,* he told himself forcefully. "The monitor is a good idea. She won't like it, but she'll use it."

"Tank can sleep with her. If she thrashes around or makes noise, I'll have him wake her," Hawk offered.

"That would be awesome." Charlie grinned in relief. "Her nightmares wake me. When I feel how afraid she is, I wake her. Usually, she's pretty still, but her hands are always clenched. Can you train him to see that?"

"Yes, easily. Of course, he'd need to be

awake himself though," Hawk added.

"Well, if he could check her whenever he wakes that would be a big help."

Sara kept telling him he had nothing to be guilty about, but he couldn't help it. They were stuck in a loop, and he didn't know if she felt bad he was going or because he felt bad. But Tank would reassure her, and if Tank could wake her before the dreams frightened her too badly that would be perfect.

"Consider it done," Hawk said. "So, where to now? I'm not going back until they're done decorating."

Charlie laughed. "We bring them a pizza, grab Tank, and really go for a run."

Two months later Charlie carried Sara into their new home. She blushed and laughed as he placed her on her feet in the empty living room.

"Home-sweet-home." Charlie kissed her, caught up in her happiness until Oz cleared his throat.

Sara broke away from him giggling. "Let's go see our rooms. The furniture we ordered should be in them already along with all our cartons to unpack. If anyone needs help rearranging, holler."

"We go shopping tomorrow for downstairs furniture," Stasia reminded them. "And you're all coming, like it or not."

Sara's and Charlie's room overlooked the back garden. Painted a soft, light gray with white trim, two large windows faced the small lawn and garden. From the windows they could see the garage and the six-foot brick wall surrounding it. An empty lot lay over the wall, part of the academy, and then the back of a stone building with a dark, slate roof. The houses on either side couldn't be seen. Two new nightstands framed the bed they'd received for a wedding present, and a Queen Anne chair with navy-blue fabric stood before the window. Two closed doors lay along one wall.

One door opened into a small bathroom and the other to a small walk-in closet. A row of built-in cabinetry covered the wall with the two doors and built-in shelves surrounded the windows. One wall was empty; Sara planned to place her desk there. She set Lucky in the window. The window enclosure was deep, not deep enough for a window seat, but the kitten would love it. Stacks of cartons teetered in uneven piles everywhere. Charlie moved them from the bed and pulled

Sara down beside him on the bare mattress.

"I love you," he whispered as he unbuttoned the top button of her shirt.

Brilliant blue eyes and a blinding smile she saved just for him were his reply. The magic made her feelings clear, but he didn't need it, her kiss told him more than words could. Her hands were under his shirt on the bare skin of his waist when Stasia called from next door.

"Hey, can you give me a hand moving this? They put the bed in front of the windows."

Charlie laughed and reluctantly sat up. "We did say holler." He heaved a sigh and went to help Stasia.

Sara followed after straightening her shirt. Her disappointment made him grin.

The rest of the day they spent unpacking. "I'm starving!" Stasia said as they gathered in the empty kitchen later that evening.

Hawk opened the cabinet beside the refrigerator and turned to his sister. "Well, we can't cook. We have no food yet."

Sara glanced around the empty kitchen. "Hmm, we can't call a cab and our cars don't arrive until tomorrow."

"I'll go," Stasia volunteered. "No one will see me leave, I'll be invisible, and I can take a cab back."

"Check in every ten minutes. You miss a check and I'll summon you," Charlie said.

Sara grinned at Stasia. "Summon her anyway. Call us when you're ready for one, just get something for tonight and breakfast. Tomorrow, when the cars arrive, we can go shopping."

Stasia left to get food.

"Man, it would rock if you could summon just me," Oz said as they watched Tank playing in the backyard with Hawk while waiting for Stasia to call.

Sara glanced at him and shrugged. "It would, but it's all or nothing. None of you can resist it." Practice had shown her Call-For Help would pull them to her even if they slept.

"That's because you're irresistible." Charlie drew her closer for a kiss.

She laughed and kissed him back.

He was happy they'd managed to get out of the guilty loop. She had spikes of worry and loneliness but mostly she seemed content and happy. He was excited and looking forward to starting school.

Major Nelson arrived early the next day.

Brenda and Joy followed with two armored cars.

"Only use these cars and pump your own gas at different stations," the major said as he dropped the keys into Oz's hand. "No one ever drives them except you guys. If you have any car problems, call Staff Sergeant Guthrie. Don't take them to a mechanic. Oz and Sara, we want you two to stick together as much as you can."

He handed them the new panic buttons. "If any of you press this button, all of them will trigger, and Sara will summon. Sara, if it goes off, wait thirty seconds or so, then summon. Give them time to get out of sight, but don't wait too long. If you hit it accidentally, call Sara right away."

"We're going to pick out furniture today. Where should we have it delivered?" Charlie asked.

Major Nelson handed him a small white card. "Use the same address you used for the bedroom furniture. Never have anything delivered here. I'm sorry, but that includes food too."

"We know, and we'll be careful," Sara said.

"Don't leave the zone without notifying us either."

Charlie put the card into his wallet as he

spoke, "We won't. We have a same zone rule for all of us. If training takes us away, they'll follow."

Major Nelson nodded. "Arrangements are in place for me to be your plebe sponsor, Charlie. When you get leave, you can go home, it's my official address. Stasia and Hawk will be assigned normal sponsors. I think you'll both enjoy meeting new friends. I'm sorry Charlie won't get a real one. Not that I won't be doing the same things, I will, but I know you need time with Sara."

Major Nelson turned to Sara. "When you and Oz receive your schedules, send me a copy. If you won't be there, let us know; call Staff Sergeant Guthrie or Major Harris. That means, if you skip a day at school, we want to know as a security measure. Your academic standing is up to you."

Sara and Oz nodded, and Major Nelson continued, "If you're called out, don't worry about coming home to get geared up just go to the airport. Backup gear will be there unless we notify you of a different location, and all of you are to call to confirm it's an actual callout. That means call me or Staff Sergeant Guthrie. The panic button will blink green and sound a tone for callout. If it's red, it's panic."

Charlie glanced at Stasia who'd made a

small eager sound before turning to the major. "What do we do if it's green? Oz and Sara can just walk out of any class they're in, we can't."

"Show the instructor your beeping wristband and get to a phone as fast as you can. We aren't anticipating any emergency callouts. This is just a precaution. We should have plenty of time to call the school and have you escorted to a pick up. If it does flash green, call first though to make sure it's not a ploy to get you off campus."

Charlie nodded and lightly punched Stasia in the shoulder. She grinned at him, and he winked. They were both looking forward to another callout.

Major Nelson stood to leave. "And, guys, I'm proud of you. I know how hard you've been working to get here." He saluted and left.

The month they took off before school was the best month of Charlie's life. Days were spent sightseeing and getting to know both school campuses. The weather was warming, and Charlie and Sara spent a lot of time lying in the garden together, reading textbooks, while Lucky, Tank and their new dog, Scrap, played.

"I could do this the rest of my life." Sara leaned over and kissed Charlie who lay on a blanket beside her.

Charlie laughed and placed his book on the ground. "It *is* pretty nice. When we're apart, I'll think of you lying here in the sun just like this." He traced a finger across the V-neck of her light-purple cotton t-shirt. "This will be so hard for me… for us. If it's too hard on you, I can give it up, Sara."

Sara put both arms around his neck, pulling him closer, the heat of her body warming his soul. "We'll be fine. Call me whenever you can. I'll miss you desperately, but it's temporary. To live the life we want, we need to do this. Eventually, you'd be bored in the garden."

"But never with you." He brushed a lock of blond hair behind her ear. "Let's go take a nap."

She smiled her special smile and they ran up to their bedroom.

Hours later loud banging and power tools pulled them from bed. "What's all this?" Charlie asked as he eyed the hole in the back door.

"I made an entrance for the animals." Oz didn't glance up from the digital locking mechanism spread out in pieces beside him on the floor. The knees of his jeans were dirty and his t-shirt had grease stains on it.

"Check it out. This is a fingerprint scanner I've been working on. Hawk is showing them how to use it to get back in. When they put their paws on it the door will unlock. I put this panel on the back door for us. Charlie, Stasia and Hawk won't have house keys on them, but they can still get in. I plan on putting a camera on it as well so we get a picture of who tried."

Oz handed Sara his phone. "Use this app. I'll put it on all our phones. It'll show us who came in and out and when. You can see any open exterior door or window. I'll be changing out the sensors for mine when I get a chance. Then we'll be able to see who opened them. I already did the front gate; I just need to program you guys in. It looks like a standard keypad, but it's not, its reading your prints. Two fingers and your thumb open it."

Hawk had the doggie door Oz was putting in standing in the grass and was showing the animals how to use it. Lucky put a dainty paw on the keypad, and Hawk slid the door up by hand. Tail waving, Lucky strolled through.

"I think they understand now," Hawk

said, "but I'll make sure of it before we leave."

They helped Oz finish the installation, everyone saddened at the reminder of their time together coming to an end.

- 4 -

INDUCTION

The day before Charlie was due to report to school, he took Sara out for dinner. His parents would arrive later that evening and he wanted time alone with her.

They toured the historic section of Annapolis after dinner. He paused on a pier overlooking the water. The view reminded Charlie of their stay in St. Vincent, and he hoped it reminded her too. Warm summer breezes, carrying the scent of ocean and fresh mown grass, wafted delicate strands of golden hair about her face. "I want you to keep my wedding ring until I can wear it again. We aren't allowed jewelry." The gold ring sat in his palm.

She turned hers nervously, not meeting his eyes.

"This doesn't mean I don't consider us

married, I definitely do." Sunset lit the sky in shades of pink and orange, casting an artificial flush on Sara's pale cheeks. A lump formed in his throat, and he had to take a minute to separate her feelings from his own. Both sad and nervous, it was her feeling of loss that pierced him. "I'd wear it if I could."

After closing her hand around his ring, he opened a small black box and took out a square cut, two-carat diamond ring surrounded by diamond chips and smiled over her relief. The ring had cost almost his entire savings and was worth every penny if it made her happy.

Her eyes smiled into his as he slid the ring onto her finger. "The first Christmas after I graduate we'll legally marry. Trust in my love for you."

Seagulls wheeled over the water, calling to each other as true night descended. Locked in an embrace, they were oblivious to their surroundings and the bystanders who stopped to gawk. Caught up in her love for him, a fierce, bright, almost overwhelming sensation, he didn't notice anything except her. With his eyes closed he could see the brightness that was Sara entwined with him, a perfect match. They were truly one. Tears filled his eyes at her response. He was the luckiest man alive.

Mrs. Morales and Charlie's parents had arrived the day before and planned to return home the day after the induction ceremony. Charlie, Stasia, and Hawk had reported at 0700 that morning. Sara had kissed him goodbye, pride fighting loneliness and worry. He himself felt eagerness, becoming an officer was a dream come true for him. Once Sara adjusted to their separation, his guilt for leaving her would fade.... He hoped.

When they'd arrived, they'd received their clothing and room assignments and went through the same check in procedure as every other cadet. Their security bracelets passed without comment although some of the other new recruits eyed them curiously.

The first thing they did after receiving their uniforms and while waiting their turn to go to the barbershop was take placement tests. Charlie finished and rechecked his papers, and then sat quietly at his desk. He rubbed the white mark his wedding ring had left on his finger pensively, blocking out Sara as much as he could.

Both had been practicing how to block their emotions, but neither could do it well. The most they could manage was muffled or focusing on something else to mask them, which made for odd emotional spikes hard to figure out. *Patience and trust*, he told himself. He was unable to lie to her, not that he wanted to, but all his emotional responses were clear to her and some were awkward to explain. He stifled a groan. Just thinking about an awkward response caused a wave of lust for her to flush his skin. Her answering desire made him squirm in his seat.

The instructor frowned and took his paper. "Problems, mister?" he asked in a sarcastic voice.

Charlie shook his head.

"All done then?" the instructor inquired as he leafed through the papers in his hand.

"Yes, sir." He'd been told not to hold back academically, and it was a relief to not have to pretend to be other than what he was. For a moment he let himself imagine he could truly be himself, but his magic pulsed so eagerly at the thought he quickly turned his thoughts away. Being a protection warrior openly was too dangerous. He hated to even consider the worlds reaction when they learned of them.

The instructor leaned down and whispered. "These tests are important; you can't just guess. If you can't hack the academics now, you'd better pack it in.

Sports won't get you through here."

"I did my best, sir."

The instructor nodded and took the test to his desk where he checked it and then frowned, one finger tapping the one hundred he'd just written on the top of the page. He made a note and attached it to the test, noting the time the boy had finished, and putting in big letters — probable cheater. At the end of the allotted time he sent this group for the next test.

This time, two kids finished early, a brother and sister. He didn't speak to them; he took their papers and graded them. With broad strokes, he circled the one-hundreds in red ink, wrote the times and a note to the commandant. 'Sir, I have three, one-hundreds, which as you know, is highly unlikely and most probably the result of cheating. How they got their hands on my test I don't know.' He signed his name with a scrawl and kept the papers to the side to bring to the attention of the commandant.

After the testing, they did simple exercises followed by a five-mile run. Charlie found it all rather boring. Stasia set the pace. He and Hawk followed, keeping easily in front of the others. The pace of the day picked up, if not the interest, as they were assigned to their rooms. He met and liked his roommates, and all were instructed on the proper way to make their beds, keep their room, and proper etiquette for greeting a superior officer, which was everyone.

Meanwhile, the test instructors were having an informal meeting with the commandant.

"They got perfect scores on every test," the instructor said as he placed his tests before the commandant.

The commandant nodded. "Yes, I was expecting them to do well. Admittedly, not quite this good, but they're presidential appointees sent here because of their academic prowess. You've all been briefed about their security bracelets. I guess now we know why. Put them in advanced courses; see how they do. We want to challenge them, not break them. So, if it's too much, let me know."

The first day ended with an induction ceremony where they'd take their oath of service in front of friends and family.

Sara's pride in him glowed as she watched the ceremony, and he was again struck by how lucky he was to know her so intimately. While he stood among his classmates, to human eyes alone in a group, love echoed between them. She was a part of his soul, with him always.

When he rose his hand to give his oath, his magic gathered in response, echoing in Sara. Immediately, he stopped speaking and coughed, trying to get Stasia's and Hawk's attention. Both glanced at him, and he gave the no talking sign, not able to do more, too busy attempting to reign in his magic and block Sara.

Her struggle to hold back the magic made his worse. This time the magic had gathered faster and more powerfully as soon as he'd said I swear. Static crawled over his arms, the magic waited to strike him and make his oath a reality.

He craned his head to see Sara run from the stands. She clutched her stomach as if it hurt but he knew she was afraid and worried, not in pain. Oz followed her, holding his phone to his ear.

Charlie didn't take the oath. Frustrated, his magic pushed, eager to be released, tingling inside his body. Apparently, his message was received, or Stasia and Hawk felt it too, because the pressure began to dissipate. A crack of thunder sounded although the sky was clear with no sign of rain. The hair on his arms stood up straight and all around him static electricity sparked off people. A streak of lightning flashed across the sky and hit behind the chapel. Charlie jumped. He wasn't the only one. Most of his classmates startled and some of the spectators screamed. The bright flash was clearly visible behind the chapel.

Stasia exchanged uneasy glances with Charlie.

Sweat beaded Charlie's brow and his hands shook. Sara was in physical pain now. Before he could decide to break formation and go to her, it passed. Tingles and static subsided, and the crowd settled down.

Oz ran in front of the podium where the commandant spoke. No one except his team could see him while he signed that Sara was fine and then ran to the back of the crowd where he regained visibility and resumed his seat.

With Sara's pain receding, Oz's reassuring nod enabled him to stand in formation when his entire being wanted her. His magic was pushing him, it too wanted to make sure Sara was fine. Sweat trickled down his face in the effort to hold his magic inside his body.

After the ceremony the midshipmen were given time to say goodbye to their families and friends who'd attended. A flurry of hugs and loud greetings confused the area as the crowd mingled.

Oz slapped Charlie on the shoulder. "Sara is fine. The lightning hit her but passed quickly. Major Nelson is coming to administer your oaths. Don't try to make any in public again. Sara went home. I'll be you until you get back. If you go fast, nobody will even miss you." Oz gestured for their family to gather around him and Charlie, blocking the view of people near them. "Invis three." He turned Charlie invisible and casted disguise on himself, the brief flickers of magic hidden in the press of people.

Charlie ran to Sara.

"Their magic was affected by the oath," Oz told Charlie's parents as they watched him run off. "They'll be fine once they touch, but they couldn't do it here, too much blue glow for a crowd. How are you two?" He turned to Stasia and Hawk.

Stasia rubbed her arms. "I had no idea what Chief meant by be quiet. Then I said I swear, and a giant weight settled on me and the magic tingled as if it were about to manifest. I wasn't sure I'd be able to hold it back."

Hawk nodded. "It's a weird sensation. Don't take an oath lightly. You can feel it like lighting about to strike."

"Well, good thing you stopped." Oz bumped his shoulder with his. "Or there would've been literal lightning, maybe on all of them. You could've killed your entire class."

Hawk shuddered. "I almost didn't stop until I remembered what happened when Charlie made his oath to Sara."

Fifteen minutes later Oz's cell phone rang. "We're coming back. Can you meet me where you left Sara?"

They met behind the building. Oz removed his disguise, and they walked out with Sara between them.

Charlie made quick farewells to his parents and then hugged Sara. "I love you. If it's too much, I'll quit. You're more important to me."

"We'll be fine, Charlie. I love you too, more than anything."

He smiled sadly and kissed her. Pride and sadness mixed with his own anticipation and worry in a confusing mix. Reluctantly, he released her and moved away.

Stasia and Hawk hugged Oz and Sara. Without speaking they returned to formation.

Oz put his arm around Sara as their friends went off to join their companies.

"We got this." He grinned at her and

pulled her ponytail. "I'll miss them too."

Sara leaned into his side, being careful to avoid touching his skin.

NOTORIETY

Within two weeks it was clear they weren't cheating and in fact found the work too easy. Their fitness instructors were thrilled with them, then horrified none intended to do any competitive sports. The football coach practically cried when Charlie turned him down. He went so far as to talk to the commandant when Charlie told him his academic schedule wouldn't permit time for sports.

"Competition is vital for a well-rounded officer," the coach argued, using the commandant's favorite quote.

"I agree, but in this case we have orders from the superintendent himself— they're not to compete. You can use them in training, but not competition."

"It's a crying shame. You should see them fence. Anastasia is easily Olympic material. I never saw anyone as graceful and quick as she is."

"I've seen them." The commandant leaned back in his black leather chair and folded his hands. "They're superb athletes, but orders are orders."

A few days later Stasia and Charlie were sitting in the grass waiting for their turns on the obstacle course. Charlie observed the other plebes while Stasia laid back with her eyes closed, enjoying the sun. Hawk stood and swung his arms, then stretched. If he relaxed too much, he tended to fade away from the instructor's sight.

"Hayes, you're up!" The instructor clicked his stopwatch as Charlie started.

Charlie didn't go fast; he went steadily.

The instructor frowned at him when he finished. "We expect a full effort, mister. Do it again!"

Stasia snorted a laugh.

The instructor, a fourth-year cadet, glared at her. "You think this is funny? You go too. The last one back gives me one hundred."

Hawk coughed into his hand, smothering a laugh.

The instructor glanced at him but said nothing. He started his stopwatch. His frown grew as they both took their time.

Charlie held back and ensured he came in last. Stasia could beat him without trying, but she'd let him set the pace. A hundred push-ups didn't make him sweat; he could do thousands.

"Miss Morales, see if you can show these slow pokes the proper grips to cross this." The instructor indicated a group of boys, all older and bigger than her, she was to instruct.

Stasia stood and saluted. "Yes, sir." With effortless grace she jumped and grabbed the bar. "Put your hand facing this way, thumb out. Use your bodyweight for momentum and release at the apogee. Make sure you know where your next move is and have a backup, there could be a wasp nest or snake where you intended to grab. You want to commit to your jump, but not marry it."

The boys laughed while Stasia repositioned their hands as needed and corrected positioning. One boy was having a hard time.

The instructor stood behind Stasia as she corrected the boy and Charlie stepped closer to listen in.

"You need more upper body strength for a quicker grab. Until you have it, go slower or you'll fall. It'll cost you more time that way. You're rushing too much."

Dejected and upset the boy shook his head, crossed his arms and narrowed his eyes. "I should be faster than you."

Stasia laughed. "I'm a lot stronger than I look. Girl's muscles don't look the same and I'm lighter. Trust me, you'll get a faster time if you don't rush."

She winked at Charlie, and he smothered his laugh, wondering if she were tempted to cast Sweet-Talk to get them to listen to her. Her aura, Friendly Persuasion made everyone she spoke with more likely to agree with her and shop keepers serve her first, giving her their best prices. Their first meal in the cafeteria had been funny with all the servers trying to serve her first but she'd spoken with them and they couldn't help but agree to make her wait like everyone else. *She'd have to speak to her professors too,* Charlie thought, suddenly worried her aura would affect the classwork they assigned her. They'd been so secluded from normal life he hadn't realized how differently the magic made everyone treat them but now that he was trying to fit in, the differences were glaring.

The boy Stasia spoke with now rolled his eyes but nodded and tried again. This time he made better time without falling and Stasia clapped.

The instructor shaded his eyes and examined his group of sweating plebes. Charlie followed his gaze. Most of them were sweating. He, Stasia and Hawk remained comfortable, neither the temperature nor the exercise here would be able to make them sweat. The instructor's eyes narrowed as he examined them, and Charlie hid his wince. There was nothing he could do about it.

"Bored, plebe?" A whistle swinging on a thin cord around his finger, the instructor stood in front of Hawk. "Or do you need a nap?"

Hawk hesitated, then opted for the truth. "Bored, sir."

The instructor choked back a surprised laugh. "A five-mile run will keep you occupied. Give me twenty laps!"

Hawk nodded, then remembered to say yes sir and ran off smiling.

The instructor returned to his plebes. "Sanchez, count Morales's laps. Let's see if I can make him sweat." The instructor glanced at his watch and resumed instructing the others. Charlie anxiously followed Hawk's progress worried his passive ability Hidden Nature would make him impossible for Sanchez to track, but Sanchez kept his eyes on him and seemed to be having no trouble.

Stasia was watching with a worried frown too and casted distract on every person who approached Sanchez.

Charlie snickered and had to cough to hide it when her distract caused an entire group of cadets to turn away from their instructor mid-word. The resultant lecture that followed captured everyone's attention, and Charlie nudged Sanchez when Hawk passed, reminding him he was counting the laps. They'd have to talk later about ensuring ways of keeping Hawk in view while outdoors. It hadn't occurred to Charlie before now it would be a problem.

Twenty minutes or so later, Hawk again stood in line, stretching, not looking at all hot or tired. The instructor scowled and gestured Sanchez over to him. "He did all twenty?"

"Yes, sir," Sanchez replied. "He's pretty fast."

The instructor called Hawk, Stasia and Charlie away from the others and faced them with his hands on his hips. "We expect full effort from you. I'm not saying you aren't doing well, but you aren't applying yourselves at all. You aren't pushing it."

Stasia and Hawk exchanged glances. Charlie started to speak and then thought better of it.

"This is just between us." The instructor

snapped his fingers. "Out with it."

"Sir, we're following orders," Charlie finally said.

"I see." Their instructor eyed them through half-closed lids. "Okay, get back to your companies."

A week later the instructor stood at the prow of his boat grinning. "This is the life, boys!" he bellowed. "Breathe it in!"

Charlie took an exaggerated breath of sea air, grinning at the six boys crewing his boat. The grin turned to a scowl as the instructor waved his arms at an approaching motorboat. A rooster tail of water sprayed over three of the sailboats.

"Pull 'em in tight now, boys, make way." The warning was heeded but made no difference.

Another motorboat joined the first and both raced illegally through the gathered sailboats, causing a wake and panic as the plebes tried not to run into each other or the motorboats. The instructor yelled directions from his boat, but two sailboats collided hard. Cadets yelled as a boom whipped around and knocked three boys into the water. One boat capsized, throwing shouting cadets into the water.

Hawk dove, cutting the surf without splashing.

Stasia jumped onto the capsized boat where she pulled two people onto the hull before the other midshipmen on her boat had time to react.

"Chief, ones trapped in the rigging!" she yelled.

Charlie dove in, warm water closing over his head. He stroked hard and used leap to propel himself through the water. A boy he didn't know struggled in the ropes tangled about him, his panicked gaze fastening on Charlie.

Charlie grabbed the rope and yanked, tearing the ropes loose, fittings and all. He pulled the boy through the water and surfaced to see Stasia helping the others into a nearby boat. Still treading water, Charlie lifted the boy out of the water and placed him on the capsized boat and then pulled himself out.

Stasia signed to him, asking if she should distract or use Sweet-Talk on the instructor, and Charlie winced when he glanced at the man. They'd been using advanced combat sign language and the instructor must wonder where and when they'd learned it. That she'd used the signs they'd worked out reassured him. The instructor would have no way of knowing what her gestures meant. He signed back for her to wait.

The instructor arrived at the boat the plebes were clinging to as Stasia examined them.

"Concussion and maybe a broken arm," she said as she gently manipulated the boy's arm. "One swallowed a lot of water and three are fine, just wet. Hawk is searching now for the last one."

"He's been down there a long time." The boy who'd swallowed the water said while leaning over the side, searching the water for sign of his missing friend. All around them the midshipmen shaded their eyes as they scanned the water for any sign of the missing boys.

Stasia flicked her fingers, casting Sweet-Talk. "Hawk's fine; he swims like a fish. Don't worry. He'll find him."

Charlie hoped he found him soon. He was worried, and Sara sensed it and was growing afraid. He was just about to suggest they move the boats from the area to give Hawk an easier time differentiating the people on his radar when Hawk's head broke the surface forty feet away. Charlie sighed in relief.

While he wasn't worried for Hawk, Hawk's ability to form an air bubble around his head would last for an hour, he was worried about keeping their secret and for the missing cadet. His magic seemed confused, pushing him and then retreating as if it didn't know whether Charlie should be protecting or not.

It took effort to keep his mouth closed when he wanted to yell directions and take charge. Only telling himself there was nothing he could do let him wait quietly but Sara was growing increasingly fearful and her fear agitated his magic. He'd have to do something soon or it'd burst from his body whether he wished it too or not. It roiled beneath his skin with increasing pressure and he gritted his teeth hard.

Hawk swam to the closest boat doing a backstroke with one hand, using the other to hold the unconscious boy's head above water.

Charlie's surge of relief eased Sara, but it was short-lived because he was still worried over the boys condition or maybe they were already stuck in a loop and it wasn't his worry. The thought made him groan, and Stasia glanced at him in alarm

"Sara is worried," he whispered as he lifted the boy onto the boat and started CPR.

She said nothing but her frown deepened. Hawk pulled himself from the water, and Charlie let him take over.

The boy gagged up sea water, and they

sat back. Charlie slapped Hawk's back, then clasped Stasia's hand hard in his a moment, hoping the contact would soothe the magic.

The instructor brought them all in and sent the injured to the infirmary. He paused thoughtfully as he passed the small sailboat and tugged one of the ropes Charlie had pulled free in the other boat but couldn't budge it. Charlie gave him what he hoped was an innocent smile and forced himself to unclench his fists.

A blue flicker raced across his fingertips and he headed to the instructor.

"I'm sorry, sir, but I need to visit the infirmary too."

"Is something wrong with your hands?" the instructor asked.

"What?" Charlie peered at his hands and winced as another flicker of blue appeared. "Oh… no. The glow is a battery warning; my security device needs a new one. The water probably shorted something."

The instructor nodded and dismissed him.

Thirty minutes later Brenda escorted Sara into the infirmary. "I'm sorry, Charlie, but I was so worried. I'm doing fine, but today I knew something was wrong," Sara embraced him, putting her hands against his face. A blue glow surrounded them then dissipated, and she moved her hand to his pulse.

"Nothing happened, just a minor training accident. None of us were involved. The worry was for the other people." Charlie put his face against her warm neck, breathing deeply to settle his pounding pulse the first sight of her had caused. "Three weeks is a long time. Don't worry about it. I'm surprised we lasted this long."

"How are you handling touching other people?" Brenda asked.

"I'm not touching them, except quickly. So far, it hasn't been a problem." Charlie grinned. "I'm not worried about it. I don't feel any discomfort. Let them wonder why they can't touch me."

"I wondered if the effect had worn off because your magic hasn't mingled." Brenda reached out and rested her palm on Charlie's hand. Forty seconds later she withdrew it, shaking and flexing her fingers.

"No idea, I should've checked. Next time I will."

"Well, your freshly primed now, so be careful."

"That's almost worse," Sara complained as

they drove away. "It's hard to only see him a few minutes."

"You haven't snuck in then?" Brenda gave her a knowing grin.

"No, we've been good, following the rules. But it isn't easy when I know something's wrong. My magic and I both want to summon him."

"How's everything going with you guys otherwise?"

"Oz and I are fine. We miss them a lot, all of them, but we're keeping busy. Guthrie got us a place to practice our magic. The magic is easier to hold back if I use it."

"Well, we aren't stationed too far away at Andrews. The Scouts can practice with you both too."

Sara grinned. "That would be awesome. Just hanging out with another girl would be amazing. I really miss Stasia too."

Brenda nodded and squeezed Sara's knee. Instead of returning to base right away, she hung out with Sara and Oz at their house for a while.

When she left, she called Major Nelson. "Sara and Oz need more company. Sara told me they have a spot to practice their magic. If some of us train with them, it would help."

"They're complaining?"

"Not at all, but I was there tonight, and

they were pathetically grateful for company. It's just the two of them all the time and they miss the others. They don't go out at all except to practice or get books or food. Female companionship is important for a girl Sara's age. Without Stasia… well, the Scouts are the next best thing."

"I'll take care of it." Major Nelson called Staff Sergeant Guthrie and arranged for the Scouts to work out with them. He also vulontold the Scouts to take Sara and Oz out of the house occasionally or go to their house.

A week later the plebes were put in new companies and taken to different locations. Given a compass, a knife and a rope, they were dropped off in a wooded area and told to find their way back.

For the first time all week Charlie was on a team with Stasia and Hawk along with his roommate Paul and three other boys he barely knew. He was sure the instructor wanted to see how they performed together, whether they'd stay on track or get distracted. Charlie grinned to himself. This training was nothing compared to what they'd learned in

New Mexico.

He stretched and shook out his shoulders. It felt good to be out from under the watchful eye of his instructors. "Okay, Hawk, what way?"

Hawk pointed, and they headed off.

"You're sure?" Paul asked doubtfully.

"Absolutely." Charlie said, gesturing Paul into the lead.

By this time most of the other midshipmen knew they were good at outdoorsmanship, so the others followed without complaint. Fifteen minutes later they reached a river.

Charlie took charge without thinking about it. "Hawk goes first, Stasia last, I'll go second. Everyone hold the line. Hawk, holler out if you hit a current."

No one needed the line. The current was mild, and it was an easy quick swim. In less than five minutes they were all across.

"Stop." Stasia held up a hand. "Traps dead ahead!" With a long stick she removed grasses covering a hole containing a paint bladder and squatted on her heels, looking the area over. "There's a backpack in that tree with a trap directly under it."

The rest of them watched as she jumped and swung herself effortlessly into the tree and grabbed the pack after making a quick examination. An easy jump landed her well clear of the trap beneath the tree. "It could be booby-trapped. I recommend using a stick or something to open it," she said as she offered the backpack to a teammate and winked at Hawk.

Charlie laughed, earning a puzzled glance from Paul. Both Stasia and Hawk could see traps without even trying. A twitch of their fingers would disarm them.

The bag wasn't booby-trapped, it held canned food, but there was no can opener. Charlie shrugged and used the knife, cutting the top off so quickly he made it look easy. Stasia handed him hers, and Hawk did the same. The others did as well once they'd tried to open the cans themselves.

"I bet there's a can opener in one of these trees or pits." Hawk gestured around at the sparse foliage.

Stasia shrugged and wiped out her empty can with grass before putting it into the pack. "Who cares? Let's move on. With Chief, we don't need one."

Charlie picked a different teammate and let him set the pace, slung the pack over his shoulder and followed. They were crossing a small rocky gully when Hawk warned of snakes.

"Hawk goes first through here," Charlie

said.

They followed Hawk through the ravine for ten more minutes. When Hawk indicated they needed to leave it, Charlie tossed Stasia and Hawk to the top and then boosted the others up to them.

"You guys knew each other before this, didn't you?" one of his teammates asked.

"Yeah, we did, and we've done a lot of training together, so we're used to being a team," Charlie said.

"Yeah, Chief has always been our team leader; it's natural to us. We don't mean to take over," Stasia added.

"Oh, it's no problem." Paul grinned at her. "I know who you are. I thought they'd doctored those pictures of you, but if anything, you're prettier in person."

Stasia smirked and purposely misunderstood. "Yeah, Chief's pretty, that's for sure."

Everyone laughed.

"Who are they?" one of the other teammates asked.

Paul said, "Team Valor, well, some of them anyway. I haven't seen the hot blond."

Stasia chuckled. "Oz isn't interested in being in the military, but you'll probably see him around, he'll be attending a few classes."

Charlie snickered.

Paul rolled his eyes. "I meant—"

Hawk interrupted, "We know who you meant, but don't call her that, she's his fiancée." Hawk nodded at Chief.

Paul blushed and mumbled, "Sorry."

"Who the hell is Team Valor?" another asked.

"Professional video game team." Stasia glanced at the boy and snorted. "We gave it up for all this." With a dramatic flourish, she pointed at the drought-killed plants around them.

Paul strode alongside Stasia. "If I was as good as you guys, I wouldn't have quit."

Stasia shrugged.

"Aren't you too young to be here?" Paul asked.

"Academic scholarship." Stasia dropped back beside her brother. "It's why we can't do sports— we can only do academics."

"Yeah, I heard you guys were acing the tests."

Stasia shrugged again.

"Hey, Chief, will your girlfriend be taking classes here too?" one of the other boys asked.

"Some maybe. She's studying medicine now. She'll be around though, using the gym and stuff."

"How the heck did you guys wrangle

that?"

"Security did. She agreed to work as a consultant when she graduates, and they agreed to let her use the facilities where she'd be safer. She's smarter than all of us put together and the Navy wants her to work for them."

"I knew there was a reason you played so well, you're like super geniuses or something," Paul said.

"Or something," Hawk agreed chuckling, making Charlie laugh again.

They came to a small brook; Hawk crossed it easily, then held the rope to give the others something to use to balance against. "These obstacles are pretty lame," Hawk complained.

"It's not like they can use live fire or mine fields." Stasia punched him in the arm as she passed him.

Hawk scowled. "I guess."

"You're sure this is the right way?" Paul asked a while later.

"Yeah, I always know what direction I'm going. It's a weird ability, but I can always tell." Hawk exchanged grins with Charlie.

Rangers never got lost. Once they'd been to a place they could return to it as unerringly as a homing pigeon. They also gave a speed buff to any group they were in. Reminded of that, Charlie slowed and made excuses to stop whenever he could.

Their group was still the first one back. By the end of the week everyone knew they'd been a professional video game team and were calling them Chief and Hawk.

- 6 -

AURAS

"So, you're the big chief I've been hearing about," a sarcastic voice said from behind Charlie on the first official day of school.

"Midshipman Fourth-Class Charles Hayes, sir." Charlie turned to face the speaker.

The firstie addressing him glowered with narrowed eyes and his hands on his hips. Both his tone and gaze were angry. The same height as Charlie, at six-foot three they stood eye-to-eye. Both broad shouldered and well-muscled, Charlie was five years younger than the first-class midshipman confronting him. Someday Charlie would be bigger than the firstie glaring at him.

"I don't think I like your tone, midi. Drop and give me twenty!"

"Yes, sir." Charlie dropped to the floor, did twenty fast pushups and then jumped to his feet.

76

The firstie ran his fingers through his short-cropped blond hair and narrowed his blue eyes at Charlie. "Rumor has it you're some kind of brainiac too. Tell me the general orders."

Charlie started to speak, and the firstie held a hand to his ear. "I can't hear you, mid, speak up!" He wasn't happy until Charlie was yelling the general orders at the top of his lungs.

"Yeah, that's not bad, but I think you need more practice. Let's say every hour you repeat that. If you're in a class, wait until after and do it twice. Come find me after dinner and I'll see if you've learned anything. Dismissed, plebe!"

Charlie saluted and hurried to his class. He'd thought the firstie's harassment was funny but quickly realized it would get old, and he worried about his aura affecting his classmates.

This is my team, he thought forcefully as he crossed the Yard. He headed to a group of new cadets and intentionally used his voice of command on them.

See, he told his magic as they saluted and scurried away to class as he'd ordered. *My team!* He wasn't sure it had done any good although he could feel the magic's satisfaction when they'd obeyed.

First-class midshipmen lurked over other plebes, having the freshmen shine their already spotless shoes and making them recite menus and do pushups. *All part of the academy experience*, he told himself and wondered how Stasia and Hawk were doing.

Sara had started classes the day before. *She and Oz were probably sipping lattes as they strolled to class.* He made it to his class on time and then felt like a fool afterward when he had to repeat the general orders four times at the top of his lungs and run to his next class. *At least his classes were interesting, and the teachers all seemed nice enough. None wanted their shoes shined anyway.*

Charlie's roommate Paul was in most of the same classes. Their other two roommates, Jeff and Dave, they rarely saw. At dinner, the same firstie cornered him and made him yell the general orders for the amusement of all.

My team, he kept repeating to himself, concentrating so hard he didn't have room for anger. Those closest gave him leery glances and moved away but they didn't run. *Progress*, he thought.

After dinner Charlie and Paul headed to the library when Charlie noticed Oz running. He slowed, hoping to see Sara but didn't spot her.

Paul paused beside him. "Toric already

has it in for you. I thought it would take him a day or two before he tried to put you in your place.”

“Toric?” Charlie turned his gaze from Oz to Paul.

“You know, the big handsome guy who just embarrassed you in front of everyone at dinner, Midshipman First Class Edward Toric. He’s the star around here, or at least he was until you showed up.”

“I won’t be a star. No sports for me; I’m not allowed,” Charlie said glumly.

“Well, true, but that’s just on the real teams, right? You can do the intramural stuff, can’t you?”

“As long as it isn’t official competition, I can participate.”

“Well, Toric holds a lot of records. I’m sure if he’s heard how good you did this summer, he’s worried you’ll break them.”

“How do you know all this?”

“My sister Emily. She graduated last year and gave me a long list of people to avoid pissing off,” Paul admitted.

“Could I borrow it?” Charlie grinned at him. “I’m aggravating people I haven’t even spoken with.” That was so true he winced. His aura was forcing confrontations or making the other students run from him every time he got annoyed.

Stasia practically followed him around to distract or cast Sweet-Talk to end the arguments. She hadn't complained but it must be annoying her.

Paul laughed. "Sure, I'll show you guys tonight, but let's not spread it around. If anyone hears they're on that list, I'm sure to catch hell."

Hawk and Stasia waited inside the library. Stasia had brought one of her roommates, and Hawk had come with two of his. They made introductions, opened their notebooks, and compared notes on their classes. Everyone was taking cyber security, seamanship, government and leadership. Charlie, Hawk, Paul, and Stasia, and Stasia's roommate Amy, were in advanced math and physics classes and everyone took different English classes.

They left an hour later. Stasia, Hawk, and Charlie returned to the dorm the long way, first going out of their way to pass by the wall behind their house. Neither Sara nor Oz were in sight. Nobody paused or asked to stop.

"I'll get us a study room tomorrow," Hawk offered as they split up for the evening.

The next day was similar except this time Toric made Charlie recite the day's menu to firsties passing into the dining hall.

All part of the academy experience, he reminded himself, trying not to let Toric or the other upperclassmen who smirked annoy him.

Charlie groaned when his intramural team formed with Toric's team the competition. Inhumanly fast reflexes and hand-eye coordination made Charlie a formidable opponent. He carried his team to victory with ease, never missing a basket or a pass. He almost felt bad about it, but these games were just for fun, they weren't ruining anyone's career or GPA. He decided to enjoy it and play, and his teammates appreciated his efforts. Charlie missed the camaraderie of sports, cheering your teammates on and being cheered on in return.

And his magic practically purred with happiness inside him. *My team,* he thought triumphantly and knew his magic agreed. These boys were his teammates, they'd gone from neutral to friendly.

Now, is all I have to do is play with everyone here, he thought sarcastically to himself and stifled his groan. *But at least the magic is learning.* It heartened him, and he headed back to class in a much more cheerful frame of mind.

Over the next week he tried a few different sports. He thought he'd like fencing, but he hated it. His instinct was to go for the kill, tapping someone's chest with the point wasn't working for him. The effort to hold his magic back made him sweat. The magic wanted him to hack and kill. While fencing, the magic magnified any spark of anger until he left the field in a towering rage.

Opponents cowered from him; his aura so strong no one around him could concentrate. The magic forced them to attack him instead of their partners, which lead to some hard to explain encounters. To avoid causing a scene he concentrated on Sara while he fenced, picturing her expression as they made love, remembering the warmth of her body and softness of her hair.

Usually, his sword swings got carried away while he daydreamed. Trained muscles fought as if he held a sword, not a rapier, and he tended to bruise the heck out of his rivals.

But at least I didn't force the entire room to attack me, he thought ruefully as he handed off the rapier to the next fencer.

Talking to his challenger worked as a distraction, and he could keep the magic happy if he helped teach instead of just attacking. The magic made no demands if it thought Charlie was instructing and not fighting. Before long, Charlie was helping teach every self-defense class he took, and the magic was accepting them. He didn't know if it understood he was training or if it just thought of them as his friends, but his aura was weakening around them. He knew it by the more casual way others approached, and Toric had begun to look smug and loom over him.

Stasia and Hawk tried jujitsu with him, and they had a great time. While sparing with each other they didn't need to hold back, but in public they had to slow their movement into a normal human range. The three of them learned to give advice as they fought to pacify the magic. Stasia used her Sweet-Talk and got the instructor to give them private lessons, and she even got him to teach Sara and Oz.

If Toric didn't harass him every single day, he would've been enjoying everything about school except for not seeing Sara. Time flew by, and his classes were going well. Everyone made new friends, and he stopped worrying so much about Sara.

She was handling the separation well. She'd had no nightmares or at least none he sensed. School work kept her occupied. Not unhappy or happy, but content and interested in what she was doing, which relieved him. He felt guilty he was happier than her and hoped as she made friends in school she'd have more fun there.

She'd never made friends quickly like Stasia did, always more solitary, less outgoing, but he was confident she'd make some in her own time. *Besides,* he told himself, *it's not like I'm happy every moment of every day either.* She had moments of happiness, and he tried to convince himself he felt guilty for nothing.

The next day, he saw Sara running and stopped to watch. The gray shorts and white T-shirt she wore like everyone else would've made her blend in if it wasn't for Tank and her long hair pulled into a ponytail. She looked so beautiful to him, his breath caught and tears came to his eyes. He turned away before he disgraced himself by crying.

Midshipman Martins commented on Tank. "I didn't know they allow dogs on campus."

"They don't," Charlie said. "That's a security dog. He's working."

"How do you know?" Martins asked.

Charlie spoke respectfully, Martins was an upperclassman Stasia had Sweet-Talked into tutoring them. "She's my girlfriend," Charlie admitted. "The dog's name is Tank. She works for the government and has permission to run here where it's safer."

"She's awful young to be working for the government," Martins said.

"Aren't we all?" Charlie said with an eyeroll that got a light laugh from Martins. "She's very smart."

"Smarter than you?" Paul turned to him, a surprised expression on his face.

"Much." Charlie hurried away.

Sara had felt him missing her and was now sad and lonely. Charlie scowled, unsure what to do. If he focused his attention on something else that might be easier for her or it might hurt her feelings if she interpreted it as he didn't care. Before he could decide how to handle it, he'd reached the library.

Paul held the door while Charlie hesitated.

Charlie glanced back, but Sara was out of sight now, and he wondered if she'd run home to cry. She was miserable enough to be crying. He straightened his shoulders and entered the library. He'd use his five-minute phone call tonight to reassure her.

They'd known this would be hard, and it wouldn't help either of them if he got into trouble by going to her now. The best thing he could do for her was to carry on like normal, so he took a deep breath and turned to Paul with a fake smile and continued speaking as if his heart wasn't breaking.

"Sara and Oz will both be taking classes here even though they don't officially attend."

"Ah, the other members of Team Valor. You'll have to introduce me; I was a big fan. It's not secret or anything?" Paul added when Charlie sighed.

"Not at all. I'm sure they'll all see her around." Charlie smiled. "I don't mind if everyone knows she's taken."

"The best ones always are," Paul heaved a disheartened sigh. He got a mischievous look in his eye and grinned at Charlie. "Maybe I can take her from you?"

"Ha!" Charlie exclaimed, but Paul's words had angered him, not at Paul who continued to smile, Charlie's aura not affecting him a whit. Paul was a friend and the magic knew it. But Paul had reminded him that people did want to take her from him, and he didn't know who his enemies were.

I'm training to protect her better, he told himself forcefully and his magic didn't press. They were in perfect agreement that she needed protecting and that he'd do it.

THE ARREST

Charlie's teacher was explaining the differences between classic physics and quantum theory when he felt Sara's surprise and then her fear. The jolts were sudden and strong enough to force an oof of surprise from him. He was already running to the door before his bracelet turned red. Without excusing himself or asking for permission, he held his wrist up, showing the professor his flashing bracelet as he ran out the door. His classmates stared in horrified fascination as he broke the rules leaving the room.

Stasia was just exiting her classroom next door. After a quick glance up and down the otherwise empty hallway, she turned herself invisible. Charlie raced into a nearby restroom. Still invisible, Stasia followed.

Sara was fighting. He didn't know how he knew it, but he was certain of it. He expected to be summoned at any moment. The seconds ticked by with glacial slowness.

"Maybe it was a false alarm?" Stasia whispered.

"It's not," Charlie clenched his fists and closed his eyes, concentrating. "She's afraid and hurt, not badly, but she's furious. I don't think she's fighting anymore though." His brow furrowed as he focused, trying to decipher Sara's mixed emotions. She mainly felt anger. "Damn it, we can't stay in here. I'm going to our house."

"Not for a phone?" Stasia asked worriedly.

"No, get home and call. I'll meet you there," Charlie said as he exited the bathroom.

No one was in sight, so he ran down the hall and jumped to the bottom floor, ignoring the stairs. Still invisible, Stasia sprinted past him. When he entered the next hallway, he had to slow to a more normal pace. He wanted to use Valorous Leap like Stasia was, but he couldn't risk being seen. If Sara had been more afraid and less angry he would've done it anyway.

Hawk caught up to him as he ran across campus. Charlie ignored all hails and ran, not going full out, but moving fast. More spikes of pain came from Sara as he raced around the back of the stone building and leaped the wall at his house. The alarm triggered as he crossed the wall, then turned off. Stasia was already inside.

"Major Nelson is sending Alpha team to her last known location. Beta team is suiting up. We're to wait here!" Stasia yelled from upstairs as he came through the door followed by Hawk.

"Hawk, how is Tank?" Charlie asked.

Hawk closed his eyes. "Furious and contained in a vehicle."

"Our car?" Stasia asked.

"No, he could open those doors."

Charlie hesitated, tempted to tell Hawk to make Tank attack. The dog get behind his target instantly, passing through walls or bars just like a rogue could, but he had no idea who was around. The car Tank was in might be sitting on a city street surrounded by innocent civilians. Hawk always kept him in defensive mode when he wasn't with him. If he was contained inside a car, Sara and Oz had let him be contained. They could order Tank to attack too. They couldn't choose what spells Tank would use like Hawk could, but the dog would obey an attack command by any of them. Charlie paced the kitchen growing angrier by the second. "Why isn't she summoning us?"

"Either she can't or doesn't want to. Calm down before you freak her out," Stasia ordered.

Ten minutes earlier, Sara had been cuffed and thrown into the back of a police cruiser.

Oz stood outside the car, holding Tank by the collar and yelling at the arresting officer. "The bracelet is shocking you. She isn't resisting. We can't take them off. Look!" The police officer who had her in custody wasn't listening. Another officer gestured for Oz to get into the back of a different police car.

The officer glared at her in the rear-view mirror. "We'll settle this at the precinct. Use that device on me again and there'll be hell to pay!"

"When I hit the red button, it triggered the defense mechanism. I'm cooperating just don't touch me," Sara said in exasperation.

The policeman just repeated her rights. "Now shut up!"

"Look,"— Sara held up her cuffed hands pleadingly— "We had nothing to do with that other than stopping them. This is a security device, and I can't take it off. If you'd read it, you'll see there's a number to call for the FBI. I'm sure they'll be here soon to straighten this out. The electric shocks are an automatic defense. I'm *not* tazing you."

"You're a liar. Your friend has that same bracelet and his wasn't giving off shocks." The policeman glared at her in the mirror.

"Because I triggered the alarm," Sara said, blaming the bracelet for his inability to touch her without getting a shock.

"Bullshit, you thought you could get away!" The police car pulled up to the back door of the precinct and he yanked her from the car. "Stop it right now!" He shook her hard when she shocked him again.

"I can't!" she yelled back. "Just stop touching me, and I'll come with you!"

The officer called for help and used another set of cuffs, twisting his baton through them, and dragged her inside using the baton.

Unable to keep her feet without pulling back, she injured her wrists as she stumbled behind the officer.

The officer who came to help opened the door and smirked. "Can't handle this little girl alone, huh?"

The officer dragging Sara snarled, "She has a weapon on her, and we'll need tools to remove it. And she isn't shy about using it either!" He tugged Sara passed his snickering coworker and opened a door to a small, windowless room with a metal table.

"I'm not going in there." Sara leaned back and braced herself. "Leave me right here; I won't move a muscle."

"You go where I say you go!" The officer tried to pull her inside as she resisted.

"Stop it! I can't go in there!" Her voice rose to panicked shrillness. "Why are you doing this? I didn't do anything!"

While his fellow officers laughed at his inability to get her into the room, he yanked on the cuffs. When that didn't work, he hit her behind the knees with his baton, knocking her off her feet.

Sara begged him to let her go as he dragged her through the door and chained her to the table.

"Stop it!" Afraid now and starting to hyperventilate, she screamed, "Let me go!" and then took a deep breath and spoke in a voice of forced calm. "Don't leave me alone in here, please!"

The officer smiled and slammed the door.

She jerked on the chains holding her wrists as hard as she could. Magic exploded from her body and swirled around the room before returning to her and reabsorbing. The chain on her left wrist gouged deep, leaving a blood smear on her shirt after she healed it. A sob she couldn't stop tore from her as she yanked again, trying to free her hands, and then stood shaking and panting. A minute later she yelled furiously to be let out.

Oz was in the other room handcuffed to a desk, furious as well." You can't lock her up like that; she's extremely claustrophobic! We're cooperating. There's no need to keep her in there!"

"She has a weapon I can't remove, which she used on me, and is under arrest," the officer said.

Oz pointed to his own wrist chained to the desk. "If you read it, you'll see there's a number to call, or call the FBI, but let her out." Oz cringed as Sara tried to break free from the room.

"Doesn't sound like cooperation to me." The officer smirked at the loud bangs and thumps and her tear-choked voice screaming to be released.

"It's a panic attack, and I promise, if you let her out or even just open the door, she'll calm down." Oz begged. "In twenty minutes this place will be crawling with FBI. Please don't make her wait in there."

"Yeah, sure… I'll worry about that later," the officer said, clearly not believing a word Oz said. "Give me your statement, then you can make a phone call."

Oz closed his eyes and took a deep breath. "Neither of us did anything wrong. The liquor store owner told you what happened. I heard him. Security tapes caught the entire incident. You can see what happened, but please, let— her— out!" he yelled, losing his patience.

Charlie was frantic. Sara was terrified and hurt and wanted him desperately. "Major, where is she?"

"Relax, I'm going to get her, you stay there. That's an order, I mean it, Charlie!"

The panic bracelets contained a GPS, and Major Nelson was in route to the police station.

"She's terrified and in pain. Where is she?" The room gained clarity and depth, and he knew his eyes had blazed to blue with his fury

"Are you sure? She shouldn't be either of those things. Angry maybe, but not hurt." Major Nelson said.

"Yes, I'm sure!" Charlie yelled. "Do you know where she is? Is Oz with her?"

"Yes, we thought so. Let me speak to Hawk," Major Nelson said.

"I'm here." Hawk grabbed the phone from Charlie.

"Go to the location where she hit the alarm. Track her from there. She should be fine now, so they might've removed her bracelet. Beta is on its way there." He hung up and called the police station. They were expecting him when he arrived.

Already suited up, Team Valor ran for the car. Minutes later they arrived at the address in question and Hawk began searching. Charlie waited inside the car, knowing his aura would cause the pedestrians to run in fear if he emerged. He was already causing them to skitter past on the sidewalk.

He closed his eyes and tried to communicate with his magic. They're neutral," he mumbled repeatedly but he knew it wouldn't work when he eyed them all as potential kidnappers too.

Eyes scanning the footprints no one could see except himself; Hawk followed the trail of Sara and Oz's movements. He fumbled for his sunglasses to cover his glowing eyes while pointing to where a car had been parked. "One man put her in a car here. Tank was in another car with Oz. The cars went down this street here. I'll track.

You follow me in our car."

The liquor store owner came out of his shop and surveyed them with narrowed eyes and a phone clutched in his hand. "Are you investigating the robbery?"

Stasia showed him her federal ID. "What happened here?"

"Two men came in and robbed me at gunpoint. When they left, they ran into two kids and their dog. The kids fought them off, and the police came and arrested everyone."

"Was anyone hurt?" Stasia asked.

"Not badly, no. The fight ended pretty quickly. Guns were fired, but no one was shot or anything."

"Why did they arrest all of them?" Hawk asked.

"I don't know. The one policeman said the girl tazed him. I told them the kids weren't involved, but the officer was pretty angry. He almost shot her dog."

"Thanks," Stasia said to the liquor store owner over her shoulder as she headed to Charlie.

"If she's at the police station, why is she so afraid? Hawk, keep tracking," Charlie ordered.

Charlie drove, following Hawk as Hawk trailed the car that had held Sara. Stasia lowered her sunglasses. The three of them wore custom-made glasses designed to hide the blue glow of magic when they became upset. Attached by magnets to their headgear, the glasses would stay on while they fought. Regular sunglasses worked to a degree. These allowed no blue glow to escape. Of course that only worked to hide the magic in their eyes. It did nothing to stop it from leaking from their skin as it was now.

Blue swirls of magic brought Stasia's anger to him clearly. Charlie eyed his team with satisfaction. Whoever had taken their mage and sun-priest would be very sorry when they caught up.

Major Nelson arrived at the precinct and flashed his ID at the front desk and was permitted to speak with Oz.

"Oh, thank God. They have Sara locked up, and she's freaking out. Get her out of there before she calls us," Oz said in greeting.

Major Nelson turned to the officer, frowning, his gaze flicking to the name on his shirt. "Is that true, Officer O'Brien? You locked her up?"

"She used a weapon on me and is safely contained," Officer O'Brien insisted.

"For the last time!" Oz yelled, "It wasn't a weapon, it was her security device! She can't turn it off. Just don't touch her!"

"Mr. Simmons is correct. Release her please." Major Nelson crossed his arms, leaning back with his lips pursed.

"Miss Mitchel is under arrest for assaulting an officer."

"I see." Major Nelson's eyes narrowed. "Proceed as you must but let her out of the room. I take full responsibility for her conduct. She'll remain seated."

"No." Officer O'Brien crossed his arms and glared at the major.

Major Nelson took out his cellphone, walked into the hallway and made a short call, then returned. "This is a matter of national security. I'm afraid I have to insist."

"Insist away," the officer said with a half-smile and one raised eyebrow. "I'm going to ask you to leave— once. If you refuse, I'll place you under arrest as well."

Fully suited up and heavily armed, Alpha team pushed by the police officer on the desk and forced open the door leading to the back room where Oz was.

"I wouldn't recommend that." Major Nelson smirked at Officer O'Brien as Alpha team surrounded Oz.

Police officers rushed into the room with

weapons drawn followed by the police captain.

"What's going on here?" he bellowed, eyeing the armed and armored men who'd entered his precinct.

"Officer O'Brien has one of my charges locked up, and I want her right now!"

"Miss Mitchel used a weapon on me and is under arrest," Officer O'Brien insisted heatedly.

"It wasn't a weapon— it was this!" Oz pointed to his bracelet, rattling the chain holding him to the desk. "Once she hit her panic button, she can't turn it off. It's a security feature and will shock anyone who touches her! She said she'd come with you. All you had to do was let go of her arm. Call the damned number on the damned bracelet!" Oz yelled, out of patience.

The captain examined Oz's bracelet, then turned to Officer O'Brien. "Let her out."

"She's uncooperative and dangerous, yelling and fighting me." Officer O'Brien crossed his arms, looking stubborn.

"Sara is severely claustrophobic, and you locked her in! It was a panic attack! Let her out!" Oz shouted.

Rick slung his assault rifle over his shoulder, leaned over and put his sunglasses on Oz who nodded absently. While everyone else continued speaking, Rick knelt and removed the cuff from Oz with a lock picking tool.

The captain held his hands out for the keys to the handcuffs.

Officer O'Brien reluctantly handed them over.

Alpha team intercepted Charlie before they arrived at the police station.

"Go home. The major is handling this," Brenda said.

Charlie took his sunglasses off, sliding them up on his helmet until the magnets clicked, holding them in place. "Not fast enough he isn't. She's terrified and hurt. I'm going to find her."

"We know where she is, and she'll be home soon." Brenda laid a hand on Charlie's tense shoulder.

"Did you see her with your own eyes?"

"No, but I saw Oz. I'm sure Sara is fine. Go home, Charlie. That's an order!" Brenda shoved his shoulder, not budging him an inch.

Charlie glared at her, his lips compressed, his eyes blazing blue. She glared back a moment, the glare fading to an exasperated expression. Brenda would never leave Sara in danger. He knew it, but his magic wanted Sara right now.

"She'll be home really soon," Rick said, "If you go there and cause a scene you'll make life harder for her."

"I know it, but I need her!"

He clamped his mouth closed and shook his head. "I need her safe," he said in a calmer voice and told himself she was safe, but he could feel her fear and need of him although the feelings were growing more muffled and he knew she was trying to block them from him. He finally got back into the car.

Stasia lifted her own glasses, revealing her brown eyes. "Oz would've said something to them if Sara wasn't there too somewhere. If she needs you, she could summon you."

Charlie nodded. Sara's fear had been replaced by anger. He felt no more pain from her now either, but she was furious and embarrassed. Or maybe that was his anger. He groaned aloud, frustrated at his inability to control his emotions.

- 8 -

HIDDEN FEELINGS

Team Valor arrived home twenty minutes before Oz and Sara. Stasia made sandwiches for Hawk and herself while Charlie paced, trying to get a handle on his anger.

He hugged Sara tightly when she came through the door. "Are you okay?" he whispered as he rested his hand on her pulse to reassure his magic.

She nodded. "I need a shower."

To Charlie's surprise, she pulled away and ran upstairs.

"What happened?" Stasia stared after Sara a moment before turning to Oz.

"Sara and I stopped for pizza on our way home. Two men came out of nowhere with guns. We found out later they'd just robbed a liquor store, but at the time we thought they were there to take us. So, we hit our buttons, and then hit them. The fight itself was

102

nothing. Right away we realized it wasn't an attempt just bad timing, but we didn't have time to call in before the police arrived and questioned us. We were cooperating. There were multiple witnesses, and I didn't think it would be any big deal."

Oz paused and winced. "Then an officer grabbed Sara's arm and it all went to hell. Tank lunged at him. I called him off, but the officer was sure Sara had tazed him or something and arrested her. The other officer put Tank with me and brought us to the station. It would've been fine except they locked her in a small room and chained her to a table. She completely freaked out." Oz winced at Stasia's appalled look and placed his arm around her shoulder. "Nobody was hurt, and she's fine now."

"She isn't fine!" Charlie took a deep breath, exhaling loudly. "Sorry, Oz, I'm not mad at you, but she isn't okay, she's furious." Sara was a lot of things. The wild, uneven spikes of her emotions scared him.

"Stay here while I check in and see about returning you guys to campus," Major Nelson said.

"Use my office." Oz slapped Charlie's shoulder and led Major Nelson to the small downstairs room he used as his workshop and study.

"I'm going up to talk to her. Tell Major Nelson I'm not returning to school until she's okay," Charlie said to Stasia and headed upstairs. He pulled off his gear as he entered their bedroom and dropped it on the floor next to his uniform that already lay in a heap by the closet. Sara had left her clothes in a pile outside the bathroom. Charlie joined her in the shower.

Face upturned to the hot water, she didn't acknowledge his entrance. Not sure what to say to calm her internal emotional storm, he held her unspeaking.

He wanted to tell her she should've summoned them, but she'd been right not to. If she hadn't been chained to that damned table, she would've been fine. Once locked in it would've taken a lot of explaining if they'd appeared in there too. But, being in that room shouldn't have caused the reaction it had either. He understood why it had, but he'd thought she was doing better than that. After another minute of internal debate, he settled for, "I love you."

Miserable and afraid, she nodded, putting her face against his neck but didn't speak. The warm water grew cool as they stood under the spray. Still without speaking, Sara left the shower and put on a sweat suit.

When he dressed in his uniform, her eyes

filled with tears.

"Don't cry," he pleaded. "I have to go back."

She turned away and hurried downstairs, speaking over her shoulder, "I know. I'm sorry."

Charlie stood there undecided on what to do. It was always hard when they parted, sharing the echoing sadness. But she seemed different now, both sad and angry.

He'd assumed the anger was for what had happened, but now wasn't sure. Slowly, he followed, stopping in the kitchen where she spoke with the major while snuggling Lucky.

"This is over." Major Nelson was saying as Charlie entered. "No charges were filed or will be filed. You don't need to do anything at all."

"Will we have to testify against those men?" Oz asked.

"Unlikely, the liquor store's security camera filmed the entire thing. Nice kick by the way."

Oz nodded modestly. "And them?" he indicated Stasia, Hawk and Charlie with his chin.

"I'll escort them back onto campus and they make up any missed work. No one will question them."

"When?" Charlie's troubled gaze rested

on Sara petting Lucky.

Major Nelson lifted an eyebrow and regarded them. "As soon as you're ready."

Charlie took Lucky from Sara and placed the cat on the floor. He grabbed Sara's hand and led her to the living room. "I'm sorry I wasn't there for you."

"And, I'm sorry this happened." She turned away from him. "I shouldn't have hit the button, but I saw the guns and panicked. I panic too easily," she said bitterly.

"No, it was the right thing to do, never hesitate." He placed both of his hands on her shoulders, trying to meet her eyes, but she wouldn't look up. "Sara, promise me you won't hesitate."

She nodded. Her emotions fluctuated wildly, and he couldn't pin down what she felt other than anger, fear and to his surprise shame. The strength of her conflicting emotions made him think he was sensing her magic as well.

"Do you think you should talk to Doctor Gotlieb?" He cringed at the rising anger and shame that suggestion generated in her.

"I'm a mess, aren't I?" Tears filled her eyes and she lifted both hands to cover her face as she spun away.

Charlie forced a laugh and smoothed her wet hair back. "Not at all. Anyone would be angry. I'm angry. Not at you," he added hastily when she tensed. "But, at that officer for scaring you. It's okay to be angry, and you'll get over the fear."

Soft and low, her voice shook when she spoke. "I hate how I feel." Shame overlaid her fear as she laid her head on his shoulder.

"And I hate that I make you so sad and angry."

"My magic is angry with me. I had to fight it to not call you. I'm not angry at you. I'm proud of you and what you're doing. I just miss you. The separation won't kill me. I'm sure they all have girlfriends who miss them."

"In the history of the world no one has ever loved someone as much as I love you." Charlie tipped her chin up for a kiss.

The shame retreated. Filled with love and longing she kissed him back, then rested her face on his, her hot tears trickling down his cheek.

"Please, don't cry, or I'll start," he murmured as he stroked her hair.

She snorted a small laugh, pulled away and wiped her eyes. "I'm fine. You better go. I love you." Her voice broke. Although she appeared calm her emotions spiked and mutated as she tried to tame them. "Go... I'll be okay... I can't help this." Both hands made a vague gesture about her as she grimaced. "But, it'll be worse if I get you into trouble." Stifling a sob she ran back to the kitchen where she gave Stasia a quick hug and they whispered together a moment. A fake smile on her face, she hugged Hawk and took Scrap from him. "Scrap's a good boy, isn't he?" she said to the dog as she cuddled him. Scrap licked her face, and she laughed.

Major Nelson examined them. "Good to go?"

Everyone agreed they were. Charlie bit his lip. The show Sara put on was convincing. If he couldn't sense her emotions he wouldn't realize how distraught she was. Both his choices sucked. If he stayed, she'd be upset he wasn't in school. When he left, she'd feel abandoned. The hell of it was, he *was* abandoning her. He did look forward to returning to school. Not that he resented helping her, he just wished he could do both.

"I'm staying here tonight," Major Nelson informed them after another moment's inspection.

Charlie wondered if he looked as conflicted as he felt. He gave the major an anxious smile and kissed Sara again before he left. By outward appearances she was fine. He was very worried. The last thing she needed was to share his worry, but he couldn't stop. He groaned in frustration.

"Problems?" Major Nelson glanced at Charlie in the rear-view mirror.

"Sara needs to visit Doctor Gotlieb. Don't let her put it off," Charlie said through gritted teeth, hating that he couldn't help her and that she needed help. He hated the people who'd scared her so badly today and the ones who'd hurt her so much to begin with. But mostly he despised himself for leaving her to deal with everything alone when she wanted him.

"She seemed all right to me; I mean after we got her out."

"She isn't okay. Not even a little bit okay." Charlie closed his eyes and leaned his head back on the seat.

Major Nelson nodded. "I'll call for the doctor right away, and I'll stay a few days to make sure they're fine."

Major Nelson escorted them onto campus. They had to wait while the duty officer informed the officer of the watch, then were issued passes and returned to their assignments.

Charlie joined his company for dinner but couldn't eat. When Midshipman Toric approached he almost growled, in no mood for Toric's petty harassment. He almost wished his intimidating aura still worked but he'd convinced his magic to well that fellow cadets were his team.

Paul sat across from Charlie at the dining table and tried to head Toric off with a friendly greeting.

Toric ignored Paul and stopped by Charlie. He loomed over him with his hands on his hips and a dark grin. "So, went on a little jaunt and lost your appetite?" Toric eyed the uneaten food. "We don't waste rations here. You took it. You eat it."

"Yes, sir." Practice with controlling his anger let Charlie keep his voice calm and even as he picked up the fork.

Toric grabbed the fork and mixed the food together before handing the fork back." Carry on." He sauntered away, taking a seat at the table across from Charlie.

Charlie ate the food without even tasting it, too caught up in Sara's feelings. Still angry, hurt confusion mixed with shame and worry, and she wanted him. Spikes of emotion fluctuated as she tried to block her need of him, which made him feel worse.

His friends at the table left him alone. His roommate lifted his brows in inquiry but said nothing aloud. Charlie shook his head minutely, indicating he didn't want to talk.

A third-year student stopped at his table at the end of the meal. "Your girl and the dog are running."

Charlie nodded his thanks.

Even though he never went to see either Oz or Sara when they came on campus someone almost always informed him, and he did like to know. Sometimes he saw Sara and Oz jogging together and knew she saw him too by the brief flare of happiness followed by longing then sadness.

Toric also heard that Sara was running. "I think I'll go for a run after dinner." He grinned at Charlie.

It made Charlie smile. Sara was in no mood to be polite, and Tank would eat him alive.

Toric paused beside Charlie and glared down at him. "Something funny, mister?"

"Something's always funny somewhere," Charlie replied with an even bigger smile. It drove Toric crazy when he couldn't get a rise out of the plebes.

Toric stalked off, and Charlie and his roommate went to join their study group.

"Toric's an idiot." Paul shaded his eyes with one hand and stared after Toric as they walked to the library. "We could cancel this and go for a run too," he offered as he paused in front of the library and glanced back.

Oz, Sara and Tank ran in the distance.

Toric and a few of his buddies followed right on their heels.

"No, I want to plot out those tangents and what did I miss in physics?" Charlie didn't glance back. Sara had seen him; the familiar sparkle of her happiness warmed him. It was enough for now. Her anger had faded and her emotions had evened out. Her flicker of annoyance made him smile. Toric must've approached her.

"It doesn't bother you at all that he's after her, does it?" Paul asked as they went upstairs to the study room.

"Not even a little bit. Sara doesn't like him, and she loves me."

"Man, it must be nice to be that confident. Toric's handsome and popular and used to getting any girl he wants. I wouldn't want him anywhere near my girlfriend." Paul gave Charlie a crooked grin.

Charlie chuckled. "Well, he doesn't have a prayer with my girl. Sara makes her feelings very clear."

Paul shrugged and dropped the subject. No one spoke until they reached the study room.

Charlie took a paper from the table and got right to business.

"Show me what you already learned." Midshipman First Class Stevens pointed to the paper in Charlie's hand. "What's the 'wave-function' $\psi(x)$?"

Charlie wrote rapidly on a separate piece of paper.

Stevens peered over Charlie's shoulder. "Very good. Now we determine if that's expectation values or normal values."

Charlie concentrated hard. It was easier to control his emotions and ignore Sara's while concentrating. So he focused intently while they traded ideas back and forth and talked over the logic of the problems until everyone was clear about the concepts. The numbers and formulas gained the clarity he was used to seeing when his eyes flared, and he knew his magic was learning them too. The thought made him laugh, and he waved the surprised glances away.

"Okay, we meet again Monday at the same time. Nice work." Stevens said as they broke up for the night.

Paul and Charlie left together. Both still had papers to work on before lights out. Charlie went the long way where he could see the windows of his bedroom at home brightly lit. *Sara must be up studying too.* Her concentration was a soothing balm to his agitated magic.

"You know the people who live there or something?" Paul asked as they both stopped while Charlie stared at the house. "We always stop here."

"I live there," Charlie admitted. Sara was absorbed in something she found interesting and it relieved him enough that he was able to give Paul a real smile. "Sometimes I like to see who's home." They headed back to their room where their other roommates were probably already busy studying.

"Oh, I thought you were from Florida. I read that somewhere when I looked up your team."

"I was. We moved here in May. Where are you from?"

"Vermont. You'll have to come home with me sometime and go skiing. I'm five minutes from a great slope," Paul offered.

"Sounds fun, but my time off will be spent at home."

"I miss my family too. More than I thought I would, actually. Especially the home cooking and loud dinners." Paul was quiet a moment. "I don't know if it would be harder or easier if they were so close but I couldn't see them."

"Then you'll have to come to my house sometime. Stasia's a great cook, but I'm warning you now, Sara isn't. Although, she's getting better, or I'm getting used to it," he finished with a laugh.

"All of Team Valor lives there?" Paul glanced back at the house.

Charlie stopped walking and laid his hand on Paul's shoulder. "Yes, but don't let that get around, okay? It's safer for Sara if nobody knows where she is."

"Man, you guys take security pretty seriously."

Charlie shrugged and looked away as he resumed walking. "We have to. I can't discuss it but believe me when I say we learned the hard way."

"I heard you had an incident today."

"A small one." Charlie gave another small shrug. "I can't talk about the details to anyone, but if our wristbands flash we're supposed to run to our assigned spot. Sometimes it's just drills and sometimes, like today, it's a misunderstanding."

"Misunderstanding?"

"You know, like someone hits your car… is it a kidnapper trying to grab you, or an old lady who shouldn't be driving? We always have to assume kidnapper and that an attempt on one of us means the rest of us are in danger."

"Jeez, that happens to you?" Paul stopped walking as they entered their dorm room. Eyebrows raised, he faced Charlie.

"Not lately, thank God. But we're careful

and safe here on campus. Afraid to room with me now?" Charlie sat and placed his feet on his desk and arms behind his head. Head tilted to one side, he grinned at Paul, waiting for his answer.

Paul entered the room, letting the door shut behind him and began undressing. "I don't know, maybe." Paul glanced at Charlie from the corner of his eye. "Should I be?"

"I don't think so, but maybe a little… I mean, what are the chances that someone comes here and tries to grab one of us right on campus?" Charlie asked after a moment of consideration.

"Not big, I wouldn't think, but honestly, I can't imagine anyone wanting you that much." Paul snickered as he jumped into his bed.

"Sara does," Charlie said smugly.

Paul threw his pillow at him.

At a little after three a.m. Sara summoned everyone. Terrified in her sleep, she woke with a scream when Charlie shook her shoulder.

"Oh, God, not again," she said when she realized what she'd done. "I'm sorry, and I'll try not to do it again." Dull and lifeless her voice was a monotone so wildly at odds with her inner turmoil it rose the small hairs on Charlie's arm. She gestured everyone away as she sat and pulled up the covers. "I'm fine, just a bad dream."

Charlie frowned at her lie. She was still frightened and now embarrassed.

Hawk ran downstairs to wake Major Nelson who was sleeping on the couch.

"Sara summoned us in her sleep. It's a damned good thing she wasn't a mage and fire balling the house."

Major Nelson sat and stretched. "Can you sneak back?"

Hawk snickered.

Major Nelson laughed too. "Okay, go back. If anyone noticed you were gone, have them call me."

"I'm sorry guys." Sara punched Charlie's pillow, which she clutched in front of her as she sat in the bed. Rumpled sheets and tousled hair showed she'd had a restless night before the nightmare. The shirt she wore to sleep in came to her thighs.

Charlie gazed in dismay at his wrinkled sweatshirt beside her. Usually, when he wasn't home, she slept in his T-shirt but the fact she was clutching his sweatshirt as if it were a teddy bear alarmed him. He lifted his glowing hands and placed them on her face.

A sob caught in her throat as she pressed his palms against her cheek, then jerked away. The terror receded, leaving a low-level fear, anger, and embarrassed shame that Charlie could see as dark streaks on her brightness. Black, red, and pink swirls settled down to wisps behind his closed eyes.

"Don't worry about it." Stasia ruffled her hair. "We don't mind." She gave Sara a hug, exchanged a worried glance with Charlie, casted invisible, and left.

Charlie sat beside his wife and rubbed her back. "Want to tell me about the dream?"

"Same old, same old. Bad guys, dark rooms, gun shots, brains on the wall yada, yada, yada. I'm sick of myself." Sara punched the pillow again and dropped it behind her.

"It really isn't a big deal. No one will even miss us."

Sara shrugged. "Always being the weakest link sucks. You guys are so nice when you should be mad I pull you out of bed and disrupt your nights."

Charlie heaved an exasperated sigh. "It isn't like you're doing it on purpose."

She shrugged again and dropped back onto her pillows. "Yeah, you better go. I'm fine."

He smoothed the curve of her eyebrow

with a fingertip. Embarrassment and anger jumped to lust as he kissed her cheek. Her desire for him instantly aroused him, and she laughed and waved him away. He smiled and left her alone in bed. Much calmer than earlier, it was easier to leave her this time.

Oz waited downstairs in a pair of sweats. "Sara okay?" he asked as they went into the backyard.

"Better than before." Charlie glanced up at his lighted window. Only a little worried, Sara was determined now, in the preoccupied state she entered when deep in thought. She was probably studying. He wasn't sure if she was using study to distract herself from lust or fear. Once again he was leaving her to deal with her problems alone. Problems he could help with if he stayed. But she wanted him to go to school too. Confused, he said nothing.

Oz nodded and casted invisible on him.

Charlie hopped the wall and ran back to the school. The Yard was quiet with small patches of light from the streetlamps lighting the darkness. The dorm entrance remained well lit. In his boxers and white T-shirt there'd be hell to pay if he were caught out of his room.

Stasia wore gray sweats and was waiting by the entrance. If found together at night, they'd be expelled. It didn't worry him though, no one would see them. Charlie spell-stole her invisible, and they were in their rooms in no time.

Dressed in a heavy sweatshirt and sweatpants Sara was downstairs with Major Nelson when Oz came in.

"Everyone's headed back, and I doubt anyone missed them." Oz ruffled Sara's hair and kissed her cheek. "Don't let this bother you; we really aren't mad."

"You're better friends than I deserve. I wish I could say it won't happen again, but I can't," she finished angrily.

Oz gave her another quick hug. "Well, don't make it a bigger deal than it is. Everyone has nightmares. Hawk probably uses his call and we just sleep through it. If you stress about this, it'll get worse."

Sara scowled and grabbed Lucky who was rubbing against her legs. "I know. And, I'm trying not to."

"Go get some sleep," Major Nelson said. "If it happens again, no big deal. We can handle this."

Oz gave Sara a quick hug and returned to his room.

"I have a paper to work on anyway." Sara made herself a cup of coffee before heading back to her room.

Nobody had noticed their absence or return.

The next morning Charlie visited the infirmary to call Major Nelson. "How's Sara?"

"She seems fine. She went to class as usual anyhow, but she's hard to read. You'd know better than me."

"Did you call the doctor?"

"Yes, he'll be here tomorrow."

"Good. Get me copies of the keys to a side door or something in case she does it again and Stasia can't help me."

"I'll see to it. How do you think she is?"

"Upset, sad, angry, embarrassed, afraid, disgusted, take your pick… she's all of those in varying degrees. I'd say genuinely miserable."

"She seems so calm and doesn't seem unhappy."

"Yeah, she would've been a great actress like her mother. If we didn't have this link, I'd have no idea either. I'm trying hard to notice these changes in case our connection fades. I never want to mistake her moods that badly."

"So, how's that going?"

"Not good," Charlie admitted. "She's

great at appearing calm when she's really upset."

"Don't worry about it, son. No one has ever been able to figure out a woman's moods," Major Nelson said with laughter in his voice.

Charlie would've laughed too except Sara wasn't a woman. She was a sun priest whose needs had powerful repercussions and his magic was making sure he didn't forget it.

RHEA

A week later Sara called Hawk. "I need a favor," she said as soon as he answered.

"Sure, what's up?"

"Could you train another dog for me?"

"Is something wrong with Tank," Hawk asked anxiously.

"No, Tank is awesome. I love him, but I'm wearing him out. He needs more sleep."

"Oh." Hawk thought a moment. "The nightmares are back and you're using him to wake you?"

"Yes, and it's too much for him. He's killing himself trying to stay awake in class too. There's too many people there for him to relax, and he's exhausted. I'd like to leave him home to sleep but it does help to have him with me. My magic feels better when Tank's near me in crowds." Sara was silent a moment. "Hawk, this is asking a lot, but I really need him to wake me at night."

"Don't worry about it, I can train a new dog to wake you in no time at all. Just don't bring her out in public until I get a chance to finish her training. And I already know just the dog we want. I've been researching a good mate for Tank. The breeder is in France though, so it'll be expensive to get her here."

"Not a problem," Sara heaved a sigh of relief. "Thanks, Hawk. How soon can we get her?"

"By this weekend. I'll call the major. He can send someone to pick her up and arrange for me to get the weekend off to train her. And we'll make our money back eventually on her pups," he added as an afterthought.

"Maybe we should keep a few and you could train some for the parents?"

"I thought that too, but I'd need time to train them, and I don't have a lot of that right now," Hawk said.

"Mention it to the major. Maybe they can work something out. Oz or I could bring them to you on campus if they'd let you train them there," Sara said eagerly.

"I'll ask. And, Sara, don't worry about, um, calling us out at night. From midnight to 0500 we're all tucked in bed. If you need us, they won't even realize we're gone. Everyone has extra uniforms at home and can sneak back with no problem, so get some rest, and let Tank rest too."

"You'll make sure all of you are in bed at those times?"

"Don't have to, it's the rules here. But, yes, I'll tell them."

"Thanks, Hawk," Sara said earnestly. "I love you."

"I love you to, Sara, and I'll see you this weekend."

Hawk hung up right as his roommate yelled attention on deck. Toric stood behind him

"New girlfriend, mid?" Toric asked.

Hawk groaned.

His roommates gave him sympathetic looks.

"No, just a friend," Hawk said.

"Sara... Hmm, isn't that your friend's girl? Does he know you loovveee her?" Toric drew the word out sarcastically.

Hawk nodded. "He does."

"Yeah, I heard she was easy. She lives with that blond kid… you know that, right? Apparently, she loves a lot of people," Toric smirked.

Hawk tensed and then smiled. "She doesn't love you though, does she?"

Toric's smirk turned to a glare and he ran a hand over the top of Hawk's desk. "This place is filthy. All of you better spend your free time tonight cleaning this mess."

"Yes, sir," Hawk's roommates said.

Toric's smug glance traversed everyone before he strolled from the room.

"Sorry, guys," Hawk said when they were alone again in the room.

"Meh, it's all good. You can help us with our homework after we clean," one said.

"The hell with that, I want one of his dogs," another said with a grin.

"Where would you keep it, knucklehead?"

The boy who wanted the dog sighed. "Yeah, but someday, when I finally get married and have my own place?"

"So never," the other boy said.

They were all laughing as they left to eat.

Major Nelson showed up at their house Friday night with a Blue Bay Shepard. Smaller than Tank and more delicately framed, her black fur was thick and luxurious and her eyes a clear gray. Both dogs possessed the same lupine build, wolfish snout and short, sharply-pricked ears.

"I'm working on permission for him to

train them on campus, but even if you breed her right away it'll be spring by the time the pups are old enough to train. Until then he'll have to come here to work with her. She's a sweetheart. I wouldn't mind one of her pups myself," Major Nelson said as he rubbed the dog's ears. He handed Oz a packet of paperwork. "All her papers. She's good to go. All of her medical records are there too."

"Hawk can introduce her to the rest of our menagerie tomorrow." Oz took her leash. "She can sleep in the garage tonight. Thanks for bringing her."

"No problem. How's everything going? Any more night excursions?" Major Nelson asked Sara.

"No, thank god. I'm being careful," Sara said.

Oz shrugged as he bent to pet the dog. "You're not getting enough sleep, but our new girl will fix that."

"It's all under control," Sara said to Major Nelson before he could respond.

Three days later, in the middle of the afternoon, Oz called Major Nelson. "Someone is following us in a dark-blue four-door, license plate 2GAT123," Oz said as soon as the major answered.

"Sara is with you?"

"Yes, we're fine, but we can't shake this car without using extreme methods. Should we?" Oz asked.

"No, let me see what I can find out first. Can you see the driver or passengers?"

"No, it has tinted windows. One person is visible in the front seat. He's wearing a baseball cap and black hoodie and we can't make out his face."

"And you're sure he's following you?"

"Yes, he even waited in the parking lot when we parked at the store. We were hoping we were wrong, but we've been zigging and zagging all over, and he's still behind us."

"Okay, I'll set off the green button and get Valor suited up just in case. Head toward the base, and we'll take this guy and find out what he wants. If anyone else shows, hit your panic buttons. I'll call you back in a minute on where to meet me."

Charlie's bracelet flashed green at lunch. Unsurprised, he went to the hall phone and called in. He'd felt Sara's growing uneasiness and she was really worried now.

"Get home and suited up. You might be summoned. I'll fill you in later," Major

Nelson said.

Stasia and Hawk caught up to Charlie as he hung up the phone.

"Go home and suit up," Charlie said quietly. "Major Nelson will call us. Sara is worried but not afraid." They exited campus by the gate nearest their house. Once off campus, they broke into a jog. As soon as they got home they suited up, putting on their black armor, facemasks, and headgear and grabbing their weapons.

Major Nelson called Sara back and told them a Mr. Eugene Robinson owned the car. "Is it still following you?"

"Yes, its four cars back. Neither of us recognizes that name, should we?" Oz asked.

"No, he isn't a known terrorist and has no criminal record. We're checking now to see if it's a stolen car. Meet me on Canal Street. Go behind the bridge abutment to summon the team and we'll take him. Use as little razzle dazzle as you can. If anyone else turns off down that road behind or in front of him, let me know ASAP," Major Nelson ordered.

Oz drove to the indicated street. They got out of the car already shielded by Sara and went out of sight of the road behind the bridge abutment where Sara summoned everyone.

"What's up?" Stasia asked as Charlie gave Sara a quick hug then bent to pat Tank.

"We aren't sure," Oz said, "We're being followed, and the major wants us to take him discreetly, no showy stuff."

Stasia turned herself invisible and went to reconnoiter. "He's here," she reported over her headset mic. "I'm going for a peek. Hawk, cover me."

Hawk slunk into the dried weeds on the side of the road and flanked the car, his gun already in hand. No one who wasn't looking for him specifically, and looking right at him, would notice him. He took a position offering him a clear shot, and stood still, fading into complete invisibility. Tank circled the opposite way of Stasia, barely rippling the high grass he slunk through. Hawk's Assassin Attack spell kept the dog invisible.

"One man," Stasia reported. "No visible weapons. He's writing in a notebook. There's a laptop open on the seat next to him and a blue book-bag on the floor of the passenger side. I can take him easily."

"Have Sara and Oz show themselves. I want to see what he does," Major Nelson ordered. "I'm almost there. When I arrive, I'll block the road behind him."

Sara and Oz slowly returned to their own car.

"He's taking notes," Stasia reported in a whisper.

"Let him know you see him, although how he doesn't realize that, I don't know," Major Nelson ordered as he pulled in behind the other car.

Sara and Oz turned from their car and approached the other car, stopping next to Hawk on the grass.

"He's getting out," Stasia warned.

Charlie remained out of sight behind the bridge, waiting anxiously. He and his magic both hated that Sara and Oz faced a threat without him. He wasn't sure he'd have been able to hold back if Tank wasn't with her. Like Charlie, Tank could force attackers to focus on him. It wouldn't take Charlie more than seconds to leap into range. He'd be close before Hawk's Focus Attack wore off. It was a tactic they'd used frequently in the game to gain an advantageous starting position and the magic seemed to know it.

"So, um, what are you doing here?" the man asked.

"Philip?" Sara smacked herself in the head with one hand. "Why the hell are you following us?"

"You know this guy?" Hawk whispered.

"Who are you?" Oz asked.

"A friend of hers. Who are you?" Philip

put his hands in the pocket of his hoody, and Stasia tensed behind him.

"We aren't friends, Philip. I barely know you. Philip's in one of my classes," Sara said to Oz and then turned back to Philip. "Why did you follow us?"

"To find out where you live," Philip said. "I had to follow you; you wouldn't tell me."

"Because I didn't want you to know, you moron!" Sara yelled. "I'm not your friend, and I'll never ever introduce you to Anastasia, not ever. It's seriously creepy that you followed me."

Philip didn't react to Sara's anger, turning instead to Oz. "I heard you live with some guy. Is this him? he asked as he eyed Oz. "Oh, hey, I know who you are. Maybe you could introduce us?" He grinned at Oz.

"Not in a million years," Oz said.

Philip shrugged again, still grinning. "So, you guys live together, then? I bet she comes over too. And, you're wrong, Sara, we are friends."

Sara sighed with exasperation. "Look, I get it, you're a fan, but please, don't ever follow me again, it freaks me out."

"More importantly, it freaks me out!" Charlie exclaimed as he came out from behind the pillar. He still wore his facemask, but he'd left his swords and shield on the ground. "Don't bother her again, don't speak to her, don't sit near her, don't even look at her," Charlie said in a soft dangerous voice as he put an arm around Sara.

"So, who are you?" Philip asked with interest, not intimidated at all, transferring his grin to Charlie.

"Her fiancé," Charlie said. He eyed Philip uneasily. Protective aura should've scared him, but he acted as if he couldn't feel it.

"Why are you dressed like that?"

"He's Special Forces and was on his way out when I called him and told him someone was following me," Sara said quickly.

"Nice, that's cool, an Army guy. It's chill, we're just friends," Philip said to Charlie.

"I'm not your friend!" Sara yelled and smacked herself in the forehead again. "We can't ever be friends; your behavior is completely inappropriate."

"I grow on people, you'll see," Philip said. "Nice to meet you, Oz. I'll see you in class, Sara." Still grinning, he got back into his car and drove away.

"Okay, so that was creepy," Sara said. "Stasia, he's like obsessed with you, always asking me questions, which I never answer. I never speak to him at all if I can help it. I'll switch classes tomorrow."

"Yeah, he has a creep factor of ten,"

Stasia agreed. "It's like he didn't even hear a word you or Chief said. He didn't even react to his aura. That guy is seriously disconnected from reality."

Major Nelson pulled up in his car and rolled down the window. "I heard the entire thing. If you need help switching that class let me know. If he contacts you again, or follows you, or does anything at all, tell me. We can get a restraining order. If anyone else is harassing you, let us know."

"He wasn't harassing me, just annoying me. Lots of people talk to me; most go away when I make it clear I'm not looking for new friends. Some persist until I give them an autograph. He's the only one who won't take get lost for an answer." Sara turned to her friends. "Sorry about all the drama. I didn't realize it was him. If I'd known, I would've just confronted him. Sorry to drag everyone out."

"No, you did the right thing," Major Nelson said. "Don't ever confront him alone. We want you all to be cautious. I'll bring you guys back," he said to Stasia, Hawk and Charlie.

Sara gave them all a quick hug and kissed Charlie quickly.

"I'm sorry," she repeated softly.

"It's okay," Charlie said, but he simmered

with anger she could feel.

Major Nelson said, "We better test to make sure your aura is still working."

Sara's anxiety spiked and she clutched his arm hard. Charlie said, "It's nothing to worry about." He glared at Major Nelson as he hugged Sara.

Major Nelson rolled his eyes and turned away.

"You're perfectly safe," Charlie whispered, wincing at the lie. He was worried now too but he hoped she thought it was her own worry she was sensing.

She remained stiff in his arms and smiled wanly when she broke away from him and hurried to her car.

Major Nelson gestured impatiently for them to get in his car.

"Major Harris will run some tests."

"Stop here," Charlie said waving at the strip mall they were passing."

"She can—"

"No. I need to know right now."

Charlie was angry now and his Voice-of-Command made the major pull over even though he continued to demure.

"This is a risk. You shouldn't intentionally try to scare civilians to soothe your girlfriend."

"This has nothing to do with her. I need

to know. If I've trained my magic not to protect her…"

Fresh rage suffused him. He was angry at himself for training the magic, begging it to not affect the people he was near when he was angry because it inconvenienced him. He hadn't once thought of how the lack of his aura would affect Sara.

He hopped from the car before it had come to a complete stop and grinned in relief when the woman exiting the store screamed and ran, dropping her shopping. Two men near the door stepped backward with their hands up.

"Get out here before you cause a riot," Major Nelson said as he yanked him by the arm. "Let Liz run the tests."

"It still works," Charlie said in relief that changed to worry as he considered Philip's lack of reaction. *The kid must be crazy as a loon,* he thought uneasily as he followed the major back to the car.

The next day Sara called Major Nelson. "Philip's leaning on my car. I'm sure I could get him to leave, but you told me to call."

"Call campus security. Tell them he won't

leave you alone. Let's make our case for a restraining order," Major Nelson said.

Sara called, and campus security came and spoke to Philip and filled out a report. The next day Philip was at her car even though she'd parked off campus. Again, she called campus police. They came but told her they couldn't in the future unless she parked on campus.

The same thing happened the next day. Annoyed and unsettled she left the car there and took a cab home.

Oz gave her a ride to school the following day, and she gave him her keys. Philip waited outside all her classes. He never approached, but he was always there. She took Oz's car home.

"Philip was at your car again today," Oz said when he arrived home. "I told him if I caught him there tomorrow, he'd be sorry. He's seriously creepy. He talked about Stasia like they were dating, and I'm pretty sure he thinks you guys just broke up."

That night Scrap set their alarm off.

Major Nelson called when he received the alert. "I'm arranging for Hawk to come home and discover why Scrap set off the alarm. It could be a false alarm."

Hawk came home and hunkered down by Scrap and then walked the property with him.

"Someone was lurking by the fence. Granted Scrap's attention span is about two minutes, but he insists he watched someone here. I can detect where they squatted, and I could track them. Should I?"

"No. It might've been someone just tying their shoe. We have no pictures. No one actually touched the fence but tell Scrap he's a good boy. Let's keep vigilant," Major Nelson said as he rubbed the small dog's tummy.

The next morning, Philip stood at their gate. "Is Stasis home? I thought she'd like a ride to class or something?"

Oz glared at him in disgust. "Were you here last night?"

Philip shrugged and smiled. "Can you tell her I'm here now?"

Oz grabbed him by the arm and foot swept him onto the ground where he held his throat in a light grip. "Anastasia doesn't live here and isn't here now. If she knew you were bothering Sara, she'd be furious with you. Never come here again!" He squeezed Philip's throat a moment and then let him rise.

Philip nodded, smiled and sauntered away.

Charlie knew Sara was annoyed and uneasy and guessed the reason was Philip.

Liz's tests had shown there was no difference in his aura except for his classmates. Sara's relief had been tremendous. Tonight, when he could make a phone call, he'd confirm his suspicion. A stalker fan wasn't that big of a deal in the scheme of things, but his anger simmered. Anger that was likely the cause of Sara's uneasiness, but maybe Philip was really scaring her. The thought made him angrier and her uneasiness bloomed to real worry. They were caught in a loop.

The phone rules his company lived under made things harder on Sara then they needed to be as he couldn't reassure her until tonight. All day she'd be worried about his anger. That thought just made him angrier, and he sighed with frustration as her worry spiked.

That night he called her, and she assured him Philip was under control. Before he could finish reassuring her that he wasn't angry with her, he had to go. His company was only allowed one five-minute phone call a night. After lights out, he couldn't sleep. Sara needed him, and he felt awful for not going to her. She wasn't in danger or afraid, she was lonely and reacted to his guilt by blocking him as hard as she could. Her emotions grew so muffled he could barely sense anything except intense concentration.

That she didn't want him to sense her hurt. Philip was driving a wedge between them.

Over the next week, Philip wasn't around, and tension Charlie hadn't even realized he had eased.

The new dog, they named Rhea, was working out beautifully. Hawk taught Rhea how to use the dog door and to wake Sara if she tossed or turned too much or her hands clenched. Whenever Sara slept, Rhea kept watch and had only needed to wake her a few times. Tank and Scrap seemed to like her fine; she was fitting in with no problems. Hawk assured Sara that she wouldn't bother Lucky who thought all dogs loved cats.

To Charlie's relief Sara seemed much better and was keeping very busy with schoolwork. She was no longer keeping him awake worrying about her, she fell asleep before he went to bed, and rose before him for early classes.

Sara left the house at one a.m.

Oz frowned out his window as she drove away. "Charlie is gonna freak if he finds out your doing this," he mumbled before heading back to bed.

Sara drove straight to Andrews. Three times a week she came late at night to meet Doctor Gotlieb when she was sure Charlie would be asleep and therefore not aware of her emotions as she spoke to the doctor.

Doctor Gotlieb opened his door at her first light knock and gestured her into the room. "While I appreciate the necessity for meeting at night, Sara, I still don't like you driving here alone so late. I'd be happy to come to you."

Sara nervously smiled at him. "No, I couldn't ask you to do that. What you do for me already is a lot to ask. And hopefully soon we can meet at more normal hours."

The doctor nodded and took a seat in one of the overstuffed brown leather chairs and put his slippered feet on the ottoman. Sara sat on the edge of the matching chair and twined her fingers together.

"So, how's the Philip situation?" the doctor asked as he reached over and poured a cup of tea.

"Good, I think. It's been a week and I haven't seen him even once. I think he's gotten the message. God, I hope he has! I hate being the one who brings the drama all the time!" she burst out.

Doctor Gotlieb handed her the cup of steaming tea. "A stalker fan is hardly your fault."

Sara set the tea beside her on the small table that sat between the chairs. "My fault or not, it's always me bringing the problems and I hate it! She took a deep breath, picked up the tea and blew on it.

"Charlie is angry?"

"Not so much this week. I believe him when he says he isn't angry with me, but he's angry because of me and that's almost as bad."

"No, he's angry because of Philip. Taking that on yourself isn't right. And, that isn't what bothers you. If you're honest with yourself, you'll see that. Are you still staying up all night?"

Sara set the tea down again, twisted her fingers together and nodded, avoiding the doctor's gaze. "Sometimes I wish I went to school with them; isn't that pathetic?" Cheeks red, she glanced at the doctor and then away. "Stasia doesn't need me following her around, clinging to her, and neither does Charlie. My need for him is already smothering him, and I know going to the school there is stupid, trading seeing him more now for seeing him less after graduation, but I miss him so much.

"Sara, it isn't wrong to want to be with the people you love," Doctor Gotlieb said gently.

"But it is wrong to smother them with my attention. No, not my attention, my neediness. I want to be an equal partner on Team Valor, not the one who always needs help or attention."

"No, we all feel that, the need for attention from those we love. Charlie needs you too, and while he loves the school and is busy and happy, the need isn't as intense as yours, but it's there. You aren't bothering him. The magic makes him able to feel your need, that isn't your fault, and he doesn't mind. The feelings aren't wrong Sara. Admit to yourself you're afraid to scare him away and then admit it to him. Let yourself have these emotions without fear, and I promise you, they won't be as scary."

Sara jumped up and paced. "What if it does scare him away?"

Doctor Gotlieb laughed. "Think about this logically, you already feel them, and as you explained to me, blocking them doesn't work well, so what could it hurt to try it my way?"

Sara stood at the dark window, leaning her forehead against the glass.

"Can you trust him?"

"I do."

"No, not believe him, trust him. Reveal

the parts of yourself that you don't like, the fear and insecurity. Stop trying to hide who you are. Trust is hard, Sara. The connection you share makes it a necessity. You're going to drive yourself crazy trying to hold back or hide your feelings."

A small snort of laughter fogged the glass. "You just want to meet in the daytime."

Doctor Gotlieb chortled. "True, but you know I'm right. How long do you think you can hide what you really feel with schoolwork?"

A week later Sara sat on her kitchen floor with a scalpel, a small handheld suction, a roll of paper towels, a textbook and a bottle of lidocaine. A stack of syringes and a microscope with prepared slides rested on the floor behind her.

"What the hell are you doing?" Oz asked, curling his lip at the bloody paper towels.

"I'm looking at the nerves in my hand. It's gross, but it's also cool. Come see this."

Oz watched in disgusted fascination as she pointed out a small white line. "My ulna nerve, and don't worry, I can't feel a thing,

144

but this is interesting, watch." Sara casted a Soothe spell on Rhea who was sleeping near her. "Did you see?" she asked excitedly.

"I'm not sure what I saw," Oz admitted.

"You have to watch closely. Hey, maybe you could film it," Sara said. "I only have about five more minutes to do this."

Oz took out his phone and held it over her hand.

Sara wiped up the blood oozing from her wrist and casted the spell again. Blue eyes narrowed in concentration, she made another incision and did it again. Caught up in her work, changing the cuts and having Oz move the camera, she lost track of time.

Finally Oz said, "Enough already, you're grossing me out."

Startled, she glanced at the blood-splattered kitchen floor and grimaced. "Sorry, got carried away, but it's so fascinating. I hope I got some good pictures. I wish Liz could help me, but she can't touch me."

Sara healed her hand and arm and cleaned up the mess. "This is gross," she admitted as she eyed their garbage filled with bloody paper towels. "I need a lab and more equipment."

"What were we looking at?" Oz asked.

"I have an extra nerve in my hand beneath the ulna nerve, and you can see a flicker of blue magic right when I cast, just a tiny little bit. She swung her arm around to get her circulation moving to dispel the effects of the lidocaine and eyed Oz thoughtfully. "I couldn't talk you into some experiments, could I? I'd wear gloves and it won't hurt; I promise."

Oz sighed. "Fine, but not on the kitchen floor either. Let's get you a real lab somewhere, and let's say, two more years of school first."

Sara laughed. "I'll admit I'm jumping ahead, but it's so fascinating. If I can find out where it comes from, think of the possibilities. Maybe we can change what we can do, or give it to everyone, or make artificial magic, or...."

"Whoa there, Einstein. How about you learn all about the regular human body first."

"I don't want to brag or anything, but I sort of did that already. I'm working on neuroscience now," Sara said.

"You've passed all those classes already?" Oz asked in surprise.

"I would if they'd give me the tests. You don't find it, well... easy? I can learn a course in a few weeks and some even faster. When I've learned what's being taught, I just move on to the next one, it's too slow in those classes."

"I hear you, but if you want the degree, you have to finish," Oz said.

"I could care less about the degree." Sara shrugged and grinned at Oz. "I just want to learn. An entire week on the nerves of the hand is four and a half days too long. I know it's my magic that makes me smarter, but I *am* smarter. The slow pace is killing me," Sara said.

"Me too," Oz admitted. "So, you just leave the class then?"

"Yep, once I feel I'm not learning anything new. I go back sometimes when they teach other stuff, but I can't make myself sit through days or weeks of something I already understand. I just go sit in another classroom and learn what's being taught there."

Oz laughed. "And no one says anything?"

"No, I'll probably flunk every class or score very badly because I'm never there, but who cares? I'm not here for a piece of paper."

"Well, you do need a certain GPA to stay in school. Let's do this, show up for every test and all exams, you'll get f's on homework and pop quizzes, but it should average to a grade good enough to stay in school. You can probably do some homework too."

"I do try to make all tests, but they don't always announce them ahead of time or post them on their websites."

"Let's see if Major Nelson can help. You really should get a degree, Sara."

Sara laughed. "And you wish you skipped out of all your classes teaching you nothing."

"Sort of, but I use the time in class to write or plan programs," Oz said. "They think I'm diligently taking notes and really I'm not paying the slightest bit of attention."

"I guess I can do that more too. Let's call the major, we need a new strategy," Sara said.

- 10 -

TRUST IS A TWO-WAY STREET

"So, school's too easy." General Campbell leaned back in the swivel chair.

"For them, yes," Major Nelson said. "Sara's been skipping classes she already understands and taking others. Oz has been attending all of his, but says he does his own work in a lot of them. This system is holding them back."

"I assume they have an idea they want our help with," the general said dryly.

"Yes, sir. They want to test out of any class they believe they're ready for. If the class requires lab hours, they'll do them. They both want degrees, so they'll finish classes for them, but basically they want to do what Sara is already doing, to be free to attend whatever class they wish."

"And, what do they expect us to do?"

"Get them official permission. If they don't finish a class, it's an incomplete. Not handing in homework or missing quizzes will lower their grade. If they knew when a quiz was or what the homework was they could do it, but they don't want to sit through classes to find those things out when they already understand the material."

"I can see how that would be frustrating, but Jesus, the professors will hate them," the general said.

"Some," Major Nelson agreed. "But, I think most will help them. After all, there's no shame in a pupil being smarter than you are."

"Are the academy students having the same issue?" the general asked.

"Not that they've said. They're doing well, but honestly, they aren't as smart as Sara and Oz. Sara and Oz are in a league of their own," Major Nelson said.

"It's funny how their game characters reflected their real personalities so much." The general rested his elbows on the desk and steepled his fingers. "Sara and Oz were always more intellectual than the others, and then they pick characters with high intellects. Charles has wanted to be a Marine for a long time and plays a tank. I find that fascinating."

"So, what character are you playing?" Major Nelson asked.

General Campbell laughed and leaned back again in his seat. "A paladin. I have a level fifty, and you?"

"I play a warrior. I did try the paladin, the heals intrigued me, but I like the warrior better."

"Major Harris wrote an interesting report on the Scouts and the characters they play. You should ask her to let you read it." General Campbell turned in his swivel seat and looked out the window. "I'll see what I can do for them, but no promises. I wonder if we're doing the right thing, educating them like this, when we don't know what the magic can really do. We might never know. They could live their lives and die and take it with them."

"Or, and I think this is what you're really worried about," Major Nelson said softly, "they could live their lives and die and leave it behind but unchained with their knowledge."

"I admit it gives me sleepless nights," the general admitted, still looking pensively from the window. In sudden decision, he swung around and said, "We'll teach them everything they can learn. They're good kids, and we'll do our best to see they stay that way. Everyone will work diligently to make this magic a blessing."

Major Nelson nodded. "Thank God General Flores lacked imagination until it was too late. If Sara is right, and it isn't an effect, but a being, a young one that is learning, we need to keep it happy with its hosts."

"Yes happy, but not undisciplined. Make sure they're in control of when the magic merges, at least as much as they can be." General Campbell swung back around to the picture window and again gazed pensively outside. "Dismissed," he said softly.

Major Nelson saluted and left, closing the door quietly behind himself.

October passed, and November arrived with midterm pressures. Charlie was out of sorts and cranky. Sara had been pushing him away. She'd said nothing, but she was withdrawn when they spoke, and her feelings seemed muffled and distant. She loved him, he knew that, but something was wrong with their relationship. He couldn't wait to finish these exams and go home where they'd have time and privacy to work out their problems.

Contemplating that Sara might ask him to quit school made Charlie nervous and sad. He hastily pushed the thoughts away and turned his attention to his test, then felt guilty. She wasn't the only one trying to hide her feelings.

Charlie, Stasia and Hawk walked home together for Thanksgiving break. Five glorious days of freedom lay ahead of them. Midterms were over, and they were sure they'd done well. Sara and Oz waited for them on the front porch with the dogs.

Hawk knelt to ruffle ears while the dogs excitedly crowded around him. Sara gave Stasia a big hug. "God, I've missed you. I have so much to tell you, and I want to hear all about your roommates."

Next, she went to Hawk and hugged him.

"Rhea's been great." Sara bent to run her hands over the pregnant dog's silky ears. "Do you plan to give her more training while you're here?"

"Yeah, I want you guys to be able to take her with you on runs too," Hawk said.

Oz laughed as the dogs slobbered on him. "If you ever want to wear that uniform again, you better go change."

"I'm going to change too," Stasia said. "And I'm cooking dinner. I've been dying for Mom's pasta sauce." She glanced at her watch and the hair rising on her arms. "Dinner will be at six, and we can catch up then," she said with a smile for Sara. "Try not to explode the house," she added with a grin at Charlie.

He grinned back. "No promises." A soft blue glow surrounded him as he followed Sara up the stairs in a fever of impatience. Sara beat him to their room and was already undressing. Her hands shook as she fumbled with her buttons.

The uniform he wore fell in a heap at his feet. "Relax, don't hold the magic in so hard. It's just us." Charlie waited until he could see her magic and then touched her hand. With a whoosh that knocked them both over, their magic collided.

Sara had the foresight to open the windows so they weren't broken, but everything in the room rattled. He crawled over to her. The blue glow surrounding her was dense and lit by small flickers of static electricity.

"Jesus, are you okay?"

She nodded and grabbed his hand.

The magic engulfing him was almost painful. Static landed with sharp shocks before dissipating.

He pulled her onto his lap and rubbed his hands over her naked back. "Holy crap, Sara, don't wait that long. You're going to kill us!"

She choked back a laugh. "It's embarrassing how much I need you," she mumbled as she pressed herself against his chest while rubbing her hands over his bare shoulders.

Charlie chuckled. "God, no it isn't." His voice lowered. "I love that you need me." He kissed her neck on her favorite spot.

She moaned softly and pushed harder against him. They managed to be on time for dinner.

"Oh, my god, Stasia, this is so good!" Charlie said as he took a third helping.

Stasia grinned. "I made a lot, so eat up. You need to keep your, um, strength up."

Sara blushed and then laughed when Hawk snickered. "It was good of your parents to let you all stay here for Thanksgiving," she said. "Oz and I were talking about Christmas. His mother wants him to come home. No way can we let him go there without us, but she could come here. We could invite all the parents here for Christmas. Rhea will be too pregnant to travel by then. If we turn the attic into guest rooms, and move Oz's office into the basement, there'll be plenty of room. Oz needs more room anyway."

"The attic? Is there enough headroom up

there?" Stasia asked.

"Plenty for two rooms and a bathroom. Sky lights and dormer windows will make it light and cozy," Sara added. "Hawk will lose a piece of his room for the stairs. Not a big piece, but still...."

"Sure, it's fine with me," Hawk shrugged and helped himself to more pasta. "But, I'm sure Mom wouldn't mind sleeping on the couch or going to a hotel."

"They're already doing me a favor by coming here," Sara said. "The least we can do is be hospitable."

"Well, it's fine with me too," Charlie said, "and they're doing all of us a favor by coming here, not just you."

"It's okay with me too," Stasia said. "I'll call my mom tomorrow and send her a ticket."

Thanksgiving break passed too fast for everyone. "In less than a month I'll be home again." Charlie said as he and Sara spent their last night together. "And, I'll make sure we can have at least three hours alone every two weeks. Longer than that is too hard on the magic."

Sara didn't respond, but Charlie felt her relief. "Sara, if you need something, ask me. There's nothing I wouldn't do for you. You know that, right?"

She sat to lean over him, her hair curtaining them. "I know, which is why I hate to ask you. I already take advantage of you guys too much. You shouldn't have to take care of me. Don't think I'm unaware everyone stays in the zone because of me. Everyone tiptoes around my issues and gives up things they want because I'm scared. Like Hawk giving up his free time to train a dog for me, and Oz taking me to class because I'm afraid to run into Philip." Sara pushed him back onto the bed when he sat up glaring. "Not afraid of Philip, afraid I'm making you angry and disrupting your day." She clarified giving him a crooked smile when he relaxed. "I want us to be equal partners."

"Don't worry about making me mad about Philip. That idiot would make anyone angry. Besides, I'm getting much better at controlling my anger. And everyone stays in the zone for all our safety." His eyes shining blue, Charlie kissed her and then leaned his forehead on hers. "I want to take care of you," he said huskily and had to stop and clear his throat he was so choked up with emotion. "I want to be the person you come to first for everything. You're never a bother. I can't help worrying about you, but you're never ever an inconvenience or something I don't want to deal with. I want to be to you what you are to me… everything!"

Sara lay in his arms deep in thought. The familiar feel of concentration began to worry him. Whatever she had to say would be important and her anxiety over it echoed his.

"Sometimes it scares me how much I need you," she finally admitted. "When I remember when we just played together and how I felt for you then, how much I wanted you to ask me out, at how afraid I was you wouldn't like me that way— that feeling is so much more now, that when I let myself really feel it… really feel how much I need you, not my magic, but just me, it scares me to death."

Charlie idly wrapped her hair around his fingers as he thought about what she'd said. He leaned over her on one elbow and traced the outline of her brow with a fingertip. "Please don't push me away or hold back your emotions. When you close me out like that, it hurts. I wish you could have the need without the fear. There's no reason to be afraid of losing me. As long as I live I'll be there for you in every way I can be. Never doubt it. Nothing will scare me away. Don't block your emotions so hard. Can't you feel my need for you?"

Sara giggled and snuggled closer. "Sometimes more than others.

"But, yes I do." The laughter fled as she blushed and glanced away. "Promise that no matter what I feel, you won't quit school or stop doing any of the things you love?"

"Can we compromise? I promise to talk to you first, but I can't promise to continue doing something that hurts you."

Sara started crying.

"What? Why are you so unhappy?"

"How can I share things that I know you won't like, that will make you unhappy?"

"Trust."

She laughed and then stilled and to his surprise became angry

"What?" He repeated, more worried now.

"Have you been talking to Doctor Gotlieb about me?"

"No. Should I?" His eyes narrowed at her guilt.

Sara sat up, pulling the sheet up to cover herself. "Trust is a two-way street. So, you'll have to trust me when I say I can handle something no matter how I feel about it."

Charlie reached over and grabbed her pillow, scrunched it behind his head, and crossed his arms. "Out with it. Why are you so guilty?"

Sara paused and bit her lip, lifting eyes shining with unshed tears to his. "Because I go at night when you're asleep to see the doctor."

"Okay… And?" While the thought of her meeting in secret with the doctor didn't thrill him, he was glad she was seeing him.

"Well, I've been avoiding anything that might upset you… or trying to anyways."

Charlie snorted. "Hasn't worked to well."

Sara laughed and threw herself into his arms, putting her face against his. Relief and love filled her now, echoing his. "Okay, I'll be more open, and you try not to feel bad about how I feel."

"Right now, you feel pretty good," Charlie murmured as he ran his hands over her soft curves, smiling against her hair at her response. Her revelations eased him, and he told himself he'd been worried for nothing. She really did want him to stay in school. Maybe now he'd stop feeling so bad about it and she could stop worrying about making him feel bad about wanting him home.

"I love you." Her breath was a warm sigh against his skin that made him shiver in anticipation.

"Show me," he breathed.

"Well, you're in a good mood," Paul said as a greeting when he returned to school.

"I had a great weekend. How was yours?"

"Good, over too soon."

Charlie grinned. "That it was."

He liked that she missed him. He hated to leave her, and it eased her to feel it, and he laughed over their struggles to hide their feelings when it felt so much better to feel them.

Paul gave him a curious glance and he waved him away, but he couldn't keep the grin from his face. Sharing made them both feel better and all he felt from her now was love.

"I think I'm getting the hang of this," he said, and Paul quirked an eyebrow.

"It sucks leaving her, she really worries, but I think we got this."

"Well good for you. My girlfriend didn't seem that thrilled to see me, and frankly, I was glad to come back. Her whining was getting on my nerves. I've told her a million times we only get one call a day and she still complains."

Paul shook his head and put his feet up on his desk.

Charlie said, "Sara was thrilled to see me. Sometimes I think she wants this more than I do. Well, not this. She wants me to be happy…" He trailed off as he realized how lucky he was. She could ask him to give up this dream and he'd do it, but she did love him and wanted him to have everything he wanted.

"My girl is the opposite. She's been after me to break the rules, sneak out and call her. It wouldn't bother her a lick if I got expelled."

"It would crush Sara. She really loves me."

"And you're a lucky bastard. Alisha likes the idea of an officer, but she has no idea how hard we work to get there, and I don't think she'd really like being an officer's wife." He grimaced ruefully. "Or maybe I should say this officer wouldn't really like having such a selfish wife. I don't think we'll be together much longer."

"I'm certain Sara and I will be together forever."

TRUTH AND CONSEQUENCES

Charlie went to bed while his roommates were still up doing homework and talking. To avoid conversation he pulled the blanket up to his chin and rolled to face the wall. He wanted privacy to decipher Sara's emotions and to savor the closeness he felt to her. The connection they shared seemed clearer than ever. He hadn't realized how much she could block him. The sadness and loneliness he'd expected, but her frustrated longing took him by surprise, exacerbating his own.

Aggravated, he groaned and rolled onto his back, throwing an arm over his eyes, and then laughed aloud. The lust echoing between them was his fault for asking her to be totally honest. Somehow, they needed to balance privacy with sharing.

Paul jumped up into his own bed. "You, okay?"

"Yeah, I just forgot something."

His other two roommates put their books away and everyone went to bed. That night he had the most erotic dreams of his life.

Okay, maybe total honesty wasn't the way to go, he thought when he woke the next morning. Usually the first one up and out for the day, today he was last.

"Bad dreams?" Paul asked. "You were tossing and turning all night."

Charlie blushed and turned away. "Something like that," he agreed.

Paul laughed. "Forget I asked."

On Sunday, Stasia had left a few hours before the rest of them, and Sara had laughed hysterically as Oz said, "Guaranteed fast coverage," and handed Stasia a small bag. Charlie found out that night at dinner what it was about.

As soon as the first girl jumped on her chair and started singing the Blondie song, he knew Stasia was involved. In minutes, half of the girls at that table sang along, tapping out the rhythm and adding embellishments. Stasia wasn't in sight, her spot remained empty. The student body watched in horrified amazement, all eyes riveted, as the girls gleefully sang out their lines. After they finished the next verse, Stasia rang a bell.

All the girls that had been singing yelled,

'Gentleman, you have been assassinated!' and then sat and continued to eat quietly. Everyone else jumped to their feet. Condiments liberally splattered the shoes of every male upperclassman, including the number nine in a mayonnaise cloud for Stasia's company. No one had ever gotten so many at once, it was worth every demerit for singing at mealtime. Stasia returned to her seat, bumping fists with her coconspirators.

"Let that be a lesson on distraction men!" the ranking midshipman said in good-natured acknowledgment. Much laughter and talking ensued by the underclassmen as their elders went to clean their shoes.

Toric paused by Hawk on his way out of the dining hall, leaning over to whisper, "Bad things happen to people who cause trouble," and then stalked away to clean his shoes.

"What did he want?" Charlie asked.

"Nothing," Hawk said. "Just letting me know he didn't appreciate my sister's joke."

Hawk's roommate said, "I did. That was hilarious. I can't believe no one noticed them doing it."

Hawk laughed and Charlie settled back in his seat. He hadn't even realized he'd begun to stand. *Stasia can handle Toric*, he reminded himself and joined in the laughter.

A few days later, the upperclassmen were training the plebes in unarmed combat in the gym, a standard, weekly practice. Hawk and Stasia were in the same company. This week, Toric was an instructor and Hawk smothered a groan. His groan turned to a deep sigh of dismay when Toric singled Stasia out.

"Don't worry, he can't hurt her too much," the midi next to him whispered. "He'll just knock her down a few times."

Hawk heaved a heavier sigh. "I wasn't worried about *him* hurting *her*."

Toric demonstrated a move and then used it, and Hawk let loose a relieved sigh. They were both acting professionally. Toric showed her a few more strikes, letting her try each one.

"Now let's see how you do against them!" Toric said loudly with a challenging grin. Without giving her time to take a defensive position, he threw a punch.

Stasia sidestepped him, easily countering his moves. In moments, she had him face down on the mat.

When Toric rose, his face was red and his lips compressed. "I see you've had some training."

Hawk sighed again. "Here we go," he whispered.

Toric put his hands on his hips. "A little training can be dangerous because you think you can handle yourself. It's our job to make sure you can." Again with no warning, he bounded at Stasia and tried to grab her arm. Fast reflexes allowed her to use his move against him, pulling his grabbing arm and forcing him by with his own momentum. Toric tried to grab her shoulder, and she rolled away, springing to her feet. Toric feigned a punch and tried to kick her and the fight was on for real. A flurry of blows followed.

Hawk closed his eyes, knowing this could only end one way, with a very irate midshipman-first class. Loud gasps made him open his eyes. His company was watching in what looked like awe as Stasia put Toric in a tight headlock with one arm held high behind his back. She rubbed his head impudently and flipped backward off him in a move Hawk had seen Joy make a million times.

"Yeah, that's exactly how I thought that would go," Hawk mumbled. "Well, I'm sure I'm in for it next."

Carl, the other instructor, got on the mat and asked Stasia to show him slowly how she'd done it. Carl worked for the school but wasn't in the Navy. An expert at Jujitsu and Krav-Maga he taught some of the more skilled midshipmen. Stasia went through the attacks and counter attacks, and everyone was set to practicing.

"You should really be on the team, such a waste," Carl complained.

"Not allowed." Stasia gave Carl a rueful smile.

"I know, but man.... You have some serious moves. I'd like to see more," he added enthusiastically.

Stasia blushed.

"I didn't mean...." Carl trailed off. "No offense, I meant your fighting moves," he finished evenly.

"I know, none taken," Stasia said with a smile and left with the rest of her company. The instructor stared after her thoughtfully and then grinned.

"Oh, god, the poor guy, and she doesn't even do it on purpose," Hawk mumbled to himself as he too left with his company.

Over the next week, Toric hounded Team Valor unmercifully. At every opportunity, he made them do pushups and run laps. He gave them extra cleaning details and had them reciting the rules and regs by the hour. In every way he could he tried to make them miserable.

Charlie called a Valor meeting. "I get it, he hates us. Toric was the top athlete around here and three plebes come in and can outperform him. I was feeling bad about that, but now not so much. I say we break every single record he has," he finished angrily.

Stasia laughed. "I'm in."

Hawk rolled his eyes. "Fine."

Within two weeks, they'd all beaten his records. It got to be a running joke on campus. "Hey, Toric!" someone would yell as the plebes lined up to run or do pushups. "How many can you do or what's your best time here?" They'd always do one more then what Toric said he could do.

The companies were so competitive that the company leaders starting betting on it. Toric's entire company tried to encourage him to beat the plebes.

The day before they left for Christmas break Toric's company commander bet Charlie's that Toric could do more pushups. "If we win, you clean our head for a month. If you win, we clean yours." Charlie's commander gazed at him in speculation.

Charlie nodded.

His commander pulled him aside, out of earshot. "I know you're strong, but Toric has been training for years. You sure you can take him? I really don't want to clean up after them."

Charlie nodded again. Speaking when angry tended to make those he spoke with agree with him. He didn't want to inadvertently use Voice-of-Command and force the bet when he knew he had an unfair advantage.

Toric and Charlie hit the deck, their companies surrounding them and cheering them on.

"The first one who stops or hits the deck loses," Charlie's commander said.

Charlie matched Toric's rhythm. They both did push-ups at an even pace, neither hurrying. Loud cheers sounded when they hit one hundred. At one hundred and fifty, Toric started to sweat. The cheers redoubled at two hundred. At two hundred and fifty, Toric's company was shouting encouragement. At three hundred, his commander was down on the ground, yelling for him to keep going. Toric's arms began to shake.

Charlie kept on nice and steady.

At three hundred and twenty, Toric hit the ground and Charlie's company cheered. Charlie did two more pushups, faster than the other ones, and jumped to his feet. He offered Toric a hand up. After a moment's debate, Toric accepted and squeezed Charlie's hand.

"You got me, Hayes. That was impressive," Toric said. "But don't think this means I'm going to go easy on you."

"Wouldn't dream of it," Charlie said, grinning sardonically.

Toric walked away, his now silent company surrounding him. Charlie's commander slapped his back. "Nice work, plebe!" He rubbed his hands together gleefully. "When we get back from break, I'll try to sucker other companies into that bet."

Charlie returned to his room to grab his duffle bag. Paul was the only one still there; his other two roommates had already left. "You can come home with me if you want," Charlie offered.

"Nah, my plane leaves in a few hours, and I already have a ride lined up."

"Well, call me when you return. I'll come get you, and you can stay with us until we have to report back. We have a guest room," Charlie said.

"Thanks, I will." Paul said, and they shook hands.

Over the last weeks Charlie and Sara had gradually worked out sharing their feelings without overwhelming the other person as much. It was harder to do than it sounded. When Charlie was angry or sad, Sara didn't know the cause but seemed to be learning not to assume that all of his negative feelings were inspired by her. Some feelings they shared had clear, unmistakable sources, but they'd come at inconvenient times and they had to learn to block them or ignore them. They were both getting better at it, but Charlie knew it would take years, maybe forever to not be taken off guard by an unexpected spike of emotion. It was harder to not let the other person's strong emotions affect their own.

Right now, as he was saying goodbye to Paul, he knew Sara waited eagerly for him. Being that privy to her feelings for him was extremely intimate. He felt bad other people couldn't share that kind of closeness with anyone. The mix of impatience, happiness and desire was for him alone.

"My girl is waiting to see me, merry Christmas, Paul," Charlie said as he ran from the room. He slowed to the proper pace inside the building but made no attempt to stifle his eagerness.

Toric waited by the gate he used to reach his house. "Going home, plebe?"

"Yes, sir." Charlie saluted.

"Not getting picked up?"

"No, sir."

"Well, I better escort you safely home; we wouldn't want anything bad to happen to such an important midshipman such as yourself." Toric indicated Charlie was to precede him.

With an internal sigh, Charlie passed him and strode home. Irritation grew with every step he took. Irritation that Sara felt and killed her bubbling happiness, which just made him angrier.

"You live even closer than I thought," Toric said when they arrived at his house a few minutes later.

Sara waited on the porch for him, wearing high heels and a dark-red knit dress that showed off her figure. Her blond hair curled loosely around her face. Whenever they were apart he was always shocked by how beautiful she was when he saw her again. He thought he was correctly picturing her in his mind, but the beauty of her in person constantly astounded him.

Her blue eye's sparkled and the dismayed look on her face changed to relief when she spied Toric.

His aggravation doubled as he glared at Toric and then smiled reassuringly at her.

"Sara Mitchel, this is Midshipman First

Class Edward Toric," Charlie said through gritted teeth.

"We've met," Toric said with a suave smile for Sara, which she didn't return.

"Your parents will be home in two hours." Sara grasped the doorknob.

"Well, I won't keep you," Toric bowed slightly toward Sara. "It's been a pleasure, Sara. One I look forward to repeating."

Charlie and Sara stood in the yard and watched him leave.

"What's with him anyway?" Sara asked.

"Who cares!" Charlie grinned at her. "We only have two hours."

Charlie paid no attention to any of the new changes in the house as he hurried to his room. They were always careful not to touch each other after long separations in the presence of others, but as soon as the door closed behind Sara, he grabbed her and kissed her hard. Both let out low moans when their magic touched.

"God, I missed you," Charlie whispered.

She pulled his shirt free from his pants and ran her hands over his bare back and moaned again. "You feel so good. Are your parents going to freak if we share a room?"

"No, they know I still consider us married. You do too, don't you?" Suddenly anxious, he pulled back to see her face.

"Forever," she whispered.

They stood, holding each other, reveling in each other's love and growing desire.

Before his parents arrived, Sara showed him around the house.

"The new bedrooms are guest rooms, and we made Oz's office back into a bedroom too. We put two twin size beds in there. Rick will be staying there with Oz's father. Oz's mother declined our invitation," Sara said as she showed him the upstairs rooms.

"How's Rhea doing with the stairs?" Charlie asked as he watched the dog waddle down the stairs after them.

"I don't let her climb them too often, usually just twice a day. If I go up quick for something, I make her wait downstairs for me." Sara glanced at her watch.

Charlie smiled when he noticed she still wore her Suunto Core.

"I promised Stasia I'd turn on the coffee pot and her dinner rolls," Sara said as she hurried into the kitchen.

Charlie's parents and Mrs. Morales stayed for a week. Everyone enjoyed the visit immensely. Oz's father only stayed three days because of his work schedule.

"You guys look fit and happy," John said to his sons as they drove him and his wife back to the airport.

"Mostly," Charlie said with a grin. "I miss Sara, but I like school. Most of the time anyway. We're all learning a lot."

"The girls seem happy too. I'm happy for both of you," John said. "I'll admit I was worried, but it seems you're adjusting well." John turned to Rick. "I'm pleased to see there were no hard feelings about your, um, misunderstanding with Stasia."

"Stasia and I are friends." Rick turned away to stare out the window.

John sighed and patted his son's knee. "Mom and I miss you guys. Our door is always open for you both, and Sara, of course."

"This summer Sara and I'll try to get to California to visit you, but we won't have much time." Charlie glanced at his mother who was frowning. "But next year we can video chat and talk longer on the phone."

"Do you have plans for spring break?" His father asked.

"Nothing official. Our breaks don't line

up, so we're still discussing options."

"Well, keep calling us a few times a week. We really miss you," Mary said.

"I miss you too, but my phone time is extremely limited right now. That's temporary though. Soon I'll be able to call whenever I'm off duty." Charlie gave his mother a quick hug.

They waited with their parents until they had to board their plane. "I'm glad you could get leave," Charlie said to his brother as they drove home together.

"Me too. It was nice to have a family Christmas," Rick agreed.

Charlie wanted to ask him about Stasia but wasn't sure how to casually bring it up.

Rick sighed loudly. "Just ask me already. Your head's going to explode from all the pressure of not asking."

Charlie laughed. "Sorry, man, I was trying to be discreet. How are things between you and Stasia?"

"Every day it gets a little better," Rick said shortly. "In thirteen months and twenty-one days she turns eighteen."

Charlie laughed and then grimaced. "Ouch, that sucks. Waiting is the worst."

Rick rolled his eyes and glared. "How would you know? You're seventeen and live with your girlfriend."

"Yeah, it's not as easy as all that. I can talk to her for five minutes a day. I see her running in the distance a few times a week. After this break I won't meet her again for two weeks and then only for three hours. And every minute of that time, I feel how much she wants to see me. So yeah, waiting sucks," Charlie finished softly.

"I'm sorry, man," Rick said. "I know you have your own issues, it's just..." He trailed off into silence.

That night Charlie and Sara went to bed early. Oz was out on a date and Hawk was with the dogs in his room, making Rhea comfortable for her delivery. Stasia and Rick were alone downstairs.

"Done avoiding me?" Stasia asked.

"I wasn't." Rick sighed and stopped speaking. "Yes. Sorry," he finally said as he leaned his head back on the couch and closed his eyes.

Stasia rubbed his shoulders, and he tensed. She withdrew her hands and stood behind him unspeaking. When he said nothing, she stepped away. Before she'd taken more than a step, he reached back and grabbed her hand. For a few moments, they stared at each other. Finally, Stasia tightened her grasp, climbed over the couch, straddled his lap and kissed him. Rick returned the kiss until they were both breathing harder.

"Oh, God you're killing me," Rick whispered as he smoothed the hair from her face. Stasia leaned back from him a little but said nothing. He groaned and kissed her again. Twenty minutes later he pulled away. "What am I doing?" he said in self-disgust.

Stasia smiled. "You're falling in love with me," she whispered and kissed him again.

When Oz came home, she went up to her room.

Rick plodded to the downstairs guest room. Stasia was right, he was falling in love with her and the wait to be with her would be worse. She had three more years of school and suddenly he felt sympathy for Charlie. Three small breaks and three weeks in the summer did suck. All night he tossed and turned until he decided to embrace his fate like a man.

The first one awake, Rick made pancakes for everyone. Charlie and Sara came downstairs hand-in-hand and it was hard not to be jealous. *Thirteen months and twenty days*, he promised himself. Stasia came down last. Rick kissed her, to everyone's surprise, including hers.

"What?" he said into the shocked silence. 'We're in love. Everyone knows that."

Stasia beamed at him, and he smiled back.

Rick kept his displays of affection light, holding her hand and keeping his kisses quick. He had to report for duty, but every day after work he returned and took her out or just hung out with her. Letting himself love her was easier than he'd imagined. It was a relief to let himself enjoy holding her. Her happiness was worth a little sexual frustration he reminded himself as he reluctantly kissed her good night before he could forget he was a gentleman.

Charlie picked Paul up two days before they had to go back to school. Sara and Oz liked him immediately. Oz dragged him off to his basement workshop to get his opinion on his latest project.

"You sure he doesn't mind?" Sara asked as Oz and Paul disappeared downstairs.

"I'm sure," Charlie said. "If they aren't back in an hour or so we'll rescue him."

"—We're still working on the power

source but have stabilized the crystalis," Oz was saying as Paul and he entered Hawk's room. Charlie knelt beside his brother examining the new puppies. He handed Hawk the puppy he held and stood.

Rhea growled low in her throat.

"Easy there, girl. He just wants to admire your babies," Hawk said.

Rhea laid her head back down in Sara's lap. Stasia held up one of the newborn puppies for Paul to see.

"Aren't they so cute?"

Rick said, "Not really, but they will be soon."

Charlie said, "Rick, this is my roommate Paul. Paul, this is my brother, Rick."

"Well, I wish I could stay but duty calls. Stasia, I'll see you tomorrow.

Charlie exchanged grins with Sara.

"They're very cute," Paul agreed.

Oz said, "Charlie told me you've programmed your school laptop to conserve power and you're getting a thirty percent increase in the battery life."

"Really?" Sara said. Her eyes brightened and Charlie chuckled.

"We've lost them now," Stasia said and Charlie burst into laughter at his wife's' expression.

When Stasia returned to school, Rick escorted her back. Before she entered the grounds, he stopped her and kissed her lightly. "Thirteen months and twelve days," he whispered as she pulled away.

"We'll see about that," she whispered back and winked. Rick smiled after her until she was out of sight.

Toric watched from the distance.

- 12 -

THE CREEP FACTOR

After Christmas break Charlie, Hawk and Stasia settled back into the rhythm of school. Oz helped Sara build herself a small workspace in the basement beside his workshop. General Campbell had arranged for them to test out of any class they felt ready for and both were progressing very fast academically.

Oz handed Sara a tablet. "The locate program I've been working on is ready. We can resume doing locates any time now."

"The two of us can handle that. No need to take them from school," Sara said.

"I agree, but they won't. So I was thinking we not mention it for a while?" Oz lifted an eyebrow.

Sara laughed. "Unless someone asks, I won't say a word."

183

Agent Lewis and Staff Sergeant Guthrie met with them and set up a time to try Oz's program.

Agent Lewis watched the pictures flickering across the screen as Oz ran the program. "How did you get the information?" he asked as he read the full bio, including arrest records and known associates.

"Don't ask questions you don't want to know the answers to," Oz warned, not glancing up from the tablet in his hand. "If you ask again, I won't lie."

Agent Lewis bit back a laugh. "Okay, where too?"

"Sara and I have the same computer program running," Oz said. "Both of us will pick criteria and enter it to see who comes up. For instance, I'll search for dangerous criminals missing or escaped who target children. The program knows where I am and will search all databases and pull up a list of suspects likely to be around here and send my list to Sara. Her criteria will be victims of said people. As you can see, we have a match already, so I cast locate for them." Oz flicked his fingers, casting the spell. "And see? This guy is south of us. The victim is deceased and also south."

Oz tapped his screen a moment. "I'll go

through all possible missing victims. This doesn't prove he did it of course, but it should cut search time down dramatically. Not only will the program cross-reference all known associates for me, the likely button will produce a list of likely victims of said associates regardless of geographical location. So, instead of just searching for people arrested or missing in this area it'll search for every person missing who fits the criteria, giving me a reasonable number to search for. Ninety thousand missing people are too many to search through in a zone but this way I search for likely ones."

Oz pressed the likely button. "Behold, more missing criminals likely to be near our first suspect. I try to locate them," –Oz wiggled his fingers again— "and yes, two are also south. One is west, three east, and one north. Now they're likely victims for Sara's computer. Okay, I have twenty people to locate, south of us, let's go."

"Won't the information overload slow you down?" Agent Lewis asked as they headed south in a helicopter.

"Normally, it would, but I've programmed it to only show me what is most likely, and as I build the database it'll get smarter. Also, I can narrow the field by doing checks on all the people it shows me even if I don't have time to actually find them. I can spend a few hours seeing if they're around. Then, when I'm in say California, it won't list those people. It'll keep track of who I located and when it happened. Say I locate Bill in Florida, but we don't bother to get him because there are worse criminals, but then I'm in Kentucky and he's listed as a likely, so I check, and, yes, there he is, we can track patterns and put together criminal organizations. I plan on doing random checks everywhere I go to build the database."

"I see," Agent Lewis said.

"That's the long-term goal. My short-term goal is to find as many as we can as fast as we can. It's quicker to search one small area at a time than to fly over a large area back and forth, so that's what we're doing."

Oz located fifty-six people that day. Agent Lewis marked the sites of bodies for later teams to uncover and took pictures and notes of live people for other agents to handle as well. They only apprehended nine.

"You're right. It was much faster," Agent Lewis agreed, smiling at his notes.

"I'll limit my searches to violent criminals and terrorists and only missing children or people who are likely in danger, otherwise we'll bog down your agents," Oz said.

"True, fifty-six cases in one day is a lot. How many are left in this zone when you narrow it down?"

"The program doesn't just recommend by zone but by the criteria I entered as search perimeters. Half of the people we found today went missing in other states, but the program correlates all pertinent data to form a recommendation. I'm searching everything from arrest records, social media, browsing history, purchases the missing and any suspects to their disappearances have made. The program is still much slower than I'd like but the hardware limits it's speed. I'm working on that now.

"Over two thousand missing or wanted people are left in Maryland. I can see if they're here in about one hour, then you pick the most dangerous and start there," Oz said. "I can do that myself at home— make you a list of missing in the zone. You let me know when your teams are ready."

Sara tapped the tablet resting on Oz's knee. "If we train another operator or two to use this program, they could enter all the information while we work doing the apprehensions and speed this up even more."

Agent Lewis sighed. "The problem with that is, and I'm just playing devil's advocate here, but if there were illegally gotten files on the computer, well...." He trailed off.

"How about if I make a new program and request access to what I'll need?" Oz asked.

Agent Lewis laughed. "While I'm sure you could whip up this 'new' program in record time, the access will be slow, if not impossible, to get. The FBI takes its criminal database very seriously. How could we explain why you needed it?"

Oz shrugged. "I'll try it and use mine until then. Let's catch us some bad guys."

Life settled into a comforting routine. School and homework took up most of Sara's time. Every day she met Hawk on the academy grounds with the pups for thirty minutes or so, sometimes more if he had free time. Hawk trained the puppies to salute people wearing white uniforms, so it could take her a while to cross the Yard as the pups sat and lifted their front paws to their foreheads. Midshipman gathered wherever Hawk did the training, Bill the goat would have competition for a mascot soon as the puppies were a crowd favorite.

Sometimes Stasia and her roommates joined the training sessions. Paul came a few times, but Charlie and Sara both avoided causal contact with each other although he thought they were getting a handle on the magic and would be able to hold it back, making it possible for them to see each other without the telltale blue glow appearing.

When Stasia turned seventeen at the end of February, Sara threw her a birthday party at their house. Rick, her roommates and a few other friends Stasia had made at the Academy attended. Stasia proudly introduced Rick to everyone as her boyfriend.

The day passed too quickly. Charlie wished they had more time, but everybody had to get back to school. When he'd arrived, he and Sara had exchanged magic hurriedly, but had no time for anything else. *Two more weeks and they'd have three hours,* he told himself as they left.

That next weekend Sara was out of sorts and cranky. "I need to run, and maybe I'll hit the gym," Sara told Oz when she'd found him in his workshop like usual.

"I could use a break. I'll join you on the run. Let's leave the dogs and have a good sparring match afterwards," Oz offered.

Sara eagerly accepted and ran upstairs to put on a gray sweat suit and black gloves. She pulled a black cap over her head. Neither of them bothered with a coat. Dusk hadn't yet dimmed the weak winter light. Usually, they jogged a circuit around the campus, that afternoon they ran. Not going full out, but running fast and jumping obstacles, racing through parking lots and leaping over railings and stairs.

When they returned to the empty field in front of their house they sparred. Surrounded on three sides by stone buildings with no windows, the small field made a great practice place, so secluded they could use their enhanced speed and agility.

Paul ran into the room where Charlie was studying. "You better come quick!" he yelled and raced back out the door.

Charlie chased him down the hall. "What's up?"

"Your girlfriend is having a serious fight with someone."

"What?" Charlie said in confusion.

"Sara and some guy are duking it out. Half the brigade is watching!"

Charlie followed Paul into a room with way too many people already in it. He wasn't too concerned, Sara was fine, exhilarated almost. The kids watching from the window made room for him. Yep, Sara's blond ponytail, a clear give away even with the black hat and nondescript gray sweat suit. Oz wore all black with a black wool hat pulled low on his neck making his shoulder length blonde hair almost indistinguishable at this distance, but Charlie recognized him.

She and Oz were fighting in what they probably thought was privacy. Both used the landscape, bouncing off the walls and flipping over each other. It looked like fun to him, and he felt an overwhelming desire to be there with her. In mid-movement she paused and turned toward the dorm. Oz's kick connected solidly, and she went down. Charlie winced in sympathy, feeling the painful echo of the kick as she bounded back up, shaking her head. Buffs or not, that had hurt. Before he distracted her more, he left the room.

"They aren't fighting, they're sparing," Charlie said as he left. For a moment he debated going to stop them, then shrugged. She was having fun, and they weren't hurting anything.

Paul followed him out. "You're sure?" he asked, clearly worried that Sara was in trouble.

"Absolutely. Nothing to worry about,"

Charlie said as they headed back to their room. More midshipmen passed them in the hallway to see them fighting. "Let's get out of here before someone comes along who notices all these people breaking the occupancy rules. How did you even know they were there?"

"I was already in Tim's room going over Doctor Lawrence's notes with him. I saw her running earlier. You're sure that was Oz? They were hitting pretty hard."

"I'm sure; if she needed help, she'd hit the panic button. They're just fooling around."

"Remind me not to get them mad," Paul said with a small laugh

Toric pushed into the crowd of boys in front of the window and sent them all to their own rooms. Frowning thoughtfully, he watched Sara and Oz fight a few minutes.

Oz and Sara fought for over thirty minutes. Finally, they both lay down on the ground, breathing hard.

"We need to do that more often. Maybe we could go to Cub Scout camp this summer," Sara said. "I want to be able to do everything, not hold back, a real duel."

"They'd never let us, we could kill each other," Oz said. But, I agree it's a great idea. We could at least cast on dummies there.

Sara sighed. "Oh well, dummies will have to do, and at least we can run all out there."

They headed home by climbing over the wall separating their yard from academy grounds. The dogs barked excitedly. "What's got into you, silly heads," Sara said as she bent to ruffle ears. "We'll take you next time. Settle down now."

She left the dogs barking in the yard and went inside to shower. The house was quiet when she finished, and she went right to bed.

The puppies woke her with their whining. The pups slept in the kitchen now with Rhea, and Sara rose to check them. When she hit the light switch, her light didn't go on. No dogs came to greet her. Tank wasn't at the foot of her bed. Frowning now, she headed into the hallway. When the hall light failed to come on, her frown grew. She changed directions and went to Oz's room. He wasn't there. She whistled for the dogs. The puppies whined louder, but none of the dogs responded. She debated another moment and then hit her panic button and ran back to her room to grab her cell phone.

"The dogs are gone, and Oz isn't in his room. The lights are out. I'm in my room," she whispered when Major Nelson answered.

"We're on the way, summon them," Major Nelson ordered. "And stay on the phone."

Sara casted her Call-for-Help and to her relief Oz showed up at her feet. Stasia, Hawk, and Charlie arrived in their night clothes. Oz was fully dressed, but unconscious. Sara casted a heal on him while Charlie suited up and gave one of his knives to Stasia.

Sara grabbed her staff from her nightstand and handed it to Hawk.

"Put him in our bed," Sara said after examining Oz and plucking two small darts from his shoulder, which she placed gingerly on her nightstand. "We've got Oz," she told Major Nelson and described his condition.

"How many, Hawk?" Charlie whispered.

"One, downstairs in the dining room," Hawk replied.

"I'm on it." Stasia casted invisible and headed out the door. In minutes, she returned. "One man dressed in black, wearing a black facemask. He's looking through everything, taking his time. I don't think he knows you're awake or here."

"He knows," Sara said grimly "When I woke, and Tank wasn't here, I whistled for him. He had to have heard that."

Major Nelson said, "Don't let him get away, but don't engage until we arrive if you can help it. ETA twelve minutes. Beta will be jumping in. Alpha is on assignment. Hawk, if you see even a hint of someone else, let us know."

"There's no one suspicious around. The neighbors are in the usual places," Hawk replied. "The dogs are alive, but asleep."

Sara let out a pent-up breath. "Thank god," she said softly and went to check Oz again. Oz was still out cold and hadn't moved.

"How the hell did he get in here?" Charlie wondered aloud.

After a moment's thought Sara said, "We let him in when we jumped the wall on our way back tonight. Oz went ahead and turned the alarm off, and I jumped over. The dogs were freaking, but I thought it was because we'd left them behind. He must've come in while the alarm was off for me to enter."

"Scrap should've hit the alarm," Hawk said.

"My fault again, I called him and told him he was a good boy," Sara said angrily.

Stasia said, "The intruder must've been

planning this and waiting for an opportunity. I mean, what are the chances he could do that accidentally?"

"Why isn't he coming for me?" Sara asked. "He must think I'm alone up here, and I have a cell phone. I don't get it."

Stasia gestured for her phone and went back downstairs to see what their unwelcome guest was doing now.

Invisible, she followed the intruder as he explored. After going through the entire downstairs, he went upstairs and searched Hawk's room, opening all his drawers and riffling through them. Next, he went to Stasia's room. The first drawer he opened was her underwear drawer. After staring for a full minute, he held up a purple lacy bra, staring for another minute before taking out the matching briefs. As the intruder held her briefs to his nose Stasia retreated from the room.

"ETA?" she whispered.

"We're here," Major Nelson said as the sound of a helicopter could be heard.

"This guy has a creep factor of ten. I think it might be Philip. I don't want to show myself."

"Agreed, send in Chief," Major Nelson said.

- 13 -

KNOWLEDGE DOESN T EQUAL WISDOM

Charlie's fury faded to angry annoyance as Stasia reported. He ran a hand along Stasia's cheek before squeezing her shoulder.

"You stay here. I can handle this," he said. He glanced at his wife who wrung her hands and watched him worriedly. "Stay behind me."

She gave him a small, relieved smile, and he bit back his grin. Her interior relief was huge. She hated the thought of being left behind when he went to fight. Not that he thought this fight would amount to anything. One man, no matter how well armed, wouldn't be able to harm him.

The black-clad man in Stasia's room still rooted through her underwear drawer. Charlie casted Waylay and appeared behind him, grabbing him with one hand and punching him with the other, being careful to keep his hit light.

The man he grasped let out a sharp oof and swung wildly. Charlie yanked off his captive's facemask, revealing Philip, as he pushed him to the floor. He hit him again in the stomach, then flipped him to kneel on his back.

Three members of Beta team entered followed by Major Nelson.

Major Nelson grabbed Charlie's shoulder, giving Sara an irritated glance.

"I got this," he said. You return to your duty."

Charlie stood as Beta team tied Philip. He gave Sara a quick hug and pushed her lightly to the door.

"Let my girlfriend go," Philip said in a monotone. "Don't bother her again. Don't speak to her— don't sit near her— don't even look at her." Philip's gaze flicked from Charlie to Sara. "I'm special forces. I'm her boyfriend."

"You're crazy is what you are," Sara snapped.

Charlie gave Philip a disgusted glance and pulled his wife from the room. She simmered with anger and embarrassment.

Hawk and Stasia joined them in the

hallway.

"I'll deal with the crazy man. You guys better get back," Sara said and kissed Charlie's cheek. She hugged Stasia. "Thank god he didn't see you, Stasia."

"Sara, he knows she lives here if he's been watching this closely." Charlie immediately regretted saying anything. Sara's spike of fear rocked him it was so strong.

"Don't worry about him. I could handle him with my eyes closed," Stasia said.

Sara hugged Stasia again as she said, "So could Oz if he were conscious, which he isn't. Don't get cocky."

Stasia exchanged worried glances with Hawk. "I'll be careful," she promised.

Sirens approached in the distance and annoyance replaced Sara's fear. Charlie hugged her tightly a moment, resting his fingertips on the pulse in her neck to ease his magic.

"Go—before we have to explain how everyone got here. I love you guys," Sara said as she stepped away from Charlie.

He followed Stasia and stole her invisible. The three of them crouched on the wall beside the driveway until the police entered the yard. Red and blue lights threw colored shadows across Sara's face as she answered the door. She didn't glance at Charlie as she let the officers into the house.

Charlie let Stasia pull him away. His wife was fine and could take care of Oz and Philip. A crazy stalker fan wasn't the worry ISIS was. *Philip posed no real threat to her, he was just an annoyance*, he told himself firmly, aggravated that his magic continued to worry.

The thought of ISIS sent a fresh wave of rage over him. It settled quickly when Sara didn't react with either fear or worry. She was still annoyed although that was fading to concentration. She was thinking hard about something. The familiar feeling calmed Charlie, and he crossed the Yard much more relaxed. He'd have to do something about ISIS and Colonel Travensky whoever he was. He couldn't let these threats to her linger.

Training first, he told himself firmly.

"She's in no danger," he said aloud more to convince his magic than himself.

Stasia pursed her lips and shook her head.

"No, she isn't," Hawk agreed and slapped his shoulder.

"School is important. Once we're fully trained we can handle the remaining threats."

"I agree. It isn't like we have any leads anyway," Hawk said

Stasia snorted softly and dropped her hand to the knife hidden in her pants. Her expression lightened, and she slapped Charlie's shoulder. "The general is still checking leads. If he finds anything, we'll handle it."

Charlie gave her a grateful smile.

"She's our fucking Sun-Priest," Stasia said.

Charlie laughed.

Sara opened the door to admit Officer O'Brien, the man who'd arrested her. Grim-faced, she led the way upstairs and handed him off to Major Nelson before going to check on Oz again. A quick trip to her basement laboratory netted her supplies to take Oz's blood to check later, and a pair of surgical gloves, which she kept on in case the officer wanted to touch her. Oz stirred, and she casted a major heal on him followed by a heal-over-time. She yelled to Major Nelson, "Can I check the dogs now?"

Major Nelson exited Stasia's room followed by Officer O'Brien.

"I'll escort her," Officer O'Brien said before the major said anything. He gestured for her to precede him.

Major Nelson shrugged and returned to

Stasia's room. Two more police officers entered, following Tony, and passed them on the stairs.

Collapsed in a heap, Rhea and Tank lay beside the backdoor dog entrance. A quick check revealed steady pulses and clear respiration. Hiding her actions with her body, Sara casted a heal-over-time on each of them just in case. The two, small darts, one in the shoulder of each dog, she pulled out and placed in an evidence bag Officer O'Brien held open after he'd photographed them.

"Scrap is most likely outside." Sara stepped out the back door.

"How many dogs do you have?" the officer asked as he took a flashlight from his belt.

Neighbors had gathered in driveways; their questioning voices could be heard over the sound of the still running police cruisers. Sara flipped the outdoor lights on. "Not enough, apparently."

Scrap wasn't in the backyard. Ten minutes of searching showed no sign of him anywhere outside. Back in the kitchen, Sara took a moment to examine the scene.

"If Philip came in the front as we came in the back, Scrap would've known. All the dogs would've, but I called them and petted them, and they thought that meant the intruder was allowed. So, where did Philip go next?" she mused aloud as she searched the kitchen.

"Oz and I went upstairs. I showered in my room, and he showered in his, and then went to his office. Rhea and Tank were down here with the puppies when I went to bed. Where was Scrap?" she wondered aloud as she pondered the sequence of events. "Scrap's friendly, so he probably went to greet the stranger while we were busy. Philip must've been hiding somewhere."

Officer O'Brien followed to help search the basement. His eyebrows lifted at the neatly stacked medical supplies and small white Formica table in the well-lit room at the bottom of the stairs.

The officer's eyebrows rose higher when they entered the shop Oz had set up in the rest of the basement. Air-conditioning hummed, keeping the room so cool that breath showed as smoky puffs. One wall was covered with computer monitors of different sizes, showing everything from lecture notes to close-ups of cells.

A row of microscopes sent images onto the monitors at over a million times magnification. A long narrow counter, covered with circuit boards and small delicate tools, sat before the monitors with two wheeled stools beneath it. White boards were lined up three deep along a wall covered with equations and drawings.

Layers of large drawings were tacked to the wall beside the door and rolls of paper were stacked beside it. Shelves covered with computer parts, tools and supplies, formed two narrow aisles. Glass boxes and jars of chemicals and beakers sat in the center of a large table. Lights were crammed and hung wherever they could be, and extension cords crisscrossed the floor.

"Jesus, there must be a million dollars' worth of equipment in this room!" the officer exclaimed.

"Try three million." Sara stifled a laugh at Officer O'Brien's expression. "We have about half a million invested in our machine shop in the garage but that has a separate alarm. Scrap must be in the guest room," she said when there was no sign of the dog in the basement.

Limp from sedation, the small dog's body laid under one of the twin beds in the downstairs guest room. After checking the Jack Russel's pulse and respiration, Sara sank onto the bed, cradling him in her arms, hiding her face in his soft fur. "Poor little guy. Mommy really screwed up. I forget you're a guard dog sometimes and need to listen to you better."

The officer gestured to her bracelet. "I'm sorry about that, but I really thought you were doing it on purpose."

Sara nodded, but didn't take her face from Scrap's fur.

"You have a lot of problems with crazies then?" Officer O'Brien asked.

"You have no idea," Sara said bitterly as she rose to go upstairs.

Even as the officers cuffed Philip and put him into the back of the cruiser he kept insisting he lived there.

Oz joined them downstairs in the kitchen, looking pale and shaken, as Officer O'Brien took her statement.

"I'm not sure if he's dangerous or not," Sara admitted. "Other than knocking Oz and the dogs out, he's never actually done anything harmful, but he *is* crazy. He thinks he's my roommate's boyfriend too, and they've never even met. Can we get the restraining order to cover her as well?"

"Seeing as how we found him pawing through her underwear, yes," the officer assured her.

Sara nodded, relieved this was all handled so easily.

"The FBI will be investigating," Major Nelson said. "These two work with classified materials. I'm assuming your department will cooperate?"

"Yes, let us know what you need," Officer O'Brien assured him. "Do you want an ambulance for Mr. Simmons?"

Oz shook his head no as Major Nelson spoke. "Not necessary. Our medics can handle it. We could use a ride to base. If you could bring one of my team back while the others stay here that would be very helpful."

Beta waited until the gray light of dawn lit the yard and then combed the neighborhood. Philip still wasn't talking sense, insisting he lived with Sara.

Sara stood beside Major Nelson with her hands on her hips, surveying the yard. "We need Hawk. He could track where Philip was all night."

Major Nelson agreed and arranged for Hawk to return home.

Hawk backtracked Philip from Stasia's room around the entire house and then outside. Philip had entered through the dog door in the backdoor.

"Philip must've followed behind one of the dogs."

Coldly furious, Oz took notes as Hawk described how Philip had breezed through his security. When Hawk left the yard, Oz went straight to his workshop and started redesigning the security.

Hawk continued tracking, following a trail only he could see, and crossed to the opposite side of the street to a house one down from them. An older woman lived there. None of them had actually spoken to her other than to say a brief hello in passing.

Hawk paused before the backdoor. "Well, he came from in here. I'm sure of that."

Major Nelson nodded and knocked on the door. No one answered. The house remained dark, so he called Agent Lewis and explained what was going on.

"Agent Lewis is on his way, but it'll be a while. Hawk, return to school; we'll need a warrant to search here. I'll call you when we get one if we need you."

"Get me some time with the dogs as soon as possible. I need to teach them nobody is a friend unless we touch the dog and the new friend at the same time and tell them. I should've done that to begin with," Hawk said.

- 14 -

STALKER

Sara and Oz skipped school for two days, redoing their entire security system.

"That ought to do it." Oz said as he ran one last computer check. "I should've made it a priority and done it sooner. I got distracted and never even added my sensors. If anyone passes this house two times, it'll flag a computer search on their face. If they pause here, the picture of them will be sent to our phones. We can now turn off every part of this separately, so if you want your window open the rest of the house is still alarmed, but with the new system even opening a window won't leave it unalarmed. Anyone bigger than Lucky passing through any window will trigger an alarm. The dog door will now alert us if anything or anyone else passes through it. Motion sensors and cameras cover every inch of our yard. It's a

208

triple system that needs fingerprints, voice and a code. Short of armed guards, this is as safe as I can make us."

Charlie nodded he understood and promised himself to double check all of Oz's and Sara's security. They did get distracted easily. He'd speak to Agent Lewis and ensure their guards knew to watch them when they got caught up in thought and make them go somewhere safe if they planned to sit motionless for hours. Oz hadn't seen Philip at all. He'd been too involved with his work to notice the dogs were missing. If Philip had been intent on killing him, he would've succeeded.

The thought angered him enough to make Sara jump.

"Sorry, sweetheart. It was just a thought."

"We're safe here, now," she assured him, and he smiled ruefully.

Oz said, "There's motion sensors in the lab now. If we get distracted, we'll still know if someone comes in the room. It won't happen again, Chief."

Charlie slung an arm around Oz's shoulder and gave him a quick one-armed hug. "It's my job to protect you guys. Not the other way around."

"Well, we're perfectly safe. I appreciate your enthusiasm, but you don't need to babysit us. Sara and I are fine here."

"We are," Sara assured him, and Charlie winced over her rising anxiety. He was worrying her.

"Just don't get careless." He kissed Sara and headed back to campus. *I'm just steps away,* he told himself firmly to stop the niggling qualms he had over leaving them undefended.

The next day, Major Nelson arranged for everyone to meet at the academy with the commandant.

"We have a slight situation here that everyone needs to be aware of."

The major informed the commandant of what had happened at their house, but didn't mention Stasia, Hawk, and Charlie had been there. "In the course of that investigation, which we believed was a just a crazy stalker, we found evidence of a deeper more serious breach of security. Philip apparently wasn't alone in his craziness. The house we, um, located across the street from theirs where Philip had set up shop gave us new evidence. He murdered the woman who owned it."

Sara paled and grabbed Charlie's hand.

Stasia gasped and exchanged grim looks with her brother.

Major Nelson placed a small stack of pictures on the table and slid them to the commandant. "Agent Lewis and my team are the only ones who've seen these. We want to keep this as quiet as we can, but unfortunately there's bound to be some publicity. That publicity could impact the school in a negative way if this isn't handled discreetly, which is why Agent Lewis and I decided to show our findings to you and let you handle the investigation. While the pictures show someone notifying Philip on Anastasia's whereabouts, it doesn't show who did it or if they even know who Philip was or what he'd done."

Major Nelson tented his fingers on the tabletop. "You aren't harboring a murderer, or I'd report this. The woman had her throat slit in one clean move. Only Philip's fingerprints are on the scene and knife. But, someone here is signaling that house. I'm concerned for Anastasia's safety."

"Yes, this is disturbing, and I appreciate your discretion." The commandant leaned forward, picked up the pictures and rifled through them. "We'll find out who did this, and why, and inform the appropriate people and ensure Midshipman Morales is safe," the commandant assured him.

Major Nelson handed the commandant two business cards. "If you require assistance, you can contact me or Agent Lewis of the FBI. Agent Lewis will be discreet. No reports need to be made unless you find criminal involvement. If you must make reports, we'd appreciate if Anastasia's name is kept out of this as much as possible," Major Nelson continued.

The commandant stood in clear dismissal. "All appropriate actions will be taken, and I'll keep you informed on what we find."

Major Nelson thanked him. The midshipmen saluted, and everyone left.

Sara paused on the steps and turned to Major Nelson. "If someone was informing Philip on Stasia's whereabouts, why did he go that night? She wasn't going there."

"We don't know. Philip still isn't talking. Doctor Gotlieb told me Philip suffers from delusions and psychosis made worse by his unwillingness to take medication. At the time Philip entered the house, he believed he was your boyfriend, which is why he wore black clothes and a facemask. That's how Philip pictures your boyfriend, so maybe, at that moment, he wasn't interested in her but you. The fact that you had a phone and called the dogs didn't bother him because he believed he lived there with you."

Major Nelson rested his hand on Sara's shoulder. "Don't worry about Philip. He'll be going away for a long time, but someone was putting those signs in the window. I want you to investigate this, Stasia. A little discreet spying wouldn't come amiss."

"I'll try, but it's not like I have a lot of time where I won't be missed," Stasia said doubtfully.

"We understand that, and I don't believe there's anything more to this than a stalker who talked a student here into helping him somehow, but we want to make sure. Beta will be watching that window, and we have a camera set up on the doorway this week just in case our conspirator isn't aware of Philip's arrest. Tell everyone you're going home this weekend. Maybe put the word out you and Sara are having a girl's night. Oz will come here and make a big production of going to see his father for the weekend. Charlie and Hawk will stay visible on campus."

Major Nelson turned to Charlie. "Try to look busy. If your bracelet lights up, either color, get somewhere discreet. Sara will summon in one minute."

The major turned to Sara. "Don't risk yourselves. If you can't wait that minute, don't. I want you and Stasia to carry guns and extra daggers so they'll have weapons if you summon them. Tomorrow, Hawk can complain his dogs are all sick and at the vet, bad food or a reaction to the sedative. We want whoever this is to try while we're prepared. No razzle dazzle from any of you unless it's life or death. It's most likely one of your fellow students with a crush who has no idea what kind of crazy Philip is."

Oz asked all three of them a million questions about everyone they knew on campus.

Charlie finally said, "The major is probably right. Don't worry about it but don't get careless either. Stasia will find out whatever we need to know."

The fact that Philip had murdered someone made his skin crawl, but Philip was safely contained, and Oz's new security would keep Sara safe.

Sara wasn't nervous or scared. Her emotions were steady and mostly unreadable. She felt nothing strongly now. Charlie led Stasia and Hawk back to their classes, confident the Philip problems were behind them. Whoever had been signaling Philip was on campus and he planned to handle that himself.

Later that night Oz and Sara stood

looking over the academy grounds from his darkened bedroom. "I don't want to say anything to Chief because I might be wrong, but Paul is right up there on my suspect list."

"Toric is on the top of mine," Sara said. "He knows where we live too, and he hates Charlie. I think he hates all of them."

"No proof, though," Oz said.

"None," Sara agreed.

"Stasia could probably find some," Oz said.

"Poor Charlie, he must suspect Paul too." Sara leaned her forehead on the cold glass. "How could he not when Paul's not only been here but knows our security and the dogs."

"What do you think about the four kids whose room the signs were in?" Oz asked.

"No opinion other than one is friends with Paul."

"Everything points to Paul."

Sara straightened. "Except motive. Why would he help Philip? Toric has motive. We need to tell them what we think even if they don't like it."

Oz gave Sara a hug. "We're lucky Philip's dad is a vet. If Philip had slit my throat instead of using a sleeping dart, I'd be well and truly dead by now. It gives me the willies to think about it."

Stasia was supposed to be studying. Her roommates assumed she was at the library. Instead, she crept along the outside of the windows to see what was going on in the room in which the signs had hung. So far, she'd seen nothing worth mentioning.

Earlier, she'd snuck into the commandant's office. Military Police had dusted the window for prints and interviewed all four boys in whose room the signs had hung and had exactly no leads. Her name hadn't been brought up during the investigation. She'd spoken to the boys at various times, trying to appear casual, but none had seemed either threatening or interested in her.

Stasia crouched on a windowsill and called Oz. "I spoke with Sweet-Talk to all four boys and none seemed guilty to me. Why are the signs in this particular window if it wasn't one of the boys who lived in that room? Why not the next room or three doors down?"

"Go break into the house next door and check. Maybe that's the only visible window or something," Oz said.

Stasia lowered herself by falling and

catching window ledges. Once she reached the second floor, she dropped to the ground, landing soundlessly. She casted Sprint and darted across the lawn, through the gate and down the street, moving so fast she blurred. Police tape surrounded the murdered woman's home. After glancing around to be sure no one would see the door open, she opened the locked door, jumped over the yellow crime scene tape, and entered, closing the door behind her. The house had a simple layout similar to theirs. Only two upstairs rooms offered a view of the academy grounds and neither was an unobstructed view. She went to find the access and climbed up the ladder into the attic. "Eww," she mumbled.

She'd found Creep Ville. Old news footage of herself, Sara and Oz papered the walls. Philip must've printed out over a hundred copies of their last tournament picture. Duplicated over and over, every newspaper or magazine they'd ever been in hung on the walls interspersed with more recent candid shots of them in their yard or on academy grounds. The small window gave a clear view of Tim's room and only his room. Trees and telephone poles obstructed the view of every other room.

The front bedrooms she and Hawk used

had drawn shades. "Man, I hope I had my shades drawn when I was home last," she muttered as she surveyed the scene with narrowed eyes.

Yesterday, Oz had put tint on the windows. Nobody would be able to see in now, even if she raised her blinds.

Find-Hidden found nothing, but at least now she knew why the signs were always in Tim's window. Before she left, she reexamined the pictures taped to the wall.

Hawk or Chief weren't in any of the pictures. Where Chief or Hawk would've been had been crudely photoshopped to match the background or Philip had replaced their face with his. There were few pictures of Oz. He hadn't cut him from the pictures but he'd hung them so Oz's picture was mostly obscured.

"So, I have zip." Stasia slapped two pictures she'd ripped off the attic wall onto the kitchen island. "Philip went to a lot of trouble to erase Hawk and Charlie. In his mind, they don't exist. There must be a hundred copies of this on the walls there. Philip must've had a good camera to take pictures so far away you could read the writing. The only thing I found was why that room, it's the only one with a clear view. Trees and telephone poles block the others.

Get me Philip's home address. I want to try there too."

Oz handed her a slip of paper with an address on it. "Want us to come?"

"No thanks; it'll just slow me down. I'll take my headset though and check-in every ten minutes."

Sara placed the photo she'd picked up face down on the counter. "Miss two check-ins and I'll summon you. I'll call and warn Charlie and Hawk. Oz and I've been talking, and our prime suspects are Paul and Toric."

Stasia rubbed her forehead. "I can't believe it's Paul. Why would he do that? Toric I'd believe, but I'll investigate them both." She glanced at her watch. "I'll have to check Philip's house tomorrow. I have to get back before I'm missed. Stay sharp you two."

"You too." Sara jumped up from the bar stool and gave Stasia a hug. "I'm really worried about you. Put something in front of your door at night that will wake you if someone opens it. I really wish you could lock it."

"I'll be fine." Stasia pulled Sara's ponytail and then gave Oz a quick hug. "I'll check-in tomorrow at seven."

"We'll be listening. I love you, Stasia. Please be careful," Sara said as she hugged her again.

Stasia left through the back door, jumping the wall easily. Still invisible, she sprinted across campus and was back inside the dorm in minutes. After taking a quick glance up and down the hall outside her dorm room she removed invisible. All three of her roommates were inside already and greeted her with smiles and casual hellos. Stasia put the headset and mic into her closet, took out a textbook, and sat down to study.

The next night, she searched Philip's home. Find-Hidden located a hidden stash of pictures and a stack of notes beneath a floorboard. The notes chilled her blood. She called the major.

"I'm at Philip's house, and I found some things you need to see," Stasia said

"I can meet you at your house—" He started to say when Stasia interrupted.

"No, I don't want them to see these. I wish I hadn't seen them. Meet me on Canal Street and hurry, okay? I don't want to be late getting back."

He agreed, and she hung up. Without telling Sara and Oz what she'd found, she checked in and then car hoped to Canal street.

When Major Nelson arrived, she got in his car and handed him the pictures and notes.

A narrowing of the eyes and a slow nod indicated an internal hunch confirmed as Major Nelson glanced at the pictures. "You knew," Stasia stated as fact.

"Yes, but would it have served anything if you guys did?" Major Nelson asked as he tapped the photos on the steering wheel to neaten them and then placed them in a folder and leafed through the notes.

"No, I wish I still didn't." She rubbed her forehead then her eyes briskly. "Okay, so the window guy is unconnected to the crazies. Well, he knows who it is so not completely unconnected, but he didn't realize it was Philip on the other end. It shouldn't be that hard to figure out who it was."

"We think it was Paul, but we also thought Philip was the only nut," Major Nelson said.

"So, someone somewhere wants to be Oz, because they think he's my lover. That someone talked someone else into letting Philip know where I'd be. This week Philip thinks he's Charlie. He doesn't know that's who Sara's boyfriend is, but he's convinced himself that's who he is, her Special Forces boyfriend. So, in his mind, Oz is his partner, so he didn't kill him, but why come that night?"

"We don't know. We had some notes,

but he wrote them to Oz. I didn't realize there was an actual pretend Oz until now."

"Well, the person who put the signs in the window is in danger. They know who the fake Oz is, and that person is majorly twisted."

"Some of this might be to connect with Philip. It might not be true." Major Nelson squeezed Stasia's shoulder.

"God, I hope it isn't true. If he's done that before... Well... we need to make sure our Oz is well protected."

"I'll notify the commandant on this development. Oz is well protected. One crazy person shouldn't be too hard to handle or catch," Major Nelson started the car and drove to the academy.

"One crazy person who thinks eating Oz's heart will let him steal his essence and become him. This guy is a serious nut," Stasia said in disgust.

- 15 -

TORIC

Stasia spent every free minute she had sneaking around spying on everyone. Unfortunately, she didn't have that many free moments. Thursday evening she headed to the library to work on a paper due Friday. As usual she took the long way, cutting through the parking lot to see if Sara and Oz were home. Occasionally, she caught up with them in their favorite sparing spot and they spent time catching up, or if Stasia had enough time, she'd spar with them.

Toric followed, hanging back just keeping her in sight. Stasia stopped to stare at Charlie's house. Toric pursed his lips. He'd thought he'd catch her meeting a boyfriend in the Yard and be able to give her a hard time, but apparently she was hoping to see Charlie's family or maybe Sara. He knew they were good friends. He was about to leave when she turned and saw him. Her smile froze. To Toric's surprise she looked shocked. The shock switched to anger with a tinge of fear, and she narrowed her eyes at him and took a defensive position.

"Seriously?" Toric held out his empty hands. Before he could say more his eyes widened. "Get down!" he shouted as a man carrying a gun stepped out from the shadows and shot her. The gun made a soft whispering sound hardly louder than a cough.

Stasia reached back to her shoulder and plucked out a small dart., She dropped it as she fumbled with the bracelet on her wrist. Toric took a step forward. She overbalanced as she reached for her ankle and stumbled. Carl smiled as she staggered.

"Works fast," Carl said calmly as she staggered again and landed on her knees.

Toric reached her and pulled her up, holding her to his chest with one arm. She grabbed at him with hysterical strength. Is all she had time to say was 'help' before her eyes fluttered closed.

Carl laughed and stepped forward.

"What the hell are you doing, Carl?"

Toric yelled as he swung Stasia's now unconscious body into his arms and backed away.

Carl rose the gun and pointed it at him. The two men stared at each other.

Toric debated for a moment. He could drop Stasia and attack, but he'd never make it to Carl's gun hand in time. Even unconscious she gripped his shirt so tightly he doubted he could just drop her anyway. His collar bit into his neck and he tried to dislodge her grip as he took a slow step back.

If he ran now, Carl would shoot him in the back. The best thing he could do was what he was doing and hope Carl changed his mind about whatever he'd planned, or if Carl shot that he'd miss or hit Stasia again.

Carl stalked forward. "To bad you had to be so nosy. I liked you, Toric. But you know what they say— curiosity killed the cat."

Toric took another slow step back, and Carl's smile widened.

"You won't make it. Drop the girl. Nothing will wake her now."

The hair on Toric's arms rose. Carl hadn't been debating. He'd been waiting to make sure Stasia wouldn't wake. Whatever his plans for her, Toric knew Carl now planned to murder him. It shone from his eyes. His only hope was someone else would see and interfere. Toric's glance darted around the deserted area. As Carl lifted the gun to shoot, he tightened his grip on Stasia and made up his mind to run.

Sara was in the shower when her alarm sounded. She ran out, grabbed a towel, and yelled for Oz.

"Wasn't me!" Oz hollered. "Tank, Rhea, come guard!"

"It's not Charlie either!" Sara ran into her bedroom, snatched her phone from her nightstand, and hit speed dial for the major. "It isn't Oz or I. We're fine and so is Charlie."

"Summon them in thirty seconds," Major Nelson said. "The team is gathering, and we'll be there as soon as we can."

"Tick," Sara replied and started her timer.

Oz ran into her room, followed by Tank and Rhea. Sara opened her closet door and grabbed Charlie's sword. Oz nodded and raced from the room.

"I'll grab Hawk's gun!" he hollered.

"Summon in three!" Sara called and began to cast.

One second Carl was pointing a gun at him, the next he stood in front of Charlie's girlfriend. Sara was soaking wet, wearing nothing except a towel, carrying a sword in one hand and a cell phone in the other.

"Put her down right now!" Sara yelled, and a ball of light formed in her hands.

She threw it at him. Toric flinched backward, but the light didn't hit him, it hit Stasia and sank into her, lighting her from within. He didn't have time to react, Stasia was suddenly at Sara's feet.

Dazed, he noticed Charlie and Hawk were both in the room for the first time. The transition from field to bedroom had happened so fast he hadn't had time to notice anything. Charlie opened his hand, and the sword Sara held appeared there, leaving her hand empty.

The towel clutched about her breasts with the empty hand, Sara squatted beside Stasia, feeling for a pulse, her wide-eyed gaze staying glued to Toric. Another bigger ball of yellow light formed in her hands, which she threw at Stasia. A silvery dome formed around her.

"What the hell is that?" Toric yelled,

backing away from the silvery sphere surrounding Stasia.

"What did you do to her?" Sara shouted furiously.

"Nothing!" Toric yelled back. "Carl shot her with some kind of dart thing."

Sara put the phone to her ear and repeated what he'd said. "Hawk, how many?" Sara asked as she rose and stood in front of the silver bubble.

"No one." Hawk knelt by his sister and disappeared.

Toric took another step back. "I'm telling you, I didn't shoot her. It was Carl Rogers."

Hawk popped into sight, standing now. "Where were you?"

"Where you guys work out." Toric indicated Sara and Oz with his chin and held up his empty hands. Hawk looked furious and his eyes shone blue. Toric wanted to take another step away but out of the corner of his eye he saw Charlie glowering at him and the sword he carried looked wickedly sharp.

"I'm going after him." Hawk held out his hand and the gun Oz carried appeared there. He ran from the room. Sara's guard dog followed him.

Without seeing him move, Charlie was suddenly behind him, holding the sword at his throat.

"Go!" Sara said. "I'll catch up. I can handle him. Oz, you stay." Sara ran to a dresser and pulled out black clothes.

Charlie lowered his sword to his side and spun Toric to face him, squeezing his shoulder hard. "If you touch my wife, I'll kill you!" Charlie hesitated, then shook Toric once and raced after Hawk.

"Get down on the floor!" Oz commanded.

"What's going on here? What are you?" Toric whispered as he lowered himself to the floor, keeping his arms raised.

"All the way down!" Oz yelled as he held his hands apart and a blue glow solidified between them, forming a dagger.

Sara turned away, dropped her towel, dressed in black armor, and pulled a headset over a black facemask, which she left up. A wooden stick in her hand, she knelt by Stasia's still form and small golden spheres of light circled her. Sara leaped to her feet and darted from the room.

"Rhea, guard," Oz commanded and the other dog hunkered down in front of Toric, growling low in its throat, showing its white pointy teeth. Oz ran to the window and then the closet and rummaged for a moment before emerging with another headset, which he placed on his head.

On one knee, he knelt beside the silvery sphere encasing Stasia and held his hands apart. A blue glow turned into long, off-white pieces of fabric.

"Where was she shot?" Oz asked Toric as he examined Stasia.

"Left shoulder."

Oz removed Stasia's shirt and glared at Toric, placing one of the cloth things on the tiny spot of dried blood on her shoulder. "Sara, report," Oz said.

Toric listened hard and could hear her reply faintly. "They're ahead of me. Nothing to report yet. What's the ETA on the major?"

"I'm twelve minutes out with Alpha. Keep me appraised of your whereabouts," a man answered over the headset.

Oz rose and stood before Toric. "I'm going to tie you. If you even twitch, Rhea will be on you."

Rhea snarled when Oz said her name, fanning warm dog breath across Toric's face. Oz wrapped the ties he'd made from blue glow around Toric's hands and feet so tightly they tingled within moments. "Rhea is a trained guard dog; if you move, she'll kill you." Oz raced from the room. Three minutes later, he returned dressed in the same armor Sara had worn with a gun strapped to his thigh and the knife he'd conjured from thin air in a sheath on his waist. A sheath opposite held a K-Bar.

Oz crouched in front of Toric, his blue eyes so furious they blazed. "Who is Carl and why did he shoot Stasia."

"He's one of the instructors hired this year to teach unarmed combat, and I don't know why he shot her. I don't know what's going on. How the hell did I even get here?"

"The jujitsu instructor? Oz's eyes widened, then narrowed even more. "How did you just happen to be there?"

"I followed Stasia to see what she was doing behind those buildings. I thought I'd catch her meeting her boyfriend or something," Toric said.

"We're coming back. He got in a car," Sara said

"I'll get his address. Don't move," Oz said over his shoulder as he left the room.

Toric flexed his wrists, and the dog's growl rose in pitch. "Nice doggie," he whispered, and Rhea snapped at his face. Toric stopped speaking.

Oz returned, carrying a laptop. "Okay, Sara, I got it."

"Come back and suit up," the man on the headset commanded. "We'll go there. You stay home but stay alert. How's Stasia?"

"Out cold still, but if it's the same stuff

he used on me, she should wake in ten or fifteen more minutes," Oz said.

"Keep Toric contained until we come for him," the man said.

Toric didn't like the sound of that. "I didn't do anything to her."

"Then you have nothing to worry about, or not much anyways. But if you did, you'll spend the rest of your life enjoying the island breezes on Guantanamo," Oz said coldly.

Sara, Charlie and Hawk returned. Charlie grabbed Toric by the collar and lifted him off his feet with one hand. Sara clutched his other arm, putting her body between them.

"He might be telling the truth." Sara placed a glowing blue hand against Charlie's face.

"How did he get into my bedroom with my wife if he's so innocent?" Charlie snarled.

"When I summoned Stasia, she was holding onto him," Sara said.

Charlie glared at Toric, then dropped him on the bed. Blue mist surrounded him as he stalked to a closet and pulled out black armor and put it on, glaring at Toric the entire time. Two swords appeared in his hands. He sheathed them on his back without looking and then grabbed a shield off the wall and placed it on his back. When he was dressed, he loomed over Toric with his hands on his hips.

Toric recoiled, fighting the urge to run. Charlie's normally brown eyes were inhumanly bright blue, much brighter than Hawk's and Oz's blue glares.

Sara rose her glowing blue hands and placed them on Charlie's face. The blue in his eyes dimmed a bit as the blue on Sara's hands disappeared.

"What the hell are you?" Toric asked, swallowing heavily when Charlie growled low in his throat and grinned, showing his teeth.

Sara grabbed Charlie's hand and pulled him over to Stasia. "Bring Stasia to her room. When she wakes she'll want to suit up." Sara whistled, and her guard dog bounded into the room and followed Charlie who'd picked up Stasia. In moments they all returned and stood glaring at him.

"Anyone around, Hawk?" Charlie asked.

"All clear, Chief," Hawk replied.

After a few minutes of silent glaring, Hawk nudged Toric's bound foot. "If he's telling the truth, what are we going to do with him?"

Charlie frowned. "He's seen a lot. A simple explanation won't do. This won't be an easy solution."

"What were your plans for after you graduate?" Sara asked thoughtfully.

Toric was scared. Something big was happening here. He'd stumbled onto a huge secret, something he shouldn't have known. He took a deep breath and licked his lips, really uncomfortable with the past tense she'd used. "I'm going to join the Marine Core."

"Of course he is." Charlie threw his hands up and started to pace. "I thought you'd try professional football."

"No, I'm a soldier. I mean to be a Marine and command troops in combat."

"Ever think about joining the special forces, doing the extra training for Force Recon?" Sara asked.

Despite the situation Toric almost laughed at her forced nonchalance.

"Yes, I plan to do that." Toric stared Sara in the eye, both to avoid Charlie's gaze— it freaked him out— but also Sara was the only one who didn't seem hostile to him.

She turned away and took Charlie's arm, turning him toward her. "So, we make him one of us. We make him a Scout."

"Sara, he hates us. There's no way—."

Toric interrupted. "I don't hate you. It's my job to make sure you can hack it. You'll find that out in a few years, but I don't know what you're all talking about either. You aren't doing anything to me!" A blush heated his cheeks as his voice rose.

"It won't be our decision anyway," Hawk said.

Sara sighed in exasperation. "So… what— we just ask him to never mention what he's seen? Get real— he'll report this the second we let him go. He'll absolutely need to talk to our boss at least."

"I agree, Sara, and I'll handle it," The man said, his voice sounding thin and far away from the headset dangling around her neck.

"It's not that I don't trust you to do the right thing… I do, Major," Sara said slowly as she eyed Toric with her hands on her hips. "But the right thing can't be that he disappears. That's completely unacceptable to me. I'll be checking on him."

"I'll be sure to pass that along," the major said dryly.

Sara nodded. "Good." With one last glance from Toric to Charlie, she left the room.

Presumably to check Stasia, but for all Toric knew she went to contact the mother ship. Toric winced at his own thoughts, cleared his throat, and held up his tied hands.

Charlie ripped the bindings off with his bare hands as if they were tissue paper. "My wife just saved your life. If you were telling the truth about Stasia, that is."

"Your wife?" Toric rose an eyebrow. "Midshipmen can't be married, and you're what, seventeen?"

"I'm eighteen. Not that it's any of your business. Sara and I aren't any of your business either. The people who need to know do. I'm not breaking any rules."

Sara returned with Stasia fifteen minutes later. Stasia wore matching black armor and looked angry when she entered.

"I'm pretty sure he wasn't with Carl; he warned me anyway. I have no idea what he was doing there," she said to Toric's relief. He wasn't certain she'd heard him warn her or not.

"If we cut you loose, will you stay voluntarily and speak to our boss?" Sara asked.

"Jeez, Sara, just leave him here," Charlie said as he pulled Sara tight to his side.

"In our bed?" she asked with a lift of her eyebrow and a small smile. "Besides, we might be working with him someday, let's not burn our bridges."

"Fine," Charlie said gruffly and ripped the bandages on Toric's ankles in two, releasing him. "Let's go downstairs; I don't want him in here."

Forty minutes later a major showed up at

the house. Toric recognized the voice as the man from the headset. "Alpha is watching Carl's house. So far there's no sign of him. We need to catch him before word of what he saw can spread. I'll be taking Hawk with me. Oz, Sara, Chief and Stasia use locate in the copter," Major Nelson turned to Toric. "Thank you for trying to save Stasia. I'm sorry your good deed is going to be repaid this way. You'll meet our boss and it'll be his decision on what we do with you. I wouldn't worry about it too much as he's aware of Sara's position." Major Nelson paused. "This will change your career plans somewhat. God knows, it's changed everyone else's who've encountered them, but it doesn't have to be a bad thing."

"Let him call the commandant. You're scaring him to death," Sara said as Toric paled. "He thinks you're going to go kill him or something." She turned to Toric. "We wouldn't let them. Murder isn't an option."

"Not any more it's not," Charlie mumbled under his breath, sounding disappointed.

"Fine," Major Nelson rolled his eyes at Sara but took out his phone. He spoke to the commandant for a moment and then handed the phone to Toric.

"Sir." Toric's wide-eyed gaze darted

around the room as he took the phone from the major. This was a chance to ask for help, or a chance to find out what was going on. He needed to decide fast. Unconsciously, he straightened his shoulders. There was no decision, he was a Marine, and it was his duty to find out everything he could about whatever the hell was happening here before he made a report.

The commandant said, "I'm aware Major Nelson will be removing you from school for a short time. What he tells you is classified.. Tell no one, not even me. Is that clear?"

"Yes, sir." Toric narrowed his eyes but quickly smoothed his expression. Whatever they were up to they'd somehow gotten the commandant to cover for them. He'd have to kiss his career goodbye and go over his head to the superintendent.

"You won't be kept away longer than forty-eight hours. Dismissed."

"Thank you, sir." Toric handed the phone back to Major Nelson.

"Okay, Hawk and Toric, with me. You four head to the airport." Major Nelson slapped Charlie's shoulder as they headed to the cars.

16

AND YET I M DOING IT

Ten minutes later Oz reported they'd located Carl.

"Can you take him discreetly?" Major Nelson asked.

"Yes," Oz said. "He's at a motel. It should be no problem."

"Take him. Dead or alive, whatever works," Major Nelson said. "Alpha is in route to your position now. Hand him off; they can handle him."

"Wilco." Oz gestured for Sara to proceed him.

Team Valor rappelled from the helicopter, letting go when they were out of sight of the pilot. Sara cast Ascension, levitating them as they fell, and they landed lightly on the ground. Stasia was already invisible.

She lowered her black sunglasses. "I'll

just walk in. He'll notice the door open, but not me. If he's alone, I'll take him."

The simple lock didn't hinder her for even a second.

"Got him," she said a few seconds later.

Trussed to the bed, Stasia had zip-tied him, hands, elbows, ankles and knees by the time they entered. The black armor they wore carried no insignia while the facemasks concealed their identities. No one spoke, either to each other, or Carl, as he demanded to know who they were. Stasia finally wadded up a bathroom towel and stuffed it into his mouth while they waited for Alpha team.

When Alpha team arrived, Joy bumped fists with them and took the captive to the car. Stasia and Rick stayed behind while the others filed back out.

"You're okay?" Rick asked as he scanned her.

"I'm fine now. Keep your eye on him. He's sick, but skilled."

"I will, and he won't bother you again," Rick assured her and kissed her lips. "I wish I could stay with you—"

"It's okay." Stasia hugged him and then stepped away.

They both pulled down their facemasks and went outside. Rick wasn't sure what he felt or how to handle this. Stasia wasn't defenseless or afraid, but he felt as if he should be with her. Awkward and unsure, he hesitated. He paused at the car door and then returned to her.

"I love you. If you need me to stay with you, I will," he whispered.

Tears filled her brown eyes. "I love you too. I'm fine. Go do your duty and I'll do mine," she said, smiling tremulously at him.

Rick hesitated a moment and then traced her lower lip with his thumb before returning to the car.

Sara put an arm around Stasia. "It sucks, I know. You can probably see him Saturday; you have a day pass already."

Stasia brightened. "True, they'll probably let me keep it. I'll call him to see if he can get time off."

"Sometimes I wonder why we put ourselves through this," Sara said as they watched Alpha team drive away. "We could quit and lead normal lives, see who we want when we want."

"What about Team Valor?" Stasia asked.

Sara shrugged. "We could quit that too. If I had Charlie, I wouldn't care if I lost my magic."

"So why do you stay?"

"Duty, I suppose," Sara said. "Magical healing is such a great gift I feel like I have a duty to use it. To learn how it works and hopefully teach others how someday."

"It is a great gift," Stasia agreed. "And I have a duty to protect you so you can do those things. If Rick and I quit, it puts you more at risk. It puts everyone in the United States more at risk. It's my duty as well."

"Duty sucks!" Sara said.

"It'll get better once we learn more." Stasia put an arm around Sara's shoulder.

Sara nodded and straightened. "I'm learning as fast as I can."

"Your boss works here?" Toric stared out the window and swallowed hard. Major Nelson had given his name at the gate and the guard had waved them in. Toric had only visited the White House as a tourist in high school.

"Yes." Hawk grinned. "Just tell the truth, and you'll be fine. Sara would kill us if we let anything bad happen to you."

Two secret service agents escorted Major Nelson and Toric to the Oval Office. A general approached and Toric and Major Nelson saluted. "I'm going to ask you to swear that everything you see and hear will remain confidential. I realize you have secret clearance already, but what you'll hear tonight is the most classified secret we have. Someone of your inexperience wouldn't normally be put into this position, but circumstances make it necessary. If you feel you can't swear this oath, you'll be escorted from the premises and returned to the school. But, I warn you now, if you won't take the oath, you'll never be assigned a position of any importance after this, but you can continue in your career. If you take it and tell, you'll not only be court marshaled, but we'll do everything in our power to discredit you. Is this perfectly clear?"

"Yes, sir," Toric rose his right hand. His earlier thoughts of reporting this being exchanged for thoughts of what the hell had he got himself into.

General Campbell administered the oath.

"I didn't realize you were in town," Major Nelson shook General's Campbell's hand.

"On unrelated business and I head back in two days. I assume everything is handled?" General Campbell asked.

"Alpha has him in custody and is returning to base. We'll investigate, and Agent Lewis will be notified. I'll keep you informed," Major Nelson said.

"This is our only loose end?" General

Campbell asked, nodding at Toric.

"Yes."

"Very good, let's neaten this up." The general spoke to the president's secretary, and a moment later she indicated they could enter.

"Midshipman First Class Edward Toric?" the president asked as they entered.

Toric saluted. "Yes, sir."

"At ease. Everyone take a seat. I've already been informed of today's events. You've been brought here to see for yourself that the head of the military knows even though none of your current officers do. This is not some secret conspiracy you're duty bound to report. It is a secret, but, I, your commander-in-chief, know all about it. I agree the easiest way to, um, neaten this up is to make you a Scout." The president leaned back in his chair. "However, the other Scouts went into this blind. I think a fully informed decision would be best. This will change your entire life after all, probably in ways we can't foresee now. If you choose not to become a Scout, we'll still expect complete silence on this and your career can continue as if this never happened."

The president gestured to the major. "Turn on the video and let him see what a Scout does."

Major Nelson turned on the video and everyone watched training clips from Cub Scout Camp. Brenda and Drew fighting hand-to-hand, moving impossibly fast. Joy and Drew doing an obstacle course, so smoothly and gracefully it looked like ballet. Marcus and Tony shooting and reloading their weapons with precision timing and aim. The entire company assembling guns while doing logic problems incredibly fast. Grainy black and white footage of a team of Scouts creeping through three feet of snow on their stomachs, dragging a covered sled.

Major Nelson stopped the tape. "This is actual footage of one of their rescues. It took the Scouts two days of crawling under barbed wire and motion sensors to get in through three feet of snow in twenty below temperatures. Those pictures were taken last January in Siberia as they rescued a defector's family. They brought out three children and his wife using only what you see there. We needed complete deniability; they were never seen. The family disappeared on a snowy night and is presumed dead. The Scouts are the best trained and best supplied group of soldiers we have. Some are Army, most are Marines. They practice long hours and their missions take them all over the world. Mostly they do rescues, but sometimes they fight."

The general turned the tape back on. Still photos of the ISIS training camp near Mosul in Iraq played next. "This was last year." The footage changed to video from Eagle Eyes One's perspective.

The Scouts held off large groups of attackers, taking heavy fire. Toric's attention sharpened when he spotted another silvery dome like the one that had covered Stasia although this one was much larger. He watched in awe as the tanks exploded. A man dressed like Charlie with two swords and a shield, cut down ten to twenty men at a time. The armor he wore must be something newly developed because bullet marks pockmarked his armor, but they didn't slow him at all. It was hard to tell from the footage, but it appeared as if all the enemy in sight were concentrating on him and ignoring the small group of Scouts following him.

Major Nelson stopped the video again. "I'm sure you noticed some inexplicable things there. We refer to them as our top-secret weapons. Only the Scouts know about them, at least we hope that's true," Major Nelson said, and the president grimaced. "By necessity, the Scouts stick together both on and off duty. The Scouts can be called out at a moment's notice. Few even know they exist, and they get no credit. They'll never be rich and will probably die young."

General Campbell stood and paced a moment. "We can assign you to that team."

Toric cleared his throat. "It would be a waste. I can't do any of that. On my best day I'm not that fast. If I practiced a million years, I could never be that graceful. I'm a good shot, but not in their class."

The general smiled.

The president leaned forward and put his hands on his desk. "If we could, um, magically make you that strong and fast, would you join them?"

"Yes, sir," Toric said as a blush crawled across his cheeks. He'd always thought of himself as extremely athletic, but those guys were the real deal. A frown crossed his face as he remembered things he'd seen Charlie, Stasia and her brother do." Charlie Hayes is training to be a Scout?"

"Yes, that was him in the video, the man with the swords," Major Nelson confirmed. "Charlie's a fully trained Scout. He's been through every course Camp Pendleton has to offer, and then attended our Cub Scout Camp."

"You sure? Charlie's only eighteen."

"We're sure," Major Nelson said with a small laugh. "When that recording was taken, he was seventeen. The youngest Scout is Sebastian Morales."

Deep in thought, Toric was silent. Obviously, Charlie was attending the academy to further his career in the Scouts. To move up in the ranks he'd need a college degree and the best one for a Marine was the academy. If he was recruited at fifteen or sixteen, he must be a lot stronger and faster than he let on. He thought a moment about that and then wondered how that could be if Charlie was a video game superstar.

"Yes, there's a piece of information missing," the general agreed as he watched him puzzle through the data. "Our secret weapons. By the way, do you play video games?"

"No, sir."

"If you become a Scout, you will." General Campbell motioned for the major to start the film. "This is Cub Scout Camp, and these are our secret weapons."

The tape showed Oz throwing fireballs at a target dummy. He switched to lightning, then rain that formed a thin coating of ice on his target. He alternated small flashes of fire with bigger fireballs. The camera panned to the next target dummy. Stasia was suddenly behind it, attacking so swiftly his eye couldn't quite follow. She disappeared and reappeared at the target dummy right beside it, again hitting with a fast flurry of attacks. The screen darkened and then restarted, and Charlie stood before a line of target dummies.

He cut his target in half with one fast blow and then was instantly beside another one. A single blow and the second target fell in two separate pieces, stuffing and metal bracings cleanly sheared. The screen darkened and lit. Another picture formed of Charlie standing before Sara and a man with a machine gun firing at him. Charlie spun his swords and deflected the bullets. Another blast of machine gun fire followed, and he held a shield in front of himself. Another blast and he yelled, *"Oorah"* and the bullets bounced off him. He said 'tick' and another blast of gunfire bounced off him. Toric watched as Charlie was shot at steadily for seven minutes. A few got through, leaving bloody red marks, but no visible wounds.

Major Nelson stopped the tape. "We have hours of this footage. Suffice it to say that Charlie is the toughest son of a bitch you will ever encounter. No one alive is tougher or stronger than he is. He has an aura that will make weak enemies run and strong ones attack him."

"That's impossible... what they just did,

no one can do," Toric said flatly.

"As Sara would say, and yet I'm doing it," Major Nelson said with a laugh.

General Campbell cleared his throat. "They can do a lot more. That was just a sample to show you the types of things they can do and why it's so important that it remains secret. What you can't see in those tapes, but saw earlier, was the enhanced performance from anyone they accept into their raid group. You can be as fast and strong as any Scout."

The president spoke up. "They brought you here to me as the commander-in-chief. I'm their boss. If you become a Scout, you'll be reassigned to General Campbell and answer only to us. We'll give you duty assignments, your commandant is not in the need to know loop. He'll be told where to assign you upon your graduation, that's it. You'll never speak of this meeting to anyone except fellow Scouts and your immediate chain of command. That would be, Staff Sergeant Guthrie, Captain Sanders, Major Harris, Major Nelson, General Campbell, and of course, myself. That's it."

"Yes, I'd like to be a Scout, but how are they doing that?" Toric burst out and nodded at the frozen video screen showing a picture of Charlie blocking a small missile with his shield.

"Magic," General Campbell said.

Toric frowned.

"We don't understand it either," Major Nelson assured him, "but we've seen it up close and personal. They use magic."

The president stood. "You can fill him in on all the details." He turned to Toric, "If you change your mind, do so before we send you to Cub Scout Camp." The president shook Major Nelson's hand as he escorted them to the doorway.

Toric saluted in a daze and followed Major Nelson back to the car.

"Met the big boss then?" Hawk asked, grinning hugely.

"Yeah." Toric frowned at Hawk. He hadn't seen him in any of the footage.

"Yeah, I have magic too. You should see your face," Hawk said laughingly.

"They didn't show me pictures of you," Toric said.

"I'm hard to see." Hawk demonstrated by going invisible.

"Holy shit!" Toric exclaimed. "Will I be able to do that?"

"No, but you'll be faster, stronger, and smarter by being with us. Plus, there's Sara."

"Charlie doesn't seem like the type who shares well," Toric said.

Major Nelson let out a shout of laughter. Hawk and the major laughed for a minute, then the major said, "Don't ever suggest that to him, not even jokingly. Hawk meant Sara's heals, not Sara herself. You can't be killed if she's with you."

"Well, technically not true," Hawk said. "You can be, but she can resurrect you if she gets to you in six minutes, before your spirit releases. She can do it three times in a row, then has to wait an hour, but yeah, if she's with you, bullets won't hurt you or at least not for long. She can heal anything, even a lost limb if we can find it. If Charlie is with you and enraged, you won't even feel any pain."

"You're shitting me! Am I being punked?" Toric asked.

Hawk lifted an eyebrow. "By the president of the United States?"

"Well, holy shit! So that explains the bracelets. No wonder Charlie is paranoid about her, he needs her. She's priceless… holy crap," he repeated this time thoughtfully.

"We all need her, but Charlie and Sara are connected in more than one way. They love each other, but it's more than that. Their magic is connected as well. She's his wife in every way except legally. Don't mess with her— ever.”

"So, Oz lives with her to protect her?" Toric asked.

"He would if she needed it, she isn't helpless, she can fight, and you saw her summon us," Hawk said.

"But, where did you get the magic?" Toric asked.

Hawk explained as best he could. "You can't talk to us about this unless we're in a secure spot like this," Hawk said when he finished telling him. "I'm sure you'll have a million questions but hold them until you're somewhere you're sure you won't be overheard."

"Holy crap," Toric said again softly. "I think I better thank Sara. I might've just disappeared tonight instead of all this."

"Maybe," Hawk admitted, "but when they found out you had nothing to do with it; they probably wouldn't have done anything, um, irrevocable."

Major Nelson interrupted. "After graduation you'll be assigned to General Campbell. I'm sure they'll send you to Cub Scout Camp, but probably not the full nine weeks. You'll have to do the regular MARSOC training. Well, some of it anyway. We skip most of the physical stuff and do that at our camp. The Scouts are learning to fly right now, so you'll do that as well. Our home base is Pendleton, but we're stationed here while the cubs are in school."

Hawk blushed and looked away. "One last thing you really need to know. The magic can be, um, sexually transmitted. What that means for the Scouts is they're allowed to fraternize only with each other. That rule might change when we learn more, but right now we're only allowed to date fellow Scouts."

"I could infect someone, like with an STD?" Toric asked in dismay.

"We don't know. It's a relatively new phenomenon. So far no Scout has ever reported seeing any magic, but keep in mind if somebody who isn't a Marine gets infected, they'd die from it. Sara can only heal Marines."

Toric nodded. "So, at the first sign of a blue glow or any other glow, I do what?"

"Well, stop whatever you're doing and call in. I'm sure Major Harris or the others could tell you more."

"How many females Scouts are there?" Toric asked after a quiet moment of thought.

"Seven, if you count Major Harris who isn't a Scout, but is in the raid. Joy is pretty serious with Drew. Rick and Stasia are an item and Charlie and Sara are married, so three available."

"Well, that kind of sucks," Toric said.

"Tell me about it. They're all way out of my league, and I have a ton of rules on who I can, err, date."

They were quiet the rest of the way home.

"Try not to treat them any differently; it's hard enough for them to fit in as it is. Call me if you have questions, but never say anything on the phone." Major Nelson paused. "Our primary duty as a Scout is to protect our cubs, that's them. We protect them and their secret. Sara would kill herself trying to save a Scout, make sure that never becomes necessary. Be swift, silent, and deadly."

A bit overwhelmed with the rapid change his life had just taken, Toric nodded. "Yes, sir," he said softly.

17

A NEW STRATEGY

The rest of Team Valor waited for Hawk's return downstairs at the kitchen table.

"Our newest Scout," Hawk said with a grin at Charlie as he hugged Stasia.

"Yeah, we heard, awesome," Charlie mumbled.

"Will he be going to Cub Scout Camp with Sara and I this summer?" Oz asked Major Nelson.

"Nothing is definite yet," Major Nelson said as Charlie stood and glowered.

"No way! I don't trust him."

Major Nelson rose an eyebrow.

"I don't trust him not to hurt Sara," Charlie clarified. "He's been chasing after her all year."

"You think I'll what, attack her? Rape her?" Toric asked in amazement.

"I don't know you." Charlie stepped toe-to-toe with Toric. "All I know is you want her, or you want to annoy me by taking her." Agitated, he swung and paced while running a hand through his short brown hair. He spun to face the major. "I won't be in the zone, and she won't be able to call me for help. I won't leave her defenseless."

"I don't hate you. It was never personal. It's the upperclassmen's job to make sure the new guys can hack it. None of the others…" He pursed his lips and cocked his head. "Your damned aura. All of my classmates found excuses why they couldn't confront you. I had to force myself to approach and was pissed a freshman could intimidate me without even trying. I was maybe harsher than I needed to be… And I thought I'd gotten the upper hand, but you turned it off, didn't you?"

Sara leaned into his side. Charlie put an arm around her automatically but moved so he stood more in front of her.

"I'm hardly defenseless, Charlie. And I won't be alone. Oz will be with me, and the Scouts, including your brother."

Major Nelson frowned thoughtfully, his gaze flicking from one frowning face to another.

Oz jerked his head and rolled his eyes, indicating he wanted to speak privately to the major.

Charlie sighed and straightened, shooting Oz a glance that said he better tell him later what he wished to speak with the major about now. Toric was likely telling the truth. He hadn't considered how his aura would affect someone determined to confront him. Despite himself he was impressed with Toric's bravery. None of the other firsties had even tried, but he still didn't want him near Sara.

"Okay, team," Major Nelson said. "Get in your uniforms, and I'll bring you back." Everyone headed upstairs, except Oz and Toric.

Oz waited until the sound of footsteps faded and glanced at Toric, then whispered, "Charlie will need some time to get over Toric being in his bedroom with his naked wife. His mind knows Toric wasn't there by choice, but his instinct to protect Sara is in full Neanderthal."

Oz spoke directly to Toric. "Stay away from Sara, and Chief too, if you can. For a while at least. You're lucky he didn't kill you— literally. I know you have officer crap, err, stuff to do, but his magic is on edge. He was shooting off sparks and they've exchanged magic two times already. I know you don't understand what I'm saying here, but it isn't good."

"I'll get him a pass for this weekend," Major Nelson said with a worried look. "Have him sit in the sun with her. I'll get Hawk a pass too. He can sit with them; his aura will help."

Toric looked from one worried face to the other. "So, that's bad then."

"Uncontained magic can be deadly," Oz explained. "When their magic touches, it can be explosive, literally. Add to that we don't know all the effects, yeah, it worries us when it behaves in new ways. So be cautious and if you see him glowing blue get away from him. Get everyone away from him. Call Sara and she can summon him."

Oz changed the subject and spoke in a normal voice as footsteps sounded on the stairs. "Familiarize yourself with the game. It'll help, but for the love of god be subtle. I'm a mage, Sara a sun priest, Stasia a rogue, Chief a protection warrior, and Hawk is a ranger. If you accept Rick's raid invitation, you'll receive our passive buffs. So get familiar with what we can do."

Stasia, Hawk and Charlie entered the kitchen.

"We're ready," Stasia said.

Everyone exchanged hugs before heading to the car.

Major Nelson drove. Charlie sat in the passenger seat.

"Good to go?" the major asked Charlie softly.

"Good to go," Charlie replied, but his fists were clenched.

Major Nelson met Stasia's eyes in the rear-view and she nodded. The major sighed and drove them back to school. He called the commandant, and after informing him about his instructor being arrested, arranged for passes for the weekend.

"While we believe the threat to Anastasia is resolved, the identity of the person who assisted Carl is still unknown. One of your students was helping, probably unwittingly," Major Nelson said.

"The investigation is ongoing," the commandant assured him. "I'll let you know when we find the person responsible."

"We still want Anastasia's name kept out of this. Midshipman First Class Edward Toric will receive credit for stopping an attack on a fellow midshipman, name unmentioned. I don't expect anyone to have to testify. Carl will spend a long, long time in prison. Any new information will immediately be brought to your attention."

Toric used his free time researching the game and watching old online videos of Team Valor raids and was impressed despite himself at their grasp of strategy and teamwork. He watched *Stasis Leroy's Underhill* five times.

"Holy shit," he whispered as it sank in that she could really do that. He was lucky she'd been trying to hide her magic and hadn't killed him instantly. Holding back had been a risk. Carl might have killed her before Sara could summon her away although he supposed the risk had been slight. Her passive buffs would likely have prolonged her life long enough for Sara to summon and heal her even if Carl had slit her throat.

What Sara could do was both terrifying and amazing and the more he contemplated it the more he understood why they were keeping the magic secret. Until they could figure out how the magic worked and make healing possible for everyone it was much too dangerous to expose her. Unsettled by his musing he watched some of Hawk's videos.

"Holy shit!" he said again louder as he contemplated his computer screen.

The full implications of what they were capable of were sinking in. Individually, they were powerful, but together, as a team, they'd be almost unstoppable. It was ironic they were susceptible to drugs made to help people, but not bullets. If they were in their armor, it would take a miracle to stop them.

"Holy shit," he said again softly.

He researched everything he could about the plane accident and their subsequent illness. The photographs in a tabloid were pretty grim, and he wondered if they'd been doctored. If they were real pictures, he was amazed they'd lived. No wonder they were concerned with it spreading. Someday, he hoped to hear the entire story firsthand.

Toric saw Oz and Sara running a few times but didn't go near them. He still gave Stasia and Hawk a few extra drills, but he cut down as much as he could, targeting their roommates instead. Toric made a serious effort to avoid Charlie without seeming too. Everyone was busy studying for midterms before spring break, so it was easy to cut back without being obvious. The day before spring break, Hawk appeared beside him while he was walking to class. One minute he was alone, the next Hawk was there.

"Chief is doing much better. I thought you'd like to know," Hawk whispered. "I'd still avoid Sara if I were you, but he's back to normal, magically speaking."

Hawk didn't wait for an acknowledgment. Toric didn't see him disappear; he just suddenly realized he couldn't see him. He made a real effort and spotted Hawk walking to his class, but it was difficult keeping him in sight, it was hard to even remember he wanted to keep him in sight, and he wondered if it was hard for Hawk to remain visible.

Magic, he thought in awe as he lost sight of Hawk again. He tried to put all thoughts of Team Valor out of his mind and concentrate on his last exams.

Charlie couldn't wait to leave school. He and Sara planned to spend all week together except when she was taking her own exams. She'd assured him they wouldn't take her long.

The week off passed way too quickly. He didn't understand how the same amount of time spent in school seemed twice as long.

Stasia and Rick saw each other as much as possible during that time. Rick had gotten leave and stayed in their guest room, which they'd taken to calling Rick's room. At least Charlie assumed that's where he stayed. He didn't ask.

Stasia was frustrated. Rick was being a saint, and it was driving her crazy. He was okay with holding her hand or lying on the couch with her, but anything other than a quick kiss and he drew away. She needed a new strategy. That evening she sat back at the kitchen table and pursed her lips, deep in thought.

"What?" Rick narrowed his eyes at her.

Stasia smiled sweetly. "Just thinking."

"Hmm," he said doubtfully when her grin widened. "What?" Rick asked again as his eyes narrowed even more.

"Well, a few things. I was wondering if my being a virgin is the problem. Because, if it is, I can fix that," she said with an evil grin.

Rick's face turned red. "Jesus Christ, Stasia, you can't just say things like that."

She shrugged. "It's not like it's a secret, and it's just us here. Is it a problem for you?"

"We aren't talking about this." Rick stood and turned his back.

"So, it is," Stasia said and heaved a deep

sigh. "Well, that's easy enough to fix."

Rick whirled and glared.

Not breaking eye contact, she took out her cell phone.

"Don't! You! Dare!" Rick shouted and grabbed the phone.

Stasia stood and put her hands on her hips. "If you don't want to, I'm sure I can find someone else who will. Then you won't have these crazy guilty feelings. You won't be spoiling me. I'll already be spoiled."

"Okay, sweetheart, calm down. That isn't what I meant. I don't want to ruin—"

Stasia cut him off. "Having sex won't ruin me."

"Having sex with a minor will ruin me," Rick said as he placed her cell phone on the kitchen counter and then resumed his seat.

"Oh, my god, really?" She glared at him. "I'm not twelve!" She took a deep breath, sat in his lap, and tried to talk calmly. "I admire how strong your willpower is, I really do, but mine isn't that strong. You're frustrating me unbearably. Could we compromise at least?"

"Like how?" he asked and grabbed her hands to stop them from wandering.

"Like that. You stop acting like we're in the Victorian ages, and I won't look for someone else to 'ruin' me," Stasia said.

"See, there's a problem with that plan.

My willpower is only so strong. You can talk me into more than we should do, and I need to be able to face my father again," Rick said softly.

"What about me, Rick?" Stasia asked in an even softer voice. "Can you keep turning me down and face me?"

Rick pushed her off his lap and backed away. "Stop, you're glowing!"

Stasia glanced at her hands, which glowed a light blue. "I want you with every fiber of my being, and you still turn me down. Keep pushing me away, and my magic will become uncontainable. My frustration will literally kill you. You say I have to hold the magic in for another ten months when I'll be acceptable for you. Meanwhile, you're physically hurting me here, Rick."

"If we do this, your magic could infect me."

"Sara could heal you."

"We don't know that for sure."

"So, it isn't my age? You're afraid to sleep with me?" Stasia whispered, turning so he wouldn't see her tears.

"Some," he admitted, "but not in the way you think. I'm afraid to face them, and I'd have to for her to heal me."

He grabbed her shoulder and turned her to face him. She glared when he brushed a tear away with his thumb. Angry with herself and him, she shrugged from his hold. She'd meant to tease him into it, not manipulate with tears but her magic was lonely or maybe it was only her. She wanted him to love her like she loved him— passionately.

The glow spread up her arms as they stood unspeaking. She tried to hold it back, but the blue continued to spread.

Rick took a deep breath and pulled her into an embrace. "Let it go," he whispered. "I'm here for you."

Tears streamed down her cheeks as she sobbed, and the glow brightened. "I can't, I don't know how."

Rick kissed her neck and then picked her up and carried her to the guest room where he set her on her feet and slowly unbuttoned his shirt. The shirt fluttered to the floor as he reached out and lifted her T-shirt off.

Stasia's pulse pounded in a mix of anticipation and worry.

"You're sure?" Deep and low his voice made goosebumps appear on Stasia's arms, and she rubbed them absently.

"Yes." Staring into his eyes, she removed her bra and dropped it on the growing pile of clothes. When their bare chest touched, she heaved a deep sigh that turned into a moan.

Rick kissed her passionately. When he

drew back, he was breathing hard and his eyes had darkened.

The sight reassured and excited her. She'd been worried he'd been holding back because he didn't desire her.

"I love you," she whispered and pulled him down to kiss him again.

"We've never talked about birth control," he murmured as his hands wandered over her back. "I don't have any condoms, so intercourse is out, but there are other things we can do."

Heat spread from her stomach until she felt flushed everywhere. The heat in her stomach moved lower as Rick caressed her breasts. She moaned his name as he showed her the other things.

Snuggled together under the covers Stasia no longer glowed.

"Did you take the magic back? I didn't notice, and I feel the same."

"I have no idea," she said with a small laugh. "I was too distracted." She rolled over until she was on top of him. "Feeling guilty?"

He smiled into her eyes. "Surprisingly, no. You feel too good."

"Well, don't regret this later, please." Stasia blushed. "I wish I didn't have to go back to school so soon."

"I love you," Rick said as he ran his hands through her hair. "There's no rush. We have all the time in the world."

"If you feel sick, go to Sara right away, and don't leave town for a few days. If they send you on a mission, you'll have to tell them you've been exposed." Stasia's cheeks heated in a blush.

"I'll be careful," Rick promised. "And I'll get us some protection."

"Tonight?" Stasia asked, her brown eyes sparkling.

Rick moaned and kissed her. "Yes," he growled and kissed her again.

18

DUTY IS A BLACK-HEARTED BITCH

Stasia's steps dragged as she walked back to school the next evening. Rick ran a hand over her dark head and laughed. "You have to go."

"I could easily sneak out."

"I know, but don't. Don't break your word for me. When you sneak out, it's because you're ordered to. The honor code is important. If you need to leave, ask the major first."

"You're right, but I'll miss you. You'll call me, right?" she asked anxiously.

"Every day, unless I'm on assignment, and yes, I'll be careful. You be careful too. I'll see you as soon as we can."

They paused before the gate leading onto the Yard. He traced her cheek with a fingertip. To many people were around for them to kiss while she wore a uniform. She reached up and touched his face too, then quickly stepped back. "Parting with you is harder now," she admitted.

He nodded and cleared his throat. Eyes bright with unshed tears, she smiled and whirled away, hurrying through the gate before he could speak. "Three more years," he mumbled and grimaced. *Duty was a black-hearted bitch.*

Rick returned home and called Liz to report his exposure. She ordered him to remain at Sara's house.

"I'm going to call Sara and have her run some blood tests and any other test she thinks of. If you're infected, we want good records. I'll inform Major Nelson of my orders. If you develop any symptoms at all, from sniffles to constipation, we want to know."

"Fine," Rick said and heaved a deep sigh. He knew how Charlie must feel now, living in a fishbowl with no privacy.

He returned to Stasia's to tell his sister-in-law she was babysitting him for a few days.

Sara took the samples very matter-of-factly. "Call me immediately if you start to feel sick."

"You're not, um, disappointed in me;" Rick asked, dreading the answer.

Sara hugged him. "No, I love you both. I'm happy for you. If you hurt her, I'll kill you, but no, I'm not disappointed, neither is Charlie. I'm sure he's threatening to kill her if she hurts you. He might feel the need to threaten you both," she finished with a small laugh.

Sara brought Rick downstairs to her small lab. While she took the blood samples, he examined the devices and equipment with interest.

"What are these for?" He pointed to a stack of small stainless-steel rods. Each rod was about three inches in diameter and two feet long, boxes of them lined a shelf.

She opened a box under the table and took out an identical metal rod and handed it to Rick. "That one's empty." She grinned and handed him one from the shelf. "Can you feel the difference?"

He balanced a pipe in each hand. "The full one is warmer and bigger maybe?"

She smiled. "Nope, they're the exact same size, but everyone thinks they're bigger when they're full. I think you feel the potential; it feels fuller. They weigh exactly the same. That one"— Sara said as she pointed to the one with the small white label— "Is full of magic."

She gestured for him to hand her the empty one. He watched in fascination as her hands turned blue for a moment. When the blue disappeared, she wrote out a label and placed it on the tube.

"It isn't full yet; it's magic storage. Charlie can use it easily, but Oz has trouble. It makes him uncomfortable. It makes Charlie uncomfortable as well when Oz uses it. The fresher it is, the more, um…" she paused looking for the correct word, "connected to me it is. I'm testing to see when it loses the connection, if it ever does. I can use it with no problem."

"How long does it take to fill one rod?" Rick asked.

"Depends. I can fill one completely in a minute or so, but it drains me. Filling a rod is different than casting, more emptying. When I cast, my magic regenerates while I'm casting, and I run out gradually or not at all if I'm careful in what I cast. Storing the magic like this empties it all at once and I have to spend time recuperating before I can cast again. Mostly, I just put a little bit in every few hours like you just saw so I don't run out because it makes me feel tired and weak if I do. The ones with the blue labels are Charlie's magic that he gives me. Oz can use those easier."

"Is it psychological," Rick asked. "Is it too intimate for him to use yours?"

"No, there's a real difference. My theory is it's twice removed, so it's easier. Charlie gives it to me, and I place it in storage, so it's not as connected to him. The good news is that I can use it when I need a magical fix from him. It isn't as potent or long lasting, but it does work."

"Can he use yours too?"

"Yes, again, it isn't as good, but it should help us stay apart for longer periods."

Rick smiled wryly. "So, good and bad news."

Sara nodded agreement. "Most of the summer he'll be far away from me on a boat in a different zone, so we'll need all these. We need to know how long and far away he can go and figured his summer tour was a great time to find out. The five days before he goes we'll spend harvesting his magic. As long as neither of us gets too hurt or scared we should be okay, for a while anyway."

Rick nodded thoughtfully.

Sara sighed. "I'm the weakest link here. If he gets hurt or is worried, it escalates my own worry. Sometimes a bad nightmare will set off a chain of worry where I just have to see him. The rods won't do. It feels like my magic will explode out of me."

"A chain of worrying?" Rick asked in puzzlement.

"I'm afraid in my dream, so Charlie worries, then I wake and sense his worry, so I worry and then he worries some more, and it goes back and forth until one of us is really desperate, usually me," Sara said discontentedly as she turned and neatened the small stacks.

In a moment, she turned back to Rick with a forced smile. "I'd let you feel the magic, but if you have Stasia's inside you it might be a bad idea."

Rick nodded and continued exploring her lab. "What is this?" he asked, eyeing the fifty-gallon glass tank filled with pink water and what he thought were bare muscles. Wires crisscrossed the back leading to a circuit board and pump. A camera hung above the tank and heaters and vials full of varying colored liquids were clipped to the side.

"Oz and I really excited about this." Sara took one of the rods she'd just shown him and unscrewed the end. She loosened a lid over a small hole in the glass tank and screwed the rod into place. A small yellow sphere traveled from her fingertips to the bare piece of muscle. Blue lights raced down the length of the muscle and disappeared and then at one end a steady, blue spec appeared.

"It's a piece of a nerve, it isn't alive, it's preserved and can still use my magic," Sara said proudly.

"Eww." Rick took a quick step back.

Sara laughed. "This is just a first step. It can't generate magic or cast a spell, but if we can make artificial nerves that can use our magic I could give a heal to take with you, or a shield, or fireball and maybe the heal could be used on anyone."

"You can do that?" Rick asked in amazement.

"Not yet, but I'm working on it. Oz made me this tank. He's making another now that can sustain life. I'm also trying to put my magic into living things, so far with no success, but if I can transplant a nerve successfully...." She trailed off in thought.

"Where do you get the nerves from?" Rick asked.

Sara sighed. "Myself, and it isn't easy to operate on yourself either. That's a nerve from my foot. I won't try to use one from my hand until I understand this better. I could damage myself permanently if I screw up my magic."

"Jesus, Sara, does Charlie know you're doing this?"

"Yes, it doesn't thrill him either, but I have to do it."

"No, you don't." Rick hugged her quickly.

"Rick, if you could learn something that would let you heal those sick children we visited, wouldn't you?"

"Yes," he admitted unhappily. "But you're cutting yourself up."

"It doesn't hurt or not much anyway. I heal myself right away and I'm learning a lot. I'm being careful," Sara assured him.

"Can't you use someone else's nerves or whatever?" he asked as he gestured vaguely around her lab.

"I do, but so far only mine will glow. I'm not worried about the surgery so much as taking the pain medication to do them." Sara turned away and busied herself at a microscope with the blood sample she'd taken from Rick as she continued speaking absently. "I'm susceptible to narcotics. If I'm not careful, I could overdose and bleed out. I'll need an assistant soon."

"Jesus, Sara," Rick said again. "You could addict yourself."

"I'm being careful, taking every precaution I can. When we return to school this fall I'll see if I can have Liz assigned to me, and maybe a Scout or two, and we'll need a bigger lab," she said as she eyed her somewhat cluttered space.

"I'm not saying your work isn't important, Sara, but go slowly. We can't afford to lose you." Rick frowned and hugged her again.

"I'm a turtle, I'm going so slowly," she assured him.

Rick wandered through Oz's lab as Sara finished up her tests. Black plastic boxes, ranging in size from two feet across to two inches, littered a long counter. The computer monitors displayed intricate pictures of wiring schematics from various angles with different magnifications and on diverse backgrounds. On closer exanimation, Rick decided it wasn't wiring it was cells or maybe electricity. He was still pondering them when Sara came in.

"I'll rerun the tests tomorrow." She joined Rick in front of the monitors and tapped a small black box. "Oz and I have been working hard on this."

"What is it?" Rick gestured to the screens.

Sara grimaced. "My skin. Well, mostly my skin, Oz has made some modifications."

"And the boxes?"

Sara grinned, the smile lighting her face. "Our new computer."

Rick picked up one of the boxes and peered inside then shook it. Sara's grin widened, and Rick picked up another and examined it closely then sighed and set it down gently. The black box only contained felt-like material with intricate gold patterns wound around blue glass specs. "No really, what is it?"

"Seriously, it's our new computer. Although computer is maybe misleading as it uses none of the old technology, but it does the same thing, it computes."

"Computes?"

"Determines by calculation."

"Well that's crystal clear."

A soft snort of laughter was his answer. Sara picked up one of the smaller boxes, this one about two inches square, and placed it on top of a monitor laying on the table. The monitor was connected to three routers, which bristled with Ethernet cables, and six small black speakers. A ring of oddly shaped glass balls surrounded the monitor, some touching it, some not. "This box is our most advanced model. Go ahead, ask it a question."

"Um?"

Sara giggled. "Ask it something you'd

perform on your computer at home."

"Okay, um, computer, what's the weather?"

Sara rolled her eyes as a computer voice recited the local forecast while pictures and graphs displaying the local weather appeared on the screen. "No, I mean ask it something you'd really do, like open email or a word processor app or check the Scout message board. Weather is lame."

"How will it know who I am to get my email?"

"Tell it…."

Rick rolled his eyes at her tone and crossed his arms. "Okay, smarty pants. This is Rick Hayes; how many emails do I have?"

"Eight thousand two hundred and thirty-nine current emails are stored under that name under three separate addresses," the computer said immediately as Sara laughed.

"I'll admit, we cheated and limited our samples to only respond to the Scouts, so it already knew you," Sara said, still laughing at Rick's dumbfounded expression.

"You gave it my passwords?"

"No, just told it your name and social security number, it did the rest. Any question relating to Rick or Richard Hayes or Sergeant Hayes, this computer will automatically assume we mean you."

"Can it show me the emails?"

"Sure, ask it."

"Computer, show me my inbox for my Google account, um, this is Rick—" he was about to say his last name, but the screen the box sat on already showed his inbox.

"Wow." Rick picked up the box, hefting it in his hand. It weighed mere ounces. "What's powering it?"

"The monitor it's sitting on. Oz and I are still working on the programing and we have a few kinks to work out, but crystalis will revolutionize the computer industry.

Rick played with the computer for an hour until Sara had to go to class.

As soon as she left, he called Major Nelson. "Sara and Oz need more security.. I hadn't realized until now how important they are, what they know and could do," Rick said without preamble.

"Believe me, we're aware of it. Is there anything in particular you're worried about?"

"No, I just saw her lab. Have you seen it?"

"No, not in person, but I've seen the reports. Anything I should be worried about?"

Rick told him about Sara's self-surgery and concerns.

"We'll get Liz there right away. You're

right, she shouldn't do that alone. And we'll move her lab somewhere more secure."

"You're sure she's secure at school?" Rick asked.

"As sure as I can be. We haven't seen or heard anything to make us worried. Agent Lewis has agents watching her. She needs to attend school. Pierce says it would be more dangerous for her to keep her locked up and bring teachers to her, it would attract a lot of unwanted attention. She and Oz are being very discreet on campus. Most people don't realize how smart they are. If it does become too dangerous, we'll arrange private study, but she isn't in danger as far as we can tell."

"What about Philip?" Rick asked doubtfully.

"I admit, he was under our radar. We underestimated the danger of a stalker fan, but believe me, we're watching everyone now. The agent who was watching her has been reassigned. Granted, he'd no idea of Sara's importance, but he shouldn't have let Philip get that close to her. He says he noticed, but thought it was a harmless flirtation on Philip's part. Lots of boys approach her on campus."

"I'll admit it worried me when she left here. Not that I was uncaring before, but it just hit me how important she is to the world. No wonder Charlie is a wreck," Rick said sadly.

"How are you doing?" Major Nelson asked.

Rick cringed in embarrassment, glad they were on the phone and not speaking in person. His blush was fiery red. "I'm fine. No signs of anything."

"Well, stay one more day to be sure. It took twenty-four hours for their symptoms to appear." The major paused, then sighed. "This is awkward for all of us. We have Stasia's schedule; I'll assume you, um, see her on all breaks, and we'll make sure you can remain near Sara for two days afterward. If you know you can't be near Sara for two days, don't, um—"

Rick interrupted. "Got it. Yes, we'll be careful, Dad."

"I wish this was only the safe sex talk, which I assume we don't need to have. Sex with a magic wielder can be dangerous in ways we can't even imagine. Sara is our only real healer and she can only heal Marines, so don't have sex near anyone else." Major Nelson huffed a small laugh. "I can't believe I'm having this conversation with my sergeant."

"I'm not thrilled either," Rick said. "Really, Charlie is a saint to put up with all this."

"Oh, we realize it's a lot to ask of anyone, and we're trying to make it easier on them," Major Nelson assured him.

"I'm sure he appreciates you all discussing ways to make his love life easier," Rick said dryly.

"Touché" Major Nelson replied softly and hung up.

Rick gently set the phone down, then reluctantly picked it back up to call his father.

The next day he had to endure the good-natured teasing that accompanied his return to his squad.

- 19 -

HARPIES

In eight weeks Charlie would be finished with his first year of college. Sara had adjusted and while she still wasn't happy with his absence, she wasn't unhappy either. The work she and Oz did kept her busy, and at times, excited. And she'd devised a way to store his magic to use whenever hers pressured her for contact with his.

He wasn't sure how he felt about that. He liked that she felt relieved but hated that she still thought needing him bothered him. Nothing could be further from the truth. He loved that she needed him so intensely. Sometimes he worried that it was his magic she loved although now with his stored magic it was just him she greeted so eagerly.

He shrugged irritably, annoyed with his insecurities.

The eight-week summer tour on the ship

didn't worry him that much, in fact, he looked forward to it. While he'd miss her, it would be nice to just be one of the guys, doing exactly what the other midshipmen were doing with no special restrictions, duties or privileges. The three-week vacation before school restarted they could spend together in the hottest spot they could find.

With a wince, he tried to think of something besides her skin heating in the summer sun. The memory of her warm body against his filled him with lust, which she sensed and found amusing.

Sara planned to spend the summer in New Mexico at Cub Scout Camp. *The lack of libraries would bother her more than the lack of me.* He chuckled to himself as he headed to the library with Paul. The only worry he had remaining was that he still didn't know who'd hung the signs in the window.

Paul was on the top of everyone's suspect list, except his, so he decided to ask him.

"So, Paul," Charlie said. "Did you hear Tim's room was searched and he and his roommates questioned?"

"Tim said it was something to do with his windows but wasn't sure." Paul stopped walking and faced him. "What was it? Do you know?"

"Someone was putting signs on the

window." Charlie tried to gauge Paul's reaction, but there was none to gauge.

"Like what kind of signs?" Paul asked as they resumed walking to the library.

"I'm not one hundred percent sure, but I guess inappropriate signs." Charlie shrugged.

"What we're inappropriate signs?" Stasia's roommate Amy asked as she joined them.

"Someone put signs in Tim's windows," Paul said.

Amy laughed. "That was me." She stopped laughing and looked worried when Charlie halted. "Tim isn't in trouble, is he?"

"No," Charlie assured her as he continued walking, "but, why did you do it, and what did they say?"

Amy laughed again. "Carl asked me to. He told me Rick and Stasia were having problems and Rick wanted to know where to find her off campus and could read a note taped to the window from her house. It worked too, they're back together better than ever," she finished happily.

Charlie debated what to tell her. She hadn't broken any rules, and she'd been trying to help, but she also knew Stasia had security issues and should've considered that.

After a moment, he stopped walking again. "Did you guys hear Carl was fired?"

"I heard he quit." A frown grew on Amy's brow.

Charlie nodded. "Don't say anything to anyone, but the school fired him for attacking one of the students, and he's been arrested. Rick had nothing to do with those notes. Carl was using you to find out where Stasia would be. If she didn't have that security bracelet, something bad might've happened to her. Something might've happened to you as well if he decided to cover his tracks."

"I never meant for anything bad to happen." Amy looked stricken. "I never thought...." She trailed off. "But I should've thought. I knew she had security issues." Amy began walking, looking troubled. Charlie and Paul exchanged unhappy glances and followed. "I'm such an idiot. I better report what I did."

Charlie squeezed her shoulder a moment. "I think so too," Charlie said softly. "I'm sorry, Amy."

Shoulders hunched and face sad, she sighed and turned back to the dorm. "It's my own fault. If I don't get to speak to Stasia, tell her I'm sorry."

Charlie nodded, and he and Paul watched her plod away.

"Think they'll expel her?" Paul asked.

"I hope not," Charlie said. "It was stupid, but she didn't mean to hurt her, and she's turning herself in as soon as she found out. That's brave. If she'd said nothing, she might've gotten away with it."

"Man, I hope not too, I like Amy." Paul frowned after Amy.

Charlie grinned at Paul and punched his shoulder. "I thought you had a girlfriend?" Charlie said as they continued to the library.

Paul rubbed his shoulder absently, still staring after Amy. "Had. She dumped me right after Christmas. Apparently, I'm not worth waiting for."

"You don't sound too broken up about it." Charlie glanced at Paul, relieved to see him smiling.

Paul trailed after Charlie and soon caught up. "Meh, I don't have time for a girlfriend, and besides, you have no idea how easy it is to score a girl in this uniform. Come with us on your next weekend pass. You're missing all the fun."

Charlie snickered. "I'll make a deal with you. You tell Sara, and I'll go."

Paul laughed, "Oh god, no way. I've seen her fight. But seriously, you two should both come. Get out and socialize— loosen up a little. There's more to life than studying and schoolwork. The place is crowded and fun.

Kids from colleges all over go there."

"I'll consider it," Charlie said.

"No alcohol is served, but best of all it's open during the day when we can go," Paul said.

"Sure, I'll ask Sara, she loves to dance, but no promises; she likes time alone with me more," Charlie said smugly.

Paul laughed.

On his next day off Charlie took Sara with Paul, Hawk, and Oz to the dance club. The idea of a real date thrilled Sara, and Charlie promised himself to take her out more often.

The dance hall was fun. Big, and noisy, a long bar ran along one end that sold sodas and expensive fruity drinks without alcohol. Waitresses wandered through the crowded hall taking orders. Buying food wasn't mandatory though; most tables only held drinks. A lot of Charlie's classmates were there already. The white uniforms made them stand out, and Charlie saw at once why they liked it here. Girls flocked around them.

After dancing a few dances with him, Sara danced with Paul and then Oz. Charlie watched her happily. She was having a great time.

"I can't get over how that doesn't bother you at all," Paul said as he rejoined him, and they watched Oz and Sara dance. "They live alone together and obviously like each other, and it doesn't worry you."

"Sara and Oz love each other, but not like that," Charlie said absently as he observed them.

"And it never worried you?" Paul persisted.

Charlie shrugged. "No, he's one of my best friends, and I trust them completely."

"I'm your friend too, but man, if I lived with her... Well, look at her," Paul said defensively when Charlie rose an eyebrow.

Charlie laughed. "Good to know."

Hawk snickered and slapped Charlie's shoulder. "Trust me, no move would work."

Oz and Sara finished their dance and returned to the table. Oz grabbed a seat by Paul while Sara held a hand out to Hawk, smiling, her eyes shining with happiness, and her cheeks flushed. Hawk took her hand to rise but dropped it once he was standing, and they headed to the dance floor, laughing together.

"Time to find me some company." Paul rubbed his hands together as he scanned the room. His eyes lit and a broad smile crossed his face as he nudged Oz and pointed to a group of girls sitting together on the opposite side of the room. "That table there, the girls change, but not their attitude. They're always an easy pick up, at least for us. Let's see how you do without the uniform," he said with a challenging smile.

Charlie laughed. "I'll time it; first one who gets a kiss, wins. Clock starts when you reach the table."

Oz rolled his eyes. "Piece of cake." With a wink at Paul, he stood and rubbed his hands together, then cracked his knuckles and threaded his way through the dancers. He was almost at the table when he halted and turned back to them, and then straightened his shoulders and continued forward.

Paul laughed. "Did you see that? he almost chickened out." The laughter stopped, replaced by an amazed expression when a group of the girls jumped up and hugged and kissed Oz, clearly very excited to see him.

Charlie chortled at Paul. "Wow, you aren't kidding, but I think they like the regular clothes better than uniforms. I didn't even have time to start my watch."

Paul frowned at Oz. "How the hell did he do that?"

Charlie laughed again. "Maybe they're Valor groupies."

"Well, he's bringing them back, so at least he's willing to share," Paul said on a happier note.

Both boys stood when Oz got closer. Then Charlie groaned— *the harpies*. Oz had brought them the harpies.

Oz snickered at his expression.

"Chief, you remember Hannah and Haley?" Oz said with an even bigger grin and introduced them and their friends to Paul. "We went to high school with them."

"What are you doing here?" Charlie asked in amazement.

"Haley and I are visiting my grandparents for spring break. We always come here when we're in town," Hannah said. "Rumor had it you moved to California. Are you both in the academy now? How did you get in early?"

"No, just me," Charlie said. "I graduated high school a year early."

Hannah stepped forward to hug him, and he backed away, holding up his hands. "Sorry, no public displays in the uniform."

Hannah glanced around at the other midshipmen, and Charlie blushed. Some were making out in corners. It was against the rules but wasn't stopping them.

Charlie shot a desperate glance at Paul. Head tilted to the side and lips slightly pursed, Paul's gaze darted between them. After one last puzzled look, Paul smiled and offered his hand to Hannah.

"Would you like to dance?"

Before she could respond, Haley grabbed Paul's hand. "I will." She winked at Hannah over her shoulder.

Paul led her to the dance floor after giving Charlie a small apologetic shrug. The other girls followed, gigging and shooting Charlie appraising glances as they crowded around Paul and Haley.

Hannah took the seat between Charlie and Oz that Paul had vacated.

The song changed, and Hawk and Sara headed back to the table. Hawk took one look at Hannah, dropped Sara's arm, and got himself lost in the crowd. Charlie wished he could do the same.

"Sara," Hannah said in surprise, her eyes narrowing as Charlie rose when Sara approached the table.

Charlie drew Sara in close to him, not hugging her, but making it clear they were together.

"Still following Charlie around, I see." Her eyes narrowed farther as her gaze rested on the diamond engagement ring glittering in the club lights.

Charlie glared at Hannah who swallowed convulsively and leaned away. He kissed the top of Sara's head, but Sara laughed.

"Still wishing he'd follow you," Sara

replied.

Hannah tossed her head. "No. I'm dating Kevin Alward. He's the quarterback now." She tried to give Charlie a dismissive look but couldn't quite pull it off. "Nice seeing you, Charlie. I'll be back to see my grandmother in July," she added hopefully.

"I'll be on the Pacific Ocean somewhere in July."

Hannah nodded, then smirked at Sara. "Guess you won't see him than either," she said smugly.

Sara smiled back. "No, but I'll be waiting for him at our house."

Oz bit back a snort of laughter as Sara took Charlie's hand and led him to the dance floor.

"That never gets old," Sara said with an evil chuckle. "She's so easy to aggravate."

Charlie kissed her neck in her favorite spot. "I like when you say our house… let's go home to our house," he said his voice deeper, his meaning clear.

20

THE FIRST SCHOOL YEAR ENDS

When Charlie returned to school that night Paul told him about his date with Hannah. "I told you that place is great to pick up girls." Paul dropped into his desk chair and put his feet on the desk.

"You're going to catch something," Charlie said.

"I used protection, and she was totally willing."

"Oh, I believe that! Hannah was totally willing in high school too."

Paul grinned. "I'll probably never see her again, but it was fun."

"I don't mean to sound conceited here, but I guarantee she calls you when she's in town again. Hannah is determined to sleep with me and will use you to get to me."

"That's cool with me. She can use me all she likes." Paul snickered and leaned back in the chair stretching. "I'm not stupid. She practically drooled when I said we were roommates."

Charlie thumped down in his chair and took out a notebook. "Hannah doesn't even really like me. I'm just a conquest she can brag about back home."

"It's cool, bro, I'll throw myself on that grenade for you." Paul dropped his feet to the floor as their roommate Dave entered.

"What grenade?" Dave paused inside the doorway.

Paul described his day with graphic embellishments.

"Damn, and I was here all day trying to figure out these differential equations. Take me next time you go."

Paul laughed. "Will do." Still chuckling, he took Dave's math book. "And we'll help you with this too." Charlie and Paul explained the math problems until they were sure he understood.

Before lights out that night, Toric came into their room and inspected, running his hands over everything looking for dust. With his hands on his hips, he surveyed the neat desks and closets. "Carry on," he said as he left the room.

Paul jumped into his bunk. "Whew, I seriously didn't want to clean this place."

"Toric must be mellowing in his old age; he hasn't made us clean all month." Dave slapped Jeff, their other roommate, with his towel as he passed him on the way to the shower.

Jeff continued towel-drying his hair. "I heard his girlfriend broke up with him and he started playing video games. Maybe he's hoping Chief will help him with that?"

"Whatever." Paul plumped the pillow behind his head. "As long as we don't have to clean."

Charlie buried his face in his book to hide his grin.

The day before school ended, Charlie went to see Toric. "You'll be working with Sara, and I'm trusting that you'll not only not hurt her, but that you'll protect her."

"I'll do my best and treat her with the utmost respect." Toric offered his hand in a handshake.

Charlie shook his hand and stalked away. Sara wasn't helpless, but Toric was a big, well-trained man and knew their weakness for sedatives. Add to that he'd been chasing her for a year, and it made Charlie nervous to leave her alone with him.

"Oz will be with her," he mumbled and

then smacked himself in the head with one hand, aggravated over his irrational fears.

School ended, and their class set a new time record for the Herndon Monument, a record Charlie realized no normal human would be able to beat but he'd been unable to resist leaving his mark on the school.

Toric graduated and was assigned to the general.

Rick issued the raid invitation, which Toric accepted, and he was on his way to becoming a Scout.

Charlie had six days to report to his ship. He and Sara spent the first three putting as much magic as they could into the metal rods. The next two they spent lying in the sun, trying to rebuild and absorb each other's magic.

When they had to separate at the end of the fifth day, they both cried. Brenda picked him up and escorted him to his ship.

"The Scouts will be with her; she'll be safe."

Charlie leaned back in the passenger seat with his eyes closed. "I don't know if I can do this. Every instinct I have is screaming at me not to leave her. If I can't hack this, the entire year of separation will have been for nothing."

"You *can* do this, Charlie. If she has to be in the same zone, we'll move her into it. We won't stress the magic more than it can take." Brenda patted his knee.

"And if my connection with her breaks when I leave?"

"Then, you'll get it back when you return." Brenda glanced at him and then back at the road. "She's been out of the zone before when you were in Iraq, and she didn't stop loving or sensing you."

"I made her crazy, and she almost killed herself and Hawk trying to get to me."

"Okay, maybe a bad example."

Both were quiet for a while.

Brenda glanced at him again and sighed. "Relax. For Sara's sake try not to stress about this so much. You know it'll worry her to feel it."

"I'm trying," Charlie said through gritted teeth. Sara was still miserable, and she reacted to his spike of anger with fear. If he didn't get himself under control she'd begin to worry that she was making him angry by being sad. To distract himself he questioned Brenda on the travel arrangements even though he'd already memorized the details.

Brenda cooperated, telling him about his new assignment and gossiping about Drew and Joy. When she'd dropped Charlie off, she called Liz.

"Charlie is really stressed. More than might be healthy for his crewmates."

"I'm monitoring the situation. I'll be onboard checking to see if his aura is negatively affecting the crew. Honestly, we don't foresee it being a problem. The magic now recognizes Navy personnel as his team. He's able to spar with Marines and naval personnel with no push from his magic now. Army, Coast Guard, and Air force still give him problems and civilians, of course, but Navy and Marines he can interact with normally."

"Can Sara heal them too?" Brenda asked excitedly.

"Yes, and before you ask, no, we don't know what changed it. My theory is when they started school and had problems sparing with their classmates they made a real effort to think of them as teammates they were training. The magic learned to accept Naval personnel because they truly believed they were teammates. General Campbell is considering having them stationed on an Army base so they can teach the magic Army is teammates too, but we'll wait until all training is finished."

Brenda clutched the phone closer to her ear. "That's huge news."

Liz laughed. "Yes, but years away and who knows what will happen meanwhile."

"Still, it proves the magic can learn and evolve."

"Terrifying, isn't it?" Liz hung up.

Brenda stared at the phone in her hand and shivered.

21

CUB SCOUT CAMP

A week later, Sara and Oz flew to New Mexico to spend the summer at Cub Scout Camp. Alpha team accompanied them along with crates of supplies from the basement workshop. Toric joined them after his leave and began his training.

He watched in awe as small black globes flowed from Sara's staff. He was familiar with the game now and recognized her Lesser Fear Spell. Seeing it in person was both terrifying and thrilling.

He gestured to the staff she held. "Can you use anything, or does it have to be hollow?"

"Anything over four feet, but this has stored magic in it." Sara offered Toric the staff to examine.

"We should all carry backups for you, maybe those collapsible batons."

"Oz is redesigning a bunch of our gear."

303

Toric handed her back the wooden staff and returned to practicing. Every day he got faster.

Camp settled into a routine. He spent mornings doing classwork and learning how to use equipment. In the afternoons the Scouts practiced together both in groups and one-on-one, and evenings were spent either online playing UBM or studying. And he had a lot to study. A year behind the rest of the Scouts, he was learning everything from how to defuse and make bombs to how to fly the helicopters. Before bed he'd watch recordings of either old Valor raids or Scout footage to learn tactics.

When he was there two weeks, he had to do a chute-less jump with Sara.

"Everyone hates this the first time," Sara assured him as they sat in the back of a small plane Brenda piloted. All the Scouts were now certified pilots. Captain Sanders gave Oz, Sara, and Toric flying lessons every day.

Toric nodded and smiled wanly.

"Jump in fifteen," Brenda said over the intercom.

Sara stood and clipped her belt to Toric's. "Hold onto me this time. If you drop me, don't panic. I don't need to be touching you to cast Ascension just be within forty yards. It's fun, trust me."

Toric took her hand.

She laughed and hugged him tightly. "Don't let me go." Bright blue eyes stared up at him framed in golden blond hair.

Not wanting to seem a coward, he didn't close his eyes like he wanted to. Brenda counted down and Toric tightened his grip and jumped when Brenda said go. The wind whistled past his ears and he tried not to think about how crazy it was to jump with no chute. His entire body was so tense it hurt.

Sara pulled herself up until she was by his ear and counted out the seconds until they were falling straight and casted Ascension. The wind stopped whistling, and they floated gently.

"Three minutes, and don't forget to mark the tick. It's always possible I'll be distracted and need to be reminded. We'll hit the ground before Ascension runs out this time but keep it in mind. If you let me go, we'll still fall together unless we push off each other."

Toric made himself loosen his white-knuckled grip on her. "I can't accidentally remove it?"

"It takes an act of will. You have to really want to remove it, not just be thinking of removing it. The difference is only perception, but the magic never makes a mistake. If you want to drop again, try envisioning clicking off the buff as you do in the game. For the next drop you can wear a chute, only one chute-less jump is required."

Toric nodded and relaxed his grip even more. Sara's face rested beside his to make talking easier. She smelled good and felt better. He took a deep breath of her scent and exhaled in a sigh on her neck, causing her to shiver and pull away. A blush crept over his cheeks. He turned his face away from hers and asked about the drop rate.

When they floated inches above the ground she gave him a high-five. "See, I didn't drop you. On the next jump, you can wear the chute and I'll catch you in midair. Pretty soon, you'll trust me."

For the rest of the jumps Toric wore his chute but never used it. The first time she used Protective Companion and grabbed him, then waited to cast Ascension until they were at treetop height, he kept his eyes closed.

She laughed and patted the hand that gripped her gloved one. "Almost everyone pulls the cord for that one the first few times. We'll do an angled jump this time. We practice these a lot as a group. It's tricky to get the right trajectory. Pick me up and hold me tight and when you think you have the angle for our target, jump."

Toric nodded and picked her up and she put her legs around him. His body responded, and she blushed.

She pulled herself higher on his waist. "Sorry," she mumbled.

He chuckled. "Um, nothing personal." A red flush crept up his neck as he shifted his grip.

Sara cleared her throat. "I'm one of five women in three hundred miles; you aren't the only Scout who notices. Don't worry about it."

Brenda announced she was starting her turn and Toric checked his watch's altimeter and compass feature and jumped. Sara casted Ascension on his mark, and they were falling at a fast angle. "Call out if you want to cancel and me to recast if we need to change the angle," she yelled over the wind whistling past them.

"Cancel two," he said and then four seconds later said, "Ascension three."

They landed within feet of the target. "That's really good." Sara slapped his shoulder and grinned at him. "We have time for a few more jumps today. Let's get some more Scouts to join us. Then, after dinner, we can work on night ones. Those can be scarier. We'll do a few tonight with just the two of us. When we're working, and the op permits, we jump at night to avoid being seen."

He nodded, and they headed to the helicopter that would bring them back for another jump. Charlie would literally kill him if he knew what he was thinking; he needed to get a grip… He needed to get a girl of his own.

Over the course of the summer they did a lot more jumps; both singly and in groups and he enjoyed it. He did learn to trust her, and it was fun floating through the air. The Scouts tried stunts and different maneuvers as they fell. They could spread themselves out and land precisely, the only tricky part was keeping in Sara's range until you had the buff, and of course being sure it would last until you landed if you pushed away from the group. Every Scout wore an altimeter and learned to do the math in their head to calculate fall speed.

Usually, they dropped in pairs hooked together. She'd buff one person in each group, and then do the unbuffed person in each group. The pairs would push off each other and take their positions. They practiced falling with only two levitated holding the rest up as they used their belt clips to stay together, releasing and dropping to the ground when they came into range. A Scout could drop twenty feet as easily as a normal person could drop four.

They even practiced fake rescues in case a Scout became incapacitated during a jump. Toric found those practices nerve wracking as nobody knew until mid-jump who Sara or Major Nelson would pick to be the faller.

When Major Nelson signaled you to release and fall as you hung off a levitated partners leg and you had to trust that not only would Sara notice, but reach you in time… well, they weren't his favorite thing, especially at night. And he wasn't the only one who stared at his altimeter with one hand on the ripcord of his chute, but so far Sara hadn't missed anyone.

By the fifth week Toric started to feel like part of the team.

Two days before they were scheduled to leave Cub Scout Camp Brenda sat beside him at the small table set up under an awning where most class work was done as Sara and Oz had taken over the building that had been designated as classroom and conference space. When he started to rise, she waved him back down and grinned wryly. While technically Toric outranked her, here he had no official rank until he passed his tests. General Campbell had spoken to him about the importance of the reputation system and how he wouldn't assume his official rank until the general was assured that he understood the magic.

"At ease. You'll be accompanying Beta to Pendleton. They'll be taking a refresher course that you'll take too and do your finals there. For now, you'll stay with Beta. We sometimes move people to different teams depending on what we're doing."

Toric nodded his understanding; he'd studied all their previous missions.

"We're also going to make a small Gamma team that you'll oversee. Beta will fill you in; I just thought you'd want to know." Brenda slapped his shoulder and grinned.

Toric grinned back. "I was worried I wouldn't get a chance at command in this small of a group.

Brenda said, "Once your training is complete, if Gamma isn't in use, you'll take over command of Alpha from me, but don't get too comfortable there. As soon as Charlie graduates, he'll assume command of that team. Glenn will retain command of Beta."

Sara came up and sat next to Brenda. "Command of what team?"

"Alpha." Brenda absently patted her hand.

Her eyes widened, and she turned to face

Sara, grabbing her arm. "Hmm, you're not painful just sort of tingly. Toric, touch her. Does it hurt?"

Toric took Sara's bare hand. "Nope. Does that hurt you?"

"No, I can never feel it." Sara pulled the brim of the ball cap she wore down lower and rose.

"Hey, are you okay?" Brenda frowned and grabbed her arm, sliding her hand under the sweatshirt sleeve.

A shiver so strong it was almost a tremor shook Sara as she yanked her arm away and pulled her sleeve down. "I'll be fine; just one more week to go."

"Stop! Go, use some stored magic right now."

"I can't. I'm out, but I really am fine."

"Damn it, I should've noticed something was off when you started wearing long sleeves! How long have you been out?" Brenda's eyes narrowed.

"A while." Red stained Sara's cheeks, and she turned away. "I won't ruin this for him!" she suddenly shouted.

"He's probably being as stubborn as you are," Brenda said in disgust and took out her phone to make a call. "Major Nelson, sir, Sara is out of rods. Make sure Chief has enough." She listened for a moment and hung up.

"Okay, you're going to Pendleton too. Charlie can be there sooner. We're going tonight. Go get packed." Brenda stopped Toric from leaving with a hand sign and waited to speak until Sara was out of earshot.

"The idiot is going to kill herself trying to make Chief happy. Don't touch her and don't let anyone else touch her. Tell Oz to stay away from her. I'll send him on a different plane with half of Alpha and take Sara myself tonight." She paused a moment in thought. "And Rick. If she just has to be with someone, better him than anyone else."

Toric frowned and shifted uncomfortably in his seat. Brenda smirked and rolled her eyes. "No, not sex. Get your mind out of the gutter," Brenda snorted a small laugh. "Her magic demands physical contact, just skin-to-skin. She's depleted magically. The sun will help, but she needs Charlie."

Toric nodded, acknowledging understanding his orders. "Yes, Ma'am, but how did she get so depleted?"

Brenda narrowed her eyes again. "On purpose, I'd guess. She must've been using it to not need to be with him so much. It worked, but now she's weak."

"I don't think I understand this."

"Magic, well her magic, wants to be with

Charlie's magic. The more magic she has, the more it wants to be with him, so if she spends it, the need isn't so intense."

"Okay, that makes sense, I guess. But wouldn't his want hers too?"

"She gave him hers. Those tubes hold her magic. She's the only one who can store magic. When she takes his magic and stores it, it's diluted by hers, she can't take it directly. The magic of hers he has is stronger, and he has more of it than she does of his."

"So, they build up magic and when they have a certain amount they need to share it?"

"Yes, if the magic feels threatened, they need to share it as well."

"Threatened how?" Toric peered after Sara, his brow furrowed, hoping he hadn't upset her enough to need Charlie.

"If either one of them is afraid or really worried, the magic wants the other one."

Toric slumped in relief. Sara had been neither frightened or upset by his impropriety. "Ah, it's trying to protect itself, be stronger."

"That's what we think too. The host is in danger and it tries to protect the host by making them seek help. If they won't willing go to each other, the magic will try to force them."

Toric turned to face Brenda again. "Once

they share the magic, they're all better?"

"Yes, but the sharing can be hard on them; it's a powerful release of energy. They've blown out windows by touching hands."

"Oh."

"Her magic must be desperate by now if she's been spending it all daily and avoiding the sun to slow her regeneration. None of the magic she has will be his. She's making herself weak. We can't let her do that." Brenda stood and headed to the barracks.

Toric followed. "Wouldn't Charlie know if she was desperate?"

"He should, which worries me even more."

"Why would she do that though? Maybe it isn't that bad."

Brenda sighed. "She's a seventeen-year-old girl in love and would do anything to make him happy. When it comes to him, she has no sense."

Toric sighed too. "Yeah, that's not good."

"No, it isn't." Brenda reached for her phone. "Go pack. Beta will follow us in case she crashes the plane."

Toric nodded and sprinted to the barracks.

22

IT LL BE SMITES WHEN SHE WAKES

The plane reached Pendleton without incident. Charlie's ship would arrive off the coast of California in six days. Sara wouldn't leave her room. "You need sun and rest." Brenda frowned at Sara as she paced the small room, throwing heals on herself.

"No, I don't. I can't spend my magic here, and I can't control it if it's stronger."

The next day Sara was edgy and cranky. "I'm fine!" Tears trailed down her cheeks, which she dashed away with the back of her hand "I just miss him so much." She stopped crying a moment later and hugged herself, before she resumed throwing heals. "It's too much this way. I need to use it. Find me somewhere to cast, please."

"He'll be here soon. Cast on yourself or

me until we get a place for you to smite. Give me a minute to make some calls; I'll be right back."

Brenda went into the hallway and called Glenn. "Sara needs a place fast to cast Smite. The magical pressure is too much for her hold back much longer."

"Call Major Nelson and get Chief back here," Glenn said. "I'll line up a place for her to cast. Keep the tranq gun handy."

"Yes, sir."

Brenda called Major Nelson. "Sara needs Charlie ASAP. The magic is really pushing her."

"It's only a few more days. Have her cast or something."

"Major…" Brenda gritted her teeth on what she wanted to say and cleared her throat. Being careful to speak in a respectful voice she continued, "I realize it'll be difficult to get him here, but she really does need him. The magic…"

"I'll see what I can do," Major Nelson said brusquely and hung up.

Brenda closed her eyes and counted to ten before returning to Sara.

At dusk Sara fell asleep, exhausted from casting all day. Brenda headed to the lounge where they kept a cooler of food and drinks and called the major again.

"Get Charlie here. I'm not kidding; she really needs him. I don't care if he only has a few days, this is an emergency."

"Brenda… it's not that easy. Tell her to wait for crying out loud."

"Sir, I can tell her all day long, but try telling her magic. Do you want her to blow up another building or two to reach him? Because that's what we're going to have any minute now."

"She's that bad?"

"Yes!" Brenda shouted then took a deep breath. "Excuse me, sir, but yes, she's that bad. If it's too difficult to bring Charlie here, take her to him, but do something soon. When she wakes, if she's still this riled, I'm going to sedate her with or without her permission."

"The casting isn't helping?"

"Yes, and no. It helps, but as it regenerates she's desperate. Keeping her from him is cruel."

"Fine, I'll get him here as soon as I can."

Brenda glared at the phone.

"Problems?" Harrison asked as he rummaged in the cooler, emerging with a soda.

"The major seems to think Sara can ask the magic to wait."

Harrison nodded slowly, his mouth in a

grim line. "You convinced him she can't?"

"I hope so. He says he'll get Charlie here anyway."

"Then he will. The major might not be as empathic as we might wish for Sara, but he's a man of his word."

Brenda hesitated and then blurted, "Is it because she's a girl?"

Harrison winced. "Not my place to say." He excused himself and left the room.

Brenda rubbed her forehead and closed her eyes.

Sara woke in the early morning frantic. Blue magic swirled about her coating every inch of her. Lines of strain bracketed her eyes and lips as she tried to hold her magic back. Brenda had fallen asleep on the chair in Sara's room and woke when she did.

"Chief is on his way to you. Can I sedate you until he arrives?"

"Yes, help me, Brenda. I can't hold it back much longer."

Brenda took out her dart gun and fired. Nothing happened. Again, she pulled the trigger and swore when no dart emerged. A hurried unload and examination showed a bent pin. Sara's expression tightened and Brenda rose slowly to her feet, backing from the room saying, "Wait right here."

Sara followed her into the hallway.

"I need Oz then." She snatched at Brenda's phone. The blue glow surrounding her intensified. Harrison entered the hallway from the room across the hall. Sara grabbed him with Protective-Companion and pressed her hand on his face, sobbing and calling for Charlie.

Brenda gestured to the gawkers in the doorways. "One of you call someone near my room. There's tranquilizers in my nightstand, or call Glenn for his. Get in your rooms and lock your doors now!" Brenda yelled as doors up and down the hall opened.

Sara screamed as she tried to pull magic from Harrison. Magic swirled furiously around her, lifting strands of hair from the strength of its twirling. Harrison shouted hoarsely and pushed her away as her touch reached painful proportions. Sara sobbed and apologized, holding trembling hands to her face. For a moment she hugged herself and then reached to Brenda, pleading for her to help.

Brenda backpedaled away. "Heal Harrison, Sara, you'll feel better. Nothing is going to hurt you. You're perfectly safe."

Sara stopped crying and healed Harrison, casting one heal after another on him. "I need...." She trailed off into sobs and reached to Harrison again. Harrison backed up and entered his room, leaving Sara and Brenda alone in the hallway.

"We have no magic to give you." Brenda held out her empty hands.

Sara nodded and the blue surrounding her fluctuated wildly as she tried to control it.

"You're fine. Charlie is fine, and you'll see each other very soon."

"Don't say his name," Sara said in high keening wail. "Don't, don't, don't!" Her magic pulsed erratically. Light flew from her fingers in a steady stream as she casted heals as fast as she could. The blue settled down into one solid color and Sara stood panting in the hallway. The door opened at the end of the hall and a fully suited Scout appeared. Her magic raced to him and engulfed him and raced back to her. She screamed in frustration.

The Scout approached, removing his facemask. "I have sedatives here that should help you." Toric showed her the needle he held. "Can I use them?"

Blue eyes glowing brightly, she pulled him to her side with her Protective-Companion spell and pressed a hand to his face, then snatched it away and healed him. "Help me! I can't hold it back much longer!"

Toric gave her the shot in her arm. White

glowing tears trickled down her cheeks. One hand outstretched as if she strained to reach something only she could see, the other clutched his armor with inhuman strength until she collapsed in a heap. Toric caught her as she fell and lowered her to the floor.

"Jesus, now what?"

Brenda picked Sara up and motioned to the door of the room with her chin. "Now we get Charlie here as fast as we can. Call the others; we'll need to take turns carrying her or her defensive shocks will get us. She's casting heals now, but it'll be smites when she wakes, and he isn't here.

23

TOO LITTLE TOO LATE

Charlie's superior officer called him aside in the middle of his shift. "Report to bay twelve immediately. Your presence is requested at Camp Pendleton. You leave in ten minutes on a Seahawk. Apparently, you're needed there yesterday. We'll forward your gear. I don't think you'll be returning— dismissed."

Charlie ran to the top deck. Excitement tingled along his spine, and with a small shock he realized he looked forward to a mission, and not just as a break in the routine of shipboard life or to see his team. He looked forward to violence.

The bracelet he wore on his left wrist remained dark. He frowned in puzzlement and slowed to concentrate, trying to sense Sara. Two steps from the copter he stopped in his tracks. He sensed nothing at all from her, not even the familiar hum of deep concentration or the faded presence of sleep. *When had that happened and how hadn't I noticed?*

He literally felt nothing from her. He'd been so caught up in his own life he hadn't even noticed the missing connection. Hands shacking now, he greeted the pilot. The last feeling he clearly remembered from her had been over a week ago when she'd been embarrassed about something.

Communication between them was almost nonexistent; she had no internet access, and he had no phone, but he'd thought they were doing okay. Both had settled into a steady day-to-day routine. Her feelings were just a background sensation easier to dismiss at this distance. He'd realized they were harder to make out but had attributed it to time apart and the dullness of her work, assuming she just felt no strong emotion. And to be honest, he hadn't tried to sense them. Work on the ship distracted him, and he was enjoying being just one of the guys. She hadn't been unhappy; he'd thought she was content. Now she was nothing. Nausea built until vomit burned the back of his throat.

"Nervous?" The pilot handed Charlie a headset, eyeing Charlie's shaking hands in amusement.

Charlie was more than nervous— he was

scared to death. "How long?"

"Five hours. Someone wants you in an awful hurry," the pilot said cheerfully.

Charlie had a sudden, terrible conviction that Sara had died. "Oh, god," he sobbed and started to cry. The magic within him pulsed, and he had to strain to hold it back. It wanted Sara desperately too. He staggered forward and dropped to his knees.

"Jesus!" The pilot exchanged a disgusted glance with his copilot.

Charlie tried to get ahold of himself, taking several deep breaths and rubbing his face with both hands. "I'm fine. Sorry, I just... I think my wife has died." His voice broke. He pulled himself up by using the side of the copter, furious with himself and his magic.

"Oh, sorry, man." Awkward silence descended as they buckled in, broken only by the roar of the engines.

Charlie tried to sense her as hard as he could and reached nothing at all, not even a misty shred of a dream. Magic flickered over his hands. He took deep breaths, breathing in the familiar scent of hot metal and diesel fuel, and closed his eyes, trying to keep the panic at bay, afraid to lose control of his magic in the helicopter.

Someone would've called me if Sara died, he

tried to reassure himself. But would they have where he might have a magical breakdown? No, they'd do what they were doing, get him home as fast as they could. Magic exploded from his body and swirled around the cabin. The pilot and copilot exclaimed.

"What the hell is that?"

"Where'd it go?"

"Was that smoke? Check the readouts. Everything's green on my board."

Charlie gritted his teeth and forced his magic back as the two pilots argued about what they'd seen.

The copilot left his headset and climbed into the back with Charlie.

"What's going on," Charlie asked, trying to project innocent questioning but unable to hide the strained grimace caused by the burning sensation of holding his magic back.

"Smoke or something in the cockpit. It looked like it went right through the wall. Did you see anything back here?"

"Nope."

The copilot gave him a doubtful glance but continued his inspection without speaking. Charlie sagged in relief when the man retreated to the cockpit and let his magic loose. It swirled around him but didn't dart off. He was able to recall it in moments and it withdrew back into his body, but it still wanted Sara with desperate intensity. Charlie didn't know if the magic was trusting he was going to her or had realized it was trapped in the helicopter, but he was grateful it had stopped trying to manifest.

The not knowing would drive him mad. He needed to find out if she was okay. If this was a callout with nothing to do with her, he was going to be seriously pissed they'd let him worry like this. "Can you make phone calls from here?" Charlie finally asked the pilot.

"I can radio, and they can call," the pilot offered.

"Can you find out if Sara Mitchel Hayes is on base and her condition?" Charlie gave the pilot his and Sara's federal ID numbers.

Twenty minutes later the pilot said, "Sara Mitchel is on base and I'm to tell you her condition is unstable."

"Oh, thank god." Charlie closed his eyes and rested his head on the seat back. "I'll be in time."

"I'm very sorry," the pilot said with real sympathy in his voice.

"She'll be okay; I'll get there in time. I can't tell you— when I thought she was dead." Charlie shuddered and relaxed his tense shoulders. *They must've sedated her,* he told himself and tried not to imagine why they would've needed to.

"I'm a fucking idiot."

"What?" the pilot asked.

"Nothing. Sorry, I just never should've left her when I knew… Never mind." Charlie clamped his lips together and stared at the ocean passing beneath them.

He knew she needed his magic, and he'd left her. "What the hell was I thinking," he muttered and rubbed his face hard. He'd left his wife, the wife whose magic needed his desperately, in a different zone. His nausea returned doubled. Guilt burned like acid. His selfishness might cost his team everything. Her magic would be panicked. It needed to sense him nearby to feel safe.

"Please, let me be in time," he murmured.

"We're at our top speed," the pilot said in a tone of false reassurance.

Charlie said nothing. He clasped his hands and prayed. Her magic would do anything to reach him. She'd fight anyone who tried to stop her, not caring who saw or who she hurt.

Sara regained consciousness without control, her magic wanted out. A brilliant white ball of light formed in her hands and she blew a hole in the side of the building and jumped, her magic making her frantic.

"Jesus Christ, stop her!" Brenda jumped after her.

Lurching and stumbling, more crawling then walking, Sara crossed the courtyard. Another ball of light formed in her hands, this one larger and brighter with an orange tint. The hole she blasted in the cement wall of the next building was bigger than the last one. Chunks of debris flew in all directions. Sara tripped, rolled, and shook her head as she pushed herself to her feet and crawled through the opening she'd created.

Toric raced after Brenda, passing her as she stopped and took her phone out, ordering whoever answered to evacuate the area.

This was Scout housing Sara was plowing through like a bulldozer, but the next buildings weren't. Toric kept calling her name and then had an inspiration. "I have Charlie. Chief is with me, come back!"

Hair a tangled mass about her shoulders, and eyes a brilliant blue, she skidded to a halt and spun to face him. Toric ran, pushing through the magic surrounding her. He jabbed the needle in and pushed the plunger as they both screamed. Bright sparks of static grew in size as they leapt between them. He backed out of the blue cloud, trying to brush it off him, gritting his teeth at the painful shocks.

A bolt of lightning forked from the clear sky and slammed into her. She convulsed and then was still. Thin streaks of white lightning formed from her body and leaped into the sky. Thunder sounded and shook the building.

"Stop!" Toric yelled, "Sara stop! He's coming, wait please."

The blue surrounding her settled into a dense black cloud. Small forks of lightning split from it and the smell of ozone filled the air. Toric hastily backed away.

Brenda ran up. "Give her another shot in five minutes. I have stronger stuff coming and we're evacuating the area. Is she okay?"

"I have no idea. The lightning hit her. You can't approach her. Good luck giving her a shot of anything," Toric said as they both backed away from the lightning forking from her. "Man, this went downhill fast," Toric said in disbelief

"It does that." Brenda called Rick. "We're in apartment complex B. Follow the trail of wreckage. You can't miss us, and hurry."

"Why him?"

Brenda shrugged. "Why not him? Maybe the magic will recognize him and calm the hell down."

Before Rick arrived with the new medicine, Sara sat suddenly and stared at them from eyes completely blue with glowing white edges. She reached her hand out to them. "My warrior." Flat and dull the words blended together.

"We have no magic to give you," Brenda said, "but Charlie is coming."

Sara tapped her fingers on the ground over and over in her Call-For-Help pattern. Bright white lightning slammed into her again, causing both Toric and Brenda to scream and jump back. Rick ran up carrying the tranquilizer gun, but before he could hand in to Brenda or use it, Sara casted Protective Companion and yanked him to her with no warning despite the fact he was standing out of her normal range. Toric and Brenda ran further away. Lightning again struck her. This time it stayed, and the blue-white glow surrounded them.

"So not good." Brenda got back on the phone. "Major, she has Rick in a lightning field. We're going to need a medic here."

"We have none close to you who are in

the know. Do your best." Major Nelson snapped.

The explosion when Charlie appeared knocked them all back. The lightning lifted off Rick and slammed into his brother. Charlie and Sara both screamed.

Brenda darted forward and pulled Rick farther back. "Back up!"

She and Toric grabbed Rick's feet. Another more powerful wave of energy knocked them over again. Saint Elmo's fire crawled over the exterior of the building. The violet light sizzled but left no scorch marks. Thunder crashed again, and the violet-blue glow traveled in a wave from the exterior of the building over the lawn and settled on the trees, outlining each leaf in purple fire.

Charlie and Sara screamed again. Thunder crashed repeatedly, but no more lightning descended and the Saint Elmo's fire dissipated. Brenda and Toric rose to their feet and carried Rick further away.

Joy ran up. "Holy Christ!" she exclaimed and hunched away from the pulsing cloud of magic.

Dark blue with intensely white threads cutting through it, the magic writhed madly about Sara and Charlie.

"We're holding everyone back, but the blue glow can be seen. We'll need a cover story for sure." Joy seemed to notice Rick for the first time and bent to feel for a pulse.

Another loud series of thunderous crashes sounded, and the magic swirled harder.

"Jesus, that building is going to come down on them." Toric ran forward, but stopped before entering the building, unsure if it would help or hurt if he tried to move them now.

Brenda ran up and grabbed his arm, pulling him back. "They need to touch."

Charlie crouched before Sara; his body outlined in violet fire that didn't burn.

"Maybe we need to back up more," Toric said nervously as Sara reached for Charlie.

She ripped his shirt as she grabbed him. The magic disappeared with a whoosh of air that fluttered the leaves on the trees behind them and made Toric's ears pop. Sara sobbed and ripped Charlie's shirt further, placing her face on his bare skin. He grabbed her arms and another explosion knocked everyone over again. The lightning returned and covered Sara and Charlie. Eerily quiet, distant sounds of sirens and yelling were muffled as if the area in which they stood was incased in cotton.

Joy ran back to help keep everyone away.

Brenda checked Rick, then her watch.

"Five minutes." Tendrils of lightning writhed from Charlie and Sara as if searching.

"I think it wants Rick," Toric said as more and more tendrils slithered in their direction.

Brenda dragged Rick further away. Six and a half minutes later, the lightning disappeared, and they both slumped over. Brenda approached and tentatively touched them with the back of her hand and then felt for pulses. "Let's get them in the grass. I'm afraid this building might fall over."

Gritting their teeth against the pain of touching them, Toric and Brenda carried them one at a time and placed them by the pool.

"Now what?"

"We wait and see if they wake." Brenda checked everyone's pulse again. "Hawk is on his way. But, it'll be a while before he gets here."

"Far be it for me to criticize military decisions, but I'm going on record as saying it probably isn't smart to separate them," Toric said in a massive understatement.

"I agree, but it doesn't matter what we think."

"If she dies because Hawk is too far away, it'll be a real tragedy. Not for Charlie, but for all of us."

Brenda nodded, then sat beside Rick and waited.

When Charlie woke, he knew he was touching Sara and sighed in relief. Dazed, he pulled her closer and put one hand on her heart, the other her neck. The steady pulse beneath his palm reassured him. Her desperate need for his magic thrummed under his skin. *No, not her feelings, her magic's,* he thought in mounting unease.

He'd felt her fear seconds before she'd summoned him but now felt nothing again. If the magic wasn't so thick about them he doubted he'd be able to feel the magic's need like he did. He closed his eyes to examine her aura, but her normal golden tones were obscured by blue.

Hoping skin contact would help, he placed her on his bare chest and ripped her shirt off to give them more contact. The blue settled into his skin, and for the first time he wondered where he was. He sat up weakly, keeping Sara pressed to him.

"Better?" Brenda asked.

"No, not yet, but we need privacy."

Charlie glared at Toric who held his hands up and backed away.

"Okay but stay out here. We'll get you a tent or something. No buildings for a little while."

"My brother?" Charlie asked, and spell-stole Sara's heal to cast on Rick who lay at Brenda's feet.

Brenda waved him back down as he awkwardly stood. "Stay there. Rick will be fine. Sara can heal him when she wakes."

Charlie hesitated then sat. There was nothing he could do. Helping Sara would help his brother and she need to touch him. "What happened?"

Toric said, "Sara ran out of your magic and waited a little too long to tell us."

Charlie winced and rubbed his forehead. "Did she hurt anyone?"

"Just Rick and herself. She caught him in a lightning field, making a warrior, I think."

"How are you?" Brenda asked.

Charlie took a second to consider. "I'm okay. Her magic is desperate though. I feel its need. Did anything scare her?"

His eyes narrowed when Toric flushed, but Brenda said, "I don't think so. I think she scared it by holding it back so hard. She was keeping it weak, staying out of the sun and using it." Brenda leaned down to feel Rick's pulse and nodded reassuringly. "He'll be fine. Want me to—"

"Don't come near her," Charlie said, shocking himself by his angry tone. Brenda had only taken one step forward, but he felt as if she'd pulled a gun. Blue magic swirled around Charlie and he knew his eyes were glowing when the world gained startling detail.

"Sorry" – he offered her a sickly smile— "I just need to be alone with her for a while." The idea of anyone else being near her right now made him sick to his stomach. Even unconscious her magic's need for his burned. With his eyes closed he could see her aura now, but it flared oddly as if sparks traveled through it. His magic seemed to sooth the sparks, letting her normal steady glow shine through.

"Okay, we won't. I'll get you water and a tent or something. We'll be right back." Brenda bent to pick up Rick and motioned Toric to follow her.

"Go get orange juice, water, and a few blankets. I'll call for a tent. I don't want to leave them alone here," Brenda said and Toric ran off.

By the time Brenda and Toric returned, Charlie had removed Sara's jeans, leaving her in her underwear. He sat with her curled in his lap covered by their shirts.

Charlie glared at Toric. He didn't need the magic to feel his guilt, it was written all over his face whenever he glanced at Sara. He'd done something, Charlie was sure of that.

"What the hell did you do?"

Toric's flush deepened. "Nothing."

"He didn't do anything," Brenda said as she gestured for Toric to hand her the supplies. "We'll leave you be for a while. I swear, Charlie, Toric did nothing. He and Sara are friends. When she wakes you can ask her but there's no need to be mad at him, or her either. She thought she had it handled. It hit her hard and suddenly."

Brenda approached slowly and placed the items on the ground beside him and then backed away, moving slowly and keeping her empty hands in sight.

Charlie watched her every move, his entire body tense, angry with himself now for his unreasonable anger.

He shook out a blanket and placed Sara on it, then used another to cover them both. Small flashes of blue from his hands disappeared as he touched her. Toric handed Brenda a dart gun and then went to check on the tent.

Brenda sat with her back against a tree,

watching them with the dart gun in one hand.

Toric returned minutes later with Joy.

"Joy and I will set the tent up for you," Brenda offered, and Charlie nodded.

Brenda picked a spot shaded by trees away from the buildings, giving an illusion of privacy.

Joy came to get Charlie when the tent was up. "Do you want help with her?"

"No, I'll manage. We just need privacy now. We'll stay here until she's more balanced. She'll need to touch me for a while."

"Rick needs healing when she can do it. He'll be fine until she is up to it. But if you want to see him…" Joy added when Charlie groaned.

"No, let him rest. She's getting better too. The magic is a bit less desperate."

Charlie carried Sara inside the tent, and Brenda exchanged relieved glances with Joy.

Thirty minutes later Rick woke and grabbed his head. "Wow, my head. Man, that's a headache. What hit me?"

"Your sister-in-law." Brenda said.

"Are they okay?" Rick struggled to his feet.

"They're alive, but no I don't think they're okay," Brenda said dryly.

"So, what would've happened if he hadn't shown up?" Toric turned and examined the two gaping holes in the buildings, one of which was large enough to drive a truck through.

"I think she was making Rick a warrior."

Toric nodded. "If he's going to be gone a lot she needs more than one."

Brenda grimaced. "Yeah, but sharing the magic is incredibly intimate. I can't see Charlie being happy sharing her, even with his brother." She eyed Toric knowingly. "Don't even think it."

"My thoughts are my own," he said lightly.

"Set some watches here. Make sure no one approaches. Keep a Scout in this yard at all times and at least two Scouts on the perimeter, making sure the barricade stays up. We have privates patrolling, but let's make sure no one disturbs them. I'll take the first watch."

Toric saluted and left to carry out her orders.

Sara awoke in a frenzy of desperation. Charlie wrestled her to the ground until she calmed. "Stop, I'm right here!" He was so grateful to sense her again his words came out hoarsely.

She stopped struggling and clutched him.

His magic went from him in a rush that caused his ears to pop.

She released her grip.

"That was horrible. I really tried, but I can't do this. I'm so sorry!" she wailed as she sat and pushed away from him.

Charlie grabbed her and pulled her in close. "You were supposed to tell me if it was too much for you, not cut me out like this."

"I was handling it. I really was. But, I ran out of magic, and you only had one more week, and I didn't want to ruin it for you, and I thought I could do it for one more week, and then I couldn't!"

He kissed her, and she stopped babbling for a minute. "Never do that again!" He grabbed her shoulders and shook her lightly. "Never do that again!"

Her magic leaked from her skin and surrounded him. He waited until he absorbed it before speaking again.

"You have to believe me, Sara, you can't do this again. If you need me, tell me. I promise you, I won't be upset about that. I sure as hell am upset about this. Stop trying to let me go, just stop! I'm not going anywhere. If I can't do something I should for the service because you need me, then to hell with them. This isn't about you missing your boyfriend! If they can't understand that, then I'll quit, and we'll go away somewhere just us. But do *not* do that again!"

Sara started crying.

Charlie murmured, "It's going to take a while to balance this out. I missed you too, not just the magic." He kissed her neck in her favorite spot and it got no response, except more tears. He kept talking softly and rubbing her back until she relaxed enough to enjoy his kisses.

Charlie heard Glenn arrive and relieve Brenda and knew when they brought a portable bathroom and food but made no effort to speak to anyone. He didn't know how he was going to balance the magic's and Sara's needs with his own.

- 24 -

GIRLS ARE TOO MUCH WORK

"Do we let the process progress or stop it?" the general asked. He paced unhappily before the president's desk.

"I'm torn. On one hand, another warrior would be great, but on another, it's more to worry about." The president paused in thought. "Dispel and heal him. See if she can stop the change."

"Yes, sir." The general saluted, and the order came to Sara.

The next afternoon Brenda and Toric brought Rick to Sara.

Charlie followed her from the tent, not at all happy about how eagerly she went to his brother. She'd never felt this longing to see him before.

Sara hesitated before casting Dispel. A frown on her face, she formed a heal in her hands, holding the yellow ball on her fingertips for a moment before throwing it at Rick, the frown deepening as she dispelled him.

When no trace of magic remained on him, tears filled her eyes and she hugged him, burying her face in his blue sweatshirt. Rick patted her back and then pulled away. "Everyone will be happier if they know the process can be stopped. Someday, we can try again in a more controlled way."

Sara nodded and hugged him again.

Charlie watched with rising jealousy. Sara wanted his brother. Not sexually, but she did want him. Her magic sought him, the familiar blue glow of her magic surrounded her.

After a few minutes, Rick stepped away from her. Blue magic followed him. Bright sparks of static flitted between Rick and Sara.

"I have no magic for you," Rick whispered when Sara hugged him again, gripping his sweatshirt in both hands.

Sara blushed and mumbled, "I'm so sorry, it isn't right to want you in any way, but I can't help it."

"Go to Charlie; he needs you."

Sara stepped away, but her magic lingered on Rick. She was headed back to the tent and him when Toric touched her arm.

"I—"

Before Toric could say more, her magic

rushed him and knocked them over. Toric grabbed her and she turned blue shining eyes to his face.

Charlie bellowed his charge and intercepted them.

"Shit!" Brenda pulled Toric away. "Get Sara away, Charlie, before her magic tries to take us all!"

Enraged with jealousy, Charlie grabbed Sara and yanked her away. Her magic swirled in a frenzy about Toric and small arcs of lightning flew between them as she struggled in his grasp, trying to go to Toric.

Without thinking, he yelled his berserk cry, a loud *Oorah* echoed by every Scout on base. Sara's magic whirled faster. Thunder sounded, and Charlie had her pinned to the ground and didn't even remember doing it. The Scouts had come running when he called, and her magic went to the ones who played warriors.

"Everyone out right now! Give us space here!" Brenda ordered. The Scouts obeyed, and Sara's magic rushed to her. Brenda batted uselessly at the blue cloud as she fumbled for her phone. "Sara is out of control here," she said when the major answered.

The magic chasing her returned to Sara, and Brenda stopped running and told the major what was happening. "The magic wants another warrior, it doesn't want to be alone, and it doesn't care what that does to them."

"Hawk will be there in an hour, quicker if she summons him, although god knows how we'll explain another midair disappearance, and he should be safe with them and calm them," Major Nelson said. "We really screwed up making the magic this desperate."

"We'll try to keep her contained until Hawk is here, but I'm not guaranteeing we can stop her from taking an innocent bystander," Brenda warned.

"Understood, do your best. Liz is on the way too. Tranq her if you have too."

"Yes, sir." Brenda snapped her phone closed and pulled out her dart gun. "I told you to get his ass here," she muttered.

Charlie shook Sara furiously. "Stop! You don't need them, I'm here." His magic surrounded her, and she stopped trying to get away. Tears streamed from her glowing eyes as she clutched him, and then she was tearing at his borrowed clothes. They made love in a wild frenzy, so out of control they neither knew nor cared if they were alone and unobserved. Afterward, he lay with her naked in the grass, holding her pressed against him. A cloud of magic lit with sparks of static covered them, so dark and dense it offered a modicum of privacy.

She'd fallen into an exhausted sleep. Afraid to move and wake her, he laid unmoving, terrified of what her magic would make her do.

Hawk found them there together.

"Could you throw me a blanket?" Charlie whispered. A fiery blush heated his cheeks.

Hawk flushed and turned away, going to the tent and emerging with a blanket.

Charlie tucked the blanket about them as best he could with one hand. She woke and started crying.

Hawk sat beside them.

Gradually, Sara stopped crying, and they both relaxed. A light blue mist of magic covered all three of them. No one spoke. Sara kept her face pressed against Charlie's chest. Charlie was afraid to disturb her balance. The unsteadiness of her aura scared him to death. Hawk and Sara were both embarrassed, but Charlie said nothing, knowing she needed Hawk.

After a few hours, Hawk whispered, "Want food or anything?"

"Yes, whatever's handy, and thanks, Hawk. We really need you," Charlie said as Sara tried to burrow closer to him, so filled with lust he worried she'd lose control right there and do something that would embarrass everyone. He flushed wildly knowing Hawk could sense their emotions while he stood in the magic.

"I'll be back in thirty minutes, maybe a bit more." Hawk rose and hesitated for a moment then jogged off.

As soon as Hawk was out of sight they made love again. Inside the tent this time. *Progress,* Charlie thought ruefully as he dressed afterward in boxer shorts and lightweight sleep pants Brenda had provided. Sara put on a t-shirt and shorts and wrapped the blanket around her shoulders.

When Hawk returned, he'd ask him to get her a bathing suit so they could have more skin contact. The brief separation of using the bathroom stressed Sara, she didn't say anything, but her hands clenched on him and Charlie felt her distress.

Hawk brought back salads, cookies and sodas, and found them sitting together outside the tent wrapped in the blanket.

Over the next three hours, as Sara picked at the food, the magic dissipated until none remained in sight. He exchanged a rueful smile with Sara when the magic stopped transmitting Hawk's embarrassment to them. He hoped the magic would remain in their bodies. Without it swirling about them their feelings would remain private.

Sara's glance darted from Hawk to Charlie and she frowned. "Can we all sleep here tonight?"

"Like a camp out," Charlie added, trying to make it less weird for Hawk, hoping to alleviate some of Sara's embarrassment.

"Sure, this is great. My bunk at sea was like a foot too short for me." Hawk told them stories that had Sara smiling as they sat together, enjoying his aura.

"Thanks, man," Charlie whispered after Sara fell asleep again in his arms.

"De nada." Hawk peered at Sara worriedly. "Close one, huh?"

"She tried to magically rape the entire platoon."

Hawk winced at his choice of words. "Not her fault the magic can't be denied."

"She shouldn't have let it get so bad." Sara stirred as his anger grew, and he tried to stifle it.

Hawk shrugged. "Well, I'm sure she didn't realize this would happen. Being angry with her won't help."

"I'm angry at myself, not her. I should've realized she needed me sooner. Way sooner. I'm a complete selfish bastard. I didn't even notice I'd stopped sensing her for a week. Don't you dare tell her that either," he finished in a fierce whisper.

Hawk nodded.

"When they sent me here, I tried to sense her and thought she was dead. She's killing herself so I can do what I want, and I don't even notice. No wonder her magic wants someone else to take care of her."

"Well, don't do it again." Hawk shrugged and stretched out in the grass, putting his hands behind his head.

Charlie snorted.

Hawk laughed. "Girls are too much work."

"I'm the worst husband on Earth, and she puts up with me. I need to do a lot better at this." Charlie pulled Sara higher on his chest. "If any of them try to take my place, I'll kill them."

It took five days before Sara thought she could control her magic enough to be near other people. After three days, Hawk left them alone at night, sleeping in his own tent nearby. The wild lust she felt had settled back into a normal amount, which both relieved and disappointed Charlie. Every time she'd dragged him into the tent she was embarrassed afterward. He felt kind of smug, not caring who knew how much she wanted him.

Charlie watched, poised to leap, as she approached his brother and sighed in relief when she hugged him as usual. She didn't try to get near any of the others and felt no need for them.

They went to Charlie's parents' house and spent a week there. Hawk spent nights at Charlie's parents and days visiting with his mother.

"Sara and Hawk are spending a lot of time together," John said in a worried voice as they watched Hawk sit with his arm around Sara on the back steps after dinner.

"She's having a magical issue. Nothing we can't handle," Charlie said quickly when his father looked alarmed. "Hawk's aura helps her remain calm. Helps us both remain calm."

"I see," his father said, although clearly he didn't. Charlie sighed and explained in more depth. "I see," John repeated in a much different tone of voice, frowning at his son. "A wife is more than a friend or a lover. They're a dependent, it says so right on the tax form."

Charlie snorted a quick, "Ha," and his father winced.

"That means we have to be dependable. Sometimes, we have to sacrifice something we want for their good."

"I know, and I'm going to withdraw. She can't be separated from me like this," Charlie said sadly.

"Well, I'd try explaining before withdrawing, but it's up to you. Whatever you decide, I'm proud of you, son, never doubt it." His father slapped his shoulder.

That night Charlie told Sara he was withdrawing and was shocked by her panicked response.

She scrambled from the bed. "No, you can't! It'll be fine. I promise I'll handle it better."

"You don't have to—."

"No! You can't. I really am okay." Her voice rose shrilly, "Don't do this to us. Give me one more chance, please!" Tears streamed down her face as she begged.

Annoyed at her overreaction, he took her hands. "This is for the best."

"No, I know I hurt you— us, but please don't do this."

Hawk came to the door followed by his parents.

"Is everything okay in here?" Mary clutched her blue robe closed with one hand.

Sara ran to his mother and grabbed her,

crying hysterically. "Don't let him. Make him give me one more chance. What do I say to stop him?"

Hawk pulled her away and held her. "Calm down. What's going on?"

"He doesn't trust me anymore even though I promised it wouldn't happen again. I'll be so careful! He can't quit— he can't! I can't ruin this! God, Hawk, I'm trying so hard."

"Quit what, ruin what? Take a breath and calm down." Hawk glanced over at Charlie who glared.

She knew he was angry with her now, but she was being ridiculous and deserved to feel his anger. He didn't try to hide it from her.

Sara took a deep breath. "If he quits because of me, it'll ruin everything forever, and he'll hate me. Please, please stop him! I promise you, Hawk, I can handle this. I know what to look for now, please!"

Charlie took Sara from Hawk. "Sara and I will work this out together." He turned to his gawking parents. "We'll work this out." His father took his mother's arm and led her from the room.

Hawk lingered uncertainly.

"Give us a few minutes, please, Hawk."

"Sure, I'll make coffee or something." Hawk gave Sara one last troubled glance and went downstairs.

"Okay, sit here and calm down," Charlie commanded in a firm voice, intentionally trying to use his Voice of Command on her. "We'll work our problems out together. Now tell me what the problem is."

Sara paced before him as she spoke. "If you quit, it'll be my fault, and don't say it won't, it will, and years from now, when everyone is in the service and doing well, you'll resent me, then you'll hate me, and I won't let you!"

"Okay, then I won't. See, wasn't that easy? All you had to do was ask."

She glared at him.

He laughed.

"You really won't quit?" Sara stopped before him, placing her hands on his hips, staring hopefully into his face.

"I really won't, I promise." He kissed her forehead. "But, I also won't leave you like that again, so I can't swear they won't fire me."

She stiffened. "I can't be responsible for that, Charlie. I just can't."

"Sara...."

"No, how would you like it if you crushed my dreams?"

"I'd never...."

"You are right now! If you quit because

of me, my dream of a happy future with you will be crushed; it'll die under the weight of resentment."

"Sara…" he said again in exasperation. "What am I supposed to do? Let the magic get so desperate you sleep with my brother?"

She slapped him and then looked horrified. "I never…I'm sorry."

He nodded, one sharp jerk of his head. "I'm sorry too. I shouldn't have said that when I know you don't want him that way, but damn, Sara, that hurt."

Tears slid down her cheeks and she dashed them away with the back of her hand, then knelt in front of him, grabbing his hands. "I know and I'm so sorry. I didn't do it on purpose. But, Charlie, it won't happen again. I can recognize the magic's need now!" She dropped his hands and jumped up and paced, twining her fingers together.

"Sara, it isn't about that. I need to know you're okay. I just can't be separated from you like that again. When she didn't stop pacing or acknowledge him, he grabbed her shoulder and spun her to face him. I can't," he almost yelled.

"Because you feel guilty." She sat on the bed and tugged him down beside her. When he was sitting, she hugged him a moment and then knelt in front of him again and placed her hands on his knees. Wide eyes blue and bright, she stared into his face. "What you're feeling isn't love, it's anger and guilt and disappointment. If you give up your dream because of me that's what you'll feel all the time for me. Please! you can't do it!"

Charlie stared at her, his lips in a tight line.

Slow tears rolled down her face. "Why can't you see...?"

"Why can't you?"

Black despair hit him. She blocked her feelings from him, and he felt it like the slap in his face.

"Don't," he whispered.

"I don't know how to fix this. Tell me how to fix this," she moaned.

"Don't close me out. Never do that. There's nothing to fix. We're fine. You're upset over something that hasn't happened."

"Yet— it hasn't happened yet, but it will."

"Why can't you trust me? I know I've let you down here, but I never will again. I could never hate you." Bright strands of hair tangled in his fingers as he stroked her hair and pulled her closer.

"Please, I'm begging you to not do this to us," she said and let him share her unmuted emotions.

He staggered backward a step, shocked by the wildness of her emotions and closed his eyes to see her aura, shrugging uncomfortably when he saw the black streaks. "What more can I say? I already said I wouldn't quit."

Blue eyes shiny with unshed tears, she stared at him. Her self-loathing felt like a punch in the gut. In horror, he saw the thin black lines in her brightness pulse.

A fine tremble shook her hands as she backed away from him. Such utter despair filled her, his eyes teared in sympathy. He reached for her, and she moaned and ran from the room, taking him by surprise.

"Hawk, stop her!" he yelled as he chased her, afraid she'd do something drastic.

Hawk already had Sara in a tight embrace at the foot of the stairs. "Whoa, calm down. Where are you going?"

Charlie stood still on the middle of the stairs watching them. *How had this spun so far out of control?* he thought, shocked by her panic.

"I've ruined everything and can't fix it. I shouldn't have lived. I've ruined his whole life," Sara gasped between sobs.

Hawk shook her. "Stop talking crazy. Charlie is fine."

"And when he quits because of me, will

he be fine five years from now?" Self-loathing boiled up, covering her despair. "He'll hate me and have nothing. I love him too much to do that to him! I won't do that!" Shoulders straight in determination, she pushed Hawk away, her gaze darting wildly around the kitchen.

"Please come back upstairs and work this out. You're scaring me." Charlie held a hand out to her.

Her face was pale and tight when she spun to face him. "I'm so sorry, so, so, sorry. I never meant to hurt you. I wanted you to be happy, to have everything you want." The words poured from her in a babble between sobs. "I hold you back— make you miserable. I should've died, not come back here, not trapped you like this!"

"Stop it, none of that is true for me..."

The black sludge oozed over her brightness as she talked over him, and he almost wished he couldn't see her aura. He wanted to unsee the lurking madness and kept his gaze on her teary face.

"I did try. I'd try forever, but I won't hurt you for myself." Her cheeks were shiny from tears and she was panting now as her voice rose. "I love you too much to take your dream from you."

Her mounting desperation made his

palms sweat.

"Okay, whatever you want." Truly afraid for her, Charlie held both arms out to her.

Fists clenched and trembling, her wild blue gaze scanned the room, landing on the knife on the kitchen counter. Charlie intercepted her as she went for it. A gasping struggle ensued while she scrabbled for the knife as he pulled her away. They were terrifying the magic. It gathered about them in a swirling storm of blue. Charlie realized he was yelling at her for to stop when she stilled in his arms. Muscles in her back strained as she tried to escape him, and her desperate fear mounted.

Her brilliant blue eyes stared into his as she shouted, "I quit Team Valor!" let loose her fear spell, grabbing the knife when the spell made him release her, slashed her wrist, and ran out the door.

- 25 -

FEAR

Charlie and Hawk crouched in the corner cowering with their hands over their heads. Charlie's mother and father ran down the stairs.

"What was that?" John stopped in the kitchen doorway, holding an arm out to stop Mary from entering.

Charlie pushed himself to his feet, offering Hawk a hand. "That was Sara. Hawk, catch her. Mom, call Major Nelson and tell him we need tranquilizers." Charlie picked up Sara's bloody bracelet from the floor and kicked the knife across the room. Hawk raced from the room after Sara.

His lips in a thin line, his father headed to the house phone while Charlie grabbed his father's cell phone from the kitchen counter and called his brother, dialing as he ran after Hawk.

"Sara might be on her way there. Sedate her right away. Don't let her do anything rash."

"What's going on?" Rick asked in confusion. "I thought she was better."

"She ran away. She thinks she ruined my life and is completely desperate. Does it matter why? Just stop her!" Without explaining further or saying goodbye, he hung up.

Hawk lost her tracks within feet. She'd casted Ascension and left no trail for him to find. Charlie assumed she'd gotten a ride or jumped on a passing truck because Hawk couldn't see her on his radar either. Hawk went North and Charlie south, neither found a trace of her.

Two hours later Hawk and Charlie stood on the bank of a nearby river as a helicopter flew over shining a light on the water. "Jesus, Hawk, how did this happen?"

"She'll go to the Scouts. She'll need one of them," Hawk said.

"I already called my brother."

Hawk put an arm around Charlie's shoulder. "No, it won't be him. It'll be one of the others. She wouldn't leave you and rub your face in it, but she'll need to share magic; she'll make a warrior."

Bile filled Charlie's throat. "Hawk, will

she kill herself?"

"God no! I don't think so."

Charlie heard the lie is his voice but let himself be pulled back to his parents' house. His mother and father waited on the porch. Charlie felt cold and sick. His magic surrounded him in dense streamers and the air felt weighted as if it were solidifying around him. The magic seemed confused. Sharps spikes of fear and confusion were followed by stretches where he sensed nothing from it, but he wasn't sure his own feelings weren't drowning it out. For the first time since they'd received the magic Sara didn't want him and her magic must agree with her to so confuse his own magic.

He forced himself to mount the three stairs leading to the back door when he wanted to fall to the ground and cry. "Mom, why would she do this?" He hugged his mother.

Mary lead him to a kitchen chair. "She's seventeen, Charlie, and under tremendous pressure. You're the most important person in her life, and she thinks she ruined it. Give her time to calm down and come back."

"The panic she feels is terrifying. I'm afraid of what she'll do."

"She'll feel that too." Hawk nodded his thanks to John for the coffee he handed him.

"What you feel will influence her, so be afraid and want her back."

Charlie declined the coffee his father offered and went to his parent's front steps where he tried to use his feelings to get her to return. All his fear and anger, his guilt, everything he felt he tried to magnify. The major came but left him alone on the steps. Both teams were searching with tranquilizer guns. Oz was on his way to find her or her body.

Everyone left the house except for Hawk and his parents. The neighborhood darkened as household lights went off, leaving only the intermittent streetlamps to light the darkness.

He sat on the front steps, leaning on the railing with his eyes closed, concentrating on Sara. She was filled with raging emotions, which although troubling, reassured him that she lived. With all his heart he hoped she'd return to him soon. When her hand touched his face, he moaned and grabbed her so tightly she squeaked.

"Don't leave again. Well work this out so we'll both be happy. I promise you." His words had no effect except to cause another stronger flurry of emotion. He knew she'd run if he released her. Wild panic filled her, and she strained in his grasp. Tears fell unheeded down his cheeks.

Still filled with desperation and self-loathing, she shook in his arms.

"Stop feeling so bad. I love you so much."

"I don't know what to do!" she wailed.

"Stay with me and together we can figure this out. I'm trying to understand. You haven't ruined anything. We're fine. Please trust me, and I'll trust you." Still crying, he pulled her into his lap and wiped his face on his sleeve. He placed his glowing blue hands on her bare skin. "Please, I need you."

Her answering flare of magic shook the doors and windows in their frames. He cried harder.

"I can't believe you left me." She was with him, but she hadn't come back to him. He felt her internal conflict, wanting him and wanting to run from him. The sick feeling in the pit of his stomach intensified.

Her shivers turned to sobs and she cried on his shoulder.

"Never again, Sara. Never run from me again, I can't take it." His magic began to swirl about them in a frenzy while hers coated him in a dark dense cloud. He was shocked to feel it's fear of him or maybe his magic. He wasn't sure what was happening. Sparks flicked through the magic where the two touched. The darker blue of Sara's magic was afraid while his still seemed confused and twined with hers hesitantly.

Despite himself he almost laughed. He was confused too. Before he could figure it out Sara said, "I promise," and the lightning hit them.

Hawk called the major. "Sara's back and the magic is freaking out."

Lights turned on in neighboring houses. In moments the lightning was absorbed by their skin. Hawk came out, careful to touch neither of them, and spoke with the neighbors about the transformer that had just blown.

As soon as the lightning absorbed completely Charlie picked Sara up and carried her into a dark pocket of trees where he sat with her on his lap. "Where were you going?"

"Away just away. I wanted you to be free of me. I can't control it; I have to go!"

"I will never be free of you, not ever. Not one hundred years after you die!"

"I almost..." She stopped talking and pressed her face on his. "Most of the time I hate how I make you feel," she mumbled.

"No, don't say that! God, Sara, it's always love for you. The other stuff isn't for you. It's for me. I feel how you hate yourself right now. Do you hate me?"

Blond hair stuck to her wet cheeks as she

shook her head. "Never!"

"Well I never hate you either. This is confusing for both of us. We'll need a lot of trust and patience. I do want to be a Marine officer, but not more than I want you. The academy is only one way to get there, it isn't the only way. The guilt I'm feeling is because I never take the time to talk with you like this. I come home, and we merge the magic, have sex and I go. I've treated you horribly, giving you crumbs of attention, being so caught up in what I want." He kissed her neck and breathed in the scent of her skin, angry with himself and knowing she felt it and it was making things worse but unable to stop.

"We both need to do better at communicating. You need to stop being so afraid to tell me what you want, and I need to stop taking advantage of you. I tell myself you're fine when I know you're not so I can do what I want to. I feel bad doing it, and you feel that and think you caused it, but it isn't you, it's me." Charlie held her quietly for a few minutes as she cried into his shoulder. His words weren't helping. Every time he thought she was calming another wave of emotion rocked her. She was practically hyperventilating, and he felt her internal conflict, wanting to both run and stay.

"I wish I could let you feel just one thing at a time. I could quit the military completely. The worry isn't for quitting, it's for upsetting you. The unhappiness is mostly for disappointing you, not for quitting. It's so complicated. Everything I think has so many different emotions attached to it you'll just have to trust me when I say something is okay. I'll trust you too. You say you can handle the separation and I'll believe it, but, Sara, I can't. I need you, not the magic, me! The thought of being separated from you makes me physically ill. This has been the worst night of my life, and I wish I could forget it."

She filched away, and he tightened his grip on her. "Feel as bad as you want to, but don't leave."

"I want to stay, but my magic wants me to run. I can't stay." Terrified, she pulled away, trying to stand.

"Okay, now we're getting somewhere here." Charlie held her tighter. "Why do you want to run?" he closed his eyes to examine her aura and gasped. His fear made her scream and struggle in his grasp.

"I don't know. I just need to be away from here."

"From me?" He didn't think she wanted away from him and was certain of it as the black fissures in her aura widened as she answered.

"No, from here. Let's go somewhere far away from here." Blackness pulsed on the edges of her brightness, and he realized it was the conflicting desires. The need to run and stay were both so powerful they were tearing her apart. Her magic would shatter her to get its way.

"Okay, we'll go." Her emotions were all over and so strong that each made him wince and shudder, sudden relief when he felt relieved, panic when she said she had to go, fear, confusion, and doubt all felt so strongly he was suddenly certain it was her magic.

She sagged weakly in his arms over his surge of relief.

"Hawk!" He wasn't surprised when Hawk answered instantly. "The magic needs to leave here. I'm taking Sara away. Get my car, please. I'll take her to Cub Scout Camp." Sara tensed as Hawk approached. Charlie did his best to block her out, afraid she'd infect him with her wild mood swings and cause him to bolt or fight.

"Make sure we're alone, okay?"

It's just Hawk," he said soothingly as she strained against his hold, trying to flee.

"I know; I'm sorry but I really need to go now." Magic was dark around her hands, lightning flared from it in little shocks, zapping him with strong static.

"We're going— three minutes." He rose his voice, "Hurry, Hawk!"

"I'm so sorry I did this to us." Sara shivered and strained in his grasp, fighting her need to flee, clutching him hard one second and straining away the next. "I was trying to help you."

"It's okay, it isn't you, and we'll learn to handle the magic better. I want to go too," he said to soothe her magic and was relieved to see the oozing black on her aura recede. She was still frantic but not fighting herself so hard. He stroked her arms and talked softly to her as they waited, trying to ignore the wild swirl of her emotions. She was calm one second and on the edge of panicked flight the next. His relief when Hawk reappeared calmed her. "Don't come near us." Afraid she'd dart off if he let her walk on her own, he carried her as he crawled out from under the trees.

Hawk nodded and dropped a backpack, then the keys and backed away. Charlie grabbed them and ran to his car. Sara calmed immediately once they were moving away.

"I don't know what this is, I'm sorry. I feel like I'll explode if I don't get somewhere safe, somewhere no can find me." Her voice rose, her calmness shattered.

"We're going. No one else will be around for a hundred miles," Charlie promised.

Sara nodded and rummaged through the bag Hawk had supplied. She took out a case of sedatives and clutched it. Then, with determination, injected herself. She slept within minutes. He pulled over and rooted through the bag, found his phone and called the major.

"It isn't Sara; it's the magic," he said as soon as the major answered. "Her magic wants to escape. I'm taking her to Cub Scout Camp. She gave herself a shot. How many can I give her?"

"As many as it takes," Major Nelson assured him. "Supplies will be there for you."

"Make sure no one else is around. Her magic wants out and its making her crazy. She almost killed herself." Tears filled Charlie's eyes.

"Yeah, we know. Hawk heard. Tell her you won't be separated or kicked out of school. We'll work this out. Everyone is learning here. We won't make this mistake again."

Charlie started his car and put the major on speaker phone. "I thought she was better, and I don't know how to help her except to take her away like her magic wants."

"We're notifying the authorities. Go as fast as you want, you won't be stopped. Brenda is flying there now. Drew is trailing you by copter. Don't let her run, Chief."

"Yeah, we're both trying to stop that. How long will these sedatives last?"

"Depends on the dose."

"She took a full syringe."

"Three hours I'm guessing, but don't take anything for granted. Can you get your bracelet on her?"

"She'll just rip it off. You have no idea of her level of anxiety here."

"Oz's flight is being diverted to New Mexico. The entire team will be in the zone."

"I'm sure my parents are worried. Tell my father I'll take good care of her. I'll try much harder." He ran a hand over his wife's tear-streaked face.

"Keep us informed when you can."

Charlie drove as fast as he could. Almost three hours later she woke. Small yellow lights flitted around her and then she casted a full heal, the yellow light causing her to glow for a moment. No longer panicked, but very worried, she sat with her head back and eyes closed.

Charlie said, "Everything is fine. I talked to the major while you were, um, sleeping. We can be together, and I can go to school.

We'll stay in New Mexico as long as we need to. No one will be there except us," he added quickly as her alarm grew. Her magic had receded, the fissures in her aura were thin black lines again; it was just them as he drove down the road.

Her emotions fluctuated wildly as he spoke— happy, sad, happy, scared. She burst into tears and grabbed for him.

"God, what's wrong with me?"

"I don't know, but we'll figure it out," he assured her and gripped her hand tightly. She cried for a few minutes, and then calmed and healed herself again.

"I'm sick," she admitted, wincing at his spike of alarm. "I need access to a lab."

"We can call Liz or Doctor Elliot." Charlie reached for his phone.

"No!" she yelled and then took a deep breath and spoke more calmly. "Don't. They can't even touch me. I'll take some samples and run them." Her panic was growing. "No people, Charlie. If I run, stop me." She calmed, then burst into tears a minute later.

Charlie made some calls. While he spoke on the phone, her emotions were all over the place from calm acceptance to wild fear and it worried him that the magic might've permanently damaged her.

Small golden yellow spheres swirled

about her followed by bigger heals and shields. The rapid mood swings scared him. He almost wished to see the black sludge on her aura, but the emotional storm was just her, not her magic. Every Spell-Steal cooldown he stole her Soothe and casted it on her.

Twenty minutes later, his phone rang, causing her to scream shrilly and then laugh as she gasped from the shock. The laughter turned to tears and she buried her face in his shoulder and shook. Once again he stole her Soothe and casted it on her.

He spoke with Liz on the phone. "Okay, we're going to, Mimbres Valley, in New Mexico. Liz will be there in two hours to help us if we need it. They're evacuating the entire building right now. There's a fully equipped lab there and no one will come near us. You'll be perfectly safe."

Charlie slowed to give them time to empty the building. He neither knew nor cared how they did it. Sara stared out the window, concentrating. She checked her pulse and casted more heals. Another round of wild emotions slammed him from her, joy, despair, pain, anger, fear, guilt, worry. Soothe did nothing to slow this round of wild emotion.

"What is it?"

She burst into tears again, took out the sedatives, and gave herself a small injection. A few seconds later she calmed and laid her head on his shoulder.

"I love you. I'm so sorry," she murmured as she drifted to sleep.

An hour later he carried her inside the empty hospital. Small, hardly bigger than a clinic, it lay on the outskirts of a rural city center. He laid her on an empty bed and waited for her to wake again.

Liz called. "If you need me, I'm right outside."

"She's still asleep. Don't come in. I don't want to spook her."

Sara woke twenty minutes later, healed herself, and then went briskly about taking blood samples, sweating and shaking as she ran the tests. Charlie stood tensely, alert for any hint of panic, a syringe of sedative already in his hand. Another round of wild emotions filled her as she examined the test results.

"I'm very sick and will need some drugs to survive this. I'll need an ultrasound right away," she said in a calm voice, belaying her raging emotions. "I'm so sorry." She took a deep breath and met his scared gaze squarely. "I'm pregnant. My hormone levels are so high I'm surprised I'm functioning this well."

Charlie was stunned. His emotions went on a roller coaster as well. She laughed and then cried as she felt them all. His relief was overwhelming. A pregnant hormonal wife, he could deal with that. A smile lit his face and he laughed as his magic darted and spun about the room. It was clearly excited, whether sharing his excitement or feeling its own, he didn't know. He was almost giddy with relief.

"A baby?"

An unsure smile crossed her face and she hugged him. Relief and happiness replaced worry when he hugged her back.

"You're really not mad," she said, sounding amazed and feeling loved.

"Mad? No— why would I be? Granted, I would've preferred to wait a bit, but having a family with you is something I want. A baby," he repeated and laughed, kissing her cheek as he smoothed her hair. "Let's get Liz in here and get you the medicine you need, and once these hormones are under control, you'll see this much clearer."

"You're really not mad," she repeated and laughed and kissed him and then began to cry.

After crying for a minute, she wiped her cheeks and smiled shakily and then grimaced. I'm sorry, I know I'm acting crazy, but—"

"Not your fault, and we'll get you help."

"I'll take another injection of sedative, and Liz can come examine me and check my results. And, I'll start some drug therapy to try to get my hormone levels down." Her fear and panic were on the rise, so he nodded and quickly injected her. When she succumbed to the drug, he placed her on the table and called Liz.

"Sara's pregnant. She says her hormone levels are way too high and wants you to come examine her while she's sedated. The magic wants her to run. She's fighting it to stay and its making her crazy. I can see the black streaks in her aura."

Sara being ill worried him but now that they knew the cause he was sure between her heals and modern medicine they could fix these hormonal surges.

"We're going to have a baby." Charlie grinned at Liz when she entered. The idea of being a father thrilled and terrified him. Relief that pregnancy was the cause of these wild mood swings left him almost lightheaded. He was sure they could reassure the magic once Sara's hormones were under control and it would stop pushing her to run. And if not, he'd take her away until their child was born, and she could stop fighting it.

Liz smiled back, but the smile didn't last as she examined the test results.

"These levels are high enough to be fatal in a regular human, Charlie. Sara is very, very, sick. Glove up and give me a hand, I need more samples. And then get Sara in a hospital gown so I can do an ultrasound and a full pelvic examine. The ultrasound will be tricky, but if you put on gloves and I guide your hand it should work."

After the examination Liz had Charlie sedate Sara again.

"Stay with her while I go order supplies." Lips compressed, Liz hurried from the room.

Charlie sat beside Sara, stroking her hair. "We're really going to be a family," he whispered and laughed. She'd have to accept him quitting school now because he was sure to be expelled, and he didn't care. Something he'd have thought impossible mere hours ago.

He leaned over to kiss Sara's brow. "I'm going to take such good care of you," He laughed again and shook his head. "A baby."

26

THE BABY

Liz called General Campbell's private number. "The pregnancy isn't viable, its ectopic."

"Can you help her?"

"Yes, I can remove the cell mass and treat the hormones, but that isn't the issue."

"By your tone, this a serious problem…"

"More than I think your prepared for, and I'm not sure what to do."

"Major!"

"Charlie is thrilled about having a baby."

"Does this mean they can't have children?"

"Not at all, and that's not what I meant. I'm sorry, I'm not being clear, but Sara is like a daughter to me and this condition is very bad." Liz took a few deep breaths and blew her nose. "The first problem will be Charlie. When I go in there and tell him, how do you think he'll react?"

"He'll be upset. The same as any man would be in that situation."

"Except he isn't a man," Liz waited a moment for that to sink in. "The second problem is worse and connected to the first. To have such high hormone levels the magic must somehow be manipulating it, ergo the magic wants her pregnant. If she won't make a warrior, it will— with or without her cooperation."

"Jesus," the general gasped.

"That's not the big problem."

"I can't wait." The general sounded grim.

"This is what I see happening here. If I go in there and remove the ectopic pregnancy, killing the child both he and the magic wants, Charlie will kill me. So, to save Sara's life, I'll tranq him and then do it, but what's stopping the magic from doing it again? And this time, Charlie won't take her to us, they'll run— I guarantee it."

"Oh, Dear Lord…" the general trailed off. "Stall. Give me thirty minutes to speak with the president."

The president, Pierce Taylor, General

Campbell and Major Nelson spoke on a video conference call.

"This might be an opportunity and not a disaster," Major Nelson said into the silence that followed the general's report.

"How so? the president straightened in his chair, leaning forward slightly.

"Project Erasure could be implemented on Sara without having to implement on the others. Her condition would be enough explanation for her death. They'd believe she'd killed herself. And while I hate to suggest such a drastic solution, it could solve numerous problems. The rest of the team is much more stable than she. None of them have ever run amok. Let's face it, it's just a matter of time before she loses control and starts taking people over."

"That's a big assumption." Pierce frowned.

"Did you see the latest footage of her trying to make a warrior?" Major Nelson asked.

"Yes, and I admit she was out of control, but it isn't that difficult to keep her in control, just don't separate them."

"This is a once in a lifetime opportunity—"

"No," the president interrupted. "At this moment, that isn't an option. Sara is too valuable an asset to waste. Not alone for the healing ability, but her mind. The things she and Oz are creating are amazing. We don't have time to go into that right now, but my decision is final. Work harder at keeping her magic happy. If she needs to be with Charlie, make that happen. Tell Major Harris to sedate Charlie and do the procedure. Get them whatever supplies they need and let them go wherever they feel safe. Have Doctor Gotlieb available to speak with both when they wake. Charlie isn't unreasonable. Explain what and why and he'll cooperate with us."

"You hope," Major Nelson muttered under his breath.

"Yes, but hope is all we have right now, so you better hope too." The president ended the call.

Liz returned forty minutes later. "Bring Sara, I need to run a few more tests."

Charlie rose uncertainly and gathered his wife in his arms. Tears had tracked across Liz's face in her absence, and she was pale and nervous.

"What's wrong?" Charlie asked as he

followed Liz into a nearby room. This room was larger with no exam tables. Workstations lined the walls, not a lab, but an office. Puzzled, Charlie brought Sara to the chair Liz indicated at the back of the room and sat.

Liz gave Sara another injection, refilled the needle, and laid it on the desk. Tears in her eyes, she kissed Sara on the forehead and then gathered a sheaf of papers and stepped away.

"What's going on? Your freaking me out." Charlie kissed Sara's brow as he watched Liz.

"Sara is very ill. Medicine is being delivered that will help her, but you need to be clear on her condition. When the medicine arrives, I'll put it in the trunk of your car along with supplies you'll need. Doctor Gotlieb strongly recommends that Sara doesn't wake up here. Take her somewhere secluded where she'll feel safe. Keep as much skin contact as you can, surround her in your magic, and, if possible, sit in the sunshine. The doctor suggests you chain her to you as she might be compelled to run."

"Okay, that's no problem." Charlie shifted Sara on his lap, pressing her tighter against him.

"Where going to talk about her condition

for a minute." Liz fiddled with the papers in her hand, taking them to a copy machine by the doorway.

"Instructions, my notes, and copies of the tests will be in a folder in the car too. If you go off grid, you can read them for answers."

Charlie nodded, but Liz didn't see him intent on the copy machine.

Charlie, it's important for you to realize that this isn't a natural condition." Liz turned from the machine and faced him. "The magic caused this. By my estimate, the first day you returned.

Charlie nodded again. Liz swallowed heavily and continued. "That means it can do so again if it becomes desperate for a warrior's magic. Don't let it become desperate." Liz held up her hands as Charlie opened his mouth to speak. "This has nothing to do with blame. These are the facts. The magic is trying to reproduce, but it doesn't know how too. The biological process of birth is complicated and can't be rushed. A hormonal imbalance of this magnitude can be fatal, even to Sara. So every precaution needs to be taken to ensure the magic never needs to reproduce this way."

"Spit it out, Liz, you're beating around the bush here."

Liz took a deep breath and her knuckles whiten on the paper she held. After placing them on top of the machine, she put her hands in the pockets of the white coat.

"Remember that I love Sara and would never do a thing to harm her. I have her best interests at heart."

When Charlie nodded, she licked her lips and continued.

"Please sedate yourself, Charlie."

"What?" Charlie's shocked glance darted from the needle on the desk beside him to Liz.

"The magic wants to reproduce, when I tell you this, it might try to force you to run, so please sedate yourself. The tranquilizer will work slower on you. I estimate we can talk for a minute or so before it takes effect."

Charlie's hand hovered over the needle and then his eyes narrowed. His gaze swung back to Liz and she shot him. Shocked, he hesitated. Fierce anger filled him. He screamed his attack cry, still clutching Sara, and leapt for Liz, but she was already through the door, which slammed closed.

Liz wanted to kill his child; he knew it with every fiber of his body. This room was a trap that he needed out of. Screaming in rage, he spun from the door. Liz would've prepared something; she'd picked this room purposefully. The baby was the priority now, he could deal with Liz later; he had less than a minute to get Sara somewhere safe. A quick scan of the room revealed no windows big enough to squeeze through. Three narrow slits high on the wall behind him let in light but were two small for even Sara to fit through.

"No!" he hollered as he ran back to kick the door, knowing it was useless. Already he felt lightheaded from the tranquilizer. "No! Don't do this, Liz! Let us have our baby! We'll go away somewhere! No one will ever see us again, I swear it! Please, Liz, this child won't be a danger to you or anyone else. Please, Liz," he whispered as he slid down the wall, tears streaming down his face, his wife clutched in his arms.

When Charlie woke, he wore only boxers. Sara laid on top of him with a hospital gown on backward, the front open so their bare chests touched. A light blanket covered them. For a moment, relief filled him at her steady heartbeat and warm breath. Then fury as he sat and placed her on the bed to examine her, knowing what he'd find.

The blood seeping from between her thighs made his pulse pound. Blue magic swirled about him in agitation. Anger— cold furious anger – suffused him at what they'd done to her. Without meaning to, he found himself destroying the room. Blood dripped from his clenched fist and he absently wiped it on his chest as he panted trying to get control of himself. Blind rage wouldn't help her, he needed to get a grip. But first, he needed to get her out of this deathtrap. The door was unlocked. With hands that shook, he wrapped Sara in the light blanket. The intercom crackled to life

"I'm sorry, Charlie, but to save Sara's life I had to do it. Please, take one minute to hear me out," Liz said. "There was no baby, none! An ectopic pregnancy isn't viable. A mass of cells attached to her fallopian tube needed to be removed before they grew large enough to kill her. No baby has ever survived from this location. Sara might survive the miscarriage but the hormone overload while the mass grew could've killed her.

"Ectopic births are so rare as to be practically mythical and only if the pregnancy attaches to a major vein or organ. No child has ever been born from the condition Sara had. Am I making myself clear to you? Without surgery, she could've died. If you have sex with her again while her hormones are so out of whack it could reoccur, and you *will* kill her. Please, Charlie. I love Sara. Please, please, let me help her. Let me help you both. Call me—"

Liz was still begging when Charlie ran from the hospital, clutching Sara to his chest.

Police vehicles with flashing lights formed a perimeter around the clinic. Three Blackhawk helicopters circled in the distance. Furious and afraid, he paused. The jeep she'd given him for Christmas was ten feet away. Liz would've put a tracking device on it, but it would still be faster than running. Besides, the helicopters could track him on foot. Once he was away from here, he could steal another vehicle, get to a phone and call Oz for help. And more than anything he needed to escape.

Two hours later Charlie called Liz, much calmer now since mulling over what she'd said. He pulled over on the dirt road leading to Cub Scout Camp and searched the car. All the supplies Liz had mentioned were in the trunk as well as the promised paperwork. He chained Sara to his right wrist using the manacles and chains he found in the trunk. Then he sat on the side of the road and read through the files from top to bottom.

Still wrapped in the sheet, Sara lay beside him, six feet of chain in a loose heap between them. Any minute now she'd wake. Despite repeated healings from him, she still bled. Not knowing what else to do, he called Liz.

"Oh, thank God!" Liz sounded as if she'd been crying.

To his shock, Charlie began to cry.

"It's okay," Liz said all choked up and paused to blow her nose. "Don't worry about anything. I'm handling everything, and no one is angry."

"The bleeding hasn't stopped," Charlie finally said when he pulled himself together enough to speak.

"No, it won't for a week or so, don't worry about that. If it does stop or becomes very light over the next day or so, then call me. That would be a problem."

"I'm sorry for the way I behaved… It's just…."

Liz blew her nose again and cleared her throat. "Forgiven and forgotten. Let's just worry about getting Sara well. Do you remember what I said?"

"Yes, I understand the magic is trying to reproduce. "

"No sex until her hormones are level."

"Will we be able to have children?"

"Yes, nothing is physically wrong with her. The magic is the problem. If it'll let nature take its course, you should be fine."

"And when she wakes?" Charlie ran a hand over his wife's dirty, matted hair.

"Tell her, and show her the test results, but be prepared to sedate her again. Do everything Doctor Gotlieb suggested. I need blood samples to monitor her condition. Supplies are waiting at camp."

"I'll keep her away from everyone, but if she really needs another warrior, we better give her one." It killed him to say it, but his jealousy wasn't worth Sara's life or sanity.

"Who?" Liz cleared her throat. "Three warriors are standing by. I'm sorry we have no woman warriors right now. Joy is switching mains as we speak but doesn't know the class yet."

"God, it can't be my brother; Stasia would freak." Charlie rubbed his eyes with both trembling hands. "I can't do this."

"I'll pick and have someone close if she absolutely needs it, but she might not. The magic has had time to calm down since your return. If she does need a warrior, it's just the magic, Charlie. Not a personal choice."

He shook his head numbly. "I did this to

us by not taking care of us. I didn't even notice our lost connection."

"One way or another she'll recover, let that be enough."

Sara woke calmly, casted a heal on herself, and sat quietly. "The baby's dead then."

He nodded, tears springing to his eyes over her pain. He held her through a flurry of emotions and crying, talking softly to her as he rubbed her back, offering what comfort he could.

"I hate my magic. I hate it!" Tears and deep gasping breaths made her shudder as she clutched him.

"The magic didn't intend harm. In the future, we'll be very careful to never let it become so desperate. Don't hate the magic. We can live with it and enjoy it if we give it what it wants."

"I feel horrible!"

"I know, me too. Once the hormones settle down, you'll feel much better." The chain connecting them rattled as she pushed away from him and glanced around.

"Keep everyone away from us. Everyone! I don't want anyone except you, and I'm afraid I can't stop it."

"I will, and we can have more children."
As soon as he said it he regretted it. Her
magic flared from her in a storm.

"Umm…"

"Oh, god, don't say that! Stop it! Stop it!
Stop it!" She tried to jump from his lap.
"No!" Wild eyed, she panted as she struggled
to dominate the magic and force it back.

Charlie grabbed her and forced her
against his bare chest. "When we're older,
we'll have children. I promise."

"When I'm older we'll have children,"
Sara agreed in relief as the magic settled
down. "When I'm ready we'll have children,
conceived naturally with no help from you!
You almost killed us!" She screamed into
Charlie's chest as his magic joined hers in the
swirling cloud.

"I swear we will when Sara is ready." He
was relieved when the lightning hit them.

"Better?" He asked after the magical
storm had passed.

"Oh, god, much better. Nothing like a
little magical entrapment to lift a girl's
spirits."

He laughed. "I'm happy, not trapped. Let
yourself be happy about it too."

She snuggled into his chest and with
relief he felt her happiness, it was still too

much, with crazy highs and lows, but she was at least happy.

"I do want your children someday." Happiness and contentment filled her at his emotional response. Proud and possessive and full of love for her, he kissed her brow and rocked her in his arms. They sat together for hours, resting on the side of the road.

"I feel so much better." Sara smiled ruefully at Charlie as they walked around the deserted camp three days later.

"How about a race then?" Charlie grinned as he dropped her hand and ran off, using Valorous Leap to outpace her. He laughed as she pulled him back to her and ran ahead. She ran over the obstacle course and he followed. She was more agile, but he was faster. They were both laughing and breathless when they stopped and flopped down in the dead grass to rest.

Sara rolled over to face him. "I'm sorry for everything I did that caused that."

Charlie was relieved at the evenness of her emotions. The hot New Mexico sun beat down on his bare back as he leaned over her, casting a shadow across her face. "I'm sorry too, and I forgive you."

She nodded. "And I forgive you too, and we'll both be more careful. I can't promise I'll never have another hormonal attack, but if I think it's starting, I'll tell you. And you tell me if you think it's happening."

He smiled sadly and smoothed the hair from her brow. The soft golden strands slipped smoothly through his fingers. "That was a hard lesson, but we're okay now."

Tears came to her eyes as she pulled him closer, letting love echo between them.

Two days later they returned home.

27

WITH GIRLS, WHO KNOWS

Sara laid the book she was reading on the grass. "I'm going to cyber commute this semester and study at home. Oz and I can work in the basement. I'm afraid to be in a crowd right now without you."

"Do whatever makes you comfortable." Charlie traced the ridge of her collarbone with one finger and smiled over her rising desire. He frowned when she pulled away. Not for the first-time Charlie wished their backyard was bigger and more private so she could relax without fear of being spied on. Sunshine, rest and privacy was what she needed.

He'd wanted to resign from school, but she'd gotten so upset he'd agreed to try again, and he had to admit, he wanted to attend. He wanted to stay with her too. He wished he didn't have to choose one over the other.

"Classes at the academy start in a week, and I think we can do it. I'll see you almost every day and have all weekend with you. At the first hint it isn't enough, you tell me."

She frowned and quickly smoothed it away. He didn't know if the frown was for his guilt or because he was going, but he didn't ask. She'd made it crystal clear she wanted him to go. Talking again about how guilty wanting to go made him feel wouldn't help. *She knows how much I love her too,* he told himself as he pulled her closer for a kiss.

She kissed him back, and he relaxed, basking in her love. Relaxed and warm in his arms, she felt nothing except love for him. His tight muscles eased, and she sighed in contentment.

The sat unspeaking just enjoying being together. She finally pulled away to glance at her watch.

"Stasia and Rick will be home soon." Sara rose from the chaise and trudged to the back door.

Charlie grinned and she scowled. "It's not funny."

"Hey, you picked him. Trying to steal your best friend's boyfriend is a serious no-no."

Her glare deepened, and then she gave him a wicked smile. "I could've picked Toric.

He was there the entire time."

It was his turn to glare. "Not funny, Sara."

She laughed, then sobered. "It wasn't me picking, not really, and I do love Rick. I just hope Stasia will forgive me."

"Yeah, me too," he said all humor gone. Her worry was real and justified. He thought Stasia would forgive her, if not immediately, at least eventually, but with girls, who knew.

When Stasia and Rick came home, Sara and Charlie were waiting. Sara held onto his hand with both of hers. She'd avoided all the Scouts since her return. A tranquilizer gun rested in Charlie's waistband. If she showed any signs of needing Rick, he'd sedate her and take her away.

Stasia was angry and Rick embarrassed.

"I'm so sorry, Stasia!" Sara burst out as soon as they came through the door.

"I know, and I'm trying not to be mad, but I can't believe you tried to take him from me. You of all people realize how I feel about him."

"I do, and I'm ashamed to say I didn't think of you at all. I was completely out of my head. If it helps, I have no urge to, um, convert him at all."

The glare Stasia aimed at Sara told everyone that was no help. Sara held out both hands to Stasia. Stasia's glare deepened and Sara recoiled.

Charlie pulled Sara tighter against him and cleared his throat. "Don't blame Sara, the magic had her. Learn from our mistakes so this doesn't happen to you one day."

"I feel it; it's so frustrating that he has no magic for me." The glare lessened and Stasia leaned on Rick.

"Stasia can't pass her magic to me, she's tried," Rick added.

"It's frustrating, but I don't have a compulsion to take yours," she said to Charlie and glared at Sara again.

"Her magic has never mingled with anyone else's." Sara glanced worriedly from Charlie to Rick. "Stasia, if it does, you won't be able to stop it from happening again."

"I'll never know. Rick has no magic." Stasia shrugged and continued to glare.

"Sara and I could give him magic," Charlie said softly.

"It would be risky in a lot of ways." Sara took Charlie's hand again in both of hers. "The change could kill him. The government doesn't want us to," she took a deep breath, "and I might, um, bond to him. I'd try my hardest not to, but we've never done this."

"I don't want you near him," Stasia spat.

Rick put a hand on her shoulder. "Sara

couldn't help it. You know she'd never intentionally hurt either of us."

"Don't you think I know that?" Stasia spun and faced Rick with her hands on her hips. "I know, but I still don't want her near you. I realize I sound like a crazy jealous person, but that's how I feel. She's a magical vampire. I understand she can't help it, but she could turn on you in a minute, and then you'd want her, not me!"

"Stasia, honestly it isn't that bad. You've seen us share magic. She'd touch his face or hand for a few minutes," Charlie said in exasperation.

"I have seen you, and you know it's more intimate than that."

"Now it is, yes. But when it first happened, it wasn't. It did feel good, but we didn't connect emotionally from it until we wanted to." He traced his glowing, blue hand along Sara's jaw, smiling over her response that was discernable only to him.

Stasia said, "You might be willing to share Sara with another man, but I'm not willing to share him. I'm not willing to risk it progressing from a light touch to sex, and you know that it could."

Charlie's face burned with anger. Sara said nothing, but a fiery blush reddened her cheeks and she was mortified. "Don't say it like that. It wasn't her choice unless she should've chosen to die first. I'd share her with anyone to prevent that!"

"Stop!" Sara stepped between them, holding a hand out before each of them. "I acted badly and I'm sorry, and I'll try to never do it again. I wasn't myself, but that's no excuse, your right." Embarrassed and upset, Sara stepped away from Charlie. "I picked Rick because I love him and feel safe with him, like a brother. I'm sorry it hurt you." Pale and shaking, Sara held a hand out to Stasia again.

When Stasia crossed her arms, Charlie turned Sara away and shook her. "You stop. If, god forbid, it happens again, do *not* pick death— do you hear me?"

"Okay, guys, everyone calm down." Rick kissed the top of Stasia's head and gave Sara a hug, exchanging worried glances with his brother. "It's over with no harm done to anyone. It's not like Sara will just turn on me, buildings will explode first— we'll have warning."

Stasia nodded jerkily, clearly not appeased.

Charlie felt how upset Sara was behind her calm façade and turned angrily to Stasia. "Would you rather she'd died first?"

Stasia met his eye. "Yes," she said flatly

and stalked away.

Sara's hurt pierced him.

"She didn't mean it." Rick gave Sara another quick hug before chasing after Stasia.

Charlie didn't know what to say; he hadn't expected that answer.

Sara hugged him, emotions fluctuating wildly from hurt to sorrow.

Charlie was angry and worried.

Sara turned in his arms and rested her face on his chest. "It's okay. It hurt, but was honest, and I'd hate to share you too. I don't think I'd want her dead, but maybe. Don't be mad at her. No way did she mean that literally. I can't believe she'd really want me dead."

"With all my soul I'd hate to share you, but I would." Charlie took her face in his hands. "Never choose death! If this happens again, you'll recognize what's happening. Hold out if you can, but don't kill yourself over this."

Sara nodded, but didn't promise. "When I thought of that, I wasn't in my right mind."

"I know, but you scared me to death." Charlie buried his face in her bright hair.

Sara hugged him back. "I scared myself too. I just wanted it all to stop, but it would've only stopped for me— you were so alone."

Charlie closed his eyes and kissed her neck, taking a deep breath of her scent and resting his fingers on the pulse of her wrist. "I hate thinking about it. Let's do something fun. We'll get Hawk to scout the dance hall to make sure it's harpy free, then go dancing."

Stasia and Rick stood on opposites sides of the bed in her room, glaring at each other. "That was a horrible thing to say," Rick said.

"Yes, but true. I had no idea I was this crazy jealous of a person, but I am." Stasia swung away from him and paced. "When I think of her taking you like that... I could kill her myself."

"No one is taking me. I'm not a toy." A small smile flitted across his face.

"It isn't funny. How would you feel if I did that with someone else?"

"Not homicidal. Sara didn't try to sleep with me. She tried to change me into a warrior to use my magic," Rick said gently, "me— her brother, not her lover."

Stasia groaned. "I know, and it makes me feel bad, but I want your magic!"

"I have none." Rick held out his empty

hands.

Stasia flared up blue all over, bounded over the bed, and pressed herself against him, trying to force her magic into him, sobbing in frustration.

"Is it worse?" he whispered as he stroked her back.

She nodded. "It'll pass, but it sucks."

"I'd help you if I could. Maybe Oz or Hawk could help?"

"My poor brother… I'll make him sit with me a while."

Rick laughed and tugged her hair. "He doesn't mind. Cook him some food and he's happy to sit and eat it." He took a deep breath. "Maybe you could give him some magic or take some from him."

"I don't want his. Charlie and Sara are wrong, it is sexual, well maybe not sexual, but intimate. I want your magic, and I want you to have mine. It's frustrating not sharing it with you. It's lonely. I don't want to share with Hawk or Oz or anyone else."

"Want to go for a run and burn off some of that frustration?" Rick asked.

She lightly bit his neck. "No, I don't want to run," she growled at him.

When school restarted for them Sara was calm and only a little sad. General Campbell had arranged for lab space on campus. Oz had set up the adjoining spaces while Sara and Charlie where recovering from the separation. On the first day of school, Oz escorted her to the new lab.

Sara hesitated at the gate, glancing down at her navy-blue slacks and smoothing her white oxford.

Oz's blue eyes were worried as he observed her. "If you don't want to go, we can work from home."

'No, I'll be fine. Besides you have classes here to attend."

"Are you sure you don't want to take them too?"

"Not right now. I hate the thought of being surrounded by strangers. And anyway, we're so close to a breakthrough. Between my online courses, working on my dissertations, and our work, I'll be just fine in the lab all day." A rueful smile on her face, she walked through the gate with Oz. "And to be honest, knowing Charlie is on the same campus helps."

Oz put his arm around her and gave her a quick squeeze. "If you need anything, or any of us, don't hesitate to call." He tapped the bulky black box strapped to his arm. "This needs lots of testing, so call me a lot."

"Man, we still have so many kinks to work out. The interface won't be really useful until we master the virtual keyboard and monitors."

"I have a great idea for that. What if we take the research we're doing on smite and apply it there?"

Sara and Oz exchanged grins and hurried their steps.

Three Weeks Later

Charlie grabbed lunch for Sara and Oz and headed to their lab. Someone brought them lunch every day. They were so involved in their research they didn't stop to eat and hardly stopped to sleep. When he arrived, they were leaning over a tank in Sara's lab, holding tools he didn't recognize, which he assumed Oz had made.

Before he spoke with them, he brought the food to Oz's workspace. The idea of eating in Sara's lab revolted him. Tanks of all sizes sat on metal tables, each filled with body parts. It always freaked him out to recognize parts of her floating in the tanks. The pieces that clearly didn't belong to her weren't as upsetting but they all grossed him out.

Whiteboards hung on the walls from floor to ceiling. Shades were drawn at all times over the rooms two windows and her door was kept locked. A retinal scanner and voice recognition panel blocked access for everyone except Team Valor. Oz assured him that the security was top notch, impenetrable. He hoped so. It looked like a serial killer's lair. The police would be looking for corpses for sure if they saw all the dismembered parts.

When Charlie joined them, Oz was applying tiny electrodes to a sliver of something that Sara was dissecting.

"Foods here."

Sara glanced at him, smiled, mumbled, "One minute," and returned to her work.

For thirty minutes neither glanced up nor acknowledged him. Charlie glanced at his watch.

"Sorry, sweetheart, have to run, I have class."

Sara glanced up again, and then down at her watch.

"Sorry, we can't stop now."

"No problem. I'll see you later tonight." Charlie kissed her cheek and hurried to class. Sara's amusement at his relief to leave her lab made him smile.

When he returned that evening, they

were still at it. Bloody liquid filled a tank by them and small racks of slides were stacked in front of a microscope. Sara had been very excited all day and was concentrating hard now. At his entrance, they both glanced up and immediately resumed poking the tissue on the table before them with long pins.

Charlie left them too it and headed to Oz's space where he found their untouched lunches. He preferred Oz's lab although he didn't recognize many of the components. Most of the varied devices littering the long tables Oz had made himself. He busied himself examining the small spheres of cloudy blue glass that had taken over the main table until Paul and Hawk joined him there twenty minutes later. They worked on homework together. Neither Oz nor Sara showed up.

Hawk and Charlie exchanged grins as they left. Sara had kissed him without putting down the bloody tools in her hand and resumed work before he'd even left the room.

Hawk snickered as they joined Paul who waited outside to walk back to the dorm with them. "Whatever it is they're working on must be fascinating because I've never seen her ignore him before."

Charlie laughed and punched Hawk's

shoulder. "They're intense about it, I'll grant you that. And excited. Give them a few days and they'll remember we exist and maybe explain it to us."

Paul grinned. "The new computer is fascinating. Such a simple concept really, but elegant. Someday I hope I find out what else they're working on that's so super-secret."

Hawk and Charlie exchanged amused glances.

Paul rolled his eyes. "Right… well, whatever it is, I'm sure it'll be brilliant. The computer Oz made is remarkable, almost, but not quite organic. He's letting me work on the programing and his programs are genius, beyond genius. It's a real honor to be included."

Paul gushed about Oz's computer and programing skill until they reached the dorm.

"Bring them food when you go," Charlie reminded Hawk before they split up to head for their dorm rooms.

"Amy is going in the morning, I'll remind her," Paul said.

"And I'll tell my sister," Hawk said.

"Has she been going?" Charlie stopped walking and grabbed Hawk's arm.

"Twice that I know of. Rick goes, and it's just killing her. Don't worry about it, Chief. She has a hot temper, but she does love Sara.

They'll work it out."

Charlie released Hawk. He hadn't realized Rick visited them and the thought made him uneasy. Sara hadn't seen any of the Scouts except Joy and Brenda that he was aware of. Those two came a few times a week and helped them in their lab. Once this latest obsessive work session ended, he'd ask her if Rick was visiting, or helping, or both.

"Stasia and Sara had a fight?" Paul looked surprised.

"Yeah, girls you know, it's nothing to worry about." Charlie slapped Hawk's back, and everyone headed to their rooms.

28

VALOR INDUSTRIES

In November Sara and Oz asked to meet with General Campbell at their lab. He arrived in the morning and toured the campus, then met with them. Team Valor was in attendance along with Major Nelson.

"We've made a big breakthrough." Oz grinned and handed the general a boxy wristwatch with a wide, blue-glass lens, a flat, blue-glass disk the size of a half-dollar, a plastic card with two different sized flesh-colored squares with small, circular, silver protuberances, and a bulky white cuff with a bumpy appearance that would cover most of a forearm and a much smaller thinner leather bracelet with a silver disk on the bottom. While the general examined the items, Oz started a projector. "This is a magnified version of the interior of the spell-bracelet."

Blue-glass balls enmeshed in fine, gold

wires rotated on the screen. The picture switched to show jars of a milky, white fluid and then a tanned piece of leather embedded with tiny silver pins. Oz described the different components as the pictures changed.

Charlie bit back a laugh, Oz had lost his audience after the third slide. The equations on the screen were wasted on everyone except Oz and Sara. After much work with Oz, he understood them… barely. Stasia kicked him under the table and grinned as he smothered another laugh.

Finally Oz got to the good stuff.

Team Valor leaned forward in their seats, grinning, when Oz said, "Major, if you'd try the white cuff. You'll feel a prickle when you put it on; we call that engaged. It's uncomfortable but needs blood to work. The smaller one needs to be on your right hand with the silver disk against your wrist, the larger on your left. Both require skin contact. Once it's engaged, run a spell pattern of Sara's."

Major Nelson casted Lesser Reflective Shield spell. A silvery sphere formed around him, and he jumped in surprise. "I did that?"

Sara laughed and clapped her hands, then high-fived Oz. "Try another."

Major Nelson casted Ascension, then

Soothe followed by a heal. He casted eight spells before the magic ran out.

"Different spells use differing amounts of magic, so you need to keep track in your head of how much magic is left. Oz plans to add a counter when we figure out how to. There's a pseudo counter in the wristcomp for now that I'll show you later."

Sara handed him a bulky blue cuff. "Charlie's spells. The magic in them isn't as strong as the magic in my bracelet, so you'll have fewer spells, but you could Valorous Leap, or Charge, or steal a weapon, or steal a spell from one of us. Any of his spells should work."

"We can't make artificial magic yet. I still have to harvest it, but we're working on it. And, I really think we'll get it eventually."

Sara and Oz grinned at the major's dumbfounded expression.

"How long does it last?" The general examined the bracelet closely.

"So far, my stored magic hasn't degraded or dissipated unless it's released." Sara started another slide show, showing pictures of her research and experiments as she spoke. "It returns to me or Charlie if released in the same zone. We haven't tried out of the zone yet, so you need to be careful with them. I don't think the magic could find us out of the zone, and loose magic might be a bad idea."

"How long does it take to make one?" General Campbell picked up the blue cuff and examined it.

"Well, the magic and nerves need to be harvested and the device itself made, and then I program it for mine and Charlie does for his. So, assuming all components are on hand, assembly time is about an hour and programing takes about thirty minutes or so. But if we needed to supply the magic to fill the bracelet, I'd say a maximum of another hour, we're being careful not to deplete either of us."

Oz interrupted, "You should only wear one cuff at a time. The smaller one on your right wrist is just mapping your hand movement to send the spell pattern to the bigger one, and if you were wearing a wristcomp you wouldn't need one. Those you can leave on. You can switch the cuffs out, but only engage one. Also, it has the same limitations of Sara's magic, it only works on the raid. It releases small amounts of m-radiation, but Sara can heal that. We keep them in lead cases, which seem to keep the radiation contained, and Sara or I can dispel the radiation from the cases before it reaches a dangerous amount."

Charlie said, "We can use them, but it

burns. I think because we have magic and it's forcing new neural pathways from ones already in place. We should keep our use to a minimum."

Sara said. "You shouldn't feel it all when you cast unless you engage two at once, but if you do, let us know immediately."

"This is impressive." The general hefted the bracelets in his hand. "I'll be honest, I don't understand a word or number of the math you showed me, but I like the results. How much is the actual cost of one these?"

"Not much, and it'll get cheaper if we can order supplies in bulk, and Sara and I will want raises." Oz laughed when the general winced. "But, about five hundred and fifty, per bracelet."

"Thousand?" The general smiled at the bracelet in his hand.

Sara laughed. "Hundred, but we can probably cut it down to three hundred or a hundred fifty dollars apiece and we can reuse them. Of course, we're still tweaking the design and we want to add some features too, which will raise the price, but again, it'll be reusable. That isn't including the cost of the case."

The general's mouth dropped open and snapped shut. "You're telling me, for five hundred dollars, the Scouts can heal themselves now?"

"They can, and they can summon us or each other— all my spells work." Sara beamed at him.

"So, what's this do?" The general grinned and held up the large wristwatch.

"It tells time," Oz said with a straight face.

Sara rolled her eyes and then laughed. "That's a wristcomp and much more expensive to make. Not including the cost of the research to get us there that cost us over fifty thousand dollars, but again the next one will be cheaper. We made a lot of mistakes the first time. I think we can do it between five and ten thousand dollars, but that price will lower if we make the parts needed in bulk. Right now, we're custom making almost every piece so it's time consuming and expensive."

She took the wristcomp from the general and put it on her wrist. "We borrowed a lot of technologies for this and are still stealing satellite access to use it. This is a prototype. We're working on design to make it more attractive and incorporate all the peripherals. The small disk there will boost the hologram in bright light but isn't needed in a room like this."

Sara lifted the wristcomp to her face and

said her name. "Now it knows me. The wristcomp won't respond for anyone it isn't programed for. Oz, show him the screen. I can see everything that screen shows you on my wristcomp."

Oz turned the laptop in front of him to show the general. "The white dot is Sara." He pointed to the map. "This will hurt a second." A blue glow between his hands solidified into his dagger and he used it to make a small cut on Sara's arm. "If we click on the picture here, we see where she's injured, all of her vitals are listed here." He nodded at Sara and she healed her arm. "And see, we see it in real time she's better now."

"Where is Rick?" Sara asked and on the computer screen another icon flashed. "Five different types of chips are being tested right now. The one Rick has is old tech we just made smaller. To access it, we're hijacking satellites around the world. No one will ever know," she said reassuringly as the general glanced at her in alarm. She held out her hand so he could see the small screen. "As you can see, the GPS coordinates are also fairly standard and will give me voice directions like any other GPS, but this one is smarter, no long winding routes unless I ask for it. It's also running a program Oz designed in the background."

She nodded to Oz, and he said, "This device is intended to help our Scouts in combat, so it's scanning and correlating all data on his location. I'm working on a satellite program of my own to help with that, but we need time to develop and test the hardware. Rick's wristcomp will notify him if it sees or learns there might be an enemy nearby. If his heartrate accelerates or he reacts in any way that indicates alarm when he's shown the information, the computer will automatically tell the satellite to track the person, which is why we need our own satellites. Right now, while we're testing, our usage is light enough to go without notice, but those systems won't be able to handle our projected draw. If he was under fire, the satellite would track every single man attacking him and warn him of position changes it deemed put him in danger, so you can see it would potentially use quite a bit of memory and processing power. Much more processing power than the current systems could handle."

Oz held out his own wrist and tapped the glass cover on the wristcomp. "This isn't glass. It's crystal and it's the brain of the machine. It's integrated with my hand and eye movement, so I don't need to enter any long commands. I can just look or point and say things like, follow that guy. Give me that guy's address. Where did I park my car, and it'll search the database and tell me, but because crystalis is so much faster and can store trillions of bits of information it'll constantly update itself to be ready for those types of questions and have an answer almost as fast as I can ask it. It's programmed to anticipate a user. Say for instance, if you always ask it to record your meetings, it'll remind you if you forget to ask it. If it knows your schedule, say you leave work at five every day and go right home, it'll warn you without you having to ask that there's a traffic accident or other delays and offer an alternate route. And there's this," he said and flicked his wrist.

The general exclaimed and Sara high-fived Oz as a hologram of a computer screen appeared in front of him.

It looked so realistic Charlie reached out to put his hand through it. The first version he'd seen had been much less substantial looking. They'd made lots of progress in just a few weeks.

Oz flicked his wrist again and the screen became cloudy and insubstantial appearing as if the words floated in air. He gestured again, and three screens appeared that he flicked with his fingers and they shrank and grew and repositioned themselves while the general and major exclaimed and leaned closer to see them.

Sara grinned at Oz. "This part is all new, all Oz. Show me Rick." A hologram sprang up around her depicting a street as seen from directly overhead; she slid her hand through it and spun it until she got to Rick.

It appeared to be a miniature scene that gained depth as Sara used her finger to touch the images and Charlie could see the buildings and people walking past his brother with enough clarity to recognize them even though they were just inches high.

Sara said, "It's not heavily detailed, but the topography is there. There are different settings from full like this or casual like this." She flicked her finger and the small buildings became boxes and the people were replaced with red dots.

She said, "In casual mode, we don't rely on satellites. People within ten feet of the device would register as red dots. We're working on the programing to color-code anyone in the vicinity. It's a complicate project if we don't want to give the user information overload. Rick can see what I'm doing. I can tap a spot like this." She tapped behind a building and an orange dot with a white ring showed up, and then she tapped on a building and another dot appeared with a small number two on it. "I could just tell him to go to position two. The dots show up on his map, and he could use the GPS directions, voice directions, or the screen to find the location. Either he or I could tap a red dot and get a real time video feed sent from his wristcomp. Oz's locate program is always running in the background, scanning faces and putting them through his facial recognition pattern, so if there was any information available it would scroll in the side screen with relevant data first."

"The locate program is always running? Doesn't that drain the battery or slow the processing time?" General Campbell asked.

Oz shook his head and changed the picture on the main screen to show a microchip on a piece of black felt beside a spec of what appeared to be shiny blue glass. "Crystalis is faster than microchips by an order of ten trillion. Actually, maybe even faster as we're just beginning to learn it. If the programing is good enough it can have any information I might want ready for my question. Unlike a standard computer, the information the program deems I might want is stored directly in the crystals. That small spec can hold a yottabyte of information, which means the system can answer me instantly and run numerous programs at once without conflict."

Oz changed the picture again to a closeup of the wristcomp. "The string of crystals there are working as independent memory storage so everything you access is stored, which makes the response very fast because the machine will learn and remember your personal search patterns— how you think— and will be able to anticipate your requests. The program Sara is running right now has a built-in directive of preserving the soldier with a secondary directive of mission parameters. That means the computer is scanning for threats and will warn Rick if it spots anything at all it thinks might be a threat. If he walked by a known criminal, it would warn him. If it saw smoke, heard gunshots, noted the people about him look afraid or are acting oddly, it would notify him."

"We're still working on that programming," Sara added. "It's a complicated one as well."

"Mostly because we aren't sure of the correct response," Oz said.

Sara shrugged and turned back to the general. "The responses are complicated because I can also make the small screen on my wrist appear as a flatscreen in front of me."

Sara pinched the hologram and shrunk it down to nothing. Then she rapidly casted heals and Ascension on them and gave her wrist a little flick and small bar appeared to float in front of her right shoulder. "Spell timers with all the bells and whistles. If you used a spell-bracelet, the computer in the wristcomp will give an approximate magic usage, but it can be off as right now we have no way to measure the potency of the magic. If you were wearing a device, I could ask for a time on a spell whether or not I'd cast it. The program is fully integrated for everyone's spells." She turned to Oz. "Ascension time on Oz."

"Two minutes and forty-three seconds remains, countdown?" the device said.

"No," Sara flicked her wrist, and the screen was suddenly much smaller and see-through. "If I'd said yes, it would count it down. Or I could ask for reminders, remind followed by a number and it would remind me to redo it. If Oz had low vitals it would recommend I heal him. If he was out of my range and on my oversee list, it would recommend I head to him. It remembers my choices, and if I always choose the same response it'll automatically notify me if I forget to set the parameter. There's a cool feature for a drop where it'll tell when to cancel and recast Ascension to reach the optimal landing zone. As you can see, the information display, how the information is displayed is a complicated project that will take time and testing to determine. If we were on a real mission surrounded by hostiles, the correct information displayed in helpful ways would be invaluable but too much displayed badly would be distracting. Oz and I will need to speak to more people who've been in combat and can offer guidance."

"That's in our request," Oz said. "We'll get to that. The wristcomp can also be used as a phone going through the satellites. With one of these I can talk to anyone else, anywhere. Using these stickycoms"— Oz tapped the small plastic card— "we can 'hear' and 'speak' using vibrations with no audible noise. Although the speak part isn't as good as I want it yet, a whisper is required."

Sara said, "but the main benefit of using our computer is the Valkyrie program."

"Meet Valory," Oz said proudly.

General Campbell gasped and leaned back in his chair, lifting a hand to the woman who stood before him. The woman smiled and smoothed her white robe with her free hand. Her wings fluttered, each feather moving independently with her breathing. She carried a glowing white sword and a diamond tiara sparkled in her hair. Her skin was pale and her eyes were inhumanly bright blue. The tip of pointed ear was visible in her long white hair.

Charlie recognized the avatar as being one of Marcy's and hoped Oz wasn't lonely. His spike of worry caused Sara to glance at him, and he smiled crookedly, cocking a shoulder at the figure. Sara's expression lightened, and she smiled reassuringly, the smile brightening when she felt his spike of love. She knew what he was worried about without him saying a thing. He laughed and high-fived Sara, loving she knew him so well.

"She looks very real." Major Nelson stood to lean over the table.

"I'm an artificial intelligence housed inside the wristcomp. My physical appearance can be set to any parameters." As she spoke the woman's sword became a glowing white pen and a sheaf of paper appeared in her hand.

Oz laughed lightly and with barely a flicker the image of the woman disappeared, replaced by that of a man. The man wore a blue suit and had the same white hair and startling blue eyes and carried the glowing pen and paper. He stepped forward, shrinking as he did so, his wings fading and disappearing as he walked across the table at Barbie doll size. He came to a stop in the center of the table and a black swivel chair and desk appeared.

He sat as he said, "Perhaps you'd prefer this appearance?" and his white hair slicked back and his blue suit became a khaki brown uniform without insignia.

Oz said, "This is the world's first real artificial intelligence. Val can anticipate and remember very much as a human does. I'm still working on the programming but it's already a thousand times faster than any processor on the market today. Crystalis makes it possible to store *and* access quadrillions of bites of information at the same time."

"What's it do?" the general asked.

Sara said, "Anything an assistant can do. Val, call Brenda and move our meeting to three. Ask her if she wants to go for dinner after and see if Harrison wants to meet us there. Display my files on limb replacement."

Sara had barely finished speaking before a screen sprang up in front of her. She moved the screen to the side with a fingertip and continued speaking. "Order us lunch, my usual, and what would you like?" she turned to Charlie, grinning.

"A double cheeseburger, no mayo, extra tomato, fries coleslaw and two pickles."

Stasia, Oz and Hawk ordered, and Sara turned to the general.

"Nothing for me, thank you," he said.

"Me either," Major Nelson added, eyeing Val doubtfully. "Is it doing anything?"

Valory lifted a hand to smooth his shirt front as he said, "Brenda agreed to the change in the meeting and recommends Harlingtons for dinner. Harrison can't make it for dinner but can meet you at ten tomorrow to go over the new plans, but Marcus has requested to take his place, so I invited him to the meeting as well. Benny G's says they'll deliver in forty-five minutes."

"Impressive," the general said." Did you preprogram the restaurant numbers?"

Valory said, "I choose the venues unless I'm told otherwise."

The general lifted an eyebrow, and Charlie laughed in delight. "Val searches for places just like you would. It checks the web and phonebook and reads the reviews."

Valory said, "I also keep track of the quality of service. If delivery is late or items are missing or prepared wrong or the food is of poor quality, I won't use that vender again. I try to anticipate and please in all ways. For instance, I know Midshipman Morales prefers curly fries so have requested them without her having to ask me."

A new screen popped up before the general.

"Perhaps you'd like to see a list of available actions? I can perform over three hundred actions simultaneously and be preprogramed to do so with command words or gestures. Programming is ongoing, and that number should rise."

Sara said, "What makes Valory so impressive its ability to use other programs with just voice commands. I can ask it to type out a report exactly as I could ask a human assistant and just like with a human assistant I can tell it to change the paper format, make text bigger or smaller or reword sections. But Valory does it all much faster because it doesn't forget a process once it's learned it and it can multitask. It can be making my corrections while preforming any other task I've set it. Valory is why we're able to get so much done."

Oz said, "Sara and I are working on the sensors so Val isn't confined to the room we're in but can access the sensors independently. Ideally, it would be able to manifest a presence away from the base wristcomp, but that programing is complex because of security issues."

Valory said, "I can leave emails or make phone calls and check message boards but I'm unable to travel away from my base."

Charlie gestured to the screen hanging before the general and said, "Just use your finger to scroll like on a tablet."

General Campbell nodded absently as he hesitantly reached for the screen hanging before him. "That's amazingly clear. How do you get the screen so sharp and real looking?"

Oz said, "Refraction. We call it hard light."

"Would you like to see the research?" Valory asked.

"Not right now, thank you."

Sara said, "Val can explain how it works in depth and show graphs and pictures. It'll respond according the level of security to the lowest clearance in the room. If it can't determine that, it'll warn before revealing classified secrets, and if it thinks the area is unsafe to speak freely, it'll warn of it."

"I'd be happy to explain any of the components, theorems or programing at your convenience," Valory said.

"Damn machine is smarter than me," Major Nelson muttered, making Charlie laugh.

Oz said, "It's not smarter than a human,

it just has access to all human knowledge almost instantly. It possesses a relatively low intellect and can't produce an original idea although it can seem too."

General Campbell quirked a brow. "How so?"

Valory said, "My ability to remember your preferences and anticipate them could seem to be original thought. I anticipate my functioning to improve until I can apply a known idea in a totally unique way, but I lack the ability to form a new idea. I am not real."

Major Nelson asked, "Do you have feelings?"

Before Valory could answer, General Campbell asked, "Are you self-aware?"

Valory leaned back in his chair, crossing his legs and folding his hands on his chest. "I have limited self-awareness but not in the way you mean. I don't possess feelings. I do have programed responses to mimic appropriate action."

Charlie said, "Val can yell to gain attention and it laughs at jokes."

"Why yell?" Major Nelson asked. He leaned over to see the screen hanging before General Campbell and a new screen appeared before him. He sat back in his seat and the screen lowered to a traditional desktop display height.

Charlie bit back his laugh at the major's expression.

Sara said, "Yelling is an important action, especially for an AI who'll be in combat. It can warn you of danger but if you aren't paying attention it will yell and the tone will be consistent to the danger you face. It might sound angry or worried. It can also be told to yell at someone, say you have to call and remind someone of something, and you want your displeasure clear you could tell Val to call and tell it the tone to use."

Charlie said, "If you said rip him a new one, Val would really yell and maybe even curse depending on the person it was speaking with, but if you said inform him firmly, the tone would be firm and less polite then if you said inform him politely. He can whisper too and will do so if he perceives the situation warrants silence. Sara is working on the programing for that, but it isn't a priority because of these." Charlie tapped the flesh-colored stickers.

Oz said, "Programing for that is ongoing and we don't foresee it being finished for years."

Sara shrugged and flicked the screen before her closed. "That's because we're working on other things. We plan on eventually having a wide assortment of voice models to choose from. Some people will need distinct avatars. Not every Valory will look the same, in fact, I think it more likely most will have unique appearances to differentiate them when in groups. It would be confusing if everyone's assistant looked alike, especially if we iron out the wrinkles that let them travel around."

"It's cool and all," Major Nelson said so doubtfully Charlie's laugh burst free.

"It doesn't just make phone calls," Charlie said. "It can research for you and keep track of your schedule but it's most important feature is its ability to monitor multiple areas at once."

He tapped one of the blue disks. "These are the new sensors and Val can keep track of all of them and it's smart enough to know if something is off. I could place one of these anywhere and it could watch for anything I wanted. If you put one in a doorway, it could tell you who went in and out and when but more importantly it's constantly running every face it sees through Oz's locate program and if someone dangerous enters he'd warn you without your having to ask."

Oz said, "It's also smart enough to recognize sketchy behavior and it'll notice if you have a weapon on you. This version of Valkyrie will be a combat assistant trained to watch your back. We have plans to integrate it into our suit and make it able to engage and disengage our bracelets if it anticipates the need. Say for instance it saw a gunman aim at your back it could engage Sara's white bracelet and yell shield.

Sara said, "I'm hoping our shield research will let it actually apply an artificial shield of his own one day."

Major Nelson said, "I don't think I like the idea of an AI being able to pull a weapon on a man."

Oz grinned crookedly. "Is it any different from an automated response from a security system that uses lethal hardware? At least it can be programed to warn first. But we have time to decide and work on that programing as the weapons aren't even designed yet."

Sara said, "We can plan now though and run simulations to track the data. We want you all to use Val and report back to us so we can see the logs of its proficiency."

General Campbell said, "Everyone will want a Val."

Oz's grin widened. "I hope so and only our new computers will have the power to run one. We're working on the sensors and it shouldn't be too long until we have one you can retrofit on any appliance so that Val can operate it. It'll be able to turn on and off anything you own with either voice commands or preprograming and the appliances won't need to be left on like they are now. It'll be able to do it from a cold start right through the sensor."

Stasia said, "We want to give Valory a physical body someday so he can interact with real objects. I've been studying robotics in my free time, not that I have much free time." She shook her head and cleared her throat, sitting forward and tenting her fingers before her. "I'd like to work on that after we graduate. There's already some remarkably advanced robots available but with the new computers we could make a much better one. Oz and I have talked about the mechanics, the limitations of the currently available parts, and we'll need to devise a better delivery system for power and information."

Sara nodded agreement, giving Stasia a small apologetic grimace. "Basically, we need to build an artificial nervous system. And we just don't have the time to do it right now. I love Stasia's ideas but they're going need to wait."

Stasia said, "It's not like I have time right now anyway."

Oz reached over to pat her arm. "It's on the list, and meanwhile you can work on the simulations and programing."

Charlie exchanged another worried glance with Sara.

Oz said, "You'll have to make do with the Valkyrie system. We're still tweaking its response program and need feedback on that. Stasia runs the models for that program, so if you're finding your Valory isn't responding correctly, either missing cues or answering when it isn't asked, contact her."

"It seems to be working as intended," Stasia said. "In fact, "I've been meaning to ask if I can hand out a few more of the newer models to get more feedback. Amy had some really great ideas."

"We'll talk after this," Oz said and Stasia leaned back in her seat, but she looked happier now and Charlie made a mental note to speak with Oz about letting her help more in the lab.

General Campbell held the bulky wristcomp in the air and scrutinized it. "What's the battery life?"

"None," Oz said. "Well, not one like you're thinking. A wristcomp uses a small ultrathin lithium battery that should last at least a year or more, but Sara made the battery the hologram uses. It isn't a leather band; it too has to engage. This is gross, but its skin, Sara's skin and nerves, solar powered with a little life force thrown in. A mix of tech and magic. We're on the verge of a breakthrough and hope to have a totally tech version soon. Right now, completely motionless in the dark, you have about six days. It can conserve power by turning off all functions and uses more for holograms. But the amount of light a normal person is subjected to in a day is sufficient to power it indefinitely. The watch is equipped with a fully programmable computer capable of running any app you could name and a virtual keyboard and twelve virtual screens. This will replace old computer tech completely. There'll be no need for a desktop or laptop when the computer on your wrist can do everything—"

Sara interrupted. "Screens can be unlimited with a peripheral projector." She slid the quarter-sized blue-glass disk to the general. "Games, Tetris, full-screen."

A twelve-by-twelve game screen appeared in front of her at eye level. Charlie chuckled when the general poked it. It looked solid as if a real screen floated before her, but it was just hardened light. The general's finger passed into the picture and he grunted, making Charlie laugh again. He still didn't understand how it worked but there was no denying it did work.

She used her fingers to pick up and turn

blocks and then played a minute. "As you can see, I don't need gloves. The tiny glass-like chips on the edge of the watch face are mapping my hand movements. The polling rate is already appreciable faster than the norm but we're working on making it even faster. The computer is using the energy and muscles in my hands to power itself and mapping what I'm doing to play the game or cast my spells. Eye movement is being tracked by this sensor." Sara peeled off a previously unnoticed flesh-colored tab from the right temple by her eye and held it up on a fingertip. "This sensor maps and sends the information to the wristcomp, letting me interact with the screen by just glancing at it. Refraction of the hardened light combined with mapping my wrist and finger motions gives very accurate results. As I use it, it'll become faster, anticipating my actions."

"Who can use these?" The general tapped the wristcomp on her wrist.

"Anyone who's tried it, but no one not in the raid has tried it yet." Sara took off the wristcomp and handed it to him. "I'm willing to make a few more, but the process of getting my skin is indeed gross. I'm not willing to make a lot of them."

"And this?" The general held up the plastic card with the tan boxes. "They look like bulky Band-Aids for robots."

Oz laughed. "Prototypes of the earphones Sara mentioned, but they aren't quite ready. We call them stickycoms. Place the larger one behind your ear and the smaller on your neck and they vibrate and record vibrations and the computer inside synthesizes voice, but right now it sounds monotone. Usable, but not pleasant. And we've sort of given up on them. Sara has a better idea for one device permanently placed in the jawbone behind the ear that will map all muscle movement, but we haven't had time to work on it really, so we're settling on these for now." Oz tapped the plastic card before General Campbell.

"You did all this in three months?" General Campbell shook his head in amazement.

"No, we've been working on it right along," Oz said. "Honestly, everything we've shown you could still use work, but we need more money and access to people we want to talk with. We can talk without revealing anything, but some of the people live far away and we need transportation, and of course, security."

Sara interrupted, "And we wanted you to know who we're talking with because some aren't friendly to America."

"If they go anywhere, we all go." Charlie took Sara's hand. "Travel arrangements for them need to take our school schedule into account."

Oz exchanged an unhappy glance with Charlie and then turned to the general. "There's one more thing to show you and one thing to tell you." Oz turned on the projector again. "We call this a stasis jar. Sara made this for Stasia, but it has real practical applications. We can't show you a live demonstration, it's too dangerous for us, but as you can see, it's sucking the magic in."

General Campbell leaned forward and stared at the screen. On screen Sara stood in a bathing suit glowing from magic. The jar lit up and her magic flew to it. She fell to the floor, and Oz raced to the jar. It darkened, and the magic rushed out and back to Sara.

"The jar will hold the magic as long as the power lasts and it's using a lot of power." Oz showed the general the power consumption graphs. "On that first test, we almost killed Sara. In later tests, we used much less magic and still sucked down the power. But, the bottom line is, the magic can be contained."

"We're working on a way to siphon it off and use it," Sara said. "No luck yet, but I'm confident we'll get there. I made this for

Stasia to trap me, but you could use it if I ever rampaged again. I'd most likely die, but the magic would be bottled up."

Oz turned off the video. "We won't tell you how we made this," Oz and Sara exchanged worried glances. "If you break it trying to figure it out, we won't make another one either."

"Maybe someday we will," Sara added. "But anyway, I also made it because we're going to turn Joy if we can, and if that works we'll turn Rick."

"I see." General Campbell tapped the tabletop with his fingertips. "So, you make a container you say will hold the magic because you plan on making more of it with or without approval."

"Yes." Sara's gaze traveled over everyone, resting on Stasia a moment, before she turned back to the general. "Stasia needs Rick to have magic too, but I need to be sure I can do it before I try him, so we'll do Joy. Joy volunteered. We told her everything we know or suspect might happen. I might kill her trying this, and I'd feel horrible, but if I killed Rick, I could never face my in-laws again."

"So, you'll sacrifice Joy for him." Major Nelson leaned back in his chair and glared at Sara.

"Yes, she knows that, and I'm not proud of it, but yes," Sara said.

"Does Rick know?" Major Nelson rose an eyebrow and curled his lip.

"No." Stasia laid her hand on Sara's as she started to speak and leaned forward. "And we'd appreciate if it stays that way."

"Because you both know he'd never let you do it." Major Nelson switched his glare to Stasia.

They didn't answer.

Major Nelson threw his hands up. "God save me from teenage hormones."

Charlie glared at the major and leaned forward in his seat. "Sara needs another warrior. Well, not her, her magic. It pushes her all the time now whenever she meets the raid. She and I will try to give Joy magic and do our best to see she isn't hurt. Stasia can't do it, she's tried. Sara could do it alone, but we'll do it together. I'm hoping we don't form any sort of bond with her, but we're aware we might. She is too. Joy will focus on being a warrior, but she was a rogue, so again the outcome is uncertain. If Joy is unacceptable to you, we're willing to consider your candidate." Charlie sat back and crossed his arms.

"Don't do anything until I inform the president." General Campbell motioned

Major Nelson back when he started to speak. "As for the money, I'm sure we can arrange some."

"Money and space." Oz gestured about the crowded room. "And I could use assistants. I'd be willing to teach them, so maybe some second or first year midshipmen if they have the aptitude. Nothing to do with magic. A million ideas are floating around in my head that I'm dying to try out. The computer programing still needs work as does the Valkyrie system and the batteries on the wristcomps. In fact, we're working on a power source itself."

Sara slid a folder to the general. "We've drawn up a plan for a building we'd like with space for all of us to work. I know it's a lot of money we're asking for, but we need more supplies and equipment."

"It's almost a million dollars just for security!" The general's eyes widened as he read the list.

Oz nodded. "The plan is to use our new products to outfit the dogs in some dumber wristcomps, much bulkier and heavier with no bells and whistles, but they'll be able to transmit pictures and alarms for us and an automatic notification if they're incapacitated in any way."

Oz tapped the small, blue-glass disk. "I'm

working on this and making sensors programmable for multiple conditions like fire and floods to be used in our security. A simulation of the system I'm working on, including the complete specifications, is on the USB. A copy of what we've spoken to you about today is on here too." Oz handed the general a USB. "An estimate cost and timeline is also in there."

"To continue our research, we need supplies," Sara picked up the discussion. "And rooms with different levels of access to store our magic and magical experiments. Everything protected by Oz's security programs and devices."

"Speaking of which," Oz said. "We agree the government gets all rights to any magical device we make, excluding the ones we make for ourselves or the Scouts, but we won't ever sell designs or knowledge of magical devices. We'll also give copies of all our research on the magic with complete transparency. For the non-magical devices, and ideas like my security system, we'd like thirty-eight percent of gross. The initial startup cost will be high, but you should see a profit very soon."

Sara slid another folder to the general. "The figures are in here, and you'll notice the notations giving credit to the midshipmen who helped us plan this."

"The math doesn't mean a thing to most people so we've, um, dumbed it down a bit on this list here." Oz passed the general another folder.

The general opened the folder, then frowned. "You're saying you can make all of these things right now?"

"Yes, if we had time, money, parts, and labor," Oz said. "We've used the prototypes in the devices we showed you. A wristcomp can be made dumbed down with a regular battery and some functionality missing, but better than anything on the market today. With that same technology, we can make interactive video games much more advanced than what you saw Sara playing. My alarm system uses magic, but it too can be dumbed down and used without it and still be better than any other system. The heads up display I'm working on will outperform anything available on the market."

"And the ones marked IP?" The general flipped through the small booklet.

"Those are in progress, JT, are just thoughts, but ones we think we could do in time." Oz leaned back in his seat. "There's so much we still want to study, but honestly, school is a waste of time for us. The learning format of a classroom is too slow. Time spent traveling to and from classes would be better spent in the lab. We'll need funding to hire professors and experts to come tell us what they know, or we can go to them."

Sara gestured to the bracelets. "If our full request is denied, we'd at least like enough funding to make enough spell bracelets so everyone in the raid gets two of them, and at least ten wristcomps, and then enough dumber ones for the rest of the raid as well as some miscellaneous things we need too numerous to list right now, but there's a list for you in the file. Things like more metal storage containers of varying sizes for the magic and specialized tools we need."

"I'll bring your proposal to the president." The general gathered the folders and tapped them on the table to neaten them.

Oz nodded. "Don't forget to mention Valor Industries will take thirty-eight percent of the profits, but we estimate over a billion in six years and that's being conservative. To reach peak performance we'll need to spend even more than the initial startup. We'll require factories and employees and lots of them, but we can build up. What we're proposing is a billion-dollar industry, it's all in the report."

"One more thing," Charlie said as the general was about to leave. "The five of us possess raid assist and can invite or remove from the raid. Rick is still the leader, but we've checked it and it works. When Sara quit, Rick invited her back, but I couldn't, and we can't let that happen again."

"Yes, I was informed already. It isn't a problem. In fact, we should've done that earlier." The general shook hands with Oz and Sara. The midshipmen and Major Nelson saluted.

"How are things going at school?" Major Nelson asked as he rose to go.

"Fine," Stasia said." Academically we're all doing well. There's some talk about our special privileges, but it died down when the other midshipmen started coming to their lab to work. The competition to be invited to work here is intense. Valor Industries is paying well for their original ideas."

"Valor Industries is almost broke," Sara said. "If the president won't fund us, we'll have to scale down and pick one product to market ourselves, which will slow us enormously on research and development."

"You've been using your own money then?" The major lifted an eyebrow.

"Yes. I put enough in a trust fund to support the house, but the rest we spent doing all of this." Sara smiled. "I'm positive we'll make way more than we've spent. More than any of us could ever spend, but we're waiting to see if we do it or the government does. Either way I'll be a billionaire by twenty-one."

"You're that sure of the products?" Both eyebrows now elevated, Major Nelson waited for her reply.

"The video game alone will make billions. Oz and I have just barely begun to put his vision to work. Crystalis is the future," Sara assured him.

"Can I buy stock?" The major asked with a laugh.

Charlie said, "No need, all of our Scouts have stock in the company. You'll receive it this Christmas when the final paperwork goes through." He laughed at the major's expression. "Regular stockholder meetings will start the first of next year. Our main goal is helping the Scouts. The offshoots of that should make us all money, but that's not the point."

"You can't just give it away. It's not like we have business experience." Major Nelson frowned, his gaze traveling them and then the devices laying on the table.

Sara picked up the wristcomp and put it on. "We can hire business managers. The Scouts input is vital for development, and they're the only ones who can supply the information we need. Why shouldn't they be paid for that?"

"The stock will go to the raid position. The person in that position will only retain the stock while they're in that position," Oz clarified. "And we don't expect the government to give us the entire thirty-eight percent either."

Sara frowned at him. "We won't accept lower than twenty-five percent, they are our ideas after all. We just have to get good managers for production if we want to R and D."

"Sounds like you have it all figured out." Major Nelson settled his hat on his head.

"Well, we are super smart you know." Oz grinned and Hawk laughed.

Sara rolled her eyes. "Oz and I will each hold twenty-five shares. Stasia and Hawk will get ten each. The rest of the raid will get one, which is sort of how we ran the guild. You'll be required to attend every vote, at least in proxy."

Oz nodded. "Input on what the Scouts need is crucial. I've redesigned their gear but need to wait for funding to implement it. Valor Industries will be a legitimate security's business. We can hide our magical research in our security research. A really good audit would show it of course, but I assume that can be avoided."

"And when Valor Industries no longer needs financial help from the government, what then?" Major Nelson asked.

"None of us care that much about the money." Oz shrugged and began to gather the samples together. "If we're happy with our working conditions, we wouldn't change them just to make more money. Everyone is okay with the government making the profits. The raid could vote us out, but I don't see that happening either, at least anytime soon. They'd need at least one officer to help them. I'm not saying it couldn't happen, but it's unlikely."

"Soldiers don't fight for the money," Charlie said. "Our Scouts don't work hard for money; they're working hard to protect the people of the United States."

Major Nelson shook their hands. "I'm looking forward to these meetings, and I can't wait to see what you have planned."

The midshipmen saluted him when he left.

Stasia turned to Charlie. "You don't mind only having four shares?"

"He has my twenty-five, so really, we own twenty-nine," Sara said before Charlie could answer. "Mr. Martin drew up the papers and almost had a stroke. Everything I have, or will ever have, will be his." Sara smiled at Charlie as he laughed at Stasia's expression.

"And anything I have or will ever have will be Sara's. We're fine with it. I know in the guild the officers had equal votes with the GM having more, but the numbers balanced this way. Are you unhappy with your shares?"

"Not at all."

Hawk grinned. "We're good. You guys do all the work, and we collect the money. What's not to like?"

Sara laughed, and she and Oz went to put the samples in her lab.

Stasia stared after them with a troubled gaze. "I'm sorry I said what I did. I know she forgave me, and we've made up, but it's still so awkward between us. She never comes to me anymore just to talk."

Charlie gave Stasia a one-armed hug. "She isn't unhappy, but she isn't over losing the baby either. The nightmares are back and she's seeing Doctor Gotlieb again. Guilt over what happened this summer still haunts her, and she both loves and hates the magic. This helps her a lot, doing good things with her magic.

"If you could speak to her so she knows you wouldn't want her dead if she connected magically with Rick that would help. She's scared to death she will." Charlie grabbed Stasia's shoulders. "I love you, you know that, right?" When she nodded, he continued. "If Joy is attracted to Sara's magic, or Sara's is to hers, I won't let her change Rick. I won't risk her guilt causing her to harm herself, not for anyone."

Stasia nodded and bit her lip. "I didn't realize she was upset about the baby. She only knew she was pregnant for a few hours."

"Doctor Gotlieb says that's normal and will get easier. The magic had her so ramped up on hormones she was desperate to run. She didn't realize why she was running until she found out about the baby, but now she feels guilty that she didn't protect it better. She's really a mess emotionally, but she's working on it. Having her girlfriend back would help her."

Stasia regarded the doorway Sara and Oz had exited with worried eyes. "I feel terrible about how jealous I am of Rick, but that doesn't make me less jealous."

"Jesus, sis, she made a trap that would kill her if she rampages again. What more do you want? I was there, she couldn't help it. It wasn't her; it was the magic."

"Don't you think I know that?" Stasia

yelled right as Sara and Oz returned. The silence in the room was deafening.

Sara sighed. "It's fine; we heard you all. I still love you. Maybe someday you'll love me back. Meanwhile, we'll be friends as much as you can be. If you tried to take Charlie, I'd hate you too."

"I'm sorry, Sara." Stasia rose and gave Sara a hug. "I really wish I wasn't so crazy about this."

Sara laughed. "I understand crazy, uncontrollable feelings." She paused thoughtfully. "Would you let me run some tests on you? Maybe do a few experiments?"

Stasia bit back a snort of laughter. "You think it's my magic? It isn't."

"I didn't think it was mine either at first."

"Sure, I'll do your tests."

Stasia and Sara exchanged smiles.

Charlie sighed in relief. "We all work too hard; we need more fun."

"I agree." Oz leaned back in his chair and put his feet on the table. "We used to have fun together all the time."

"Let's try a new MMO," Hawk said eagerly.

Sara and Oz frowned.

"Oz and I'd never have time for that."

Oz glanced at Hawk and grinned. "A compromise then, let's make our own for the new game system— work and play.”

“It would be fun to design boss strategies.” Charlie pulled Sara into his lap, pleased with how happy the idea of playing together made her.

“We’ll need artists.” Stasia rubbed her bottom lip with one finger while she thought. “None of us can draw well enough.”

Sara laughed in delight. “We can play on paper and then Oz and I will program it. I’m sure we could find a few artists willing to work on spec. We’ll start with five zones and each design one. This will be fun.”

“Let’s pick our own artists to give each zone a distinct appearance,” Hawk said. “Oh, and we can all make one dungeon and collaborate on one raid.” Hawk sounded excited.

Charlie glanced from one happy face to another and grinned, his team needed this.

“First, we need to lay out classes and specs.” Oz tapped his wristcomp opening a virtual whiteboard and for two hours happy, excited talk flew around the table. “This is fun; we’ll meet at least once a week to discuss progress. Do as much or little as you like all week just like a game.”

“I know who I want as my artist.” Sara jumped up from Charlie’s lap and ran from the room laughing.

"She's *my* roommate!" Stasia yelled and bounded up to chase her.

Oz and Charlie exchanged grins.

Hawk laughed. "So much better."

- 29 -

ENCOURAGING PROGRESS

Word spread like wildfire that Valor Industries was hiring artists to work on spec, and they were called into the commandant's office. Sara's anxiety rapidly escalated to real fear when he just swiveled slightly in his chair frowning at them.

Torn by his duty to obey the rules of conduct when facing a superior and his wife's fear, Charlie broke protocol in his wife's favor.

"You're scaring her. Sara it's fine. We can handle this. You can go home," he said futilely, knowing she wouldn't leave him to face anything alone.

Hawk took her gloved hand and pulled her into his side, trying to use his aura on her.

The commandant stood suddenly.

Sara jumped, and he frowned at her.

Still clutching Hawk's hand, she

452

straightened and stared back.

"The student body is being disrupted by your game. I'm sure your government funding doesn't cover making a video game. You're allowed here on campus to protect your classified work, not play games."

Oz glanced at his quiet friends, then the commandant, shrugged and spoke up. "We aren't using any funding because we have none yet. The game research is on our time and we're doing it here for security reasons. It's much more secure for people to go there than our home, but we can do it somewhere else if it's an issue." He paused a moment, then added. "We're almost finished hiring. It should settle down soon, and we're helping the students who work with us enormously academically. When we're done, you'll have some first-rate programmers able to use the new systems we're designing. I'm not sure how informed you are on our security systems, but I assure you, the Navy will be using them in the future and need experienced people."

Oz wore a new prototype wristcomp that was much sleeker than the original model. "Show me academy grounds." A hologram formed in front of him. "Show me Amy Vlase. The reason I picked Amy is she's wearing a tracker we're testing."

The commandant rose and examined the hologram, waving his arm through it to no effect.

Oz placed two fingers in the hologram and moved them apart, zooming in on Amy's location. "Amy's in a classroom and the red dots are people within ten feet of her. I can tap her once and all data on her location will scroll by me." He reached out and tapped the image of Amy and another screen popped up with scrolling text. "With a small peripheral sensor, I could easily see within thirty yards. We're teaching your midshipmen to program this. Imagine how useful it'll be for a ship commander to instantly see where his crew is on his entire ship. It has the capability to follow a target seamlessly without switching screens as the target moves leaving and entering range of placed sensors. This isn't a real-time holograph, but an actual reproduction with exact sizes and dimensions to scale, but we can do it in real time and actually see the current condition of the room Amy occupies."

Oz turned off the picture and didn't mention the battery life was total crap on the non-skin wristcomps, they were working on that.

"The game uses the same programming?" His frown gone, the commandant returned to his seat.

"The same computer language yes, similar components, but not identical, it's a completely new language."

"New hardware as well," Sara added. "This new system will make the computers we use now obsolete."

"So, I guess I shouldn't discourage it, but encourage it." The commandant tapped his lips with one finger. "Maybe even offer a class to learn it?"

"We're waiting for funding and approvals," Oz said. "A lot of our work is classified. This system will be used. We'll develop it whether or not the government chooses to fund us. So, even if it doesn't end up being used by the military, it'll still be a viable skill for the midshipmen."

"If you like, we could fill our available positions with civilians," Sara offered. "They'd only need to occasionally meet us in person. It shouldn't pose too much of a disturbance to have them on campus."

The commandant regarded his quiet midshipmen. "Do you have anything to add?"

Charlie spoke up at once." Our orders are to protect them. Those orders supersede any other orders we receive, and we work with the classified materials too. I have no idea what your orders are or what you know. I'm sorry if I seem rude or disrespectful, but those are my orders."

Stasia interrupted, "Sir, you should be aware we've asked for a new building along with our funding and plan to staff it with your students as much as possible. Oz and Sara will both be teaching. I have no idea if they've told you anything yet, but I'm sure they will."

"All this so you three can attend the academy?" The commandant leaned back in his seat and tented his fingers.

"Yes," Hawk said. "It would be easier for them to work in Pendleton, but we're here so they have to be."

The commandant frowned. "When you graduate, what then?"

"I don't know," Hawk admitted. "We'll go where we're assigned like any other lieutenant."

"And you two?" The commandant turned to Oz and Sara.

Oz shrugged. "We'll go wherever we want, but we could do that now. The reason we stay is to be near them. So, I guess it depends where they're assigned."

"So, if you get a new building it might be empty in a few years, and any of your students left behind?"

Sara cleared her throat and looked down, avoiding everyone's gaze. "Yes, but they know we'll go with them."

The commandant eyed Hawk still holding Sara's hand. "You'll follow him, you mean." A small smile crossed his face.

"No," Charlie said. "Sara and I will marry the first Christmas the year I graduate."

Charlie winced at the commandant's confused expression.

"She's trying to not get me in trouble; Hawk doesn't care if he gets in trouble." Charlie sighed. "It's hard to explain, almost impossible without revealing classified secrets. The simple version is you scared her. Hawk is trying to comfort her, that's it."

The commandant straightened and faced Sara. "Excuse me, that wasn't my intent."

"I'm fine," Sara said.

Hawk kept a hold of her gloved hand, and she made no attempt to pull away from him.

The commandant nodded and let it go. "You have my permission to carry on as you planned on campus, but if you need more students, I'd like notice before you search for them."

Oz nodded and made a note on his wristcomp. "That's fine, we'll send you reports on our plans as they evolve," Oz agreed.

"Dismissed." The commandant returned the salutes. "Mr. Hayes, a moment please." Charlie stopped and closed his eyes, then turned smartly and returned to the office, ignoring Sara's spike of renewed alarm as best he could, trying to project confidence to her.

"Miss Mitchel is easily frightened. Extend my apologies. Will it be a problem for her to deal with the students?"

Charlie had to resist rubbing his forehead. "The students here don't frighten her, in fact, she feels safe with them, which is why she and Oz are using them to staff their projects. She's afraid she'll do something that gets me in trouble or expelled. Right now, she's afraid you called me in here for that. She knows how important this is to me and is extremely sensitive to things that upset me. Much more than she should be. Especially if she perceives herself as the cause of the upset. She's seeing a therapist, but that doesn't lessen her fear now."

The commandant leaned back in his chair and narrowed his eyes. "I see. I hadn't realized she had emotional problems, but I suppose an IQ as high as hers has its drawbacks. Her actions won't affect your standing in the academy. I didn't mean to scare her more by calling you in here, I was concerned the students would frighten her."

Charlie smiled. "Midshipmen possess no power over my career, so she can handle them. If she gets overwhelmed, she'll tell one of us. Sara isn't a coward; she's just worried she'll affect my career negatively. She does her best to follow the rules here, but sometimes her worry escalates to a panic attack, which is why Hawk held her hand, it makes her feel better. She'd rather hold mine, but she knows we aren't supposed to, and like I said, Hawk doesn't care, or I should say, doesn't care as much," Charlie finished.

"Very well. In the future, if she needs to hold your hand to prevent a panic attack, she may— dismissed."

Charlie saluted and left.

Back at the lab, everyone crowded around the table in Oz's workspace. "Everything's fine. He just wanted to know why you went to Hawk, not me, and said it was fine to come to me if you need reassurance." Sara's relief made him smile. "I know you're working on this, but you really need to stop worrying so much about getting me into trouble."

She grimaced. "I'm trying. But I can't help worrying, then I worry you'll be mad I'm worrying. I'm really trying to learn to stop those loops."

Hawk laughed. "Just say to yourself, if he doesn't like it— tough, and feel what you want too."

"I know," Sara agreed miserably. "I just care so much what he thinks of me."

Charlie hugged her, mock glaring at Hawk over her head. "Hey, don't tell her to not care about me. I want her to love me desperately."

Sara laughed and snuggled her face into his neck with a happy sigh.

- 30 -

THE RIDE TO THE TOP

"Well, General, we've examined their proposal." The president gestured General Campbell to a seat. "It's a complicated project with different levels of secrecy. I've read your recommendations and talked with Doctor Gotlieb. Sara is both our greatest asset and our weakest link. We need to keep her happy. Fortunately, she doesn't require much to be happy. A pile of books and a sunny quiet room would do it. But then there's Charlie. Unfortunately, Charles won't be happy sitting around near her and his unhappiness will make her unhappy."

General Campbell sat and crossed his legs. "Yes, it'll be hard to balance. She won't be happy unless he is, and he won't be happy unless he's in a combat unit. A fake unit will fool neither of them. Charlie will need real missions."

461

"Exactly, we'll be putting our greatest asset at risk on every single mission." The president poured coffee from a silver urn and offered it to the general who accepted with a thank you.

He continued speaking as he poured a second cup. "You propose she try to make another sun-priest, a backup, if you will. Someone more stable emotionally. To do that we'd need to recruit someone new. None of the Scouts play a sun-priest. Brenda is as close as we come with a moon-priest. The problem is, we think the magical link cause's most of her emotional problems. Any priest might potentially experience the same issues. Sara is working with us as she learns to deal with them, a new priest might not, and I hate to disrupt the balance we have now."

The president cleared his throat. "Since Sara's issue Liz reports four more Scouts have rerolled warriors. While I appreciate the enthusiasm with which they support her, we don't want them all to be warriors. We were leaving the choice of character up to them, but some guidance will be called for if the trend continues."

"I'll see to it." General Campbell assured him. "Do you have an optimal number in mind for warriors or any other class?"

"No more than five or so of each type. That would give us a good selection. Meet with Major Harris, discuss who the best warrior candidates would be if Sara needs another one, and have the others change back."

The president leaned back on the sofa and continued. "Pierce has run some scenarios we're really concerned about. We could easily go from cooperation to a magical war if we introduce someone who disrupts their unit. Pierce assures me Stasia would fight anyone she thought threatened her bond with Rick, and Charlie and Sara most likely would as well, so if the new priest wanted one of them, well, magical war. Look what Sara did to the base without even trying, now imagine she was in her right mind and desired an army of warriors and to tear the base down. Now imagine another group forming and fighting them. I tell you, it gives me nightmares."

"They did give us the stasis box."

The president snorted softly. "One box, if it really works like they said it does, and we both know they could drain the magic if she wanted to."

The general waggled his hand side-to-side. "I've examined the specs on the box and their reports. Draining the magic would let it regenerate. We'd need to remove the caster's m-nerves to ensure the magic couldn't regenerate. But I *would* like to know how they keep the magic linked to them and in stasis.

"I agree she could forcefully rip the magic from them, but a situation would need to be very dire for her to agree to permanently steal one of her friend's magic." The general sat back and sipped his coffee. "I bring up the box as proof they're aware of the security issues and are willing to overcome them. I believe they could make another box quickly but won't give it to us because we could then take one apart to duplicate it."

"Pierce agrees with you and thinks they might possess more ready to go right now. He also thinks it would show extremely bad faith if we asked for more without cause."

"And what happens to our rep with them if we don't give them everything they asked for?"

The president smiled slightly and slid a folder across the coffee table to the general.

"Not only is it imperative to keep them happy for reputation but it's just good sense. Are you aware all of them send me updates?"

General Campbell straightened and his eyes widened. "No, I was under the impression they only communicated with you through me."

"Since the day we sent them home I've been receiving emails from all of them. A practice I encourage. The point is, I'm probably the most informed person on their plans and progress. Every time they get a new idea I receive a note. And I have to tell you, the list they gave you doesn't cover half of them. Some of their ideas are so far from anything I've imagined possible, well…" the president leaned back in his chair and swiveled from side-to-side. "The United States would be foolish indeed to let these assets slip from their fingers."

"While I agree with you, what they're asking for isn't chump change. How the hell will we be able to sneak that amount of funding through congress?"

The president threw his head back and laughed. He leaned forward still grinning and tapped the folder. "For once concerning them, I've told the truth. Not the entire truth, mind you," he added when the general looked alarmed. "Pierce and I prepared a presentation that even William Fierns could understand."

The general winced then chuckled. The head of the fiancé committee, William Fierns, and the president had a history of butting heads.

"The facts are irrefutable. Change is coming and we either embrace it and grab on, riding it to the top, or someone else will. The ride is bound to be wild and it'll be hard to keep hold but it's our only option. Magic is here. Whoever controls it will control everything. The world has already changed beyond our wildest imaginings. The effects are just starting to be seen. What they imagine, how quickly they're learning...." The president shook his head, his eyes on the distance. "The magic is the least of it. Oliver's work on energy, Sara's work on communication…" The president trailed off, shaking his head. "What their building will change the world as we know it. Already talk of their genius is spreading. The papers they're publishing are so outside the box, so brilliant, so controversial in the scientific fields that being recognized as the great minds they are is taking time, but soon it'll be unmistakable and undeniable. When that happens, offers will roll in to them. The United States needs to keep them in a firm grasp."

The general rubbed his chin with two fingers. "The ride to the top?"

"Exactly!" The president tented his hands on his desk. "Congress agrees and is only too happy to sign contracts, especially ones giving the United States ownership of their ideas. Pierce worked long and hard to protect Team Valor's rights in those contracts. While the United States will retain full control of weapons, control remains with them for everything else, and let's face it, that's a piddling amount of money for the potential gains. The hardest part was legally giving them the Scouts."

"How did you manage it?"

The president snorted a small laugh. "I didn't. Sara and Mr. Martin did. Pierce and I were being too complicated, and they simplified it. The contract Valor Industries has with us specifies they get the right to choose one hundred personnel from any branch of service to work with them and that for no reason can those chosen be ordered away. There's a bunch in there about how the men and women they chose are not subject to military law unless fired from Valor Industries. Basically, Valor Industries will attempt to design a new way of warfare and congress is letting them try. Everything from the clothes they wear to the weapons they use will be new. Some of the old-timers squawked, but most had no problem with the contract as so few personnel were asked for."

The president tapped the folder on his

desk. "We're giving them everything they've asked for, including a government contract for securities. Most of the components they need can be supplied by companies we already deal with. The building they want will be built by next fall's start of term. That was an easy one. The school was already asking for expansion and had plans in place. We'll just customize the building. The school will own it. Team Valor will rent it. Paying them is where it gets tricky. Security devices are easy. We pay for what we order. They'll receive an exclusive contract with us, prices agreed upon in advance just like any other contract, but their real job won't be securities but magic research and development. What we pay them must withstand an audit. Some money can be hidden in a research grant, but not in the quantities they need."

"You're aware they're making games?"

The president set his coffee cup beside General Campbell's. "Yes, they'll be free to do whatever they wish with their developments, excluding contract violations of course."

"They'd probably be able to fund it themselves with the profits from the game."

The president sighed. "The United States government must own the rights to every magical device; we must pay for them. I'm still examining my options. Right now they don't need much for their magical work, the research grant will cover it. Pierce is working on setting up the business offices. The more time they have for research the better."

The president handed the general a folder. "Team Valor will be assigned to the same carrier this summer. Oliver and Sara will be aboard as private consultants for the security firm. It'll be our test ship. Congress recognizes the genius of the new computers, thank god. It's the only thing that pushed them into signing on so quickly. They're afraid Oliver and Sara will take their work elsewhere if they don't act quickly. Many details remain to be worked out. Congressional squawkers need to be soothed. What I'm concerned with is the security of the ship. Send either Alpha or Beta on board with them with the other team in the vicinity."

General Campbell leafed through the folder. "Will the captain be informed?"

"Not the particulars, no, but he'll be informed that their security needs to be tight, and he'll be on a yellow alert status while they're on board and be notified of the increased danger to his ship. He'll also be notified, and I sure it'll stun and amaze him, that Midshipman Charles Hayes can at any time take over command of the ship. If they are attacked, they could defend themselves, but would need to be able to order witnesses away as well as the crew into positions to help them as they needed."

The general glanced up from the folder in his hand. "I assume we're using the secret weapon explanation?"

"We are, and sooner or later someone will notice we're using it." The president stood and paced to the window, standing with his hands behind his back as he surveyed his garden. "The longer we can put off revealing anything, the better. We're learning a lot, but we need more time."

"And, um, their quarters."

The president returned to the couch and sat. "Other midshipmen who worked on the security project or Oliver's new computers will be assigned there too. Our five will be assigned quarters as close together as possible. Oliver will bunk with Sebastian and Charles. Sara will bunk in their office. They'll have permission from us to share their quarters, but instructions to not be caught sharing them. It's hypocritical, I know, but there's no way to justify a midshipman sharing his quarters with her. If they're caught, we'll bail them out, but we'll cross that bridge if we come to it. Anastasia will berth with the rest of the women. The Scouts will be in regular crew quarters."

"Will they be ready by June to install a live system?" The general tapped the folder resting on his knee.

"I guess we'll see. The worst that happens is it isn't ready and they take notes to do an actual install the next summer. The midshipmen can perform their regular duty."

"And the lucky captain is?" the general asked with a rueful smile.

The president grimaced. "Captain Williams on the *USS Harry S. Truman*. Won't he be thrilled to receive these orders." The president rose and returned to the window. He spoke without turning to face the general. "In one more year I'm up for reelection. If I win, we might have enough time to get this magic under control somewhat— have the time to learn more and prepare. If I lose, I'll inform all heads of every branch of service. Again, it's hypocritical of me, but Team Valor is too powerful to be left to one man's use. I trust myself to not abuse that power, but I don't trust my opponent. I won't go public, but I will make it hard for him to use them for political gain or worse."

"You'll just have to win," the general said softly.

The president nodded.

"Well, it seems you have everything well in hand," the general said as he rose.

"For the moment, thank god." The president rose and shook the general's hand. "For the moment."

31

PERMISSION TO PROCEED

Major Nelson met with Team Valor to discuss the plans for Valor Industries. "I've spoken with the general, and you'll be hearing from official channels about your contracts, but I've been sent to fill you in." He passed around stacks of folders held together with thick rubber bands.

"Okay, first, your building will be built here on campus by next fall. The school will own it, Valor Industries will rent it. Second, you'll receive a contract for your security devices. Any changes to the design must be pre-approved if the changes affect the cost upward. I have here the complete specs for the *USS Harry S. Truman,* which all of you will be assigned to this summer. If you can have the devices ready, then you'll install them, if not, you'll work from there."

Major Nelson opened a new folder. "This

is a list of vendors who have clearance to supply the items you need. Pierce is lining up businesspeople for you. Everyone you hire for any position has to be vetted by him, excluding the midshipmen here and raid members."

He opened another folder. "We've already located office space for the office workers, but we'd like visits there to be kept to a minimum, make them come here to meet with you."

Major Nelson paused and folded his hands on the folder. "Pierce is trying to help, not control your company; you can change any of this except the security and confidentiality agreements. They'll be lawyers and contracts for all of this."

The major continued, "As for the finances you'll need, you'll be given access to eighty million dollars at very low interest rates. That money will be audited, so can't be used on magical supplies or research unless it's also used for the securities or other auditable items. You can use the money for supplies, employees, building rentals, or purchases— pretty much anything you want. You're free to develop whatever you like as long as the interest payments are made. You'll have eight years to show a profit or the loan will be canceled. The president is still working on funding for magic R-and-D. You'll receive a two-million-dollar grant that can be used for that. The president realizes you'll need a lot more, but for now that's what we have."

Sara rose her hand. "I have a few questions. What's your priority for us?"

"Magical R-and-D. As soon as possible make spell bracelets for the raid. Wristcomps, well, seven for now, but we require a few changes, the biggest one is design. Make them harder to remove. They also need to be clearly marked as official security devices just like the ones you're wearing now are. Next, we want smaller magic traps. Not ones big enough to contain all your magic, but enough to stop another, um, incident." He frowned at Sara a moment before clearing his throat and smiling around the table.

"I'm not sure that can be done, but we'll look into it," Oz promised.

"If you have time and money left, Oz can start on the new improved Scout uniforms," Major Nelson said. "If something else you think of would be better just let us know."

"And our game?" Hawk asked.

"Free to do whatever you like within the security and confidentiality constraints, of course. Security devices must be sold exclusively to the government for the time being. The proposed prices in this report are based on components and employee wages. If it isn't correct, you'll have to resubmit the bill with complete accounting on expenditures. Do that as soon as possible."

Major Nelson stood to go and waved the midshipmen to their seats as they made to rise. "This is a huge undertaking. It's okay if you decide you're not up for it. Ask for any help you need. Everyone wants this to succeed."

After the major left, they held a private meeting.

"So, what's the plan?" Hawk glanced from Sara to Oz.

"Once we get the components, I can handle the spell bracelets and wristcomps," Sara said.

Oz frowned and tipped back in the chair, putting his feet on the table. "I'm not sure how long it'll take to tool up to make them in bulk, and we'll need bulk."

"I have a suggestion," Charlie said. "Let's hire our parents as managers. They're trustworthy and fully informed; they make the perfect choice. My father would be perfect for getting the best contracts for the components we need. Stasia, your mom could work with Sara. She'll need help in her lab and Camila is a trained nurse. Oz's dad manages a small shop now and could be put in charge of fabrication of your specialty tools."

Hawk nodded, leaning forward eagerly. "I bet we could use some of the Scouts as well in Sara's lab. The more help we have, the more time we'll have for fun things like our game."

Stasia placed a hand on her brother's arm. "Don't forget the primary goal here. Valor Securities needs to run without any of us there. At any time a mission could arise that calls us away for indeterminate amounts of time. When we graduate, we could be assigned anywhere. Valor Industries needs to be able to function without us here. We should put Mister H in charge of the entire thing."

The chair screeched as Oz let his feet hit the floor with a loud thump. "Sounds good to me." He turned and grinned at Hawk. "And we should get the game platform going as soon as we can."

"We'll need at least three different divisions." Sara tapped her chin with one finger and closed her eyes deep in thought, then opened them and leaned forward. "John can run the security division. Oz will have to run the game division, at least until we find someone else we can all agree on, then we'll have research and development. My lab will have to be hidden in that accounting."

Sara turned to Charlie. "Maybe your mom could run that? She's been an accountant so long she must know some tricks to fool audits. Liz can run the actual lab. With Liz and Mrs. Morales and a Scout or two when needed, I'll have enough help, at least for a while."

"The divisions need to be separated both legally and financially," Sara went on. "The money from securities should go to employees and back into the company to expand it. The money from games goes to the raid and expansion. Both divisions should put some back into R-and-D."

"Fine, but we'll need four divisions," Oz said. "We'll be making other things not in securities that we can sell to the general public. Not at first, but we should plan for that."

Charlie rapped his knuckles on the table and waited until everyone faced him to speak. "We do this like we ran the guild. Officers agreements, then we pass it to the raid, which in this case is the Scouts. Then it goes to the guild in general, which in this case will be our employees."

Charlie waved the file in which Pierce had listed employee salaries. "We already know what our managers starting salary are. If everyone here agrees, I'll call my parents and offer them jobs."

"Beg them," Sara said with such sincerity Charlie laughed.

"None of us care about the money from that division, right?" He glanced around the table. Everyone nodded agreement. "Okay, we'll let my father decide then, he's managed a big company. We'll tell him we want the company's profits to go to the employees after all expenses and expansion. Oz and Sara will receive a salary from that division, but it won't be huge. The game division is where we'll make our money. We all know this will be enormous. Again, I say we pay our employees very well with Oz at the top then the raid. Give yourself a huge salary from that division Oz."

"I agree," Hawk said. "We can make money so many ways from that division none of us could spend that much. Oz needs enough of a salary to live on from the security's division though because it'll take a few years to get the games launched. We can live on our military pay. He'll have no income except that."

"I still receive my E-1 pay, but I assume that will stop when we go live with Valor Industries." Oz nodded at Hawk. "Assuming all of our parents agree," he paused and frowned at Stasia. "The parents will likely live with us, at least for a while. So, we won't have a guest room available for Rick."

Hawk patted his sister's hand and then gave her a quick hug. "There's no way Mom will be cool with Rick staying in your room, sis."

"Sucky, but not a big deal. I am super sneaky after all." Stasia snickered.

Oz laughed with her a moment. "And I'm sure my dad won't stay with us long. He'll want his own place. We'll have to put our head of security on finding him one."

"Who is that?" Sara asked.

"I was thinking Guthrie, if we can get him," Oz said. "We all trust him, and he knows everything already. He's in the raid so can use all our security devices and can hire who he pleases to fill any positions he deems necessary. We have a million dollars budgeted for our security this year. Let him handle the entire thing. If he agrees, I'll go over all of our plans with him and let him take over."

"Sounds good." Sara turned to Charlie. "Your parents can have our room. We'll move into one of the attic rooms."

Charlie grimaced. "I love my parents, but I don't want our bedroom over theirs."

"Fine, we'll take the downstairs guest room then."

"Don't be silly, let them have my room. I can take an attic room," Oz said.

Charlie smiled at Oz and took Sara's hand. "Appreciated, Oz, but we'll take the downstairs guest room. It's the farthest one from them."

Stasia flipped through the order for the *Truman*. "We have a ton of things to do."

Oz opened his copy and glanced through it. "I'll do my best to get this ready, but Sara and I are both working on our dissertations."

"Mines almost done," Sara said. "And I can handle all the setup, Oz. Take whatever time you need to finish yours. I'll even take over the midshipmen. I can show them the programming as well as you can."

Oz dropped the folder onto the table, a surprised expression on his face. "Really, you've solved the keytons without a magical element?"

"Solved with solid proof. It's actually a simple process similar to photosynthesis. The electrolytes need—."

Stasia interrupted. "While I'm sure that's fascinating and all..." She trailed off.

Sara laughed, "Just to us," she admitted. "What it means is I have more time than Oz right now."

Charlie stood. "Let's break for today. Everyone calls their parents and get them here as soon as we can if they agree. Valor Industries will pay for moving expenses. We'll aim to start production for the New Year."

By Christmas the house was crowded. The parents had agreed to work for Valor Industries and moved into the house. Charlie's father had been busy lining up suppliers and hiring all month. Sara and Oz spent all their time in meetings of one type or another. By December twenty-ninth Valor Industries was an official company with a three-million-dollar contract for the *Truman* and two years to install the new systems. If it went well, they'd receive another contract to do more of the fleet.

32

THE FIRST BOARD MEETING

Valor Industries held its first board meeting January first. Oz had a slide show prepared to show them what changes he had in mind for their gear.

"We want everyone to have extra magic on them." Oz indicated the flexible tubes they were now using instead of the metal ones Sara filled with her and Charlie's magic. "You'll be given at least two of these spell bracelets, which, per your suggestions, have undergone extensive modifications.

"Sara can recharge the bracelets if she has magic available. So everyone needs to carry extra magic. I've designed these collapsible rods for us. One end is a high-powered Taser, the other a standard flashlight. The center will hold enough magic to resupply a white bracelet. A quick connect like the one in the cuff of your sleeve will be on the interior of the small side pocket above the ring for the Taser. It's meant to be used if Sara can't reach you. Using the quick connect will slow the cast time of your spells by approximately four point eight seconds because the magic has to travel through the tubing to your wrist cuff. The Tasers can also be opened and used as a staff for spells that require a staff but can't be used while connected. So only use the magic from the cuffs themselves to cast spells that require a staff or be prepared to hold the staff extremely awkwardly so it doesn't lose its connection.

"We want to send a supply of Charlie's magic with each of you as well. His magic will be weaker, about half strength, figure four spells max in the same space that holds eight of Sara's. In almost every scenario we've ran that lasted more than ten minutes we've determined having eight spells instead of four quadruples your effectiveness. So the backup canister would need to be bigger, or two canisters. We really don't have a plan for that yet, so anyone with any ideas speak up. Ideally, it would have another obvious use like the taser light."

Sara took over the presentation, standing and changing the picture on the screen. "Because we're weak against sedatives our clothing must be resistant if not impervious to darts. We'll be changing all our gear as time and money permit, starting with us five. As you can see, no skin will be exposed anywhere in our combat clothes."

Pictures of the proposed new gear flickered across the screen. The original bulky cuff that was the spell bracelet had been replaced with a much more streamlined one. Flexible tubing meant to resemble trim work attached magnetically to the sleeves. Three panels that appeared to be thick armor but were hollow reservoirs for magic covered the breastplates. Sara tapped the left breast and zoomed in.

"This is actually a gel filled fabric that should self-seal if pierced by a bullet. It offers minimum protection from bullets. The idea is for the gel to stop the escape of Charlie's magic. A magical shield will work better than any armor on the market. If you run out of magic, or think the magic in the piping on the sleeves will be enough, you can remove this armor and replace it with one from your pack that looks identical but is composed of real armor. Both the gel fabric and the armor are impervious to even high velocity darts. The underlay is the same material as the rest of the uniform and should stop needles and knives. If we do somehow get sedated though, the wristcomps will notify all others."

Oz interrupted. "If the panic button is tripped on one, all of them will instantly link and your combat HUD will activate. Anyone with a wristcomp will have all relevant data, including location and condition and, of course, who hit the button. It'll also immediately open a voice line with all wristcomps. Keep the line as clear as possible. We don't want a babble no one can hear."

Guthrie interrupted him. "When we receive the wristcomps, we'll be practicing and running drills." He nodded at Oz to continue.

Charlie cleared his throat. "Sara quit the raid and was able to be invited back with no loss of magic. Since then, we've moved everyone around to different parties within the raid with no loss of magic. That means we can use empty group six to summon individually.

Oz held his hand up to quell the excited talk and took over the presentation. "Major Nelson has been working with the team leaders on scenarios, and when everyone receives a bracelet we'll be practicing and running drills. When planning pay special attention to getting Sara to everyone to recharge the bracelets during fights. She can be pulled from group-to-group or summoned then summoned back. To optimize will take planning and organization. As Charlie said, we can now summon all or any of us using the white bracelets and the empty slots in group six."

Sara pointed to the blue bracelet. "You're most important spell for that one will be Spell-Steal. Everyone needs to practice that. You could steal Stasia's invisible or use Hawk's air bubble or Oz's polymorph or fireball. To use it to the best advantage will require a lot of planning."

Drew laughed and rubbed his hands together. "This is going to rock. I can't wait to throw twenty fireballs at once."

Sara opened a cardboard carton and handed out much smaller cuffs than the original prototypes. "These bracelets are dummies to practice putting on. You'll need to be fast. We have three methods of application and want feedback on which you prefer. One of which I don't like as it's very slow. That's the buckled one; it does have the advantage of pre-application and secure fastenings. All the pros and cons need to be weighed. We have another one here that's good but can be accidentally engaged. Not a huge problem, but it is uncomfortable to engage them."

She demonstrated the band that she applied to her arm then slapped down. "It does take a pretty firm hit to engage it and has the benefit of being able to be pre-applied but it's slower to remove to exchange for a blue one then the next model. This method is a bit tricky, but if you apply it fast and correctly, it works well." A stiff piece of plastic with very small metal pins on the flat side conformed to her wrist as she slapped it down hard. "Once applied, the connection to the magic canisters takes mere seconds. Both ports are magnetized so a flick from your thumb is all that's needed if it doesn't catch on its own. But weigh the advantages and disadvantages and let us know by the end of next week for the final design."

"Sara and I are working on smart bullets using magic, and we have some theories on a shield, but it'll be a while before we have time to work on it." Oz appraised his Scouts. "Do any of you have any ideas you want us to work on?"

Joy rose her hand. "Can you make a rogue bracelet?"

Sara's nervousness made Charlie take her hand for a moment.

She said, "In theory I could, but I don't want to touch anyone else's magic, so I won't try. Oz has a remove magic spell, but can't store it, at least not yet. So, he hasn't tried to take any magic from us. We don't want to become any more magically entangled.

Brenda leaned forward and tapped a bracelet laying on the table. "Is using all your magic this way hurting you or making you weaker?"

"Doesn't seem to be," Sara said. "As far as I can tell it works just like when I cast a spell. Unlike a stasis chamber, I regenerate it when I place it in a rod. It's casted magic, not captured magic. Keep in mind we have no idea how the bracelets will affect you long term. In the short term, I'll heal everyone after using them and dispel the m-radiation. I don't think you're in any physical danger, but there's a chance you could become magically addicted. Inform us at once of any side effects."

Oz turned to Major Nelson. "That being said, we think it'd be a good idea for some of you not to use them at all unless it's an emergency, a control group, but everyone should keep exposure to a minimum until we have a better handle on this. Sara and I'd hate to hurt any of you in any way."

Brenda picked up the bracelet and slapped it on her arm. "We understand the risks. No one here will blame you. Everyone realizes this is experimental with unknown dangers. The contract we signed to work here specifically states that we understand and accept the risks of working with experimental technology."

Charlie frowned at Sara's twinge of guilt. Her guilt deepened when she glanced at him, and he sighed in exasperation. Her emotions fluctuated wildly as she tried to hide them. Or maybe change them. Charlie wasn't sure what she felt now about anything. He took the folder from her hand and placed it on the table, then took both her hands after signing to Hawk to continue the meeting.

"Sarge will head our security," Hawk said. "Major Nelson is still in charge of raids, same as before. Everyone is free to come and go to our workspace as you like, and Sara will need some of you as guinea pigs. If you want to volunteer for that see Major Harris, she'll be running Sara's lab. The reason I mention it is that you'll need excuses to be there if questioned, so everyone will be learning to run, install, and program the security systems."

While Hawk spoke, Sara's emotions steadied. She was only a bit nervous when Charlie released her hands. He still didn't know if she was afraid of upsetting him or worried about setting up Valor Industries, but she was handling it.

He was excited, but then again, he wouldn't be doing much either. She glanced at him and frowned as his worry spiked. Running a major corporation wouldn't be easy and her stress was already high. He probably should've talked them out of this. His worry morphed to guilt. He hadn't even tried to talk her out of it. He liked the idea of her being too busy to miss him.

Sara flicked him a worried glance but reached into her carton and pulled out notebooks that she passed around. "Classes for that start this week. The contract we signed with the government specifies we get exclusive use of you. Actually, we can have as many as one hundred service personnel assigned to us to use as we see fit. We get to decide everything from training to where you're stationed. In reality, General Campbell will still be setting your missions, and Major Nelson will be in charge of your training. With our input, of course. There's copies of our contracts in here for you to see."

"Does anyone have any questions for us?" Charlie asked.

"Can Sara recharge a bracelet directly or does she need the magic containers?" Drew asked.

"I can do it directly, but it uses my magic,

so it isn't unlimited. To refill Charlie's bracelets, Charlie and I would both need to be right by the bracelet, or rage potion, which is what we call his storage containers. It takes me one minute and two seconds to do it with a thirty second cool-down. The spell is channeled so I can't move and do it and while Charlie can call his magic out and make it easier for me to harvest it, it's not as easy as it sounds and sometimes he can't at all. And while I can rip magic from them, it hurts them for me to do it and it slows their magic regeneration."

"I'm pretty sure I could call my magic out for her in battle," Charlie said. "The magic comes easiest when Sara needs me. We can't fake it though. I can't just tell myself she needs me. I really have to feel her need."

"We'll have to practice." Sara rubbed her eyes a moment. "So, the answer is yes, I can recharge mine, maybe I can recharge Charlie's."

"We'll have to time how many you can recharge before you need a rest and how long the rest needs to be before you can cast again," Brenda said.

Charlie felt Sara nervousness and this time knew the cause; they'd talked about this privately and he knew she didn't want to do that and why. "Sara doesn't want to run her magic that far down, for a while anyway. She's timed how much she can place in magic rods until she starts to feel depleted, it'll have to do for now."

"Are you still having issues from this summer?" Major Nelson sat back and narrowed his eyes at her.

"No, I'm fine, but I want to keep it that way. You have no idea how scary that was for me, to be so out of control. That mistake will haunt me the rest of my life. I won't do anything that would bring about a repeat. But the magic does want a warrior. I feel its want every time we meet. Making myself weak might make it as desperate as it was, so I'm being careful."

Major Nelson frowned, his frown smoothing when Charlie glared at him.

Charlie took Sara's hand and placed it on his wrist so she could feel his pulse. Just talking of last summer upset her and speaking of making a warrior excited her magic. The conflicting emotions were strong enough that he realized they had different sources. He placed his glowing hand on her cheek.

Stasia flicked them a glance but rose to give her presentation. "Okay, one last thing to cover," Stasia said as she changed the picture on the screen. "Raid positions. Just like in a guild there are members who raid and some just hang out in the guild. Raiders get perks that non-raiders don't. That's true for Valor Industries as well. Right now, we have seven empty raid spots. Mr. and Mrs. Hayes have left the raid. All raiders will have a bank account that is totally theirs. If they die or quit or are removed from the raid, a new account will be opened for their replacement and no further money will be added to theirs. It's your money, do whatever you want with it, but just like in the game come prepared to raid. That means gear repaired, the best weapons you can afford, back up gear and specialized gear. We'll supply the potions. We're going to be running this entire thing like we did our guild, loot rules and all. That means high performers or people in key positions get the good gear first. We don't expect to have any money in the accounts for a while, but we do expect it to happen."

Stasia turned to Major Nelson. "We do have a request in regard to the empty raid slots. The magic seeks companionship. If we do eventually turn our Scouts, they might want a magical companion. We don't know if it always has to be a sexual relationship, two examples aren't enough to give a good analysis, but we think it's likely because the magic manifests when you feel lust and love. The raid is unbalanced right now with more men than women. I really think we need to save those spots for future mates."

Liz cleared her throat and stood. "All of you need to think about that and its repercussions. If Sara changes you, well, it's likely you'll eventually desire someone with magic of their own. It'll severely limit your choice for partners. No one who can't pass a security clearance check will even be considered. We want everyone who receives magic to be in the raid as well, at least at present. Really think about this hard. Charlie and Sara cannot be parted. It would be unfair to pick a spouse who'd be unhappy going to battle because they'd have to at least be in the zone. Charlie and Sara feel each other's emotions. If you're changed and pick a magical mate that might happen to you. That means if you're walking down the street with your mate and are sexually attracted to someone you pass, they'll know it. They'll know if you lie and your most intimate feelings. You'll never be able to say 'no, honey, that dress doesn't make your butt look big.' It's a really big deal. With a magical spouse, you'll be completely and irrevocably married. I wouldn't do it, and I expect most of you would choose not to. Oz and Hawk seem to be managing staying single well. So maybe this desire for the magic to mingle is only when you feel love, but we don't know that."

She took a breath and scanned the Scouts. "Sara didn't mean to try to change anyone, but she almost did, and it could happen again. She could stop the process but maybe if it had progressed farther she wouldn't have been able too. So please, think about this. We don't want decisions made in haste." Liz sat and folded her hands.

"I'll speak with the general," Major Nelson said. "Temporary raid members are an option as well. If any of you Scouts wants out, there would be positions outside of raiding available. I'm sure Valor Industries will have spots for people already in the know to work where you could lead a more normal life. The risks in this position continue to grow. Think about this carefully. We'll be reforming the teams again. Alpha will be made up of raiders willing to undergo the change and assigned near Sara just in case. Beta will be doing more away missions. Both teams will still be using the new gear and gadgets Oz and Sara make with all the risk that entails."

"Oh, one more thing worth noting," Liz said. "If you do plan to leave the raid and take a position in civilian life, you'll lose your buffs, including the intelligence buff, but you won't forget anything you've learned, you'll just revert to learning at a more normal rate. So, take advantage of your buffs while you have them."

Charlie and Sara walked home together after the meeting. Sara leaned into his side, and he was amazed as always how simply being with him made her happier.

"You were really nervous in the meeting. If this is too much, we don't have to do it," Charlie said.

Sara shrugged. "You don't have to do it, but Oz and I do. We need money to research and this is the best way to get it."

He narrowed his eyes when she felt guilty and nervous. "What?"

To his surprise she giggled. "We could steal what we need. We talked about it. It'd be so much easier."

Charlie snorted with laughter.

Her amusement fled, replaced by a low-level aggravation. "It's not funny, I really wanted too." Her aggravation faded to guilt. "I still want too."

She laughed when he grew alarmed.

"Don't worry, we won't. The rest of the world will already hate us so much when they find out about us—"

Charlie silenced her with a kiss. "No one knows. You're perfectly safe."

She rested in his arms but felt uneasy.

"For now. And Oz and I have some ideas to make us safer, but we need time. We need Valor Industries to be successful and well respected. Someday, when we do manage to make heals available to everyone, we need the public to be using and liking our products— to know and trust us. Then, when they find out the truth, maybe they won't turn their backs but be accepting."

"You've really been planning this," Charlie said in approval.

"Oz and I have been running scenarios on his new computer. I don't think anyone else realizes how much our mere existence will change the world. If we don't prepare, it could precipitate World War Three.

Charlie stopped walking." Your serious?"

When she nodded, he frowned. "Maybe we should rethink making a heal available then. As much as I'd like to help everyone, it isn't worth a world war."

"It's too late. Our secret is bound to get out. To many people know. Our only hope is to prove we aren't dangerous."

"What do you mean too late?"

"Charlie…" Sara half-laughed and tugged him forward. "Try to remember what it was like before this happened to us. Imagine you're a normal human man and found out about five aliens living on Earth who have superpowers. We can deny we're alien all we want but we're too different to be considered human anymore. Wouldn't you be terrified? It'll be obvious the government knew and covered it up. But we can truthfully say we were trying to help, that keeping our secret wasn't for selfish gain but to prevent panic while we learned. If we have a heal to offer them, it'll be much easier."

"I see," Charlie said thoughtfully. He thought about what she'd said for a few minutes and realized he'd never really considered the big picture. He was concerned on a personal level while she was thinking globally.

"It's a good thing you're a friggin genius," he muttered, and she laughed.

"I like the research. It isn't a hardship. You don't need to be so worried."

"Running a business is a full-time job. I was worried the stress would be too much for you, and now this… How will you have time to research?"

That's why we got your dad. Oz and I already spoke to him. We're in charge of our labs, and he's doing everything else. I invited him back to the raid and he accepted for the intelligence buff. He says he'll quit again once Valor is running smoothly. Oz and I will help get things going before returning to research. The security system is simple really. It's the power sources that we need to work on, but we can power them the old-fashioned way until ours is ready."

"You're sure the new security system is ready? It seems awful fast to me."

"It's just programming. If you're asking if the new computers work than the answer is yes. I admit, the leap from microchip to crystalis is huge but it makes perfect sense. The leap from transistors to microchips was huge and world changing too. Our energy source will be another giant leap forward."

"I read Oz's notes on his ideas for transportation. I can't wait to see them," Charlie said with real enthusiasm.

Sara hesitated at the gate, and Charlie followed her glance to their well-lit house. A sense of peaceful contentment settled on her, and he grinned. He liked coming home to a full house too.

"I really hope Camila stays a while," he said.

"Me too, but everything moves so fast for us. The election next year could change everything."

She said it so worriedly he stopped to hug her again.

"We can worry about it if it happens. Once we're older and done training, our lives will settle down." Charlie gave her a quick squeeze and released her.

"Where do you want to settle down? We could set up shop anywhere."

"Honestly, it doesn't matter to me. My home is where you are. I just assumed I'd be assigned somewhere, and you would come too, but now, with all this, it's more complicated. Assignments don't generally last years, and you can't move the entire company every time I move."

"True, but I can cyber commute and go with you. Most of my research can be done long distance. I'd need to set up experiments, but someone else can send me results to study. And if I need to, I'll just move my lab around."

"Your career should take precedence, it's more important than mine."

"I can do it anywhere. If I need to stay in one spot, I'll tell you. Besides, I have a pilot license now and can take myself where I need to be."

She'd been more worried over the election than moving around and he relaxed. President Carmichael was well-liked, and he was happy to let housing worries go. "On my next break, I want to learn how too," Charlie said.

"I'm learning helicopters now. It's really fun. Brenda is teaching me," Sara said with enthusiasm. "Poor, Charlie, I'm having more fun than you are now."

"True, but I don't mind. I'm glad you're happy." He kissed her cheek. Now that they saw each other every day she was so much happier he realized how very unhappy she'd been. He wished he had more time to do other things, but his time was still very limited with school.

Sara had stopped going completely except for exams. She did the homework and papers and had special permissions for lab work and already had a bunch of papers published in different medical and scientific journals. This May she'd graduate with a double doctorate. One in medicine and the other in languages. The diploma meant nothing to her, the knowledge meant everything. It seemed like the more she learned the more she craved it. Every idea and insight she and Oz had seemed to lead to ten additional ones, each more brilliant than the last.

Both she and Oz spent hours reading, then hours more contemplating what they'd read. Since being published, calls came in with greater and greater frequency asking for their opinions and advice. They'd need a secretary soon to field them.

She spent her days doing things that interested her. He spent his following orders. He smiled wryly. Soon, he'd be the one giving orders, doing things that interested him, he just needed patience. Most of his classes were ridiculously easy. His physics classes were still challenging and interesting and he loved his political science class. Sara had sat in on a few then filled their bedroom with textbooks for a month, but she was over it now.

At the moment astronomy books filled their bedroom, but he was sure that would change in a week or so.

One of the things he loved about her was she never tried to show off how smart she was. He was sure she not only understood all his classwork but could do it while writing an essay on geo-economics in Sanskrit, but she never tried to make him feel inferior about it. She'd help if he asked, but never offered. Even pre-magic she'd been like that.

When they'd raided together, she'd never

criticized other priests who weren't as good, she'd always complimented and offered help only if asked.

As he watched her put on his t-shirt to sleep in, he was overcome with how lucky he was to have her. This beautiful, brilliant girl loved him. A dazzling smile lit her face and she dropped the shirt and held out her hand.

Two hours later, he was starving and went to raid the refrigerator, leaving Sara sound asleep.

"Meeting went well?" His father glanced up and then returned his attention to the sandwich fixings on the counter.

Charlie blushed and busied himself at the counter, turning his back so his father wouldn't notice. He found meetings like this at night very awkward. It wasn't like his parents didn't know they had sex but having sex in the same house as them was weird. "Yep, is everything at the office good?"

"Smooth as silk. The people Pierce Taylor sent us are working out great so far." His father handed him the mustard.

Charlie nodded his thanks and slathered the mustard on his ham sandwich. "Sara will need a personal secretary soon. Mostly to screen calls for her. A Valory believes everything it's told and can't weed out the nuisance calls. Do we have anyone available for that? Oz could probably use the same one for the time being."

"I'll find them one," his father said agreeably and poured a cup of tea. "Sara seems much better, but I'll admit she's still hard for me to read."

"She's better, completely recovered from her lack of magic. She's still dealing with what happened because of it, but she and Stasia are much better now too."

John sat at the kitchen island, quietly drinking his tea. "Your mother had a miscarriage once," he finally said. "It devastated her, and she's still sometimes sad about what might've been. Out of the blue she'll say things like 'our first child would've been twenty-three today,' or 'I wonder if she would've resembled the boys.' She'll cry or laugh, but I doubt she'll ever forget or get over it. I feel bad admitting this, but it really didn't upset me that much. We hadn't known she was pregnant for very long and that baby never seemed real to me. I was more upset that your mother was so upset."

"She never mentioned it." Charlie sat beside his father, placing his plate of sandwiches, soda, and a bag of chips in front of him. "It's a weird thought that I should have another sibling."

"Don't mention it to her either. She only

speaks to me about it. I'm telling you because we see how upset Sara is about this. About two years after your mother's miscarriage she'd see a baby and burst into tears. That stopped after Richard was born healthy, but that was a bad time in our marriage. I wasn't as patient or understanding as I should've been. Now I regret that a lot. I wasn't mean, just..." He shrugged. "I wasn't hurting about it and thought she was being overly emotional. A miscarriage in the first trimester is common. To me it wasn't that big of a deal. Sad, yes, but not heartbreaking. To her, well, it was heartbreaking, and I was too young and stupid to see it." John stood. "I find myself a bit overemotional myself as I get older." He placed his dirty cup in the dishwasher. "I wonder now sometimes if she would've had your mother's eyes," he said as he walked away.

Charlie finished his sandwich and cleaned up the kitchen, thinking about what his father had said. He was back in bed and almost asleep before he wondered why he'd said it.

33

THE TRUMAN

Charlie lifted Sara from the helicopter onto the deck of the ship. The dark-blue pencil skirt she wore made climbing out herself impossible. Wind from the rotors caught wisps of her blond hair, disarranging them, and she reached up one manicured hand to smooth them back into the braided bun on the nape of her neck. The other hand clutched the handle of a large box.

Brenda handed out a stack of boxes and both of their duffel bags to Charlie.

Oz followed, wearing a dark-blue business suit, his shoulder-length blond hair caught in a ponytail on his neck. Brenda handed him his duffel bag and another stack of cardboard boxes.

Stasia and Hawk jumped to the deck and Brenda passed them their duffels. Five more midshipmen got off and took their own bags. Brenda passed down more boxes.

Another helicopter, flown by Drew, was unloading right next to them. Before long a mountain of boxes teetered around them.

The officer of the deck approached and greeted Sara and Oz. "Doctor Mitchel, Doctor Simmons, Captain Williams sends his regards and invites you to join him for a short tour of the ship. I'll assure the boxes are stowed." He eyed the growing heap with a raised eyebrow.

"Thank you," Sara said. "Fit as many boxes with my initials in my room as you can, please. And make sure they're kept secure. I assume our other supplies are on board already?"

"Yes, in cargo hold four, ma'am. Anyone can show you the way there."

"No need, I know the way, but thank you." Sara gave Charlie a smile, and Stasia and Hawk a wink, and followed the officer. Charlie took Oz's duffle bag, leaving him carrying a much smaller bag over his shoulder.

Doctors Mitchel and Simmons met the captain in his office. Captain Williams shook both of their hands but eyed them doubtfully. "So, you're my new security team."

The two doctors didn't appear to be old enough to have one doctorate between them, never mind four. They appeared to be teenagers who'd worn their best clothes for a trip they were excited about. Their eyes were bright and gazes active as they examined his ship.

"Yes, sir," Dr. Simmons said. "As soon as we unpack we can show you a demonstration."

The captain had reservations, but orders were orders and he'd been ordered to be welcoming. Someone with real pull had arranged their stay and he'd been told in no uncertain terms that the doctors were to be treated with respect or heads would roll. So he smiled politely as he said, "I've seen the reports, and it looks impressive— if it works."

The doctors exchanged glances the captain couldn't read.

Dr. Simmons winced and said, "Thank you, sir."

"I thought you might like a short tour, and I'll introduce you to my officers."

Captain Williams led them from the room and showed them where the cafeteria and the infirmary were. When they reached their rooms, he pointed them out, but didn't stop. Sailors made way, huddling against bulkheads as they passed.

On the bridge, Captain Williams introduced the officers.

"We've seen pictures and video and even built a mockup, but this is more impressive in person," Dr. Mitchel said as they toured the room.

A forty something man, fit, with jet-black hair, entered and saluted.

"Commander Carmin, my Xo." Captain Williams smiled and slapped his commander on the back.

Both doctors shook his hand.

"We're looking forward to a demonstration," Commander Carmin said.

Hands on her hips and lips pursed, Dr. Mitchel peered around the room. "The plan was to install our system here by your existing one. We have the exact measurements of this room, of course, but not where the people stand. Is this a pretty typical representation?"

Captain William's glanced around and nodded. "It is."

Dr. Mitchel flicked her wrist and a glowing panel opened in front of her. "*Truman* bridge, quarter size." A holographic simulation of the bridge formed in front of her. The watching crew talked excitedly amongst themselves, some stepping closer to examine it.

Wrist out held she paced the room, stopping on the other side. "Half size," she said, and the hologram doubled in size. "*Truman* engine room twenty-seven B." The picture changed to show the room. "This might be better positioning. Most of you could view it without leaving your posts from here." Dr. Mitchel turned to the captain. "We'll need your input."

Captain Williams leaned over her shoulder and put his hand through the picture. She put hers in and twisted the angle, giving them a different view. "This is just a replica. We'll put yours in real-time. You'll be able to see everything in the room as it was one-point-two seconds ago. We're working on the lag; it's mostly a server issue."

"This looks cool and all, but how is it better than cameras?" Captain Williams asked.

"The operating system is smart. I can ask it what I want to see. I don't need to scroll through the pictures myself. Also, it's small." She handed him a black shiny device about the size of a nickel, rounded with one flat side. "This sensor can monitor and transmit video, audio, heat, light, radiation, humidity, and temperature. If you require another measurement of some kind, I'm sure we can make something. The sensor will connect wirelessly to the rest of the system. The battery should last two years. Then the sensor would be replaced with a new one. Hopefully, by then, we've mastered the power issues and can install more permanent versions."

She flipped the sensor over to show him paper coating the back, pulling the paper away to reveal the adhesive coating.

"The sensors are super easy to install and if anyone messes with one, the system notifies you. If you place these in a secure location, they can be set to administer a shock. The one's designated for crew quarters, bathrooms, and the infirmary will be somewhat different in that they'll flash green to give warning when they breach privacy. That way your crew has privacy, but you could still see in if you needed to for a fire or flood or fight."

A blue screen appeared before Dr. Simmons. "We also made a few things we want to test. This is live; we dropped it on our way here." He tapped the screen and the hologram of the engine room changed to an ocean view.

"What is that?" The captain leaned

forward, peering at the gray-black circle with weird waving round something's in the holograph.

"I have no idea," Dr. Simmons admitted. "I can give you coordinates to where it is. And tell you the temperature, radiation, and all the stuff Sara mentioned, but I don't know what that is."

"Looks like a sea anemone to me." Dr. Mitchel leaned forward, examining the image. "That's definitely a sword fish. Can you raise it, Oz?"

Dr. Simmons reached out and pinched the little white speck in the circle of darkness with weird swirling somethings and the giant fish and pulled his fingers up. The fish disappeared, and the black got grayer, but they couldn't identify anything.

"Give it a ping, Oz. Let's check if we can see it from here." She leaned over the radar man's shoulder.

"Sound one ping," Dr. Simmons said.

Captain Williams watched the radar screen with interest.

"Got it, give me two." Dr. Mitchel flicked her wrist, and a screen popped up in front her. She slid it to the side with a fingertip and made a note.

"Sound two pings," Dr. Simmons said.

Dr. Mitchel peered at the two circles on

the radar screens and then glanced at the display in front of Dr. Simmons. Another wrist flick and another screen opened in front her. She frowned in concentration and tapped on air for a few moments, hitting barely visible keys that appeared to float before her. "Okay, it sees the fish under it still. Give us a flash."

Dr. Simmons made the sensor flash and opened a small screen before him. Captain Williams made a soft surprised sound when a three-inch winged woman appeared and fluttered beside the screen. White wings seemed to gust loose strands of hair about the tiny figure's pale face. It wore a white gown and carried a glowing white sword that transformed to a glowing stylus as he watched. It looked solid enough to touch and when he leaned closer he could see a shadow beneath its feet when it perched on the edge of the floating screen.

Dr. Simmons said, "Monitor this. I want a full report on what you think each sound is and why." The tiny fluttering figure punched keys a moment and then opened a new screen before the doctor. The figure saluted and sat cross legged, floating in the air before the monitor.

Dr Simmons said, "A lot of research will be needed to identify these sounds. Valory is telling me the probability of it being all natural is sixty-nine percent. That's a crap number, we need much better intel. But look, we attracted some fish."

Dr. Mitchel said, "What's the power readout on that? I'm showing multiple life signs, all small. Can we up the gain there?" Dr. Mitchel's fingers flew over the virtual keyboard and images scrolled over the screen in front of her. In moments three screens were in front of her displaying different graphs.

"Excuse me," Captain Williams interrupted, and both doctors flushed when they turned from their screens.

"Sorry, got carried away there. We've been dying to test those." Dr. Mitchel straightened and turned her screens off with a flick of her finger.

"That was a mile out at twenty fathoms?" The captain asked.

"Yes, it needs a lot more work." Dr. Simmons turned to Dr. Mitchel. "Infrared, we could do that, but we need to narrow down those noises."

"How is it transmitting this far?" Captain Williams asked.

"Water is conductive," Dr. Simmons said absently as he made notes with his virtual keyboard. "Transmissions are limited by programming, not power. The ocean supplies unlimited power. The movement of the water is enough for what we just did, but what we just did was crap. We want to really see what's around it or at least know, not guess. Sixty-eight percent," he finished in disgust.

Dr. Mitchel laughed. "We'll get better. That's the first attempt after all." A glance at her wristcomp was followed by one to the captain. "I don't know if we should bring it in or not. How fast are we going in what direction?"

He told her, and she turned to Dr. Simmons. "Leave it. Let's make some recordings and we'll call it in in a few days."

"The water can power it for days?" the captain asked in amazement.

Dr. Simmons said, "The water can power it indefinitely. The motor inside the buoy uses the kinetic energy of the water itself that the small panels on the outside harvest. It isn't very fast except for short bursts but we're working on batteries. Right now we have to dump the excess power those burst generate as we have no way to store it."

Dr. Mitchel said, "All movement not only takes energy but produces friction. Friction produces its own sort of energy that we can harness but we can't store it. So the buoy gathers what it needs and then the computer turns off the receptors. One of the things we're testing is the accuracy of the computer. Because water movement is completely random— the water temperature, consistency and motion all fluctuate, the computer has to estimate the power gains and balance them to the expenditures. The programming needed for that is complicated and needs more research."

She opened another screen and showed him a schematic.

"The motor itself is simple. Once we master the energy storage issues we can apply that to bigger motors that could power much bigger vehicles than this buoy."

"Is it dangerous? "Commander Carmin asked.

"Not at the size we're testing. We could blow the buoy up but the power it contains would release relatively slowly, about the equivalent of a quarter stick of dynamite. So while it could cause damage, at that depth and distance it's unlikely to harm anything at all. Valory monitors it continuously and will notify us instantly if the specs change from our parameters."

Dr. Simmons pointed to his screen. "See that jitter? We need to find out what's causing that. I'm betting it's the nitrous core. This water is colder than—"

Dr. Mitchel interrupted. "Later, Oz. We're being rude." A slight blush on her cheeks, she smiled at the captain and began closing her screens by tapping the top right corner. "Sorry, where were we? Oh, yes, your internal security. The sensors are only one step. The programming, the operating system of the new computer is what makes the system so good. It's smart, real smart, and can recognize sketchy behavior and flag it for inspection."

Dr. Simmons gestured to the fluttering figure, "Meet Valory, the operating system."

The captain took a quick step back when the figure suddenly became life size.

"It's a pleasure to meet you, Captain. I'm a Valkyrie 1.6 and capable of multiple tasks at once. I've been programed to monitor the security on this ship and assist you in way I can."

"That's, ah, nice…" The captain eyed the image doubtfully. It looked slightly cartoonish with brightly glowing white eyes, sharply pointed ears and the flowing hair.

Dr. Simmons said, "You can set Valory's appearance and size and program it with simple voice commands. For instance, say there's a locker I use every day in a monitored space. Valory would know I do and would flag it for review if someone else did. If someone lingers too long, it'll flag that too. You can set it to flag for almost anything you want. Say you have a compartment only one hundred people have access to, tell it who they are and if anyone else enters or tries to, it'll flag that. Large groups of people too close together will flag an alert. Loud voices, cursing, screaming will all flag alerts. But that stuff is minor. This is a fighting ship, the outside and the deck of the ship is where you need security."

Dr. Mitchel took up the explanation, looking excited. "The sensors will show you every square inch of the deck and hull in real-time and Valory has been programed to continuously monitor those results. It will inform you of any changes that it deems significant."

"I can show you my programmed parameters," Valory added. "Getting information is as simple as requesting me to look for whatever you wish."

Dr. Simmons handed the captain a sensor from the bag he carried. This sensor was much bigger than the others, the size of a small pizza, and formed of thick, cloudy-blue, glass-like material.

"With these hull sensors you'll be able to see almost a mile out in the water. Air is harder. We've developed a great program to identify and target threats, the problem is it's slow and short sighted. At the speed of the fastest incoming missiles and the distance the sensor can see, the math says it can destroy the missile, but with less than two seconds to spare. I'm not happy with that, we need to give it glasses somehow to show them coming further away. Ideally, I want two shots to knock out any missile. As it is, missiles will blowup ten feet off the deck."

"Wait, what?" Captain Williams said in surprise. "I wasn't informed you'll be installing any weapons."

"We just made this. It's a prototype and we only have one at the moment and need to test it," Dr. Mitchel said. "I'm sure you'll receive orders once it passes the committee. It's good science, it will pass. For now, all we need is a boat to mount it on and missiles to shoot at it, but no hurry, there's plenty to do while we wait for permission."

Dr. Simmons smiled crookedly and smoothed his suit jacket. "I brought computer generated simulations, and I can show you the math."

"I'm interested to see it." Captain Williams quirked an eyebrow at his XO. "The, um, buoy you were using earlier, that was an actual picture?"

"Yes." Dr. Simmons nodded and opened

the picture again.

"And you can move it around— send out pings and lights?"

"Pings, lights, any audio we want," Dr. Simmons agreed. "What I want it to do is search for incoming submarines and torpedoes and any potentially dangerous shoals or obstructions. We're still working on how to stop an attack. The ray gun won't work well underwater."

"So far, the only thing we have to stop a torpedo is the buoy itself," Sara admitted. "And it's too slow, so we need at least a double ring around the entire ship. The outer ring sees it and sends an inner ring buoy to intercept, but even that won't be really practical until we master the battery power." Sara frowned. "We might be barking up the wrong tree here, trying to use the buoys this way. I think we need a better ray gun."

"It's all crap though, it's to chance related. Sixty percent chance is just poop," Dr. Simmons finished.

"So, the buoys aren't part of the security you plan to install? None were on the plans you sent," Captain Williams said.

"The buoys are new as well and not ready, but we received permission to test them. You should've been notified." Dr. Mitchel frowned and flicked her finger.

"Valory, find me the emails pertaining to the buoy's testing," she said to the tiny fluttering figure that appeared.

The Valkyrie saluted and disappeared.

"I was informed you'll be testing an unnamed, unspecified, device in the water and would require a small boat," the captain said.

"We'll that's it." Dr. Mitchel pointed to the hologram still floating in front of Dr. Simmons. "It's unnamed because we haven't named it yet. It needs a lot more work to be useful. I'm afraid you're stuck with the hull sensors for now. They'll tell you all particulars about the condition of your hull, but they can't stop damage."

"The goal is to make this ship as secure as we can," Dr. Simmons said. "To see the damage is helpful, but stopping it is secure."

"How vulnerable is this security system to hacking?" Commander Carmin asked.

Dr. Simmons said, "As secure as I can make it, which is much more than a conventional computer. The sensors can't be reprogrammed without both a code and the correct computer and any reprogramming is sent to the main terminal, in this case on your bridge. Enter the wrong code or use the wrong computer and the sensor is FUBAR. If a sensor is moved after being placed and activated, it'll just broadcast its location, nothing else, all other programming will be wiped. If the shell is broken, the device will cease to function, but the shell is extremely durable. Someone would actively have to try to break it. A fire wouldn't be enough to do it; they have a class 350 rating. You should still be able to use the sensors in rooms on fire or full of smoke."

Dr. Simmons replaced the bigger sensor in his bag as he spoke and pulled out one of the small ones from his pocket. He tapped the small sensor on the wall beside him, then dropped it and stamped on it before handing it to Captain Williams. "If any sensor goes down, all nearby ones will call for help, sending pictures and every other type of information they can. The systems weakest link is the server that connects them. If that's destroyed, you'd be blind. We'll be using three, so all three would need to be taken out to blind you. Any tampering would cause an alert. But let's assume, by some miracle, someone gets a sensor away, they'd not only have to feed you lies, but make Valory believe that lie. They'd need to encode it perfectly. I suppose some super genius, much smarter than I could do that on his mystery supercomputer, but it's extremely unlikely. He'd need to rig every sensor. It would be easier to hack the main computer, which is guarded by your officers every moment of every day. The computer can't be remotely accessed, so someone must enter the data manually. That could happen, but they'd be here, right in front of you, doing it. They'd need the access codes and the know how to do it. The computer won't turn on or accept new programming without retinal scans, fingerprints, and voice ID. It's as secure as I could make it."

"What we're aiming for here is ease of use for you," Dr. Mitchel said, laying her hand on Dr. Simmons arm. "We want you to be able to ask, what's the temperature in the engine room, and have the computer tell you. You could say tell me if it rises or drops. How many men are in there? Is there radiation, and it would just tell you. But say men were trapped in there you could ask to see it, either by flatscreen, or holograph, then you'd know exactly where they were, what walls to cut through to reach them safely or yell, 'Hey stupid, the other door is open!' and get them out."

"It'll be completely voice activated then?" Captain Williams asked.

"The entire operating system works on voice commands and it's much faster than computers you're used to. You can ask to see your files on a traditional desktop or rearrange them in any way you like." Dr. Mitchel tapped the display before her and said, "Valory, color code my files by date and display them on a white board."

A whiteboard sprang up behind Sara with neat rows of colored files.

"Actually, color code them by how often I use the file and only display files I've used within the last month."

The board shuffled, the files resizing and rearranging themselves.

"Add tabs and label them by type."

"It certainly is fast," the captain said as the display shifted again.

"It takes up a lot of room though," Commander Harmin said as he stepped closer to examine the small files on the board.

Dr. Mitchel said, "Valory, display my files inside a filing cabinet using a traditional format."

Commander Carmin laughed as the whiteboard disappeared and a sleek metal box appeared. Dr. Mitchel opened the box by tapping the front and the drawer slid open to reveal a row of manila folders labeled alphabetically.

Valory said, "Would you like file size to be consistent to traditional folder size?"

"Yes," Dr. Mitchel said and giggled when Commander Carmen swore softly as filing cabinets surrounded her to the ceiling, filling all the open space around her. The crew exclaimed, some reaching out to try to touch the images. The exclamations changed to awed laughter as the drawers opened or locked when their hands neared.

Dr. Mitchel said, "I can display my information any way I wish. Resume normal display format." The cabinets disappeared and a small ten-inch screen floated before her left shoulder. "You can ask Valory to display your work however you like. It can find files by keyword or date and the program is smart enough to weed out obvious false results if you're searching for a file. If I ask for the file on the current supplies in stock, it'll show me the supplies for the project I have open or the one I opened most recently, weeding out all files it knows I'm unlikely to mean, like those same words in passages of books or emails or supplies ordered for projects I haven't worked on in a while. It gives me search results by probability of both what I've asked for and what I'm doing while I ask."

She flicked the screen, making it bigger. "I keep my files on tabbed desktops and as you can see, they're both color coded and labeled. Changing the color or label is as easy as telling Valory to do it."

"My programing is ongoing," Valory said. "You have many machines I'm unfamiliar with. I estimate it will take a minimum of three months for my systems to integrate seamlessly."

"What's it mean," Captain Williams asked.

Valory said, "I can label some of the machinery present in this room but lack the programs for most. As such, directions to me regarding them will require explanation and likely specific programming for peak performance."

Dr. Simmons said," It means things like the radar and whatever that is." Oz pointed to a screen displaying wavy yellow lines. "It can't anticipate directives regarding machines it has no programed knowledge of. But it can estimate the time needed to learn the machines functions."

"Why does it need to know what the radar machine does?" Commander Carmin asked.

Dr. Simmons shrugged. "It might not need to know. I can't foresee what you'd find useful. That's one of the things we'll be monitoring. I have no idea how often or how you interact with your equipment. But, obviously, the better the Valkyrie system understands what the machines around it can do the better it can anticipate your requests. If you ask it to do something that it doesn't understand it will ask for clarification, but some clarification would be difficult to supply. It might need access to the manuals to offer correct responses to questions you might pose. This is a very specialized environment. I assume it'll take us a few years to get the program working at peak performance."

Sara said, "We'll go over the programing in more depth once you decide who the users will be. I recommend you read the security files before giving clearance for its use as we'll be collecting all the data, questions and commands given and the responses, to tweak the programing."

Dr. Simmons said, "You'll set access by introducing people to it. The first introduction will take two of you. You and your Xo will both give permission, then it'll take retina, finger, and voice prints. After that, it'll just use voice commands unless you specify it needs more. Say, for instance, the woman's crew quarters. To ensure their privacy, require a fingerprint to turn on those monitors, or limit who has permission, or give everyone permission, but have all such instances sent to you. The options are totally up to you or whoever else you give access to. The Valkyrie system is unable to break a law but because we can't foresee what a fighting ship might find necessary to reach its objective the programming for that is much laxer than the civilian models will be. It would be possible for one of your users to order Valory to spy where maybe it shouldn't. It's one of the things we'll be monitoring."

"What if we screw it up?" Commander Carmin asked. "Say we do something wrong giving access?"

Dr. Simmons shrugged. "It's a simple process, but if that happens, return to the home screen and tell it you screwed up. Name the mistake you made if you know what it was and ask it to restart. Valory can walk you through every program it has. It understands the command restart or ignore that last request. It'll require two people with admin privileges to sign a new user in. We recommend four to eight people on the ship retain admin privileges, but that's up to you. Sara and I will make sure you're comfortable using it before we go."

Dr. Mitchel said, "Programming would be more complicated. Call for one of us or a trained programmer if you need a program change on the sensors. Valory will tell you if it requires a programmer if you ask it to do something it isn't capable of doing. We'll leave you manuals, but if you need to do something different than it's already doing, call us. If the computer blows up or breaks in any way, call us. A backup system will be in place that works exactly the same way. We need to decide where to install it. If this main computer goes down it'll most likely be because the entire bridge is compromised from a bomb or something, so it shouldn't be here. It should be somewhere secure, but accessible. Let us know where that is."

Dr. Simmons said, "We'll be leaving you four wristcomps that can access the main computer. Wristcomps have no programming capability at all but work exactly like Sara's and mine. The wristcomps can show you the entire ship and have the Valkyrie program which can answer any questions you have. The battery life sucks. Eight-hours at full use, twenty-four at just audio, and it takes two hours to charge them, but we're working on that."

"Once you decide who can use them, we'll program them for the user," Dr. Mitchel said. "A six to eight-hour class will be necessary to learn all the features. If one breaks, send it back for repair. The only hard part of the wristcomp is programming a new user, other than that you really can't screw it up. You might get lost trying to use it, but you couldn't screw up its programming."

"Why only four?" Commander Carmin asked.

"You can get more, but they have complete access to all information, unless specifically programmed not to. So, anyone who has one can view any part of the ship anytime they wish. The missile rooms, the locker rooms, the bathrooms, the captain's cabin, everywhere. How many people will need that access?" Dr. Simmons asked.

Dr. Mitchel said, "We're in the process of making commercial wristcomps but the security program won't be included. If you just wanted the wristcomp to use as a computer, they can be preordered. But for the security system you don't really need all that many. You won't need to have men sitting at desks watching screens because Valory will be watching. One man could do the job of ten or more. If your man spots suspicious activity he just tells Valory to monitor it, asking for any details he wants. He could easily watch twenty people in different areas because the computer will be doing the actual looking. Your security agent just has to tell it what to look for. Like if he thinks someone is loitering with an intent to steal he taps the screen and says watch that guy and tell me if he takes anything. Or maybe you have a crew repairing a leak. Your security agent just tells the computer to watch vitals on all of them and monitor for any change he wants. There'd be no need to keep watching himself.

"Or say someone reports a crime. Your agent tells the computer to search and then only has to watch relevant footage. Valory is smart and would weed out all pictures it deemed of no consequence, suspects who couldn't have done it because they're on camera in a different area while the crime was committed, or instantly weeding out people who don't match descriptions, things like that, and only show images it thinks are relevant, cutting work time drastically. One small desk would suffice, and we'd planned to install a non-mobile system wherever you want one. The wristcomps are for you and your officers. If there is any other feature you want, ask. We'll try to accommodate all requests," Dr. Mitchel said.

"I'm really interested in your buoy." The captain peered over Dr. Simmons's shoulder at the display in front of him. "Eyes in the water would be great."

Commander Carmin moved closer and

waved his hand through the image. "Are they very expensive?"

"This one was, but the next one will be cheaper." Dr. Mitchel exchanged a rueful grimace with Dr. Simmons. "Our first tries always cost a lot more as we figure it out. I think we could duplicate it at a fraction of the cost, about twenty thousand dollars in parts, assuming the parts were made in bulk and not fabricated individually as these were. But we aren't done making it, so the cost could double."

Dr. Simmons laughed and shrugged. "Or, it could be less if we decide it doesn't need features we built in. We're just learning this. We just figured out how to send the information through the water."

Dr. Mitchel interrupted. "No, we just figured out how to decode it; sending it was easy, understanding it wasn't."

A frown settled on Dr. Simmons brow. "And we're still getting gobbledygook. We'll be swimming around trying to figure that out." He turned to the captain. "We'll be happy to show you the full specifications on it and what we hope to add. And it would help us tremendously if you tell us what you'd find helpful to Give 'Em Hell."

The captain smiled at Dr. Simmons in what he hoped was a calmly professional way and strode to the doorway. The new operating system had shocked him. The ramifications of the Valkyrie system were just setting in. Awe prickled the skin on his arms as he considered he was watching the birth of the future.

"I'll let you go settle in. Please, Dr. Mitchel, Dr. Simmons, join me for dinner tonight, and we can discuss it. It's been a real pleasure meeting you both." The captain and commander shook their hands. "I assume you can find your way to your rooms?"

Dr. Mitchel laughed and flicked her wrist, touched one section of the holographic screen hanging before her, and the screen disappeared, leaving a glowing red arrow in its place. "Not a problem, Captain. You can call us Sara and Oz. The doctorates are too new to feel like our names. The *Truman* is mapped on our wristcomps already. Is there any area we shouldn't go without informing you first?"

"A midshipman will accompany you if you're working. You're free to use the gym and visit the cafeteria or any other public space as you wish," Captain Williams said.

"We'll work up a schedule so you can assign your crew. The midshipmen who came with us want to see how this works and most are competent programmers already. Most of the installations can be done during regular business hours, but some night jobs will be necessary, and we want to do some tests at night on both the sensors and our buoy," Oz said.

"Just let them know. The midshipmen are available around the clock."

Sara and Oz thanked him and headed to their quarters. Valory shrunk to its smaller size and fluttered after them.

Captain Williams turned to his XO. "I don't know what to make of that. They're so young and talk so matter-of-factly about things like ray guns." He understood his orders now though. He could see the genius in their designs.

"What they showed us was impressive if it works."

"They seem sure it will," Captain Williams said.

"This is bound to be an interesting cruise at least," the XO said.

"I want to meet Midshipman Hayes. If he can take over this ship on a whim, he must be something special." Captain Williams returned to his chair and sat.

His XO laughed. "It'd better not happen; we'd never live it down."

The captain snorted and grimaced, then called for Midshipman Hayes to report to the

bridge.

Midshipman Hayes saluted and stood respectfully, waiting to be recognized.

"I've received my orders," Captain Williams said finally. "I will, of course, follow them, even though I don't understand them. Do you have anything to add? Permission to speak freely."

"Sir, I've been given permission to take over only in the event of an emergency that threatens Sara or, um, Oliver's safety. The reason I hold that permission is because they'll listen to me and I'm familiar with the secret weapons they possess and will use in the case of such an emergency. It's my job that no one, including you, find out what those weapons are. A security detachment on board is also aware. I'll be as discreet as possible and use only them if an emergency arises and it's possible to carry out my mission doing so. If I did take command, I'm most likely to order such improbable things you'll think I'm trying to kill us all."

"For instance?" Captain William's eyes narrowed.

"The clearing of the decks, or part of

them. Using only one or two helicopters instead of the entire fleet. Taking them and Alpha team away or toward the enemy. I really can't say until it happens, and I hope I never need to do it," Midshipman Hayes admitted.

"I see." Captain Williams finally said.

"If an instance occurs, I'll call and ask for whatever we need. I'm sure you were notified that this ship and everyone on it are expendable, but they're not. I can't reveal the secret weapons, but I've seen them, and they do work. We can't let either of them be taken or harmed." Midshipman Hayes flushed and rose his hands then dropped them at his side, resuming his at ease position. "I'm sorry, this is as awkward for me as it is for you."

"That, I believe," the captain said with a small smile.

"They did tell you my orders to protect them supersede all other orders?" Midshipman Hayes asked anxiously.

"They did. Midshipman Anastasia Morales, Sebastian Morales and Charles Hayes all have orders to protect Doctors Mitchel and Simmons that supersede any other order by anyone. The group you call Alpha team also has those orders." The captain drummed his fingers on the armrest of his chair. "Your Alpha team isn't under my command but under the command of Doctors Simmons and Mitchel. I've never heard of orders like these before."

"I'm sorry, sir. The only explanation I have is we've been trained to use the weapons."

"Imagine how thrilled I am to have weapons on board I know nothing about." Captain William's fingers picked up tempo for a moment before stilling.

Midshipman Hayes shrugged apologetically and repeated. "I'm sorry, sir."

"You say all the Scouts on your Alpha team know about these weapons as well, why wasn't Major Nelson put in charge?"

"I assumed he was," Midshipman Hayes said in confusion, "I assumed I was the backup and that he'd take charge in an emergency."

"I have no orders to that effect," Captain Williams assured him.

Midshipman Hayes frowned thoughtfully and then spoke hesitantly. "If he contacts you and requests something, I hope you'll allow him to do whatever he asked for."

"Is that an order?" The captain asked softly.

Midshipman Hayes grimaced, obviously not happy ordering the captain to do anything. "Yes, sir," he finally said.

Captain Williams sighed. "Very well then, return to your duty— dismissed."

Midshipman Hayes saluted, clearly relieved the interview was over, and hurried from the room.

"Not what I was expecting," Commander Carmin admitted when Midshipman Hayes had left the bridge. "I thought he'd be all braggart and obnoxious."

"Me too." The captain rose and stretched. "None of them are what I expected."

"I wonder about the other two."

"We'll meet them tonight at dinner in the officer's mess," the captain said.

34

WORK AND PLAY

Sara opened the door to her room and sighed. Boxes were stacked to the ceiling, filling the entire space. She hauled them out, stacking them in the hallway, earning annoyed glances from the crew who passed. After locating the boxes with her air mattress and the reinforced ones that went underneath it, she set up the small compartment. An hour and a half later she stood in the doorway surveying the room with satisfaction.

Neatly stacked boxes sat on two of the three narrow bunks remaining in the room. Inflatable pillows lined a double bed made from the reinforced crates and the bunk already in place against the left wall, letting it be used as a comfortable couch. She'd removed the top bunk to give enough head room. One large crate had been unfolded into a long counter and placed over the last bunk, leaving a narrow aisle. Four rolling stools slid under the counter when not in use. Sara had unpacked her clothing into one thin locker and Charlie's spare uniforms into another. The other two held supplies. Mostly components of things she and Oz were still working on.

Oz showed up as she was admiring the room. Together, they placed a giant sticker printout of the ship on the counter and then taped drawings and schedules to the walls and boxes on the beds.

Next, Oz set up their computer, which comprised setting a three-inch square black box with the Valor Industries logo on it on the counter and placing five blue glass disks around the room by removing the plastic backing to reveal the adhesive and pressing them down.

"Ready?" Sara asked.

When Oz nodded, she pressed a button on her virtual keyboard projected by her wristcomp in front of her and the room transformed.

Holograms covered the furnishings making it appear as if they stood in Oz's workspace back home. They exchanged high-fives, sat at the counter, and began working on the buoy.

Dinner was more fun than he thought it would be, Charlie thought happily. Everyone was polite, and the talk was interesting. Sara enjoyed it too. Stasia and Hawk appeared bored. Hawk seemed sad, probably over leaving the dogs, but his mother would take good care of them.

After dinner, they went for a walk on deck. Stasia had duty, but Hawk and Oz accompanied him and Sara. Sara gave Hawk a quick hug before they returned to their rooms for the night, and Charlie felt her worry. He gave her a reassuring smile; glad he could join her and they'd have a chance to talk privately before her worry over Hawk would put them in a loop.

Charlie joined her in her room and chuckled when he saw the air mattress. "You really are a genius. I was thinking we'd be stuck on the floor and now I pity the guys wedged in those tiny bunks."

"I feel bad for Hawk," Sara said as she changed into sweatpants, hung her clothes away in the closet, and released her hair from its fancy braiding. Long again, the braids had made her hair a crazy, curly mess.

"Yeah, he'll feel better in a day or so. He

misses the dogs and hates being on the ships. There isn't enough plants here for him, but we won't be here too long." Charlie stretched out with a contented sigh. "You're the best wife in the world," he murmured as he drew her down beside him and smoothed his fingers through her curls. She drifted to sleep, her contentment a soothing background to his own as he fell asleep beside her.

They settled into a steady rhythm of shipboard life, and Sara had never been happier. The only thing she missed was Lucky and Rhea and he wished he could bring them for her. He spent every night with her. Every morning both ran and worked out with the Scouts. All day she installed or programed sensors or worked on one of her myriad of projects but she scheduled her free time to coincide with his.

Charlie smiled as he left her after their morning workout. Life on board ship with Sara here and happy was perfect. Busy with Oz, she was working on so many projects she didn't have time to miss him during the day.

In blue jeans and a white T-shirt with the

Valor Industries logo, a V crossed with a lightning bolt, over the left breast pocket, Sara sat cross-legged on the floor of the bridge connecting the computer to the underside of an excising desk as the captain discreetly observed.

The captain smiled as holographic screens sprouted around her and her fingers flew over the barely visible holographic keyboard. She didn't look old enough to work so competently but he was impressed with the new system.

From where he stood he couldn't hear her whispered conversation with Oz. When they'd shown him the small stick-on they used instead of earphones he'd been doubtful, but since then he'd used the stickycoms himself, many times, and they worked well.

Sara glanced up and caught him staring. "Would you like to hear this go live?"

When he nodded, she smiled and tapped a corner of her screen. The screen appeared to split into two and one tumbled through the air until coming to rest before him. He was familiar with the virtual screens now and adjusted it to the height and size he wanted. A note sounded, and she waved her hand when it reached the desired volume.

"Okay, Oz, I'm live here. Diagnostic

begins on my mark. Tick." Rows of green lights raced around the computer image of the ship. The small Valkyrie that fluttered beside her said, "All readings are consistent to set parameters."

"Good to know, but I need to check them myself," Sara said.

Valory settled into a chair that hadn't been there a moment ago and put its tiny feet on a tiny desk, leaning back and yawning broadly as it closed it eyes. Tiny Zs floated above it, fading away into nothingness and the captain bit back his laugh. He'd been using the Valkyrie operating system for weeks now and hadn't yet seen all of its programed responses but he was amazed by how helpful the program was. His productivity had increased by tenfold and he could see how the program would revolutionize almost every industry.

"All green, Oz," she said after fifteen minutes of checking the readings against the master list. "I'm running the program now." The flatscreen changed to a holographic image.

She turned to him. "Captain, I'm going to go compartment by compartment. The static picture will change to a live one indicated by a green border. It can take seconds or minutes depending on the number of sensors and room size. Each sensor will be tested independently, and I expect this to take about a week because we'll be teaching your assigned crew how to check the readings too. Our first room is this one." A hologram of the bridge filled the empty space allotted for it. Sara rose and checked the readings for heat, light, temperature, humidity and radiation levels of every sensor in the room, trailed by the miniature Valory that now wore a lab coat and carried a clipboard making exaggerated checkmarks as Sara checked the sensors.

Back at the hologram she typed for a moment and people appeared in the image.

She grinned and turned to face the captain. "Captain, you are now live."

"How big can you make that?" Captain Williams gestured at the hologram floating near the middle of the room.

Two fingers made a pinching motion, and the image grew. She tapped the image of the Xo who stood at the helm watching.

"Any size I want. I could make it half size or magnify the picture by a hundred percent without losing any resolution. In this small space that isn't practical. I've set it for one tenth of actual as standard but that can be easily changed at your discretion. Double tap the image to get a full bio on him. Or ask for a report and the nearest sensors will try to determine his condition. If he was wearing a wristcomp, I could get all his vital signs. Using the sensors, he'd need to be within three feet of one for accurate readings but Valory could interpret data from further away. It would be an educated guess though and not exact, but it could tell you if it saw injuries and estimate if the person it was monitoring needed immediate medical attention by observing wounds, breathing patterns, facial expressions and body language. That's a program we're still working on and likely will be for a while. We're designing a sensor meant to be worn into combat that will transmit all data to Valory and the team's medic. You could request them if you feel you need to monitor your crew's health."

"That little box is the actual computer that's running this?" Commander Carmin pointed at the four-inch square box with the yellow V crossed with a lightning bolt she'd just mounted under a nearby console.

"Yes." Sara kept running her programs as they talked. "It doesn't really need to be that big, but we thought if we made it too small it might get accidently damaged. As soon as it's all live, we'll introduce you and whoever else you choose. You can set the hologram or your screens to single use or open or list the users who are allowed to interact individually. Say you wanted one person to be able to change the size of the screen but not be able to dismiss it or maybe you want one able to tap for information but not be able to move your screens. The choices will be up to you and easy to set and change. The midshipmen can place the sensors as well now and we plan to leave you a supply in case you decide you need more coverage in the future.

"We estimate three days to do the exterior of the ship and a week to get that up and running because of the time need to manually check everything. Valory has been tested in the lab but we need to be certain its performing as expected."

The image shifted to a view of a nearby compartment. "Stasia is in there, checking the readings manually." Sara continued to work quietly. The captain and his Xo observed a while longer before returning to their own duties.

Commander Carmen said, "The Valkyrie operating system is impressive."

"It is but I worry about the stability. It's so new and untested."

"So far it's worked flawlessly." Commander Carmen held out his wrist and tapped the wristcomp. A three-inch man wearing a standard uniform without insignia appeared and saluted. "I've been working with Dr. Simmons and he gave me this personal model. He wanted feedback on what we'd find useful in the Valkyrie program. Learning to use the device is simple and I was able to reprogram my avatar myself in seconds. This wristcomp doesn't have access to the security system yet but he told me we could give it access. I think the operating system is more valuable than the security."

Captain Williams laughed softly. "Dr. Mitchel gave me a personal model as well, and I agree. I plan to send in a report pushing for extensive testing of it. I imagine it will be replacing all of this soon." Captain Williams gestured to the computers his men worked at.

Commander Carmi said, "I imagine it will replace half of the people too. Valory can manage most of these tasks unsupervised."

The captain said, "And that worries me a bit. The operating system won't just be available to the military. Private companies of all sorts will be downsizing too. What will all those secretaries and assistants do when their jobs become obsolete?"

"It won't happen overnight. As you said, the system is too new and still needs testing."

The captain nodded his agreement but remained uneasy. Change was coming. Big change. The future had arrived and if they weren't careful it would roll over them and crush them into the ground. The kids of this generation believed in a Star Trek-like future— that they could develop devices that would bring them to the stars. *And maybe they could*, he mused as he eyed the small Valory typing at the virtual desk beside his XO. Maybe ray guns and water powered ships were just the tip of the iceberg. *Who knew what these two doctors were capable of?*

The next day Oz requested a small boat to run tests on the buoy. "Did we receive clearance to test our ray gun yet?" he asked when the captain gave him permission to take a boat.

"I did, and I'm to offer full assistance," Captain Williams said.

Oz nodded and cleared his throat. "Sara and I had another idea we'd like to try completely unrelated to security. We'd need to use some unoccupied deck space for a few hours a day and access to your shop."

"What will you be testing?"

"Well, basically a game. A training tool

for our Scouts." Oz pulled up the relevant file on his wristcomp and showed the captain. "We got the idea when we hardened the light and have been working on this for months. The goal is to make a full-sized hologram that appears as a real room. A real life holo deck." Oz laughed. "But, right now, because of space constraints, we're going to cheat and use glasses to give the effect of harden light. This is the game system we've been working on. Work on this won't impact the schedule. We'll only work on it at night after working hours," he finished, staring eagerly at the captain for approval.

"Write me up a report on what you'll need and what changes you'll make to my ship and I'll get back to you." The captain grinned at Oz's enthusiasm. It was reassuring to see him so enthused over a video game like a kid his age should be. It worried him that the doctor's genius would be pushed into designing weapons. *If at eighteen Dr. Simmons could design all this, what would he be capable of at age fifty and what kind of man would he be if he spent all of his time now on serious things?*

Oz nodded and tapped his finger in the air above his wristcomp to send the report. "It's in your inbox, and thank you, Captain. We'll be going out tonight to check our buoy. Since we have permission to test our ray gun,

I was hoping to try that tonight too. We'll need permission to fire on it."

"Dummy rounds?" Captain Williams asked.

"Yes, that's fine," Oz agreed. "Eventually, we'll need to check it against live fire, but right now we want to test its real speed. I assume you've read our reports and what we expect to happen?"

"I did. I'd like to observe tonight if that's okay?" the captain asked.

"Sure, but it'll happen fast and be hard to see. We'll be filming it for later study as well." Oz worked out the details and left to set up the experiment.

When they'd completed the tests, Sara contacted Captain Williams. "We're going to try our gun now, Captain. Drew will fire when we've cleared the area."

Captain Williams joined the doctors, both of whom still wore wetsuits, at the stern.

A helicopter circled a smaller boat just fifty yards from them.

Everyone moved back, shading their eyes, as both Sara and one of her Alpha team ran recorders. The helicopter pulled away and Sara counted down softly. A light flashed from the small boat and the missile disintegrated. The ball of light kept going.

"I'm tracking it," Oz said in a worried

voice. "Damn, it's a mile up, Sara. We need to fix that." The captain peered over Oz's shoulder, reading the range with him.

Oz said, "It was almost two miles before it broke up. It's too hard. We need to make that light weaker."

Screens flashed to life around them as they argued the math.

The captain listened to them argue for a while. "Can't you just turn the power down?"

Oz answered absently, without glancing up from the screen he was frowning at. "No, we don't actually use power per se; that just runs the targeting system. We're using photons- light. We need to use less of it and make it less dense to disperse faster. It would've destroyed anything in its path."

"I'm sorry, Captain, this system isn't anywhere near ready." Sara gestured to the graph in front of her. "We'll need time to work on it. We might want to run another test, but not for a while."

"The tracking system worked well." Oz replayed the video in slow motion.

"That's your ray gun? that little box?" Captain Williams pointed to the screen.

"No, that's the computer. The ray gun is the thing that resembles a flashlight." Oz pinched the screen and moved his fingers apart, making the picture bigger and pointed at the components. "The power is the big box. The gun itself doesn't use it, it works on a battery, but the targeting system does. You might be right, Sara. This might be a dead end. The buoys sent the warning and it was almost too slow. We're just so close I hate to give up."

Sara shrugged. "So, we work on both theories as time permits, but I'm sure mine is right."

Oz rolled his eyes and pulled her ponytail, then turned back to his screens, a deep frown creasing his brow. "I'm sure it is too, but I don't know how to do it."

"We'll get it; we're part way there now," Sara said cheerfully.

The next night after work Charlie joined them on deck to try the game. Four metal frames sat side-by-side on the deck. Oz fussed with a mesh harness, adjusting it on Joy while Drew fiddled with a cable that lowered and rose him. He wore an identical mesh harness and balanced atop a wooden board.

"Does it feel stable?" Sara asked.

"Yep. Feels like floor."

"We're still working on this, so don't try

to climb yet but we want feedback on the realism of movement. You should be able to run and jump or squat and crawl, but it might be buggy." Sara handed a customized gun to Joy and one to Drew.

Oz placed thick, blue, glass balls the size of bowling balls around the frames while Sara handed Drew and Joy black glasses. "The scene will move as you do, so when you get to the end of a corridor or climb out of a window or door you'll see a new room. Chain link is out of bounds, so don't try to get through it. We hid a treasure chest and there'll be enemies. First one to find it wins."

Sara handed a pair of black glasses to the captain who observed with interest. "You can go through it too, if you like, but I warn you, they know these grounds inside and out."

The captain grinned. "I'm an academy man myself. That's amazing detail." He paced forward, turning his head side-to-side.

"The harness should allow most motions, but it lacks total interactivity. We're working on adding sensation so that you'll feel the flooring and walls." Oz glanced up from the field of screens before him. "It needs atmosphere to feel lifelike. Breezes, smells, sounds. Some of that is simple programing but we need hardware that can perform so quietly and unobtrusively you forget you aren't really there."

"This is a good start," the captain said as he slowly turned. He removed the glasses and examined the framework. "It doesn't look that complicated."

"It's not. It's basically a swing on a treadmill but the computer will be reacting to your movement, hopefully giving the illusion your moving, not running in place while the gloves synthesis the feel of objects."

"And it's safe?"

"You could get motion sick, I suppose, although to your eyes and mind it should appear realistic. That's something we'll be monitoring for." Oz taped a small circular protuberance on the harness.

"The computer is much faster than any you've worked with before," Charlie said as he offered the captain the harness. "The pictures should retain relative perspective to your position, which should limit the motion sick effect."

"It shouldn't be like riding in a car and turning your head but like running," Sara said. "If your running and turn your head but continue to move the setting will continue to move, hopefully in a life-like way."

The captain said, "It must take immense processing power to keep the movement balanced."

"Oz's computers can handle that with no problems," Charlie assured him as he handed the captain a pair of gloves. He was tempted to get in the remaining harness, but he wanted to see this first test.

Sara handed the captain a gun and leaned forward to whisper, "The gun works just like a real one. You have to rack it back and reload it. It'll sense if you don't. I didn't tell them. I thought it would be funnier to watch them try to figure it out."

"Reload with what?"

"Just make the motion of reloading; it's all pretend. The sensors inside the gloves will read the motion and reload." Sara pretended to load the gun and handed it to him. "One more hint, locked doors require keys or alternate methods of entry and can be alarmed just like in real life. Good luck, sir."

The captain stepped into the harness and donned the glasses.

Oz opened three screens to show what each of the players saw.

"A purely simulated environment would be more engaging," Charlie said as Joy ran through an empty classroom.

"I agree, but we already had this one worked up," Oz said. "We just had to make the guns and enemies. The walls will appear solid to them, but the characters will be cartoonish. We'll need to pay actors if we want the characters to look lifelike. I have John looking for graphic artists for us who can draw lifelike models that Valory can animate but I think real actors will be better, more lifelike. Valory can run the photo editing software and put the actor into any costume we want. We just need to build up a database of clothing being worn so Valory knows where it should crease and flow."

Sara grinned as Drew ran into Joy. Joy shot him and then complained because her gun hadn't fired, and he killed her. He immediately pretended to rack another bullet into the chamber and saluted her.

Joy slapped herself in the head and did the same. They continued searching the grounds together.

"They look ridiculous," Charlie whispered to Sara, making her laugh.

"We're working on that too. We plan to add a screen around the equipment."

"Not a real screen," Oz said without glancing up from the screens before him. "We'll make a hologram that hides you while you play, and you'll be able to pick the setting."

To everyone's surprise, Captain Williams won the game, acquiring the most kills and receiving the least as well as finding the treasure.

"That was fun," he said enthusiastically as he wiped his sweating face. "I can see training potential here and it's a good workout. The glasses take some getting used to, mostly in the darker rooms where you think, 'I should remove my sunglasses to see better,' and then remember they aren't sunglasses. And the guns don't really feel like guns but that could be because they're so quiet. It would be cool if they had sound effects, so you knew when it had been racked and fired."

"We could easily add that. We could even add sound to opening doors and background objects, but it would consume more power." Sara opened a screen in front of her and began typing. "Not a lot more, but more than our batteries have unless we used just the two harnesses, and I really wanted to add more."

"I think we should make a scenario requiring the group to stay together and add in sound." Oz opened his screen beside hers. "I was thinking, with Captain Williams's permission of course, we could use one of the ship levels and program a scenario where a group of four has to find and repel invaders."

"How long would that take to program?" the captain asked.

"About an hour. We already have the layout, which is the hard part. I just add the enemy's and they're easy," Oz said. "In no time at all I could whip up some fires or other disasters to help train your crew. Send me a list of ideas, and I'll work on it in my free time. I'll need more time to make smart enemies who will look realistic and hide, or wait, or use hostages."

"First, we should work on the depth so you can climb up things," Hawk said as he peered over Oz's shoulder at his screen.

Team Valor gathered around, talking excitedly.

The captain walked away and left them to it. The math they used was way over his head. In minutes, all five of them had their wristcomps open, comparing screens and arguing equations. Once on the bridge he used his new security to observe.

Commander Carmin stood beside him, viewing the screen. "I find it interesting that everyone defers to Mr. Hayes. All disagreements end when he steps in. Everyone seeks his opinions about their theories, and he guides the discussion."

Captain Williams gestured to the screen where Charlie was setting assignments. "Sara and Oliver are smarter, but Charles is clearly the leader."

- 35 -

COLONEL TRAVENSKY

The next day Charlie accompanied Sara to the bridge. "Sara can show your officers how to use the security program at any time. It's almost completely installed. Oz has already made a few small programs for the game and would like permission to mount a more permanent harness rig on deck. The space needed is minimal, we can stack the rigs, but it'll require power."

"How much power?"

"A regular two-twenty outlet with a draw of about three hundred watts is good enough for what we're doing," Charlie said.

They worked out some details and soon had the game running twenty-four hours a day with scenarios picked at random from places already mapped. Only eight people could play at a time and a long waiting list developed to play.

Charlie was at his desk when Sara's sudden fear hit him. He jumped to his feet and began to run while hitting the icon on his wristcomp that would connect them.

"One minute," she said, and Charlie growled low in his throat, overriding her wristcomp controls in time to hear a man say, "Sorry, ma'am, it's classified."

Sara said, "I'm okay, Charlie. Someone mentioned Colonel Travensky. I can't find out anything, it's classified." Her voice rose when she said, "Oz and Stasia are on the boat with the buoy."

Charlie's HUD flashed red; she'd hit her panic button.

He examined the map. Stasia and Oz were with half of Alpha about half a mile from the ship.

Sara said, "Oz, Stasia, get back here!"

"What's going on, Sara?" Major Nelson asked.

She repeated what she'd heard and added. "Get them back here right now! Get them back here, Brenda."

Brenda answered calmly. "We're fine, Sara. Drew and I are with them, and we're coming in."

Sara said, "Wait, Oz, set the buoy for radio signals. Bring it to the surface. If you spot anything...."

"I know. I'll call," Brenda said. "Calm down, we're okay."

Charlie ran onto the bridge and saluted the Xo. "I'm sorry, sir, but we need to know the context of that name, classified or not." He grabbed Sara by the wrist, holding tightly enough to feel her pulse. Her initial fear had faded, and it faded more as he held her, or maybe his excitement just overpowered it. Either way was okay with him. He was in perfect accord with his magic. It thrummed inside him eagerly, as ready as he was to destroy her enemies.

The Xo nodded and told his officer to report. The officer said, "The message is encrypted, sir. I picked up a radio signal. It sounded Russian. There might be a boat in the area."

Sara manipulated her wristcomp.

"I'll need to hear the transmissions. Oz, there could be a sub near you. Send the buoy on a circuit; say fifteen miles in a half-circle in front of you."

"Don't ping, Oz," Charlie said thoughtfully. "I have an idea. Let's just see if we can spot a ship without it spotting us. Stay there." He took Sara by the shoulder as she started to protest. "We need to find him, Sara. This is our chance."

"No, we're not giving them Oz and Stasia!"

"We are," he disagreed gently. "Everyone has a white and a blue bracelet, correct?"

"Yeah," Oz agreed grimly.

"Major Nelson, get Alpha team ready to roll and get Hawk. If there's a sub, we're going to take it."

"Sara, calm down, it'll be fine. They can all call us, and we can call them." Charlie gave her a quick hug. She was angry now and not afraid.

Sara glared at him, pulling away, and leaning over the radio man's arm. "Do you have any other recordings?"

For ten minutes, she listened over his headset. "How often do you listen for things like this?"

"This post is manned twenty-four hours a day," the officer said.

"Do you keep records of your radar sweeps?"

"Forty-eight hours only. Unless we spot something, then it goes to permanents."

"I need access to them. Charlie, I'm going to run my own program. I don't have time to oversee that myself. There's a ship out there for us, I'm sure of that. The program will alert you of any suspicious ships if it spots one in your records. How did they know we're here?" she asked as she connected the recordings to her wristcomp. "Never mind, stupid question— that would be incredibly easy to find out. The real question is how did they know we leave the ship for the smaller boats?"

"I'm going to do something incredibly illegal here," she whispered a moment later as she sat on the floor and used her wristcomp as a flatscreen, her fingers flickering over virtual keys.

"You're searching the satellites?" Charlie crouched beside her, reading the information scrolling across the screen.

"Yes. I want to see who's watching the boat. I'm going to put a worm in all of them." Sara said, "Stasia, you guys should be safe there for now. They're waiting until Oz and I are on the boat." She grimaced as she sent the copies of the audio to Major Nelson. It sounded like gibberish to Charlie but her passive ability to understand languages made even code understandable to her. He wished they'd spoken more but she only had the three small clips of recordings.

She said, "Finish up and head back. Oz and I will go back out with, um, Marcus and Toric. They should metabolize sedatives fastest. I wish Manny was here. Toric, can you hear me?"

"Yes," Toric answered immediately.

"Report to the infirmary with Marcus. I'm going to make up some fake skin I hope will stop a dart. When they shoot you, you'll have to pretend to be unconscious. Can you do that?"

"No way!" Charlie said as Toric said, "Yes."

Sara gave him an exasperated glance, but it was her anger that made him snap his mouth closed.

"A minute ago you said we need to catch them. The radio transmissions said they won't try unless it's Oz and I. Obviously, they'll use sedatives. So, we'll give them a clear shot at fake skin, but it could still work. When they catch us, they'll probably remove all our devices and keep Oz and I heavily sedated. Toric and Marcus can hopefully use my call. They'll need to keep the bracelets on. I'm thinking we use skin-tight wetsuits hard to cut through with the bracelets engaged on their hip or something."

"No way, Sara, you're not going!" Charlie glared, angry she'd even suggested it. She ignored him and ran off the bridge to the infirmary.

Charlie faced Commander Carmin. "We

have a situation here. You'd better notify the captain."

"What did the transmissions say?"

"I have no idea," Charlie admitted. "Sara is a language expert though and thinks a submarine is in the vicinity and she's trying to track it now. She's really skilled with languages and code breaking. If she's correct, and it was sent to kidnap them, we'll take it." Charlie turned from the surprised XO and spoke to his team. "Stasia, Hawk, suit up. I need to go suit up to and stop my crazy wife," Charlie said as he ran from the bridge.

Charlie found Sara in the infirmary applying a paste to Toric's bare back.

"Don't shrug your shoulders if you can help it," she was saying as she smoothed it over Toric's shoulders when Charlie entered. "The paste isn't very flexible. Once this dries, carefully put on a white shirt over it. A tight one, so they can see you have nothing under it."

"Sara, this is a crazy plan!" Charlie grabbed her gloved hand and she yanked it away.

"You were willing to let them take Oz and Stasia with no plan. This is a plan at least." Sara spread more of her concoction on Marcus's bare back. "Have the Scouts ready to follow. Once we're on board they can use any means at all to enter the ship and then summon us off if we haven't already been summoned. As long as one Scout is outside the ship with my bracelet, you can save us all. Toric and Marcus can summon you on board if they wake with my bracelet engaged."

She smiled suddenly. "Won't they be surprised with what they've caught if you still have your bracelets? I'm worried they'll kill them outright." She held Toric's and Marcus's hands in her gloved ones. "I really believe they won't. You're too valuable as both a hostage to our good behavior and as a raid member, but I could be wrong. You don't have to do this."

"We won't let you go alone. We're your Scouts and a Scout protects its cub." Marcus ran his free hand over her blond ponytail.

Toric squeezed her hand. "I'll be there for you in any way you need."

Sara hugged them both and continued getting them ready. Charlie eyed Toric thoughtfully, realizing for the first time that Toric was interested in Sara, maybe more than interested. He'd assumed the interest he'd shown when he was in school was just to get a rise out of him, but apparently he'd been wrong. Sara was oblivious and had no reciprocal interest; he was sure of that. Then he remembered when Toric had touched her when she was trying so hard to control her magic. Anger built in him as he realized that had been a purposeful touch. Toric wanted to be her warrior.

Sara glanced at him as his anger grew. "I'm sorry, but if we want to catch them, this is the best way."

"I'm not angry with you. Go, get your wetsuit on and wear the bracelets too. Take a knife." Charlie pulled her close, staring into her brilliant blue eyes. "I'll meet you on deck. I love you, Sara."

She hugged him hard. "I love you too." She ran from the room.

Marcus and Toric started to follow. Charlie put his hand out to stop Toric and nodded at Marcus. "Go get ready. We'll be right there."

Marcus nodded and left.

Charlie turned an angry face on Toric. "She's my wife! Mine! I can't blame you for wanting her, but I sure as hell will blame you if you ever try to influence her magic again. She doesn't want you. If I told her you'd tried to become her warrior, she'd be furious. Never let it happen again!"

"I can't promise that," Toric said evenly. "Yes, I do want her, but I'd never disrespect her by trying to seduce her. What I will do is be the warrior she needs if she wants me too. That's why we're all on Alpha; we're all willing to be whatever she needs." Toric pushed past a fuming Charlie.

"Damn it, I don't have time for this shit," Charlie mumbled under his breath as he raced to his quarters to suit up.

Charlie saluted when he entered the bridge and the captain waved him forward. "I'm sorry, Captain." Men on the bridge turned and stared. The swords and shield on Charlie's back got interested glances and a few snickers, which he ignored. "The Scouts require two helicopters fueled up and ready to go. Commander Carmin informed you we're hunting a submarine?"

"Yes."

"My, um, Sara has a crazy plan to let them kidnap them. Team Alpha will follow and take the submarine, or ship, or whatever goddamned thing takes them. Anastasia and Sebastian Morales and I will assist. One team member will remain here in a helicopter. Beta team is on its way here. You should be prepared for attacks. I don't think it likely, but it might be part of their plan to slow and confuse us."

"Charlie," Sara interrupted over his wristcomp. "The worm has a hit on the satellite. A Russian one is transmitting the pictures to these coordinates. I'm repositioning the buoy as we speak. The captain should be notified as soon as we get confirmation. I'm giving him access to the buoy's images on his system. He can just ask to see it like any other sensor. I'm still running the radar checks, and if anything pops, it'll go to you. If the buoy spots a ship, the program will attempt to identify it, but Captain Williams might be better for that. Oz and I go in forty-three minutes. The time matches for a regular night check and shouldn't rouse suspicions. We're going through the motions of a normal launch now. I love you." She disconnected.

Charlie's wristcomp pinged and a flatscreen with a long scrolling list of information appeared beside his combat HUD.

"Show me the buoy," the captain said into his wristcomp and a hologram formed. He made it a comfortable size for viewing and let it run.

"Chief," Oz said. "I'm sending you a list of probable ships. You should be seeing it now. Unfortunately, eighty-six percent of them possess nuclear warheads as well as ballistic capability. I don't think they'd fire on the *Truman*. Is all they need to do is grab me and Sara and run. Hawk couldn't track them in water. I think they'll use the smallest, stealthiest ship they have."

"How sure are you they'll make an attempt and who are they?" Captain Williams asked.

"Ninety-eight percent sure and Colonel Travensky," Oz said. "As of this moment the only intel we possess on him is his name, so we can't afford to hide. We need information. No records exist of a colonel of that name in any national service. We aren't even sure he's really Russian. We don't know what he looks like or who he's associated with."

"And twelve of you are going to take a submarine if there is one?" Captain Williams asked doubtfully.

"Well, we don't need all of us," Oz said completely missing the point or ignoring it. Charlie wasn't sure which and choked back a laugh. "But it's hard to hold the Scouts back when we're threatened. We're heading out now. Stasia is coming with us. Don't let them see you scrambling; we know they're watching by satellite."

"Oz—" Charlie started to say when Oz interrupted.

"I know, man, and I'll take good care of her."

"Both the girls and yourself." Charlie

muted his wristcomp. "I'm going to keep you in our audio link for the time being, and I apologize in advance if I cut it to protect classified secrets."

"The buoy has a hit," Oz said, and a new screen popped up in front of Charlie. "The buoy found it, and you should see the data now." Oz read aloud as the screen scrolled before Charlie. "A Yankee Pod, possibly one hundred and twenty on board more likely fewer. Unlikely to have nukes. More likely reconverted to carry more torpedoes. Damn, I wish I'd made the buoy able to latch on."

"We're just going to pretend we're here as usual. Toric and Marcus, try to look more bored, please," Oz said in an aside to the people with him.

"I'm going to the helicopter, sir." Charlie said to the captain.

"Good luck," Captain Williams said softly and offered his hand.

Surprised, Charlie shook his hand and then ran from the room.

- 36 -

OLD ENEMIES

Captain Williams eyed the submarine swimming through his bridge with unease. "Let's get the crew in position quietly. No alarms, no running, assume battle stations. I want gunners and repair crews standing by," he ordered.

"Aye, aye, sir." His XO got on the intercom and informed the crew while the bridge crew stared at the hologram in horrified fascination.

On board the small boat, Oz and Sara began a normal check. They both jumped into the water as usual and swam down where they took the regular sensor readings. Stasia floated near them invisibly.

"Radar contact. A helicopter is approaching your position," the radar man reported.

"Looks like one of our birds coming." Toric lifted a hand to his brow, shading his eyes. Sara and Oz surfaced and climbed back into the boat. Stasia tread water beneath them still invisible.

Everyone knew it wasn't one of their helicopters but acted as if it was. Oz and Sara sat on the diving platform to remove their swim fins and began to remove the rest of their gear. The helicopter swooped over them, releasing a noxious green gas.

"Well, shit!" Toric dove for the oxygen tank Oz had just placed at the bottom of the boat as the gas hit them. Everyone dropped except Stasia who was still using her oxygen tank. Sara had reached for hers, but let it fall from her hand at Stasia's grim nod.

"Readouts show everyone is unconscious, except Stasia." Charlie opened a screen by him and set it to run constant updates on their vital signs. He was surprised his magic wasn't at all agitated and wondered if it had even sensed anything had happened to her. He was angry but no angrier than he'd been when he heard Travensky was here for her. He mostly felt cold anticipation now.

"Backtrack that helicopter. There must

be a bigger boat out here somewhere," Captain Williams ordered.

Stasia was busy. Men in gas masks had dropped from the helicopter, and she was doing her best to avoid them as the helicopter hovered low over the boat, kicking up spray and making the small vessel sway in unpredictable directions. The men zip tied their hands and legs and passed them aboard. A simple jump and Stasia swung herself onto a landing strut and wrapped both arms around a brace.

"I'm on board," Stasia whispered. "Let it go."

Charlie gritted his teeth and waited. "Don't lose sight of that copter."

"Heading, Foxtrot, Niner, Zulu— at its current speed and bearing it'll intersect the submarine in thirteen minutes, sir." The radar man glanced at the captain and then returned his attention to his screens.

Captain Williams stood over his radar man's shoulder, staring at the picture the buoy transmitted. The darkness surrounding the sub lightened as the submarine surfaced.

A few minutes later Stasia reported being in sight of the submarine. "As soon as I'm on board I'm calling."

Charlie waited aboard the helicopter with growing impatience.

"Okay, let's get these birds in the air." Major Nelson waved two fingers over his head. The Seahawk lifted off and headed at full speed to the submarine's location.

Charlie glanced at the screen showing their vitals in safe zones. "Wait until all four are on board, Stasia."

Stasia dropped off the helicopter from twenty feet up and landed on the hull of the ship on the balls of her feet. She pulled a knife from its scabbard on her thigh and crouched.

Two men, both wearing khaki brown uniforms, stood talking by an open hatch. Nobody was in sight at the bottom of the hatch, so she jumped to the deck. Four men carrying two stretchers approached. She braced herself between the wall and the ceiling to avoid them in the narrow space, and they walked beneath her never knowing she was there. As soon as they passed she ran down the corridor and ducked through the first open hatch she passed.

"Can you find me schematics of this ship?" Stasia whispered.

Captain Williams tapped his wristcomp, making a holographic keyboard and screen pop up in front of him. "We have that. I'll send it to you." A moment of scrolling through his files brought up the relevant file, which he forwarded to Charlie.

"This is the most current information on a Yankee Pod we have. They could've changed things, but this is its basic configuration."

Charlie forwarded it to all the wristcomps. "The plans are in your inbox, Stasia."

"I'm placing sensors," Stasia said as she took a minute to check her wristcomp to examine the layout before sneaking back into the corridor. "Two men are outside unloading and six remain aboard the helicopter. Eight are waiting down below to secure them. I could take out all eight, but that will give us away. I'm going to take a quick look around." Stasia opened hatches and peaked inside, casting distracts as necessary, placing a sensor above the door and retreating. In the first concealed spot she came across, she dropped her air tanks.

"How did she get aboard unseen?" Captain Williams asked, sounding perplexed.

"Holographic technology," Charlie lied.

Stasia reported on crew members she passed and placed more sensors.

"Hawk, pick up Joy before Stasia calls us. Group one is now officially Charlie Hayes, Stasia Morales, Sebastian Morales, Mark Nelson, and Todd Jones."

"I'm in the room prepared to hold them and placing sensors now. I'm also replacing the sedatives with saline," Stasia said. "Sara is going to freak if she wakes up here," she continued in a worried voice.

Charlie pressed his lips together. "Make sure she doesn't!" His wristcomp pinged softly, notifying him Sara's program had run its course. Two possible radar contacts over the last week were highlighted.

"Captain Williams, I'm sending you some data, which I also sent to my Beta team. Both contacts need to be checked. We want the ships intact and crews taken alive. This isn't one hundred percent; the vessels might be innocent."

"Someone's here," Stasia whispered. "Going silent."

"Hawk, get Joy." Charlie checked his weapons more for something to do than because he needed to. His attention sharpened on his displays when two men carrying a stretcher holding Oz entered the room Stasia waited in. With brisk, practiced moves, they placed him on one of the metal tables, strapped him down, and injected him with the sedative that Stasia had replaced with saline.

As soon as they exited, two more men entered carrying Marcus who received the same treatment. Both men left, and another two brought in Toric. He was being restrained in the same way when someone else came in with Sara. One man gave her a shot of the saline while two restrained her and placed a board under her hands. The board had clamps built in which pressed her fingers down, locking them in place at all joints. When they finished with Sara, they did the same to Oz.

An older man entered and rubbed his hands together, grinning, while two men began cutting off the wet suits, leaving them in their underwear. Their spellbracelets and wristcomps had already been removed.

The man said something Charlie couldn't understand, smiling and patting another's back, obviously happy and excited. He took pictures of everyone and left, locking the door behind him, leaving one man behind taping Toric's and Marcus's hands. As soon as the hatch closed, Stasia sapped the man and reported.

While she was talking, she grabbed the bottle of Ritalin next to the sedative. With a small shrug, she gave Marcus the injection and engaged her white bracelet.

"Call three." Stasia started her cast, gritting her teeth against the burn. Charlie, Major Nelson, Todd and Hawk, carrying Joy, appeared in the room.

Hawk set Joy on her feet.

Charlie ripped off the bindings holding his wife to the table and carefully removed the boards from her hands. When her hands were free, he stole her chain heal and casted it. Small bright-yellow balls bounced between the unconscious figures and settled into them.

Marcus twitched, so Stasia injected Toric. "Should I give this to Oz and Sara?" She held up the bottle of Ritalin.

Major Nelson took the bottle from her hand, read the label, and handed it back. "Give them a quarter dose."

As the major spoke, the man Stasia had sapped recovered, but before he could say anything, Charlie hit him and knocked him to the deck. Todd grabbed the tape and tied the now crying man as Charlie held him down. Charlie didn't know if the tears where from pain or fear and didn't care. He wanted the man terrified of him.

Once he was tied, Todd grabbed a fresh bottle of sedative and injected him.

"Shut up," Charlie said, and the whimpering man nodded frantically, his terrified gaze locked on Charlie.

Charlie dropped the man on the table that had held Sara and began ripping Oz free.

"Captain Williams, we're on board the submarine and have retrieved our personnel. We'll take this ship, but I'm turning off our audio link until we do." He turned off the link to the captain.

"Brenda, hang back." Major Nelson ordered. "If we can't handle this, call them out of here, and we'll worry about catching them later."

Ten miles out and keeping ten feet off the deck, staying off radar, Brenda continued circling the submarine in the Seahawk.

"Hawk, is the hallway clear?" Charlie glanced at his combat HUD in which red dots were appearing.

"One in the hallway to the right of the door," Hawk reported instantly, continuing to tap the schematic of the submarine wherever he saw people.

"I'll get him." Stasia opened the locked door. "Clear," she reported a moment later.

"Stasia, did you find a place we can leave them to recover? I don't want her waking in here." Charlie glanced around the room with its metal tables and restraining equipment. *This room would be sure to trigger a panic attack and nightmares.*

"Hawk, come with me." Stasia tapped a spot on the schematic, marking it for everyone. "The closet where I left my air tank will do. Let's make sure it's clear."

Hawk followed his sister. Two hatchways down, a small, dark, storage room half filled with cartons of packaged food made a perfect hiding spot. Charlie carried Sara and set her down, then went back for Marcus.

Todd brought Oz while Major Nelson carried Toric over his shoulder.

Charlie helped Marcus walk to the room; he was awake and disoriented but recovering quickly. The major handed Marcus his sidearm and a white bracelet. "Stay with them until they can fight and then join us."

Toric twitched and coughed. Joy engaged her white bracelet and healed him, then checked everyone's vital signs and nodded reassuringly at Charlie. "They're fine. Let's go."

Stasia, Todd, and Hawk headed to the engineering room. Charlie, Major Nelson and Joy headed to the bridge. One man stood by the hatchway leading to the bridge. Charlie casted Waylay, intercepting the man, appearing right behind him and slapped his gloved hand over the man's mouth. Joy raced up and zip-tied and gagged him, and Charlie dropped him on the floor.

Hand on the handle, he nodded to Joy, held up three fingers, and swung the door open three seconds later. Joy rushed through the door and went right. Major Nelson headed left. Charlie ran straight in.

Two men jumped up, pulled their sidearms and opened fire.

Charlie yelled his drop weapon area-of-effect, drew his sword and leapt to the closest man. "Get on the floor right now!" he bellowed, putting the point of his sword in the man's face. The man's gaze flicked to the gun he'd dropped at his feet. "I dare you." Charlie leaned into the man's face, pressing the sword into his cheek until a drop of blood appeared and laughed when the man shrieked and cowered from him.

Joy knelt on the back of the other gun wielder, zip-tying his hands, his gun tucked into the belt on her waist.

"US Marines! On the floor now!" Major Nelson shouted as he tracked the room, peering over his gun sight.

The three other men in the cramped room dropped to their knees and then to floor, placing their hands behind their heads cowering as far from Charlie as they could get in the cramped quarters.

The man in front of Charlie took one slow step backward and lowered himself to the ground in small increments as if afraid every movement would make Charlie attack.

Joy rose from the man she'd bound,

scooped up the gun from the floor, and placed it behind her belt with the other one before zip-tying the man kneeling before Charlie. When he was securely tied, she secured the other three.

Major Nelson and Charlie left Joy guarding the men and headed to the engineering department.

Hawk stood before the closed hatch of the engineering room, held his gun to his shoulder, and motioned for his sister to open the door. "There are ten men inside."

Everyone engaged the white bracelets and used one of Sara shields. Stasia opened the door, the lock not hindering her, and they rushed in.

Hawk used his Stun-Shot, and then his Knock Back-Shot, which pushed a man into the side of the ship with a loud thud audible over Todd's yells for everyone to get on the floor. Hawk winced as the man collapsed.

Todd had stolen Hawk's Stun-Shot and used it while Stasia sapped one man and used her Knock-Out-Punch on another.

Todd yelled again for everyone to get on the floor.

Five men in khaki uniforms held their hands up and dropped to their knees.

Todd holstered his weapon and began zip-tying them.

One of the men reached for a knife in his boot. Stasia appeared behind him, kicked the knife from his hand, and forced him onto the ground. She zip-tied him while Hawk covered the room. By the time Charlie and Major Nelson arrived they had the men in the room tied and laid in a neat row.

Stasia, Hawk and Todd went to clear the remainder of the ship while Major Nelson and Charlie headed back to the bridge.

"Who here can get this tin can to the surface?" The major pointed his gun at each bound man in turn. When no one responded, he squatted before the tied men huddled on the floor and said in a soft voice full of menace, "If you can't raise it, you're useless to us." He lifted his gun and pointed it at the nearest bound man.

The man babbled frantically in a language the major couldn't understand. The major cocked his gun and the babbling man jerked his head toward a nearby bound companion.

"You speak English?" the major asked.

The man glared, giving a sour glance to the man who'd given him away, but said yes in a thickly accented voice.

"Tell whoever can do it to raise this ship now."

The bound man let loose a spate of Russian.

"One of Stasia's sensors just tripped," Joy said.

"Joy, Chief, go check the corridor," Major Nelson ordered. "Then clear the rest of this level. If this ship doesn't start to rise in five minutes, we scuttle it."

Joy and Charlie left the room.

The major tapped his wristcomp face. "We can get to the surface without this ship. Can you?"

"Alfonzo will raise the ship," the man who spoke English said angrily.

Major Nelson cut Alfonso loose, and gestured with his gun for him to go to the helm.

"Crew quarters first," Joy said.

While she and Charlie cleared the top floor. Hawk and Stasia cleared the crew quarters. Back in the room Sara and Oz were in, Toric and Marcus were alert and waiting.

Toric reported, "All vitals are good. I expect them to wake any time now."

"I'll, check them," Hawk said. "We have the bridge," he said as he examined Sara and Oz for himself. "We're going to clear the rest. Toric, come with us. Marcus, guard them. When they wake, take them to the bridge."

Hawk and Toric ran through a hatchway and dropped down a ladder onto a lower deck.

"People in both directions." Hawk marked them on the ship schematic and handed Toric both his bracelets and his sidearm.

On the lower deck, Todd covered Stasia as she ran down the hallways unlocking hatches for both teams. A siren rang three short blasts then Major Nelson said, "This ship has been used in the abduction of United States citizens and is now under the control of the United States Marine Core. You won't be harmed if you exit your room and kneel in the nearest corridor with your hands behind your heads."

Major Nelson repeated his request twice more while doors up and down the corridor opened and scared looking men appeared.

Charlie left Hawk and Joy tying them, knowing his presence would make them bolt and went to help Stasia.

"Wait," Stasia whispered to Charlie after she'd opened a compartment where six people hid.

Invisible, she ran through the room to see what weapons, if any, they had. She returned to the doorway.

"The gloater is in there. Two men have guns but no real ammo just rubber bullets."

Charlie nodded and motioned Stasia to go for the gloater. "Put down your weapons and surrender!" Todd called.

Rubber bullets smacked into the walls with sharp cracks.

"I won't ask again. In three minutes, this compartment will be sealed, and when we scuttle this ship, you'll still be here."

A spate of angry Russian answered him. The men stood slowly with their hands up. Todd zip-tied them quickly. When he got to the man Stasia wanted, he gestured him to leave the room, leaving him untied. The man glared but obeyed. Stasia pick-pocketed him and removed his camera and wallet. She handed both to Todd when the man had passed them, and she faded into sight. Charlie grinned and slapped her shoulder.

Within twenty minutes of boarding the ship, they had the entire boat secure. Charlie returned to Sara who was just stirring. He turned his audio connection to Captain Williams back on as he carried Sara outside of the submarine.

"The ship is secured. Brenda, bring the rest of Alpha here. We're going to question our captives as soon as Sara is up to it. Beta, report your position."

"Approaching the first ship from the radar sweep now. We have back up and plan to drop in and conduct a search."

"Don't leave that ship until we're sure of its status," Charlie said. "Send us info on all the ship's officers. Captain Williams, if you could send a security team here, Alpha will go for the second ship."

Charlie turned the audio off and gave his attention to Sara. Calm in his arms as she woke, her magic didn't appear. His magic was more insistent to touch her. He let his magic settle around them.

TYING UP LOOSE ENDS

"It worked then?" Sara yawned and pushed away from him to rub her head.

"Mostly," Charlie agreed. "Loose ends remain. Once you're up for it, we need you to question everyone, but we have time. Nobody on our side was hurt. Beta is checking one ship now and Alpha will go to the other. Stasia and Joy are with Oz who should be waking soon."

"We can go. I'm okay." Sara kissed him and rose.

"Not yet. I need a minute." Charlie didn't want there to be the slightest chance her magic would feel threatened, worried it would leap to the major or Toric for protection. They both played warriors.

He rubbed his hands up and down Sara's bare legs and arms, letting his magic touch her. She snuggled into him, placing her hands on his face, the only bare skin she could reach, the rest was completely covered in armor. She kissed him, and the kiss grew deeper until they were both breathing harder.

Charlie drew back and cupped her face in his hands. "I love you." Still holding her, he leaned his foreheads on hers, enjoying the echo of the love they shared. He finally sat back and pulled his gloves on. For another minute, they sat together in their magic, letting the physical desire fade. When they were both even in their emotions, he took her hand in his gloved one and led her back inside.

Marcus met them at the hatch to the bridge and handed Sara a black T-shirt and sweatpants. "Oz is awake and fine and working on the computers now. I'm going up top to meet the security crew."

Sara touched his hand with her glowing one and Charlie shared her relief Marcus was well. Marcus smiled and pulled her ponytail before leaving them.

Sara and Stasia questioned everyone while Joy recorded.

"They all know Oz and I are scientists, but none mentioned a thing about magic," Sara reported to Major Nelson. "Stasia and I have separated the ones we think know what we are. I can't guarantee the rest are ignorant of our true abilities, but Stasia's Sweet-Talk works pretty well."

"Beta is joining Alpha." Major Nelson made his combat HUD larger and pointed out the positions as he spoke. "Drew is on his way for us. We haven't found any of your stolen equipment. Oz is locating it now. Captain Williams can handle these men. Chief can order they be secluded until arrangements can be made for them.

"Our priority is catching everyone who knows," Major Nelson continued. "After we remove the personnel, we're going to scuttle this ship. Its existence would help prove our capabilities. There isn't a scratch on it to explain how we got aboard or subdued the crew."

"Have Drew get my gear, all of it, and Oz's too." Sara glanced down at the black sweats she wore and curled her lip. "We have programs we can use to hack the computers."

"Already did. Oz finished that while you were doing the questioning." Major Nelson assured her. "He says we need to go to Russia to hack their databases if we want to use his locate program. We might do that if we can't figure out who's who without it."

"I'm done with these people for now," Sara said. "Let's find our missing gear. The less time they have with it, the better I'll feel."

"It's been almost four hours." Major Nelson glanced at his wristcomp. "Neither ship you flagged appears to be involved. Neither have a landing pad for a helicopter and both had legitimate manifests. We lost radar contact with the helicopter but plotted its course. Brenda returned to the *Truman* and, um, borrowed a jet and she's following the ship we believe is involved. We were waiting for the team to be ready before we pursue. Alpha has your gear on the helicopter."

"Let's go," Sara said.

She glanced at Charlie and grinned wryly. He smiled and smoothed her hair, not trying to hide his eagerness to fight from her.

Back on board a Seahawk piloted by Drew, Sara and Oz donned their backup armor and new wristcomps. Drew headed to Brenda who'd located the helicopter. The *Truman* followed slowly.

"Okay team." Major Nelson rose and faced them, hanging onto a strap in the ceiling to keep his balance. The small stickycom he wore on his throat carried his voice clearly without the need to yell over the rotor noise.

Every Scout and Team Valor wore the

small devices on their throats and behind their ears that transmitted the barest whisper into clear sound directly into their auditory canal.

"Try to take a few alive if we can."

Brenda said, "I have a ID. The ship is called The *Valdamir Hanke*. It looks like a cargo ship, but it's riding high in the water."

"Got it," Oz said. A minute later a picture popped up on Charlie's HUD.

"This is a standard schematic of the ship class," Oz said. "I'm still searching to see if any modifications have been logged for this ship. It's out of Arkhangelsk Russia with a corporate owner. The officially listed crew is twenty-six, but it has the capability to hold thousands."

Charlie gazed eagerly from the open door of the Seahawk. The crew of the ship was aware of their approach and lined the rails, holding automatic assault rifles. The scene sprang into the clarity that told him his eyes had flared blue and small wisps of magic careened around the cabin. He knew Stasia was as eager to fight as he. Hawk didn't share the eagerness, but he was intense, focused on the schematic. Oz was angry and Sara worried.

"Keep it under control," Major Nelson warned, batting uselessly at the wisps.

Charlie recalled it, a bit surprised the major was so nervous.

He eyed him thoughtfully, wondering if it were Valor or the enemy he was nervous of.

Major Nelson avoided his gaze, leaning over Hawk's shoulder to view his schematic even though he could view the same exact thing on his own HUD. Charlie shrugged and turned back to the open door.

"Forty-three men aboard, sir." Hawk tapped his combat HUD pinpointing every man on the ship by touching the image of the ship where he saw them, and small red circles began to blink on the map. Matching dots with small numbers lit on all their screens.

A glassy blue disk on the left shoulder of their armor projected the HUD in the air in front of their right arms. Text scrolled across the bottom of the picture. New information flared red on the screen before fading to black and white. The screens constantly updated as Hawk added information.

The Scouts could position or size the screens however they wished. When they separated, the wristcomps automatically added their positions to the image and mapped the surrounding area. Small glassy disks embedded in both shoulders of their armor front and back scanned and transmitted data to their wristcomps.

Nickle sized, matte-black, glass sensors that could be removed and placed to monitor whatever they wished lined their left legs, automatically transmitting data to all HUDs, updating in real time.

"We have two areas of concentration." Major Nelson examined his HUD, which he'd made into a thirty-inch widescreen before him. "Twenty-four men are at the rails. Six men are on the bridge and eight in the engine room. The rest are scattered."

"Missile Inc," Brenda warned as a man with a hand-held rocket launcher aimed at the incoming helicopter. She whizzed between them and the ship, dropping chaff but not engaging.

Major Nelson flicked his wrist and the thirty-inch screen resumed its usual proportions of a six-inch box in front of his right arm.

"Disengage and return to the *Truman*, Brenda."

"Yes sir," she said, and Charlie grinned over her disappointed tone. She loved to fly the jets and now she was missing the fight and the flight. He made a mental note to request more flying time for her. Maybe they could even requisition a jet to train with.

Brilliant white light and a thunderous boom distracted his line of thought as Hawk blew the incoming missile out of the air. Hot air buffeted his face, so he pulled down his sunglasses.

"Tick," Sara said and began casting shields.

The men on the topmost deck of the ship opened fire on them.

Charlie and Stasia both used their intercepts and were at their selected targets instantly and the fight was on. Rick used his blue bracelet to Spell-Steal Charlie's attack command and yelled, *"Oorah,"* as he jumped, the spell buffing everyone, casting Waylay in mid-air and landing beside Charlie who grinned as he swung his sword. Alpha team followed except for Tony who flew the Seahawk.

He peeled away out of range of the guns, heading back to the *Truman*. His sole job now was to summon everyone out if the fight went badly. Beta would arrive in moments and drop in.

"Alpha, clear the top deck for Beta," Major Nelson ordered.

Toric waved his squad forward and Rick slapped Charlie's shoulder before going to his assigned sector.

This is what I was meant to do, Charlie thought happily as he fought his way across the top deck. Gunshots gouged holes in the metal decking and clattered against his shield. The guns of the Scouts were loud in his ears as they returned fire. The noise was slightly disorienting because of the noise canceling properties of the stickycom in his right ear.

He wasn't sure it was a good design feature, but this was its first live fire test.

Sara's voice came through nice and clear though as she said, "Rick, tick, Toric, two." She continued to call timers and adjust positioning in a soft voice, and he supposed the trade-off of stereo sound was worth hearing her commands so clearly.

He was glad to see the Scouts listened instantly, falling back when she commanded and waiting on her timers.

"Woot!" Drew yelled and Charlie turned as three fireballs soared into the air and impacted the helicopter that was trying to lift off. The helicopter exploded with a blast that rattled Charlie's teeth and tumbled into the sea where it sank like a stone.

Joy and Rick high-fived Drew, and Rick said,

"I love this bracelet," as he used Charlie's Valorous Leap to jump to the bridge level.

Major Nelson said, "Sara, hang back. I'd like to see how we do with just the bracelets. If anyone is fatally wounded in your squads, summon Sara for a rez, otherwise keep yourselves alive."

"Yes, sir," Sara said and used her Protective Companion spell to reach Charlie's side and began to fight beside him.

He didn't mind her so close. His aura made it impossible for anyone near them to target her, and she was standing on his shield side and his shield would pull ranged attacks to it so even stray bullets were unlikely to hit her.

She wasn't fighting with magic but with her staff. Every swing made her feel satisfied. The strength of her satisfaction told him her magic was satisfied too. These were the Enemy and the magic wanted them dead.

The two of them killed the five men attacking and Charlie glanced at his HUD to see where the remaining enemy were.

Only three men remained on this level and he casted Waylay, landing among them, not caring if they saw him using magic because they wouldn't live to tell anyone. He killed them in seconds while they screamed and cowered from him.

Major Nelson said, "Stasia, take your squad to the lower level. Chief, clear the stairs for her and then clear the second deck. Oz, stay with Toric's squad. I want every squad to try to capture some for questioning but don't risk yourselves or the cubs."

"Bridge secure," Joy reported.

Charlie ran down the narrow stairs, followed by his squad. His combat HUD showed fifteen men spread out on the second floor. The gunfire overhead petered off, either the Scouts had killed them, or they'd given up. He hoped they were dead, and the viciousness of his thought shocked him for a moment.

"They deserve what they get," he muttered.

"Damn straight they do," Manny said. "Kidnappers, terrorists— they have it coming and more."

Marcus muttered agreement as Drew said. "Let's give 'um Hell," and he shot past Charlie's shoulder at a man crouching in the doorway at the bottom of the stairs.

Charlie jumped the last few feet, ignoring the bullets that thudded into his chest, and decapitated the man firing with one swing.

Three men crouched at the end of the hall and fired as soon as Charlie reached the last step. He ran forward, holding his shield before him, yelling at them to drop their weapons. Marcus fired from behind Charlie, and one of the men dropped. Another man opened a door as Sara yelled a warning.

A machine gun fired, echoingly loud in the confined hallway. Bullets tore through the metal bulkhead, small pieces of shrapnel clattering against Charlie's armor.

"I got him," Drew said.

"Two more in the next room," Sara warned as Marcus fired again.

"Stay with me," Manny said, and Charlie glanced back. Manny had followed them into the hall and now stood before Sara, holding a hand out to keep her back.

"Fucker," he snarled and yanked Drew back as a grenade went off right in the doorway. Drew stumbled back but didn't fall. Brilliant yellow light surrounded him for a second. *It had happened so quickly he probably didn't even feel it,* Charlie thought in satisfaction.

A mirror bright dome encircled Marcus a moment later. Charlie turned to go to them when Manny laughed and grabbed something from the air. He tossed it back into the room and half turned to hunch over Sara.

Fire and smoke billowed from the room, cutting off the yelling men inside.

"We got this," Manny said and waved Charlie on.

Charlie laughed and turned back. The last man had entered the hatchway behind him and sealed it.

He glanced at his HUD, then flicked the red icon that connected him to Stasia.

"Stasia, we have a locked hatch here. I think there's only one man inside. I'm taking Sara, Drew, Marcus and Manny to the bottom deck. Out."

He ran back to the stairs where Sara crouched with a screen opened before her.

"Hawk confirms one in that room. Six remain beneath us in the lowest level," she said.

Charlie ran down the next set of stairs and through an open hatch. A closed door lay to the left and three closed doors lined the right wall before the next hatch.

"When we enter, there'll be two to the left and one directly to the right," she added.

Drew reached out and tried the handle, then shook his head. He and Charlie kicked the door together. In three kicks, the wooden frame tore loose and tumbled to the ground. Men yelled; the sound lost in the loud clang as the door hit the deck.

Sara shielded her teammates as they entered, followed by an application of her heal-over-times. Charlie went left, and Drew went right. Sara stepped inside and began opening filing cabinets, ignoring the commotion.

Marcus and Manny kicked open the door across from them. Both shouted for the man inside to drop his weapon. The sound of a scuffle broke out. Charlie hit his target and ripped the gun from his hand. The man grunted and fell backward. Charlie followed him down to half kneel on his chest while he grabbed for the zip ties in his back pocket.

"You guys good?" Sara called.

Charlie didn't hear their answer. The man Drew had pinned was yelling obscenities too loudly. He glanced to the doorway where Sara stood as he yanked the tie tight. She'd left the filing cabinets and peered through the open door, and Charlie laughed as he felt her frustration. She wanted to be searching this room. Full bookshelves lined the room from floor-to-ceiling. The sight was like catnip to her.

Bullets smacking into his shoulder made him turn. A man had dropped through a hatch in the ceiling and was shooting at him.

Charlie snarled and ran at the man firing at him.

"Clear," Drew called, echoed a moment later by Manny.

Charlie wiped his sword on the corpse at his feet and headed to the door. He reached it in time to see Sara slam her staff on the ground and a silvery shield spring up around her. His eyes widened as Marcus exclaimed and he saw what Marcus had seen. A man holding a smoking rocket launcher knelt in the doorway of the last room on the right.

Charlie casted his invincible spell on Sara as Manny grabbed her. The smoking rocket circled the mirrored dome and streaked back down the hall. It blew through the man holding the gun and the wall behind him. Shrieking metal and a thunderous blast obscured Manny's laughter.

Fire and smoke billowed. Roiling black clouds smelling of burnt metal filled the hallway.

Charlie ran down the hall to check the damage.

Marcus slapped Manny on the back and rolled his eyes at Sara. "This ship is going down."

"Don't worry about it," Charlie said to Sara, amused by her guilt, as he leaned over to peer into the hole. The rocket had deflected and tore through the ceiling, then out of the wall of the floor above them. Water rushed through a gaping hole partially below the water line. "We have a few minutes."

Charlie returned to Sara. "How many are left down here?"

"Just the two unless they have another way out through that last hatch. I'll message Hawk to double check. We've had a few blips in the health monitors, but they all read green now. Oz and I need to tweak his programing so we can tell at a glance how current the info is.

Charlie stifled his laugh a moment, then burst into loud peals of laughter when she felt offended.

"What? Can I help it if I get a great idea?"

Still laughing, he said, "Go search the cabins for any intel we can use. I'll get the last two." He pulled up his facemask to kiss her cheek, then turned to holler through the next hatch. "Come out right now with your hands up!"

Sara didn't wait to see what they did. "Call for a summons when the water reaches you!" she called back over her shoulder as she ran for the bookshelves. Drew, Manny and Marcus followed her down the hallway to the room he'd just cleared.

Charlie headed through the open hatch. "How current is this list, Hawk?"

"Two left about fifteen feet ahead of you," Hawk said. "Sorry, I got a bit distracted earlier. Oz found a computer terminal and we're getting some good intel."

"Keep on that. Get everything you can before this ship goes down," Charlie said as he ran down the corridor.

"United States Marines! Come out with

your hands up!" he hollered. He had to brace himself from sliding on the slanting deck. Load creaks and groans of bending metal muffled any noise the men might've been making. Water sloshed around his ankles, rising rapidly.

Two men exited the flooding room with their hands raised. Charlie gestured for them to precede him, when they tried to jump him. He knocked one into the bulkhead with a well-placed elbow to the face, grabbed the other one's wrist, and twisted sharply. The man screamed as his wrist broke and tried to hit him with his other hand. Charlie blocked the blow with his forearm and punched back at his attacker. The man fell back onto the floor either dead or unconscious. Charlie turned back to the first man as a sharp needle pierced his cheek.

"Damn." He reached for his panic button as darkness took him.

Sara's wristcomp notified her the moment Charlie lost consciousness but she'd already felt his dismay and was casting Call-For-Help.

Charlie appeared at her feet surrounded

by the rest of Team Valor. She casted a heal and a cleanse on him and felt for his pulse more to touch him then check. The HUD in front of her right arm displayed his vitals.

"Where are they, Hawk?" she asked as she straightened.

Hawk marked the positions on the map. "We need that guy." Sara indicated the one moving away from them down the hallway. "Drew, go with Stasia and check on the one who's not moving. If he's dying, leave him, if not, bring him up top. We're going after the one running away." Sara hugged Stasia quickly as Marcus lifted Charlie.

"This guy knows about us," Sara warned as they chased the fleeing man. "Keep your facemasks down; let's not make it easy for him." She pulled her own mask down as they ran down the tilted hallway. The ship was sinking fast.

Oz ran beside Hawk. "The tranquilizer dart is proof he knows about our weaknesses, so he must know Hawk and I can find him anywhere on this ship. He must be trying to get off the ship."

"Where would he go to do that?" Hawk asked.

"The next deck," Oz said immediately. "Inflatable rafts line the sides and he can jump from there." Oz touched the glowing

Beta symbol on his HUD. "Beta, we're looking for a man heading to the water. To get there, he'll use one of the ladders leading to the next floor. He's the blue dot on your map. Take him alive," Oz said as he changed the man's icon to blue to distinguish him from the others on the HUD.

The man they chased halted at a hatchway. A loud pop sounded, and a canister emitting a green gas flew through the doorway.

"Back!" Sara shouted, and slapped her arm to engage Charlie's bracelet. She stole Hawk's Air-Bubble, pulled the bracelet off and reapplied it, but didn't engage it again, and began casting shields on everyone.

"Get Hawk's bubble!" she yelled. "Hold your breath and run through it." She ran through the thick cloud of green gas, and casted Protective Companion to yank Marcus to her as soon as she was through, trying to limit the time Charlie breathed the gas in. They raced after the fleeing man.

"He has more gas canisters," Sara warned.

Hawk yelled, "Down!"

Everyone dropped, and Hawk fired at the man. The man tumbled to the ground, stunned. Hawk ran by Sara and tied him. He threw his trussed captive over his shoulder, and they headed to the top deck, staggering on the uneven flooring.

"Tony, we need a pick-up ASAP." Sara climbed to the top deck where Beta waited. Over half of the ship was underwater now and the prow of the ship stuck sharply from the water at a steep angle.

Oz did a quick head count, then checked his wristcomp "Toric and Rick, report!"

They made no answer.

"Team leaders, summon Toric and Rick," Sara said.

Major Nelson gave her an annoyed glance and repeated the order.

"I'm the team leader if Toric is incapacitated and I can't summon," Brenda said.

"It's me," Marcus said as he slapped his white spellbracelet down.

Major Nelson said, "Don't summon yet. We need to change the teams, or we'll crash the damned Jet."

Sara said, "Team Valor is going for them." Major Nelson was still speaking when Sara grabbed Stasia's hand to stop her from running off alone. "Marcus, get Charlie on the first helicopter. Stay with him. They must've been hit by the gas or a dart. Their wristcomps should've notified us. Get everyone off. We'll be right back," Sara said.

"We'll go. You stay!" Major Nelson ordered.

Sara didn't listen. Major Nelson cursed as Team Valor went back for Rick.

"Oz, locate him," Sara said as they ran back into the sinking ship where their wristcomps said they were.

"Rick is this way, not where his wristcomp is." Oz pointed ahead of them. "They must've removed his wristcomp. Damn it, Toric is the other way."

"Go for Rick first!" Sara grabbed Stasia's belt and clipped herself on, offering her hand to Oz as she casted Ascension.

"I see him," Hawk said as he leapt past them, surefooted on the uneven flooring and Stasia followed, towing Sara and Oz.

The power went out, leaving them in darkness lit by Sara's Hand-of Sun. The deck tilted drunkenly beneath their feet and louds pops and groans warned the water was forcing its way past closed bulkheads. They found Rick in a forward hold inside a wooden box. Sara casted a heal on him, which stopped the bleeding of his severed limb but had no effect on waking him.

Stasia swore viciously before saying, "They must've put the wristcomps on their own men. Find his hand, Oz." Tears rolled down Stasia's cheeks.

Hawk threw Rick over his shoulder and everyone followed Oz back the way they'd come, using the doorframes and walls to pull themselves back up the corridor. Inside a closed, empty room, two left hands lay on the floor in a pool of blood. Stasia picked one up, held it against Rick's wrist, and turned pleading eyes on Sara. Sara casted her biggest heal and everyone held their breaths and leaned forward, watching as the limb reattached.

"That must be Toric's hand," Sara said in horror. "Where is he, Oz?"

Oz paled. "His dead body is this way. Hurry, Sara!"

"Stasia, take Rick up top. Go!" Sara raced after Oz. They had to swim. Toric was underwater in a similar box in the aft hold. Oz kicked the box apart, breaking Toric out. Brilliant white light illuminated the water from Sara's resurrection spell. Hawk held the hand to Toric's stump and Sara casted a heal. Toric woke and thrashed wildly until Sara grabbed him. She casted another heal followed by Soothe, saying, "Pull us out." She patted Toric's back while he examined his shaking hands.

"You're okay now."

"I drowned," Toric said in remembered horror. "They cut off my hand and drowned me."

"I know. I'm so sorry. You're safe now." Toric let her take his hand and grabbed her in a hard hug. Oz and Hawk towed them back to the surface.

Major Nelson and Marcus pulled Toric atop the small section of ship still above water and helped him into a harness that dangled from a line attached to the Seahawk hovering above them. Sara casted Ascension on Toric, blocking the spray whipping into her eyes with one hand.

"Go," she said firmly when he hesitated.

He grasped the line and let himself be pulled into the copter.

"How many missing devices?" Sara turned to Oz, grabbing his arm to balance herself. The helicopter hovering above them thrashed the water into a white froth, making the roof they stood on slippery.

"Four, one of each type of bracelet and their wristcomps. Ours were recovered."

"In the ship still?"

"I think so," Oz replied. "Beneath us anyway."

"Let's get them." Sara glanced contemplatively at her blue bracelet. "I have two more spells on Charlie's, I think. How about you?"

"Same."

"Okay, let's go."

Major Nelson nodded shortly. "We need them back, I agree. If you get into trouble, we can summon you. Get them and come right back here. This ship will sink to the bottom any second now."

Sara, Oz, and Hawk headed back into the ship using Sara's Hand-of-Sun as they swam through the murky water.

"Toric's and Rick's wristcomps are reporting no vitals. The men wearing them have died, but we need to tweak that programing to inform us on changes in users even if the clasp remains untouched," Sara said, Hawk's air-bubble allowing her to speak normally. The water deadened sound but her stickycom transmitted it clearly.

Hawk said, "The men must've been smart enough not to try and use them, which would've triggered an alert."

"Or they've been spying," Oz said grimly.

"We have prisoners and we'll find out," Hawk said reassuringly.

"Is anyone around, Hawk?" Sara asked.

"I don't see anything alive at all, no humans, no animals, no dragons or demons," he finished with a snort of laughter.

Sara laughed too as she checked her wristcomp for the duration left on her air-bubble. The ship suddenly sank, pushing them against the ceiling. "We're fine," she reported. "Is everyone okay up there?"

"Yes," Major Nelson reported." Keep us apprised of your condition."

"The wristcomps haven't been tested to this depth. Don't panic if you lose us," Oz warned as they continued to sink.

"Noted," Major Nelson said in exasperation.

"Sorry about disregarding your order earlier," Sara said. "I don't think a summon will work if the parties are changed after the person has been rendered unconscious. The magic works on perception and can't be fooled. I think being unconscious would work exactly like being kicked offline because of our perceptions. You can't change parties around without the party members being present. You can remove from a group but not invite a player who can't respond. It's something we need to test for, but I didn't have time to explain then."

"Apology accepted. A summons would have worked if we'd acted fast enough and they'd been conscious. But we'll rework the teams to work out scenarios for just that situation. I want all team leaders to meet with me tomorrow to discuss it."

The ship creaked and groaned as it settled to the bottom of the ocean. They waited until all movement had stopped and continued the search. It took them a while because they had to backtrack and find ways through the partially crushed hull, but they found them.

"We're coming up slowly," Sara said. "I'll be healing us, but I'm not sure how the air-bubble will work for depressurization."

"*Truman* is on its way here. Can you stay under for three more hours?" Major Nelson asked.

"Yes," Sara said. "I think we can safely come up though."

"Stay just in case," Major Nelson ordered. "The *Truman* has a hyperbolic chamber. When they get here, come up slowly."

"Okay," Sara agreed. "You better keep Charlie somewhere away from people when he wakes. If I'm not there, it could be, err, stressful for him."

"We'll move him to a small boat with Stasia and Rick." Major Nelson called Captain Williams and had Charlie sent back to his location by helicopter.

- 38 -

BE CAREFUL WHAT YOU WISH FOR

Stasia, Rick, and Major Nelson waited with Charlie aboard a small inflatable raft for Sara, Oz and Hawk to surface. Everyone else had returned to the Truman to oversee the prisoners.

"Take off Charlie's white bracelet so he can't summon them when he wakes," Major Nelson ordered.

"Shouldn't he be awake by now?" Stasia removed the bracelet and patted his cheeks.

"Between the green gas and being injected, I'm betting he's out for another hour at least." Major Nelson didn't glance up from the computer screen opened before him.

Forty-five minutes later Charlie woke, vomited over the side of the boat, and grabbed his head in pain. Major Nelson used his white bracelet to heal him.

"Sara's fine," he said before Charlie could ask.

"I'm fine," Sara agreed.

To everyone's relief, Charlie was calm and controlled with no signs of magical panic. The major reported what had happened and why they were waiting.

Charlie examined his brother's hand and then hugged him. "You're okay?"

Rick shrugged. "I will be. The heals worked, but I'm sure that memory will stick with me a while."

"How'd they catch you?" Charlie took his brother's hand and examined it again.

"Toric and I were up top with Joy and Major Nelson, clearing room-by-room." Rick gestured for his brother's wristcomp and pointed to the room. "That room had three men inside lying on the floor with their hands behind their backs when we entered. I was covering Toric. He approached and zip-tied one man's hands and then staggered. I didn't think anything of it. I thought he'd tripped on the uneven flooring. Then I tried for a better angle and couldn't get my legs to work. I was perfectly aware but couldn't move or speak. The men jumped up, and we realized they wore breathing tubes and knew exactly what they were doing. They gave us each a shot of something right above where they cut off our hands and put the wristcomps on themselves and took our bracelets, then gave us another shot. The next thing I know, Stasia has me. Toric woke in the box drowning." A small shudder rippled Rick's skin.

Charlie's alarm grew as Rick told the tale. "They must've thought they could still take you. There must be another ship. Did you hear them say anything?"

Rick repeated something in Russian but added in English. "I have no idea what that means."

"It means we'll come back later if we get away," Sara said. "No other ship. They were just going to float you away. I'm returning to check to see if there's a beacon on the box."

"Don't," Charlie's hands flared blue.

"Don't," Major Nelson ordered Sara. "She won't," he assured Charlie.

Charlie nodded, but his hands stayed blue.

"Sara's fine," Major Nelson whispered. "The bad guys are contained, and no one is permanently injured. In a few more minutes, she'll be with us."

"I'm fine," Sara agreed. "While we wait for the *Truman*, we're going to run buoy tests."

Charlie tried to wait patiently, but fine or not, his magic wanted her. Finally, he leaned way over the side of the boat and trailed his blue hands in the water. Blue magic left him to seek out Sara. A surprised snort of laughter sounded when the magic reached her. "Look how pretty the magic is here, like sparking blue gems." Her voice sharpened. "Oz, look! We need to study the magic like this, it's an entirely different phase."

"Nobody except you better touch that," Oz said. "I'm recording though."

"Better?" Major Nelson lifted one eyebrow and eyed Charlie as he sat back in the boat.

"Yes, for the moment," Charlie agreed unhappily. A tap behind his ear turned off his stickycom, and he gestured the others to do the same. "I'm not used to it being my magic that seeks her, and I can't control it as well as she can. When she comes up, we'll need to be alone." A red flush climbed his neck, heating his cheeks. "Usually, she needs me and draws my magic to her, not the other way around. I'm trying to stop it, but..."

"No problem." The major slapped his shoulder. "When they rise, if they don't need the hyperbolic chamber, we can leave her with you and take Oz and Hawk with us."

Charlie nodded and clenched his glowing hands again.

"Start coming up slowly," Major Nelson ordered when the *Truman* was closer.

Completely blue again, Charlie rubbed his hands together, and frowned in annoyance. "I'm going to her." Flushed, he stripped to his boxers, leaving his armor on the bottom of the boat, and dove over the side. The blue glow of his magic illuminated the water.

"Just as well," Major Nelson peered over the side until the glow disappeared, then turned to Stasia. "Maybe they won't notice on the ship if he's underwater."

Charlie swam down as fast as possible, using leap and charge to propel himself downward through the water. Sara pulled him to her when he entered range. He stole Hawk's air-bubble and hugged Sara, his frustration mounting when he could only touch her face. The armor she wore covered her from head-to-toe and he growled in annoyance as he rubbed her clothed back. He wanted to touch her skin. He needed to feel her heartbeat against his.

Sara placed her face against his. His urgency to touch her, had sparked hers to touch him. The magic surrounded them in the water in a roiling blue mass.

"We're going ahead." Oz and Hawk

exchanged amused glances, laughing when neither acknowledged them.

Charlie removed her facemask and let it fall away into the dark.

"This suit cost a fortune." Her soft laugh changed to a moan as he kissed her neck, his urgency transformed to a fierce desire for her.

"Your mics are on," Stasia said sweetly.

Charlie turned his off, then Sara's. "Take off the suit," he said in a deep voice, trying to remove it himself.

"I don't think I can." Sara laughed as she struggled with it. "It's wet and doesn't want to come off. Hold on a second."

The wet fabric clung to her. Charlie lost patience and ripped it off, letting the pieces sink to the ocean floor. Boots and pants followed a minute later. They both glowed bright blue as he pulled her naked body against his. The resulting explosion rocked the boat above them. Concentric blue rings traveled through the water around the boat then back to them, causing another smaller, soundless explosion, rocking the boat above them.

"Better?" Sara asked a few minutes later.

"God, yes. I'm sorry about the suit." Charlie wrapped his wife's wet ponytail around his fist to pull her head back and kiss her neck.

Sara shrugged. "No worries, I'll buy another one. I'm not going up there naked though."

Charlie laughed. "Sorry about that. I'll call for clothes."

Sara moaned again as he continued kissing her neck while running his hands over her body. "I like that you need me too sometimes," she said.

Charlie called the major's private line. "Get us bathing suits or something, please."

The major sighed. "Fine, I'll handle it." With a raised eyebrow, he turned to Stasia.

Stasia laughed. "I'll get them something to wear and send it back here," she said before he could ask.

"Thanks, I was wondering how I was going to explain that request," the major admitted.

"Did Oz and Hawk surface alright?" Sara asked the major on her own phone.

"Perfectly fine and we're headed back to the *Truman* now. Stasia will return for you with the boat."

"Thank you." Sara hung up. "I need to surface for air." She giggled as Charlie kissed her neck, working his way down her body.

"We'll go slow. Use my air." He pulled her closer. She wrapped her legs around his waist as he kicked slowly toward the surface. "It'll take at least forty minutes for Stasia to go and get back here." He trailed his hands up his wife's bare back, smiling at her response. He loved the magic.

EPILOGUE

Major Nelson changed into a clean uniform before reporting to the captain.

"Midshipman Hayes and Doctor Mitchel are my only crew unaccounted for," Captain Williams said without preamble. "I assume they're safe or you wouldn't be here?"

"Perfectly safe," Major Nelson agreed. "Midshipman Morales will retrieve them as soon as they're finished running, err, experiments."

The captain cracked a small smile. "Experiments— right." He tapped his fingers on the desk. "I'm aware of the situation between them," he finally said. "They've been discreet, but I'm not an idiot, and I have surveillance everywhere now."

Major Nelson winced.

Captain Williams held up his hand, forestalling any explanation. "I get it— she's a genius, and he has special privileges for her sake. I have no proof and don't intend to do anything about it as I'm sure you'll all lie your asses off to cover for them."

"We don't need to lie." Major Nelson sat back in his chair, grinning.

Captain Williams nodded. "I assumed as much. The government has a lot to lose if Valor Industries takes their inventions elsewhere. I can overlook this as they're discreet about it, but speaking of their devices" –the captain leaned forward and punctuated his comments with a fingertip poking the table— "Is there any chance of them harming my ship? Even a slight chance? We tracked a small underwater explosion at your location. I understand you have classified weaponry on you, and I'm not to ask about it. Keep your secrets, but—"

Major Nelson interrupted. "No danger to the ship. Midshipman Hayes and Doctor Mitchel are defusing the situation as we speak. I can't speak to the danger holding the criminals will bring here, but our weapons are under control."

"And what exactly am I supposed to do with these criminals?" Captain Williams asked sourly.

Major Nelson shrugged. "Whatever you would normally do with such people, I guess. If something else needs to happen, I'm sure you'll be informed after we finish making our reports."

Captain Williams leaned back in his chair and rubbed the bridge of his nose. "I assume I'll be getting a report?"

"Absolutely," Major Nelson said cheerfully. "You'll be a hero, stopping the abduction of two brilliant scientists working on classified military secrets. One or two of the criminals might quietly disappear, but most you can keep. From our point of view, this cruise was a complete success. More than we'd hoped for actually. Not only did we clear up a long-standing threat against them, but we got some good intel. The security devices worked well. Already they have plans for better versions and different things to make. I know they hope to return here next summer to test them out."

Major Nelson chuckled. "I don't know if I'm sorry for you or jealous they like you and want to help you."

Captain Williams snorted back a laugh. "I hope they do come back. I can't wait to see what they do next."

Major Nelson gave Captain Williams a crooked grin. "Be careful what you wish for."

THE END

- Book 5 -

COMING SOON!

A ROGUE S PASSION

Charlie fights his nature as a protection warrior and learns all fights aren't fought with a weapon.

Learning at an ever-increasing rate, Sara and Oz begin putting their security devices in action and not a moment too soon. An overheard conversation soon pits Team Valor against Mr. X, an unknown enemy who's willing to kill to keep his secrets. Every layer of deceit they unravel leads to deeper, more troubling ones, and Team Valor doesn't know who to trust.

The magic is making demands of its own, and the pressure on Charlie increases as he tries to keep it satisfied.

To make Stasia happy, and keep the magic content, Charlie and Sara attempt to transform Joy. An attempt that has repercussions they didn't expect. The magic and Sara's needs aren't compatible, and Charlie finds out sometimes stepping back to let others fight their own battles is the hardest fight to face.